D1561375

My Particular Friend
A CHARLOTTE HOUSE AFFAIR

Jennifer Petkus

A Mallard Classic
Published by Mallard Press
Denver

My Particular Friend
A CHARLOTTE HOUSE AFFAIR

Copyright © 2012 Jennifer Petkus
The cover photo is © 2011 Jennifer Petkus
All rights reserved, whatever that means.
For the Kindle:
ASIN: B005UF4Z6U

For the printed book:
ISBN-10: 0615597467
ISBN-13: 978-0615597461

visit www.myparticularfriend.com

Mallard Classics

Acknowledgements

I would like to thank my various proofreaders, including my husband, Jim Bates; my particular friends Lee Thomas and Susan Chandler; fellow Sherlockian Jaime Mahoney; fellow Janeite and JASNA member Maryann O'Brien; French Janeite Catherine Godfroid; my sister-in-law, Shel Bates; and my promoters at the Tattered Cover bookstore in Denver, Jackie Blem and Kathleen Schmidt.

Apologies

It may be foolish to cast Sir Arthur Conan Doyle's characters of Sherlock Holmes and John Watson as two women in Georgian England, whilst further eschewing zombies, vampires and cross dressing (although I have enjoyed very much stories that incorporated these elements). Women of the time would have been restricted as to what they could do, and I tried to keep those strictures in mind. Thus even though the temptation was great, there are no explosions, sword fights or bare knuckle brawls in these stories. I thought love could provide sufficient danger and excitement.

I apologize for ransacking Jane Austen, Conan Doyle, P.G. Wodehouse, William Shakespeare, Oscar Wilde, Edmund Blackadder and others, but at least I steal from the best.

And finally, I apologize for my clumsy American attempt at period punctuation, grammar and spelling.

Notes on the Period

This book is set in Bath, England, during the Napoleonic War. George III (the king during the American Revolution) is still on the throne and relatively sane. The Kennet and Avon Canal is not yet completed.

Notes on the Cover

The book cover is a photograph of Ralph Allen's home Prior Park in Bath, looking up from the artificial lakes and the magnificent Palladian bridge, which admittedly serves little purpose other than ornamentation. Twenty-six acres of the estate became the Prior Park Landscape Garden maintained by the National Trust. The buildings are now Prior Park College, a coeducational Catholic senior school.

Notes on the Royal Crescent and Bath

The Royal Crescent is a row of 30 connected homes in Bath, England, laid out in a crescent, designed by John Wood the Younger and built between 1767 and 1774. It is a stunning example of Georgian architecture. Many of the homes were let out to visitors who came to Bath for the season. Two of Jane Austen's novels, *Persuasion* and *Northanger Abbey,* take place in Bath.

Footnotes

Throughout the book, you may see this symbol: #, at the end of a paragraph. This will indicate to you that an online footnote exists at www.myparticularfriend.com/?page_id=2523

TABLE OF CONTENTS

The Start of the Affair

You know you'll never get away with it,' a soft voice said. I turned with a start toward the voice and saw a tall, elegant woman standing next me, but not facing me. I could not believe it was she who had addressed me, for she seemed solely intent on studying the variety of caps and bonnets before her, but then she said, still not addressing me directly, 'Those gloves look very nice on you, but not at the cost of the ensuing embarrassment.'

Then she turned and looked at me and gave me a quick, brilliant smile. She continued in a louder voice: 'Why don't you allow me to repay you for the kindness you did me last summer? I insist on buying these for you.'

She reached for my hands and before I knew her purpose she had removed from my fingers the gloves I wore and draped them over her arm. She then laid her other hand lightly on my arm and moved me toward the counter and what I feared would be the certain accusation of the shopkeeper. I don't know why I obediently followed her—perhaps I feared a commotion; all I knew was that her will could not be denied.

'Ah, Mr Bruce, don't you agree these gloves look charming on my friend?' the woman asked, moving her hand behind my back and encouraging me ever closer to the counter. Only now did I notice the shopkeeper had been looking steadily at me as I approached. But my companion's address commanded his attention.

'Oh, Miss House, I … of course. You are the arbiter of taste.' The shopkeeper said, seeming startled. Then a crafty gleam shone in his eyes. 'Shall I put these on your account?' #

My companion laughed lightly and said, 'Yes, my account, Mr Bruce. By all means, put them on my account. Good day to you, sir.' She turned quickly, not acknowledging his hasty bow, and immediately placed her hand behind my elbow and moved me to the shop door.

Once outside she released her hold on me and laughed again. '"On my account!" The man is priceless. And you, my dear, really should pay more attention to shopkeepers if you plan to turn to a life of crime. Despite your healthy complection, I do not think transportation would suit you.' #

I felt my face flush red and to my shame, rather than explain myself or plead forgiveness, I asked, 'How did you know?'

She smiled and said, 'You entered wearing very threadbare gloves and I see you trying to leave wearing new gloves. Oh, I'll credit you with enough sense to chuse an almost identical pair. But come, let's have a dish of tea, rather than loiter outside the *locus delicti*.' #

She attempted to move me again but this time I held firm.

'I cannot thank you enough, Miss …'

'Miss House. And you, I believe, are Miss Woodsen.' We curtseyed, or rather she seemed to regally accept my existence while I clumsily tripped on my skirts.

'You have me at a disadvantage, Miss House. I apologize that I was unaware that we are acquainted.'

'Again, let's not stand forever in front of Mr Bruce's door,' Miss House said. 'Walk with me, please.'

I agreed and together we walked down the street, slowly, for the rains had made the street muddy and because Miss

House had to stop several times to acknowledge friends. And each time she kindly introduced me to her friends as if I were her equal.

'And it's not your fault, Miss Woodsen,' she said, as we paused to allow a street sweeper to clean our path. 'We were introduced many years ago, here in Bath, although I have not seen you since. So your lapse is excused, although I must admit to chagrin. Once met, I am not easily forgotten.' #

I smiled and had to agree. She was easily as tall as any man I knew and with her golden hair and deep, blue eyes very striking. And now that my fear of arrest had waned, I found it hard not to observe her.

'I'm sorry, Miss House. There is much about my last visit to Bath I have tried to forget. I regret I lost my memory of you as well. But again, I really cannot thank …'

'Tut. Think no more of it. It is my fault really because I allowed you to be in that position. I could see Mr Bruce watching you the whole time and it amused me to let the scene play out. I am afraid he's suffered from a very persistent thief lately. Why only yesterday someone took a very pretty scarf practically from under his nose.'

'But how would you know that?' I asked.

'It's simple. I am his thief. Oh here we are.' She stopped us outside Molland's and said, 'Come, Miss Woodsen, it's my treat.' #

But I could not move. 'You … you …'

'Yes, I. Now let us go inside. I think tea will do you good.' She led me inside to a table and while settling on tea, scones and jam, I awaited a chance to question her further.

Once alone, I asked in a hushed voice: 'How could … why would … why would you'—I lowered my voice even further—'steal?'

'Like any skill, thievery needs practicing. Besides, it's a small enough repayment for all the times Mr Bruce has "put something on my account" without my request. By the by, these gloves would look much better on you.' She then produced a pair of gloves from her muff. I had seen them in the milliners but hadn't dared take them because they were of so much better quality than my own gloves.

I must have appeared stunned because I heard a voice asking Miss House: 'Is your friend all right, Miss House? She looks unwell. I do hope nothing is wrong.'

'Nothing is ever wrong here,' Charlotte said. 'It's just the exertion of the walk. No doubt something to eat will set her right.' The woman was obviously anxious to please her guest.

'Oh where is the girl?' the woman said. 'Oh here she is. Please see to Miss House and her friend. It's always a pleasure to see you, Miss House,' she added, as she backed away from our table, almost colliding with the girl. The image of the woman backing away brought a rush of memory.

'I do remember you at the ball. You were so kind to me and my mother. And everyone was so deferential to you. I really am most ashamed that I ...'

Miss House reached across to me. 'Please, if you apologize or thank me one more time, I shall begin to find you tiresome. Now, take the gloves and put them away. I don't want them and I can hardly take them back. And then we can address what is obviously on your mind. You are thinking, "Who is this extraordinary woman? And why is she being so kind to me?" Is that not so?'

I nodded.

'Good. I am Miss Charlotte House and you are Miss ...'

'Jane,' I supplied.

'You are Miss Jane Woodsen. And I watched you come into the shop with a look of resignation on your face that was then replaced by a look of determination. It was writ plain on your face: I must do what I must do. And then you'—she lowered her voice—'slipped off your gloves and put on the new ones. And you did it remarkably quickly.'

I nodded again, reliving my crime, this time with the pretence of shame.

'You had obviously practiced. And you kept your back to the counter to block Mr Bruce's view of what you were doing, which was a good tactic for an amateur. When stealing, I always try to be as brazen faced as possible. But you unconsciously brought up your shoulders to further conceal your activity and that brought you to his attention.'

'That's amazing,' I said, a little too loudly, and in a quieter voice, added, 'you are a professional thief.'

'I am nothing of the kind. Thievery is a mere *peccadillo*, and my, what a fun word that is. And it's a *peccadillo* that I have found useful from time to time. No, what you see before you is a wealthy—and I am very wealthy—bored, beautiful—and I am very beautiful, am I not—member of the *haut ton*. My brother believes himself someone important in the government while I believe myself someone important in Bath society. And what about you, Miss Woodsen? You are here for the season?' #

'Me? I am nothing interesting.'

'Oh please, I find you very interesting. You are pretty enough, if in unconventional fashion. Your hair alone deserves comment, it being quite full and lustrous with a curious mixture of hues of black and brown and some red. You spend much time out of doors without a bonnet? Which also explains your unfashionably tanned and ruddy complexion. Your hair colour and charming green eyes, with a touch of brown as well I see, hint of a strong Celtic ancestry. You are of less than middling height, which could be improved if you did not slouch, a consequence of too much reading and writing with too little light. Candles are very dear in your home, are they not? But must I continue my conjectures? Do I not merit full disclosure?'

I dropped my head in shame. 'Yes, of course,' I said, looking up. 'You do. And I am eternally'—she gave me a warning look—'I am at a low end. My family ... my father has ... he has died and the estate, what there is of it, goes to my cousin, but because of the entail and my father's debts, it will prove more burden than boon. There is only my younger sister, Elinor, who is staying with my Aunt Edith in Bishopstone, and myself.'

'And where do you stay in Bath?'

'With other friends, Colonel and Mrs Wallingford. But I fear I have overstayed my welcome with them, now that I am no longer of their station.'

'Your prospects then are bleak?' she asked.

'It would be charitable to call them bleak. I had come to Bath to gain a position as a governess but have been repeatedly rejected. Nothing discourages an employer more than someone who needs to be employed. I fear I have the stink of poverty.'

'Nonsense, pretty young girl like you. There are many men who would find you ... you shake your head.'

'I misled you. My father did not simply die. He killed himself, rather than face the wrath of his creditors, or the humiliation of debtor's prison. My life is over, Miss House.' #

Miss House said nothing while I wiped my tears. After I composed myself, she said, 'It is a sad story. But I have the cure, or at least a temporary solution. Rid yourself of the accursed Wallingfords and stay with me. Find yourself a husband or a position as a governess. I would recommend against pursuing your career as a thief, however.'

A Singular Woman

I quickly moved my very few belongings to No. 1 Royal Crescent, which Miss House had rented for the season. I found everyone eager to welcome me, the housekeeper and the servants being very concerned for my comfort. But Miss House was not there to greet me. #

'No miss, she's away,' Mary the maid told me, while she saw to my things. 'She's off on her calls and was very sorry that she could not be here. But she told us, "Make sure that Miss Woodsen is very comfortable and has everything she needs." And, of course, we are all delighted that Miss House has some company.'

'Does she have many guests?' I asked.

'She has many visitors, but apart from her brother, not many guests.'

'You like your mistress, I think?'

'Oh we do, miss. She is very kind and fair to us. And so we are happy to see her with a friend.'

Mary's words took me aback. 'I only met Miss House the day before, and although she has shown me great kindness, I don't know whether I can claim her as friend.'

Her posture stiffened slightly. I couldn't tell whether Mary was offended by my words or doing an imitation of Miss House's impeccable posture. 'She certainly thinks of you as a friend, miss. She told us, "Treat Miss Woodsen as my particular friend and see that she wants for nothing."'

'It is a great honour then that I can claim her friendship, Mary.'

She turned to me and smiled and her posture relaxed. 'I'm sure you'll be the best of friends, miss.'

I might now call Miss House friend, but she was certainly an absent one whom I did not see again for another two days. And despite the kindness of the servants, I could not help but feel an interloper in the house. That feeling and the novelty of my situation confined me to my room, even at dinner, which over the protestations of the servants, I asked be sent there. But by the second day, curiosity got the better of me. I spent my time acquainting myself with the house and learning a little of my benefactress.

In the drawing-room, I found miniatures of Miss House and her brother, whose name I learned was Michael. In their likenesses, I found them not alike. His hair was dark to her light, and the artist had caught a jovial, almost fatuous good humour at odds with his sister. I also found a framed, quick pencil sketch of a naval officer with a lock of dark black hair pressed against the glass. Closer inspection of a pencilled note revealed the subject of the drawing to be Midshipman Edward Brashears. #

The pianoforte keyboard was open and the sheet music displayed a difficult piece, Bach's *The Art of Fugue,* with many notations in what I believed to be Miss House's hand. The sheet music was incomplete, with several pages handwritten. On the writing desk, I found scattered another incomplete printing with similar notations, and several pages on the floor. The effect was that of an artist, caught in the embrace of a muse, who dashes out the door with strict instructions to the servants not to tidy her work, although the rest of the room was immaculate. #

The library was similarly instructive. It was well stocked by the owner for the use of his renters, with the perfunctory classics that had never been read, a ladder that had never been moved and a globe that had never been spun. But the fine furniture in the room had been moved aside for two large, plain deal tables on which were spread newspapers and other periodicals going back at least six months. There were Bath, Bristol and London papers, even one from America. Several clippings were scattered on the table as well, primarily betrothal and wedding announcements, again with many notations, such as 'This will not do!' and 'But what about the previous engagement?' and 'How do we know a living is ensured?'

There were also other more curious clippings: ship arrivals, war despatches, the death of a baronet and even postings in the agony column. In the announcement of the baronet's death was penned, 'Could M__ be his child?'

In several piles, tied with bright red ribbon, I found Miss House's travelling library, which was again singular. In one untied bundle, I found Laclos's *Les Liaisons dangereuses,* of which I had heard but never read, and *The Monk* and *The Castle of Otranto,* both of which I had read. At the top of another bundle was an Italian translation of a Galen anatomy text. And next to the textbooks were two large cases of pinned butterflies. #

Most prominent, however, were about a dozen large books composed of past clippings. The most recent chronologically contained an announcement of my father's death.

I abruptly sat down at the table and stared at the page that contained the announcement. The clipping was a month old but the page to which it was pasted was dated the day we had met. *What sort of woman is she?* I wondered. *I am a complete stranger to her and yet she invites me to her home and immediately catalogues me with the other esoterica of her mind.*

I could not dislodge the feeling that I was a butterfly pinned in Miss House's collection. Whatever my feelings, I earnestly wished for her return, hoping that I would find reassurance in the pleasant manner she had earlier shewn me.

It was not until late that evening, however, that Miss House arrived. I was in my room, reading the Laclos, when I heard a commotion. I hurried downstairs and found my benefactress and another woman in the hall, being attended to by the servants.

'Oh Miss House, you are wet and cold.'

'And hungry, Mary. Ask Mrs Hutton to lay on something substantial, despite the hour.'

'We know your habits by now, miss,' Mary said, while helping Miss House remove a very travel-stained cloak, to reveal mud-stained skirts. Her companion was equally begrimed.

Miss House noticed my presence upon the stairs. 'My dear Miss Woodsen, please forgive me. But as you can see, I've been away and busy.' She gestured to the older woman. 'And before I forget my manners, I would like you to meet Mrs Fitzhugh, a family friend.'

We acknowledged each other, and then Mrs Fitzhugh stepped toward me. I could see that though she was older than Miss House, neither her dark hair nor her cheerful smile betrayed her age. 'Miss Woodsen, it is a pleasure to meet you. Miss House has told me all about you.' As she spoke, she took my hand in hers.

'The pleasure is mine as well,' I said, overcome by the warmth of her greeting.

Freed of her travelling clothes, Miss House joined us. 'Miss Woodsen, I apologize for not greeting you on your arrival, and I hope Mary has not been horrible to you and has not put you in some dank room.' She flashed Mary a smile, who quickly cast down her eyes while lifting the corners of her mouth.

'No, Miss House, Mary and everyone in this household have shown me the greatest kindness.'

'I am glad of it. Now please forgive me while I change, and although you've doubtless already dined, would you join me later while I do so?'

'Of course, it would be my pleasure.'

'Good,' she said, and then rushed up the stairs, leaving me behind. I looked at Mrs Fitzhugh and Mary, still holding her mistress's cloak.

'She does leave one rather breathless,' I said softly to myself.

Mary nodded and said, 'An't it wonderful, miss?'

Mrs Fitzhugh also left, and I retired to the drawing-room to wait what I thought would be a considerable time while they composed themselves, but it seemed only minutes before Miss House joined me, dressed like a lady who had spent the entire day doing nothing more exhausting than answering her correspondence.

'Mrs Fitzhugh does not join us?' I asked.

'No, she's rather tired after our labours, and she also had the wisdom to eat; while I can never suffer food when travelling.'

We went into the dining room where we found a meal sufficient for an army awaiting Miss House. I limited myself to tea while she attacked a cold roast.

'Pardon my manners, Miss Woodsen, I am famished. I can't remember when last I ate.'

'You have been travelling this whole time?'

'Yes, my enquiries led me to Bristol.'

'Bristol!' I said, intrigued. 'Whatever could take you to Bristol?' I had assumed she was about Bath. #

She stopped eating and looked at me intently.

'I'm sorry,' I said. 'It is none of my business.'

'No, no, I like your directness. Perhaps I'll tell you of my business in Bristol someday. Why don't you tell me instead how you find the house?'

I told her that I found my situation agreeable, without mentioning the feelings I had experienced in the library.

'Then everything is to your liking? Your room?'

'Yes, of course, it is more than I could have hoped. I have never slept in such a bed.'

'I hope you felt free to have the run of the place. There is an excellent library.'

I nodded.

'And when you saw the clipping on the death of your father?'

I froze and for a space said nothing. 'How did you know I had seen it?'

'Before I joined you, I looked into the library and saw the Laclos was missing. You'll find it an enjoyable read. And I ask again, what did you think when you saw the clipping?'

'I confess I did not know what to think,' I said, trying to hide my discomfort by lifting my cup.

'You did not think yourself a butterfly pinned to a collection?'

I spilled my tea and I fear I stared at her open mouthed. She laughed.

'Oh Miss Woodsen, I am sorry. It was a guess and I did not think it would affect you so strongly. You are the victim of my machinations. I staged that tableaux like a trap and then waited for you to spring it.'

I put down the cup and said, trembling, 'You are most unkind.'

My statement wiped the smile from her face. 'I am,' she said with a look of concern that did her credit, 'but I wanted to know the measure of my new friend, whether she is made of glass or of iron, whether she will wilt before my nature or will rise to challenge me even in my own home.'

She has done it again, I thought. She has played upon my emotions as if I were her instrument. Already she has turned the kindness of her hospitality into rudeness by her absence. And by calling me friend she has turned my righteous anger over her manipulation … into eager forgiveness.

'You forgive me. I feel it now, Miss Woodsen. I have turned the corner in your estimation.' She said this with a pleading in her voice that was so charming and already her smile was returning.

I still did not know what to say, but I gave her a slight nod in return.

'And now it is your turn. Tell me what you think. Tell me your impressions about me.'

'You are the most singular person I have ever met,' I ventured to say.

'Hah! That is not helpful. In a long life, you might say that again and again, giving lie to it each time. Give me details.'

Thus challenged, I said, 'You must be a gifted pianist to tackle so challenging and obscure a piece as the music I found in the drawing-room. You devour the news like you devoured that roast. You like the sensational, witness your choice of reading material, and you have an interest in the social news that matches the most inquisitive spinsters of my village. You read Italian medical texts. And I almost get the impression that you have … an employment.'

'Oh this is fun,' she said. 'But you should remember to distinguish between observation and conclusions. A bad pianist can murder Bach as easily as a gifted one can praise him. Although you are correct, I am judged a gifted pianist. And I do read Italian, badly. And you are correct in your most important conclusion. I do have an employment.

'But the hour is late and that roast you say I have devoured weighs heavily on me. And I did journey to Bristol and back. Let's retire and we will continue our talk to-morrow.'

VISITORS

I awoke the next day with an optimism I had not felt for a long time. My apprehensions had been replaced by curiosity and I hurried to breakfast. Miss House, however, was again missing, but Mary provided me a letter.

Miss Woodsen,

*How it grieves me to continue to fail in my duty
as hostess, but again Mrs Fitzhugh and I are off.
However, I shall be gone only shortly, I promise. In
fact, it would give me great pleasure if you would join
me at the Lower Rooms at three o'clock. #*

*Yours in friendship,
Charlotte House*

*PS There may be callers asking for me—or you—
throughout the morning. If you would be so kind as
to see to their comfort—no matter their station—and
relay any messages when we meet?*

Curious, and even more curious still, I thought to myself.
And the visitors to the house that morning were very curious
indeed. Calling early at eleven was a portly gentleman who
did not stay but simply left his card; at twelve a querulous
old woman with a cat who required tea, for both her and the
cat, and did not leave a card or name; and at twelve-fifteen
a small boy who came round the servants' entrance with a
parcel addressed to Miss House. And finally at two arrived
a richly dressed, older woman, who did not give her name
to the servant to be announced. She was attended by a meek
young girl—whom I judged to be a species of niece—and
demanded to see Miss House or myself.

'You must be Miss Woodsen,' the older woman said, inspecting me through her lorgnette, and sniffing slightly, as if
she had caught a whiff of my straitened circumstances.

'I am,' I replied. 'How may I help you, ma'am?'

'You are the confidante of Miss House?'

'I am,' I said again, unsure of the truth of the matter, but by this point I was willing to agree to anything.

She took a long time to reply, perhaps doubting the veracity of my statement. 'Very well, please relate to her that I am … done with the matter and that I consider this contretemps at an end.'

'And who should I say makes this statement, Madame?' I asked, trying in a small way to match her hauteur.

'Do you not know who I am?'

'I do not,' I said, 'as you did not offer your name to the servant who answered the door.'

At this she fluffed up like a pigeon taking a chill. 'I am Lady Dalrymple, as you should know, child.' #

'Indubitably,' I replied, although I think I may have mangled the word slightly. Lady Dalrymple wouldn't have noticed, however, for she had already swirled round to collect her niece and was making for the door.

I sat, feeling that I did not need to attend her on her way out, and tried to collect my thoughts. *Whatever does all this mean? In what … business, for I cannot call it anything else … is Miss House engaged?*

But I no longer had apprehension, just curiosity. I eagerly awaited the next visitor, but no one else arrived. Nevertheless, I delayed my departure for my date with Miss House until the last moment and in consequence was in a considerable hurry.

I arrived at the Lower Rooms flushed by the cold and my exertions and found my hostess already waiting for me.

'Goodness, you look very excited, Miss Woodsen,' my friend said, after we had called for tea and buns. #

'Yes, I am sorry to keep you waiting, but we had such a number of visitors and I waited until the last possible minute to leave.'

She gave me a quick smile, so fast I would have missed it during a blink.

'Good, tell me then of our visitors.'

'First came a gentlemen about eleven o'clock. He said little, but left this card.' I handed her the card, at which she glanced for but a moment.

'Can you recall exactly what he said?'

I closed my eyes to recollect and quoted him, 'Tell Miss House I have no opinion on the matter. Here is my card, good day.'

'And that is all he said?'

I opened my eyes and looked at her. 'Well, he might have said, "*Please* tell Miss House I have no opinion on the matter."'

'Good, excellent. And do you have a parcel for me?'

'Yes,' I said, producing the parcel, and passing it to her, added, 'although I did not receive it myself. A boy delivered it to the servants' entrance.'

She looked up at me and shook her head slightly. 'My erstwhile housekeeper Mrs Hutton needs to be chided again. The boy had instructions to deliver it personally to me, or my agent.' She returned her attention to the parcel, unwrapped it and produced several letters tied as a bundle. 'No matter. I have what I wanted.'

'And a rather disagreeable old woman named Dalrymple came.' Miss House's raised eyebrow reminded me I was wrong not to give my visitor's title its due; that I did not was a testimony to my dislike.

'Ah, now we come to the heart of the matter. What did she say?'

'Lady Dalrymple considers the matter to be at an end … excuse me … she said precisely that she is "done with the matter" and considers "this contretemps at an end."'

Miss House absorbed all this and then smiled broadly.

'Thank you, Miss Woodsen, I knew that you would serve me well.'

'Oh, I almost forgot,' I cried. 'A strange woman with a cat arrived and insisted on tea for both herself and her cat.'

'Odd, I had expected no woman with a cat. No matter. I'm sure you were all politeness. Now, we are done with our tea and I must leave you again for a short time. However, I should consider it a great pleasure if you would join me again at eight, in the Upper Rooms, and you will see the outcome of all your efforts to-day.' #

I looked down at the table. 'I would like to join you, but ... I have nothing suitable for ... I left my home ...'

'I understand, Miss Woodsen. Please do not think it presumptuous of me, or of my servants, but I know that you arrived with comparatively little and I have arranged to have something suitable available. Mary has been busy all day and I hope that using your other clothing as a guide, she has found something for you to wear. If it does not fit or you find it not to your liking, then don't come. You must not feel any obligation.'

'You are too kind, Miss House, and I should decline.'

'But you won't?'

'I hope that it will fit,' I said.

THERE IS DANCING

It fit; and I thought it more beautiful than anything I had ever worn, and I thanked Mary for her efforts. 'It is a lovely colour, Mary.'

'The green matches your eyes, miss. I couldn't help but notice.'

'Green! You call this green? It is emerald; it is the sea; it is the forest primaeval. But how could you find this?'

'Oh, that was easy. Miss House told me to go to her dress-maker and see if they had anything that would suit you. It's actually parts of two different dresses. The pelisse is a bit heavy, but I thought you might like it, being it's cool to-night.' #

'You are a wonder, Mary, and a very clever girl.'

'Please miss, don't move, it needs just a few more stitches to make sure you don't pop out all over. There, done!'

I admired myself in the mirror and couldn't help but think of the shift in my fortunes.

'You'd better hurry. I'm sorry it took me so long to make those changes,' Mary said.

'You are right. I shall have to run to make it in time.'

'Run? No, the chair is waiting outside. We can't have you running.'

Mary hurried me out and the chairmen brought me swiftly to the Upper Rooms with time to spare. Miss House and Mrs Fitzhugh were waiting for me just inside. #

'My dear, you are a vision,' Mrs Fitzhugh said.

'I agree,' Miss House said. 'Clearly Mary has outdone her-self.'

'Thank you both. I feel … I feel …'

'Yes, my dear?' Mrs Fitzhugh prompted.

'I feel that anything is possible.'

'And so it is,' Miss House confirmed.

'Let us go in,' Mrs Fitzhugh said. 'There is dancing.'

Her words proved to be an understatement. I had never seen so many people in one place, for this was the height of the season; and the day and the clemency of the weather ensured that all of society gathered in this one room. We entered as the couples marched before the start of the country-dance, unfortunate timing as it might mean that we would be denied partners for a full thirty minutes, but I did not mind. I enjoyed watching the leading couple as they assuredly set the tone of the dance and feared I would never match their skill and grace. But Miss House was eager to claim seats and she firmly held my hand as we navigated the room. I turned to look for Mrs Fitzhugh but she had left us at some point.

I was soon glad of Miss House's firm hand as we threaded our way through the crowd and claimed what looked to be the last two seats available. We were only barely seated, however, when Mrs Fitzhugh returned with a pleasant young man in tow. We rose and Mrs Fitzhugh said, 'Miss Woodsen, may I introduce Mr Harrington, a very nice young man whose family I have known since the Flood.'

He bowed and I returned the favour. 'Charmed, Miss Woodsen.'

Turning to the gentleman, our companion said, 'And you, of course, know Miss House.' They acknowledged each other as well and exchanged pleasantries before Mr Harrington addressed me again. 'Miss Woodsen, may I have the pleasure of the next dance?'

Obliged as I was to his invitation, I stole a look to Miss House for I also felt an obligation to her and did not wish to precede her enjoyment. She quickly nodded her assurance with a smile and I returned my attention to the gentleman.

'Of course,' I said. 'I look forward to it.'

And the course of the evening was set. I danced the cotillion and the reel and even the quadrille, of which I had no familiarity, and to my relief but not my surprise Miss House was not unaccompanied, though she towered over her partners. We several times exchanged smiles and I laughed at the pleasantries of my partners and clapped at the success of the dances.

The room grew ever hotter and we retired for refreshment and joined a group obviously well known to my friends. Mrs Fitzhugh especially knew everyone, and soon Miss House and she were exchanging confidences with those at the table.

So happy was I to be free of the worry and despair of recent days that in my inattention I fear my face may have appeared vacuous.

After a time Miss House returned her attention to me. 'I'm sorry, my dear, I've ignored you.'

'No, I am glad of a moment to enjoy my own thoughts.'

'I'm glad you can keep yourself amused. But if I may ask a favour, would you decline the next dance? I had promised that you would see the outcome of your efforts this morning.'

'Yes,' I said, louder than I had intended. 'I wish to know what you are about.'

'Good. Mrs Fitzhugh, might we return and attend to our friend in need?'

Mrs Fitzhugh agreed and we returned to the ballroom, which by this time had quieted somewhat in favour of dances that would allow the participants to cool themselves. Thus our progress through the room was quicker and we soon found ourselves in a corner where a family was seated. They rose as we approached and Mrs Fitzhugh addressed them.

'Mr Williams, Mrs Williams, Miss Williams, Mr Wallace, may I introduce …'

Etiquette and Mrs Fitzhugh were ignored however, when Mrs William asked, 'Do you have them, Miss House?'

Seeing her distress, my friend quickly said, 'I do. All is well.'

'Thank God!' Mrs Williams cried loudly, drawing everyone's attention, but as I was closest to her, I saw Miss Williams swoon. I rushed to her side, however her weight was unsupportable and I staggered. Suddenly I felt strong arms holding me upright and then relieving me of my burden. Then the gentleman, Mr Wallace, was carrying Miss Williams to a chair.

'Thank you, sir,' I said to Mr Wallace, who merely nodded

to me, his attention to the young lady. Her mother, however, pushed him aside and sat beside her.

'Catherine, it is all right. We are saved,' she told her daughter, patting her hand. Catherine opened her eyes and smiled faintly at her mother. The tension was drained from our group. Within a few minutes everyone was smiling and they thanked Mrs Fitzhugh and my friend. Mr Wallace, however, turned especially to me.

'I apologize Miss …'

'Woodsen … Jane Woodsen,' I said.

'John Wallace,' he said in return and bowed, and I curtseyed.

'I apologize for …' and he made a vague gesture with his hands. His discomfiture was quite becoming in contrast to his sturdy, capable appearance.

'There is no need. Thank you for …' and I made a similar fumbling gesture.

He started to laugh but was cut short by a voice.

'You! Miss House!'

I turned and saw Lady Dalrymple approach, trailed by the woman I took to be her niece.

'Lady Dalrymple, so good to see you,' Miss House said, and curtseyed, followed by myself and Mrs Fitzhugh, but not Mrs Williams, who returned hostility with hostility. Mr Wallace and Mr Williams bowed but I could tell they did not like it.

'I thought I made clear that the matter is at an end,' Lady Dalrymple, oblivious to our presence, told Miss House.

'But the world turns regardless of your wishes, Lady Dalrymple, and your saying black is white does not make it so. And if your nephew chuses to marry Miss Williams and she chuses to accept, then you can have no objection, for there is no impediment to their union. I repeat: there is no impediment. If there ever had been one, it no longer exists.'

She was magnificent. Boadicea herself could not have appeared more magnificent. Lady Dalrymple shrank. She opened her mouth to speak and thought better of it after noticing the attention her words had attracted. She turned quickly, almost colliding with her companion, and walked away. #

The Williamses again thanked Miss House, and Mrs Fitzhugh and me, although they could not have known what little part I played. Hands were pressed and kisses were exchanged—Mr Wallace was excessively charming—and when it was over, Charlotte, Mrs Fitzhugh and I watched the Williamses, now a happy party, leave.

Miss House leant her head toward me and said quietly, 'And that is my employment, Miss Woodsen. That is what I do.'

An Explanation

'You have questions from last night, no doubt,' Miss House said the following morning, after we had breakfasted.

'Yes, Miss House, you confirmed last night that this is your employment. But what is it exactly? What is it that you do?'

'I suppose you could say that I am an intermediary. Mothers come to me and ask my aid in the matter of their daughter's matrimonial prospects.'

'I see,' I said, puzzled. 'And for this service …'

'I am not in trade, my dear.'

'Of course not,' I said, hurriedly, with a shake of my head. 'There was no question. I merely meant …'

'I get satisfaction, you see, when a suitable match proceeds.'

'And if an unsuitable match?' I asked.

She made a face that suggested displeasure and shook her

head. 'I never seek to stop a match. I try only to further love's interests, not impede.'

'It is a noble calling.'

She smiled brilliantly and said, 'I thought you would understand.'

'And as to last night,' I said, 'who was …'

But she stopped me with her hand. 'Alas, I can answer few questions as to the particulars of last night. Although I know that I can place my confidences with you, Miss Woodsen, the Williamses and the other players in this … affair … do not know you. They did not have an opportunity to form a good opinion of you and in all frankness, I should have not included you in the matter. But you arrived at such an opportune moment to act as my agent when I could not remain home, and I wanted to show you the happy outcome. However, with that caution, if you ask questions that I can in good faith answer, I will.'

I sat quietly for a minute, arranging my thoughts before asking. 'The parcel—the letters that you received—that was the impediment?'

She also thought a moment before answering. 'I confirm that to be a reasonable hypothesis.'

'And the contents of the letters were such that …'

She wagged her finger at me.

'Very well,' I said. 'I think I can arrive at my own conclusion. But the means by which you obtained the letters?'

'I cannot tell you the particulars, but you will in time meet some of those … er, means.' She wrinkled her nose at the awkward construction and smiled. 'I hope they will also place their faith in you as they have placed theirs in me.'

'But why me?' I asked, getting to the question that I had been too long in asking. 'Why do you place your faith in me?'

Miss House stood and smoothed her gown, turned away from me and walked about the room, stopping beside the miniatures of her brother and herself and lingering at the sketch I had noticed earlier.

'I have no particular friend, Miss Woodsen. My position in society, my natural reticence and disinclination to favour the vain, stupid and petty have left me, apart from my brother, without a confidante.'

'Mrs Fitzhugh …' I supplied.

'Is a dear friend and one in whom I have complete trust, but she is not a … she … she has never been desperate, except possibly from worry of me.'

She put her hand on the mantelpiece, near the sketch. 'But you have known sadness; I have felt it. You have thought your life and prospects were over. As have I.'

I was startled that she should confide such to me, and that she should ever have been brought so low.

She retook her seat. 'In short, Miss Woodsen, I seek a friend with whom I can be honest and on whom I can depend and to whom I would provide the same benefit.'

'I would be happy to be your friend, Miss House,' I said.

'Then perhaps you should call me Charlotte.'

'And I should … would be happy were you … will be …' I shrugged in frustration, and said finally, 'Call me Jane.'

We laughed and a bond of friendship was formed that although severely tested at times, has never faltered.

I soon learnt my friend's employment carried considerable burdens, although I know many women in society would find it odd to call them burdens. In the morning, we went out in the company of Mrs Fitzhugh and called at the homes of those who had announced a betrothal. But we also called at homes where Charlotte had anticipated an announcement and none had been published. We also called at homes that had suffered a bereavement or a good fortune to offer comfort or congratulations.

And we did not restrict ourselves to homes of quality. As

part of our good works, we visited many of meagre means and brought them such comfort as we could. It was obvious Charlotte was not unknown to these people and they welcomed her warmly, and she, to her credit, returned their warmth. But also in return, Charlotte would make clear, not through a base promise or threat but still undeniably, that she could expect those she helped to feel an obligation to her.

Of course, we also received many callers. Most were merely the compliments of other members of society returning the favour of our calls. But some calls were prompted by the concerns of mothers who feared for their daughter's prospects. In most of these situations, Charlotte merely reassured them, for in truth, most of these women fretted for no real reason. In some situations, Charlotte simply offered her advice. And in a very few situations, Charlotte offered to act on their behalf, but only after extracting assurances that her efforts would remain private.

Our callers also included those who arrived by the servants' entrance. Charlotte interviewed many cooks, maids and footmen under the fiction of employment—'If I have one stain upon my character it is that I am accused of stealing good help'—but her actual goal was to learn the customs and tenor of their current or previous employers.

In all her interactions, Charlotte's attitude was always kind and friendly, but at times I noticed a certain detachment, as if her smile were but a veneer or an artifice. Once I caught her eye at such a moment and later she told me, 'Thank you, Jane. I told you that I needed a friend who would keep me honest.'

Our mornings began far earlier than our calls, of course. Charlotte needed little sleep and often I think she slept not at all, judging by the sound of the pianoforte that might reach my room at any hour of the night. And so increasingly I found my day beginning earlier and earlier, and Charlotte soon had me helping in her researches. I learned to peruse the periodicals for those items, from the *outré* to the mundane, that would interest her. She taught me her method of filing these items in her commonplace books as well, and soon we were pinning butterflies together.

Of course occasionally a candle burnt at both ends will give out and Charlotte would spend days in bed, when it would fall to myself and Mrs Fitzhugh to continue our calls.

Social obligations consumed the bulk of the morning. We three spent a great deal of time at the Lower Rooms, which Charlotte called the *agora,* circling endlessly and absorbing the gossip of Bath. #

Naturally we also attended a number of dances and balls, but even these, I soon found, were not opportunities for pleasure but for information. Very quickly that which I had found a great joy became merely work. In reward, however, my social standing improved considerably, for I was the particular friend of Miss House, and I was to be the entrée of many a young man eager to meet her. She flattered their attentions, but never danced more than once with each and never shewed one more favour than another, and I followed her lead.

In fact I wondered at Charlotte's disinterest in any particular young man. From our meeting five years previous, I knew her to be older than my own one and twenty years. She had seemed so mature and so sure of herself then that I judged her several years my senior; and the tragedy to which she had alluded only served to deepen her sense of wisdom and worldliness. So naturally I looked upon her as an older sister—albeit one with flawless skin, sparkling eyes, hair the colour of wheat and honey and the bearing of royalty.

Perhaps her tragedy ill disposed her to thoughts of love. It was a romantic notion and filled me with speculation as to the nature of her tragedy; but her course seemed ill-conceived for a woman approaching five and twenty, or more. However her fortune, her beauty and her nature would ensure that age would never wither her charms. #

As mentioned, I found our social schedule tedious, even though many a young woman would find it to their liking. It also led to some unpleasantness between Charlotte and myself when I felt ill one evening and begged her go without me.

'But who shall be my accomplice, my dear? Who shall be Pollux to my Castor?' #

'Please, Charlotte, all eyes are on you. No one shall notice my absence.'

'Nonsense, this will not do. I cannot go without you and I *must* go.'

'I am unwell and should be miserable company,' I lamented.

'Very well, stay,' she said. 'I should hate it to be said that I force anyone to enjoy themselves.'

She left abruptly and I felt very low that I had failed in my duty, and that night I took a violent fever. I awoke late the next day and found Charlotte sitting beside my bed, looking very tired, but she smiled when she saw me stir.

'You are awake! Oh, Jane, please forgive me. My behaviour was unpardonable. How could I doubt that you would not join me only if you were greatly unwell? I am so sorry, I ...'

I stopped her with a plaintive—and I must admit overly dramatic—cry for water, and I did enjoy the way she hurried to attend to me. In fact, she did not leave my bedside that day and all that week she abandoned her usual routine. The incident left me knowing that beyond doubt my friend cared for me greatly, but that she could also be unkind when things did not go her way.

The Poison Pen Affair

The next week I resumed my calls with Charlotte and Mrs Fitzhugh, and the first person upon whom we called was Mrs Ashby, whose daughter had been engaged to the Hon. Frederick Hickham, son of Lord M_. A week later, we received a call in return from Mrs Ashby.

'Miss House, I am sorry I was out when you called,' Mrs Ashby said to my friend, who then introduced Mrs Fitzhugh and myself. Mrs Ashby was a stout woman of fair complection and hair and I could see that she was probably a great beauty in her time, but it was obvious that she had been under a great strain of late. She held a small linen that she twisted and untwisted while talking.

'I am so very glad to meet you and I am sorry that I have been so remiss in paying you a call, but after the announcement of my daughter's engagement, I have been … I have been so busy. And so many kind things have been said of you, Miss House, that I felt I must … I hoped that you might …'

'My dear Mrs Ashby, it is obvious something is troubling you. Please, if we may be of service,' Charlotte said. 'You are among friends.'

Mrs Ashby dabbed her eyes with her linen. 'My friend Mrs Willoughby said I should call, that you had been very kind to her.'

'Of course, it was very good of her to suggest it.'

'And then I saw that I had your card,' Mrs Ashby said, casting her eyes downwards and dropping her hands to her lap. #

'Yes. It was providential,' prompted Charlotte. But Mrs Ashby continued to stare downwards.

Charlotte sighed and turned to Mrs Fitzhugh. 'Margaret, would you please call for some tea?'

We waited awkwardly for the tea. Mrs Ashby occasionally repeated her gratitude and again mentioned Mrs Willoughby and the fortuitousness of our call. It was not until she'd had some tea that we could progress.

'Mrs Ashby, please tell us what has happened,' I said.

'Letters. Horrible letters.'

I confess I leant forward with interest, as did my friend. Even Mrs Fitzhugh stopped with her cup halfway to her lips.

'What do these letters say, Mrs Ashby?' Charlotte asked.

A sob of anguish escaped the poor woman. 'They accuse my daughter Sophia of indiscretions. They say that she is not … she is not a maid.' #

Charlotte sank back in her seat and I saw that the accusation had affected her deeply. Mrs Fitzhugh left her seat to comfort Mrs Ashby, but I noticed that she too seemed more interested in our friend.

Charlotte then let out a long breath, brought her shoulders up and then slowly relaxed them, and I saw detachment steal her expression before she addressed the poor woman. 'Mrs Ashby, I do not wish to be unkind and you can be sure of our sympathy and help however you answer, but I must know, is there any truth to this accusation?'

'No!' cried Mrs Ashby. The clarity and strength of her reply startled Mrs Fitzhugh. 'My daughter may not be the model of discretion, but she is a good girl.'

'And why is your daughter not here with you?'

'The strain of it keeps her at home. She is excessively upset, as am I.'

'I quite understand,' Charlotte said, 'but I need to know more if there is to be any hope. Have you the letters?'

'Yes, I brought them.' She opened her reticule and produced the letters, much folded to fit in the bag. #

Charlotte took the letters and examined them quickly. 'A woman's hand,' she said. 'Left-handed I think. The paper is fine. No watermark. Cut from a larger sheet.' She passed them to me and I saw that they were identical:

> *We read that Mr Hickham seeks fallen fruit. Is it not wiser to take the apple from the tree? For fruit that has fallen may already have been sampled, perhaps by Mr Howard? Best to put it back and chuse another before it is too late.*

'To whom were they sent?' Charlotte asked, wearing now a bemused expression.

'To myself; my sister, Mrs Landsdowne; and my cousin, Mrs Mapplethorpe.'

'And you are sure there are only the three?'

'That is the matter! How would I know for sure?' Mrs Ashby wailed.

'Precisely,' Charlotte said. 'Now, how were they delivered? Were they in the post?'

'They were found in the morning, slid under the door.'

'And your sister and your cousin immediately brought them to your attention?'

'Of course,' Mrs Ashby answered.

'When was this?'

'Two days after the announcement,' replied Mrs Ashby.

Charlotte paused in her questioning, and Mrs Fitzhugh

used the opportunity to refresh Mrs Ashby's cup, which she gratefully accepted.

Charlotte resumed. 'You are very close to your sister?'

Mrs Ashby nodded.

'And to your cousin?'

'Yes,' Mrs Ashby answered, 'she is a widow with no children and has always taken a special interest in my daughter.'

Charlotte asked, 'And it is well known that you are close to your sister and cousin? You are frequently seen together?'

'Yes, of course, but what bearing can that have?'

Charlotte ignored the question and continued: 'And the gentleman in the letter, is he known to your daughter?'

'What, Mr Howard? They have been introduced, but he is not comely and does not dance well and is a younger son and my daughter has always been rather particular.'

Charlotte gave one of her quick smiles at this. Then she asked, 'And what does your daughter say of this?'

'She says nothing, of course! She is in a very nervous state.'

'And you have no ... enemies? Neither you, your husband, your daughter? Any members of your family?'

'Enemies? No, that is absurd, we are universally well liked.' That remark produced a sound from Mrs Fitzhugh remarkably like a laugh. Mrs Ashby did not seem to notice, and asked, 'Do you have any advice for me, Miss House? Oh, I feel so silly, asking such a young woman advice for so delicate a matter.'

Mrs Fitzhugh took Mrs Ashby's hand. 'You can have every confidence in Miss House. I have known her a very long time and can tell you there is no more capable person than she.'

'And I will do everything I can to help as well,' I added, much affected by the poor woman's plight, although I did not think my assistance would amount to much.

'I think I can offer some hope,' Charlotte said.

We all looked at her and Mrs Ashby asked, 'But how? Who

knows how far this slander has spread? If Lady M_ hears of this ...'

'Please, Mrs Ashby, do not distress yourself further. You must keep up appearances that all is well. Rest assured that we will do all in our power to help and again, I think I can offer some hope that the slander has not spread—yet.'

'Oh, Miss House, if I could believe you,' Mrs Ashby said, 'but your words do give me some hope.'

Charlotte stood. 'I am glad that I can at least offer that aid. Now we must begin our enquiries and you must return to your family and try to reassure them.'

We all stood and I stept out to see to Mrs Ashby's things. When I returned, I saw that she was much improved in spirits and was thanking everyone profusely. But before she left, Charlotte cautioned her.

'One last thing, Mrs Ashby. Immediately inform us if you are aware of any further letters. And under no circumstances are you to inquire about the letters. And I shall need to retain these.' Charlotte fanned the letters before her.

Mrs Ashby had been nodding her assent the whole while until the last statement, when she suddenly clutched her reticule to her bosom.

'I have been so afraid to let them out of my sight and yet I was about to leave without giving them a thought. Yes, keep them if need be but I would rather see them burned.'

'Which they will be once they are not needed,' Charlotte assured her. We saw her to the door and then returned to the drawing-room.

'What do you make of it, Jane?' Charlotte asked me.

'A terrible tragedy to befall them,' I said.

'Yes, but what strikes you as relevant? Do you see no inconsistencies?'

Charlotte looked at me intently and I shifted uncomfortably beneath her gaze. 'No,' I said meekly.

'Tchah!' she said. 'Think of it, why send letters to the three people most likely not to believe them?'

'But there are other letters!' Mrs Fitzhugh said.

Charlotte said nothing and looked at me.

'There aren't other letters?' I ventured to ask.

'No, I don't think there are. Also note the peculiar construction of the letters. Although the accusation is quite clear, there is a reluctance actually to make that accusation. And there are other more obvious reasons why I offered her some hope.' She saw the confused look on my face and sighed. 'Why do we go to the assembly rooms? Why do we talk to maids and cooks? Why? To gather information. And even if the daughter has been indiscreet …'

'But,' I said, 'her mother most vigorously denied …'

'There is something you must learn, Jane. Everybody lies. They do it as unconsciously as breathing. But as I was saying, even if the daughter has been indiscreet, we have heard no news of it, and it is a very advantageous match. Lord M_'s son? The envy of it should fan the flames of a rumour like this. The fact that we have heard no intimation of it gives me some hope.'

'But then why send the letters at all?' Mrs Fitzhugh asked.

'Yes, that is a mystery,' Charlotte confirmed, 'and it will remain so until we gather more information.'

I sighed and said, 'So it is to the market again.'

An Ever-Rotating Wheel of Information

I earlier recounted that I found our social obligations a burden, but I felt differently on this visit to the Lower Rooms, because this time I was directly employed on someone's behalf. I began to understand why we visited these rooms again and again.

We joined the society taking a turn in the large ballroom and whereas before the image of prisoners pacing in their cells came to mind—when in my dark mood—to-day I saw the crowd as an ever-rotating wheel of information, like some vast clockwork mechanism that will reveal its secrets if only the separate gears can be aligned. As usual, we three started as a group but over time we became two parties, alternately sharing Mrs Fitzhugh, so that we might converse with as many people as possible. #

Of course, we had to be discreet in our enquiries: 'Mrs Compton, so nice to see you again. We were just speaking of you last night to Mrs Ashby. Why yes, I had heard of the engagement' Or: 'It is a pleasure to make the acquaintance of so fine a gentleman as yourself, but stay; are you not a friend of Mr Hickham? I believe him to be recently engaged.'

These enquiries were repeated again and again, but we heard little detrimental other than envy about Miss Ashby and her family. After we became three again, we even asked our master of ceremonies about the match.

'Ladies, ma'am, a great pleasure as always,' he said. 'And it is good to see you well, Miss Woodsen.'

'Thank you, Mr King,' I said. 'You are kind to notice.' #

He gave a little bow and then Charlotte said, 'We do not see Mrs Ashby here to-day. We had hoped to offer our congratulations on the engagement of her daughter to Mr Hickham.'

'Hickham, yes,' he said with a harrumph, 'high time that young man found himself a wife.'

'There are many who think the match most advantageous for the Ashbys,' I said.

'I dare say it is. But Hickham ... Mr Hickham I should say ... has remained single far too long for an eldest son. *Noblesse oblige,* as the French would have said.'

Mrs Fitzhugh returned, 'And why is that, I wonder?'

He looked at her puzzled. 'Well, the revolution might have …'

Charlotte stopped him. 'No, I think my friend wondered why Mr Hickham is so late in marrying.'

'Oh, sorry. Well, I don't know. There have been … Miss House, I take you into my confidence. I …' He stopped and then looked at me.

'You may depend on Miss Woodsen's discretion as you do mine, Mr King.'

'Well that's all right then,' he said, looking at me before turning back to Charlotte. 'We have cooperated before on matters of some discretion, Miss House. As I was saying, there had been earlier expectations that Mr Hickham would take a wife and that came to naught.'

'I was unaware of this,' Charlotte said. 'Doubtless those families are now disappointed.'

'Yes, the Spensers and the Winslowes especially. Don't see much of them as a matter of fact. I should call on them. Speaking of which — if you will excuse me ladies, I have some duties to perform.'

Mr King left us with something to think about.

'I don't think Mr King will have much luck with the Spensers,' Mrs Fitzhugh said. 'They stopped coming to Bath two seasons ago.'

'I vaguely remember them,' Charlotte said. 'Pretty girl but a little too high spirited.'

'And the Winslowes?' I asked Mrs Fitzhugh.

'They are here in Bath, but I do not recall seeing them lately. Mr Winslowe died, I believe, which may be the reason for their seclusion.'

'Our next step then is clear,' I said. 'We must call on the Winslowes.'

☙

Which did not prove easy, because although the Winslowes did, at least at one time spend the season in Bath, we could not find a present address. We enquired again in the Upper and Lower Rooms, at the Pump Room, at the theatre and at every occasion we attended, but no one seemed to know where the Winslowes lived. #

In the meantime, Mrs Ashby again visited us.

'Another letter!' she cried, once seated in the drawing-room. 'We are ruined!'

'Calm yourself,' soothed Mrs Fitzhugh.

'Yes,' I added, 'we have found no proof that this rumour has spread.'

'But it has. My best friend Mrs Clausen brought me this letter only this morning.'

Charlotte looked briefly at the letter and handed it to me. Mrs Fitzhugh joined me in reading it.

> *Tell Mrs Ashby that her cat wants to be let out of its bag. Tell her at once or the cat will be lost to her forever.*

'That is quite … odd,' I said. I looked at Charlotte, who appeared amused.

'Ruined!' Mrs Ashby said again.

Charlotte dropped her smile before addressing the hysterical woman. 'Courage, Mrs Ashby. There is nothing to fear if the recipient has not received the previous letter. And besides, you say Mrs Clausen is your best friend.'

Mrs Ashby nodded vigorously. 'We have known each other since childhood.'

'And she can keep this secret?'

Another nod.

'And no one else has come forward with letters?'

'No one.'

'Then I think the matter remains contained,' Charlotte said. As before, her measured, soothing voice had a calming effect on Mrs Ashby.

'You really think the rumour has not spread?'

'Yes, after our enquiries, I think I can safely say that you are the only intended recipient of these letters. Now, if you are calm, perhaps you can answer some further questions.'

'Yes, of course, Miss House.'

'Now, can you tell us how your daughter and Mr Hickham became acquainted?'

'It was at the start of the season, one of the Monday night balls.'

'And how were they introduced?' Charlotte asked.

'By Mr King, after my husband ...'

'After your husband had a word with Mr King?' Mrs Fitzhugh supplied.

'Yes, exactly.'

'Were you aware of Mr Hickham's previous understandings?' Charlotte asked.

'No, I do not know what you mean.'

'You are not acquainted with the Spensers? Or the Winslowes?' I asked. Charlotte shot me a look of annoyance, which puzzled me, but Mrs Ashby did not notice the exchange. I also caught Mrs Fitzhugh shaking her head at me.

In answer to my question, Mrs Ashby said, 'I don't know the Spensers, and I don't think I know the Winslowes ... although the name does sound familiar. We have not been too many seasons at Bath, you see. We were at Tunbridge Wells last season. Are these people important?' #

'We believe that Mr Hickham had understandings with the daughters of these families,' I said.

'That cannot be. Mr Hickham is quite charming and

forthcoming and told us that he had no interest in marriage until he met our daughter.'

'Perhaps he ...' I started to say, but stopped when I again saw Charlotte give me a look.

'Of course, Mrs Ashby, I must be mistaken. Mr Hickham sounds a delightful man and I should like to meet him,' Charlotte said.

'Yes, that would reassure you, Miss House. I had thought it best not to go to the next ball because of these ... but if you are really sure.' Charlotte nodded. 'He has been out of town lately but returns for the ball and I shall introduce you.'

After the plans were made for the ball, Mrs Fitzhugh saw Mrs Ashby out, leaving Charlotte and me behind in the drawing-room.

'Really, Jane, you must not interfere when I am questioning someone,' she said, as soon as we were alone. I could see that she was quite annoyed.

'Is that why you gave me that look?' I asked. 'I am your accomplice, am I not?'

She sighed when she heard her own words echoed back to her, and the annoyance left her face. 'Yes, Jane, you are my partner in crime. But you must recognize when I am trying to induce a state of susceptibility.'

'Come again?'

'You must have noticed the effect that I can have on people?'

'Of course,' I said. 'I have noticed it upon myself.'

'It is a practiced skill. With a commanding tone I can control or by patient questioning and soothing words I can put someone at ease, especially in an intimate setting. I needed Mrs Ashby in a calm state to ask my questions and I wanted her to hear only my voice.'

'Mrs Fitzhugh asked a question,' I said, petulantly.

'I know, I know; it made yours that much more annoying.'

I decided to broach a subject that had been bothering me.

'Do you truly want a friend on whom you can rely, or someone who merely agrees with you?'

'That is a frank question.'

'And one I must ask. I realize my position is perilous. You are my benefactor; I exist on your generosity. But I must be allowed to speak my own mind.'

'And I want you to. Just not when I'm …'

'… controlling the minds of the susceptible?'

Charlotte had looked quite cross until now, but now she laughed as I heard the drawing-room doors open. 'Are you two still friends?' Mrs Fitzhugh asked.

'I think we are,' Charlotte said.

'Did she upbraid you for interrupting her—what d'you call it—Mesmerism?' #

'You mean her penetrating gaze and commanding tone?' I added, and laughed.

'Yes, she can be quite forceful,' Mrs Fitzhugh said, also laughing.

Charlotte looked at us both, this time with mock annoyance. 'Ha, ha, very droll. But it does work.'

We ignored her and instead gave each other penetrating and commanding looks.

IRREGULAR MEANS

Although we had to wait to be introduced to Mr Hickham at the ball, we continued our efforts to find the Winslowes.

'I think it is time to employ other means,' Charlotte told me the next day in the library, 'and judging by the noises I hear from the kitchen, those means have just arrived.'

We soon heard a knock at the door, followed by the housekeeper Mrs Hutton leading a group of children. They were a dirty, ragged lot, but eager looking and noisy.

'Here they are, Miss House. Why you would want them in the house is beyond me, but I brought them to you just like you asked.'

'Thank you Mrs Hutton, I am much obliged. Now if you might return with some cakes and tea?'

The children were listening to this exchange with rapt attention, their eyes darting back and forth to each speaker.

'Yes, Miss House, as you say,' the housekeeper said through clenched teeth.

The housekeeper left the library.

'Close the door, Jane, if you don't mind,' Charlotte said. After that was done, she addressed the children.

'Please sit, children. We've only four chairs so two may sit with us on the edge of the tables.'

The oldest and largest children took the chairs, leaving two very small children, a boy and a girl, looking up at us. I judged them to be about the age of the children of one of the servants at my home, but they could not match their country-bred wholesomeness. They could never get up on the tables on their own so I lifted each child—a very light burden indeed—and placed them side-by-side on the table. They immediately separated, I assumed to make room for me in the middle, and so I joined them. It had been a long time since I had so carelessly sat on a table edge and I unconsciously did what I always did as a child—I started swinging my legs, in which my two companions joined.

'Please Jane, set a good example,' Charlotte said in mock seriousness. I stopped swinging my legs and meekly said 'yes, miss,' and the children followed suit.

At this time Mrs Hutton and Alice returned with tea and cakes, served with the household staff's mugs and plates, I observed. Mrs Hutton ordered Alice to dole out the mugs and add prodigious amounts of milk and sugar. It took full ten minutes for the children to eat and drink their fill with much spilled tea, cakes and biscuits on the floor, all the while Mrs Hutton muttering: 'Look at the mess. It'll take forever to clean this. Oh, not another mug!'

Eventually Mrs Hutton's ordeal was over and the surviving mugs and plates were removed and Mrs Hutton and Alice left. The children looked pleased and covered in crumbs, which they were slowly transferring to their mouths.

'Thank you all for coming,' Charlotte said. At her words they stopped fidgeting and gave her their full attention. 'And Charlie, many thanks again in that matter of the letters. I have another request of you. I need to find the whereabouts of the Winslowe family. Do any of you know where they live?'

The children looked at each other and exchanged shakes of their heads.

'No, miss, we don't,' the oldest girl said.

'There was a family by that name,' the oldest boy said, 'but they moved last year, miss.'

'Very well, Donna, Charlie, I need you to find the family for me. There was at least a father, mother and daughter. I do not know if there were other children. The father may be named Robert and he is—or was—a barrister. I believe him to be dead. The daughter's name might be Catherine.'

'That's them,' Charlie said. 'I remember the old man died.'

'Good, Charlie, I'm glad to have that confirmed.' The boy smiled. 'Now I want you to find where the family has moved, and be discreet.'

Donna and Charlie looked confused.

'It means don't let on that you are looking for them,' I added. Charlotte looked at me and nodded. 'Yes, don't let on that you are looking for them, just get word back to me.'

She got off the table and presented Donna and Charlie two

small bags and the coins inside them chinked as she placed them in their hands.

'Distribute this as usual. And the usual reward to whoever first obtains the information. And return with that information immediately, day or night. Now, off with you.'

Mrs Hutton, who was obviously eager for them to leave and had perhaps been listening, immediately opened the library door. The older children moved to the door while I helped the two off the table.

'Irregular means indeed,' I said, after the noise of the children had retreated.

'Yes, I find those little Arabs quite useful. They can go anywhere without being noticed and from their situation they've developed resourcefulness. Let us hope that they can find the Winslowes, and let us further hope that information will do us good.' #

I Seek a Position

All that could be done now was wait. We learned from Mrs Ashby that Mr Hickham had returned to town and that we would have the opportunity to meet him at the ball, but until then our avenues of inquiry were closed.

I did, however, have an opportunity to meet with a potential employer. I had been remiss in attempting to find employment because of the obligations I felt I owed Miss House and because of my illness, but I had recently renewed my efforts and had lately received an answer from a Mrs Danvers, to whom I had written. We were to meet the next day.

'Who is this Danvers?' Charlotte asked me during dinner.

'I thought you should know her, Charlotte,' I said.

'I know everyone important.'

'Yes, well Mrs Danvers may not be important but her husband is a very successful … '

'He's in trade, then.'

'He owns a quarry near Bradford-on-Avon.' #

'Bradford!'

'Yes, Bradford. I am sure you are acquainted with it. I have heard it is a pretty sort of town.'

'And they have wretched children they want you to teach?'

'I thought you quite liked children. You treated your little street Arabs very sweetly.'

She gave me the look she uses when she meant to be disagreeable for its own sake. 'I like to employ them. It does not mean I desire their prolonged company.'

'What of your own children?'

'What?' she asked sharply.

'Had you children of your own,' I said, somewhat taken aback by her tone.

'That would be an entirely different matter. Fine then, see this Danvers woman and mind that you don't track dust back here.'

I will admit to being dismayed by my friend's lack of encouragement, but I had by now learnt to accept her changeable moods. Nevertheless, I looked forward to meeting Mrs Danvers. The situation she had described sounded well suited to my own accomplishments and her daughter's age of ten made me think fondly of my own sister at that age. And despite my friend's generosity, I felt I should make my own way in the world.

The next day, as I was preparing to leave for the short walk to meet Mrs Danvers at the home of her friend in Bath, Charlotte surprised me.

'Leaving to meet Mrs Danvers, I presume?' she asked.

'Yes,' I answered, still irritated at her comments the night before.

'I feel the need of some fresh air. Might I accompany you? For if you leave, we may not have many more opportunities.'

She said this so wistfully that I could not remain mad at her and begged her company. We walked arm-in-arm, she chatting happily and making the best of the situation, telling me that I should be the best governess imaginable, while I felt miserable that I might soon be leaving her house. #

A quarter of an hour found us before the house of Mrs Danvers's friend. We stood outside for several minutes while Charlotte gave me instructions on how to comport myself.

'You should get no less than £20 a year, but try for £25, and no less than a week's holiday.'

'Thank you, Charlotte. I will always remember this kindness.'

'Tut, it is nothing, and of course you will get this position. After all, you have the gloves for it.'

We smiled at the remembrance and I proceeded up the stairs, Charlotte motioning me toward the door when I faltered. I gave her one last look as I raised the knocker and saw her retreating down the street.

The door opened and a footman beckoned me in. I gave my name and he was preparing to announce me when a woman flew down the stairs.

'You are Miss Woodsen?' she asked.

'I am,' I said. 'Mrs Danvers?'

She paused before answering. 'Yes. It will do you no good. The position is filled. Thank you. James, please show this woman out.'

I stared helplessly at her. The footman's approach broke my inaction.

'Please, Mrs Danvers, I do not understand. How could the position be filled?'

'James, please show her out.'

'Please miss,' the footman said, not unkindly. He led me to

the door and I stood without and felt my hopes crumble. It took me a full hour to return to Charlotte's home.

'Whatever is the matter?' Mrs Fitzhugh asked me after I entered.

I gave a weak smile and explained my trip to her and I confess I cried a little and she put her arms around me and let me put my head on her shoulder.

'There, there. It was not meant to be this time, that's all. Obviously the position was filled by another before you arrived.'

'She gave me a look like I was some ... some objectionable thing.'

Charlotte entered the hallway.

'What is all this?'

'She did not get the position,' Mrs Fitzhugh explained.

'My dear Jane, I am so sorry. But all this means is that I should not lose your company. And remember, to-morrow night we meet Mr Hickham.'

WE MEET MR HICKHAM

I started my preparations for the ball with a gloomy outlook, but Mary would have none of it.

'Shouldn't you be helping Miss House, Mary?'

'No miss, Alice is helping her to-night.' She said this with a tone that implied Alice's help might be more of a hindrance. 'Miss House said that I should help you to-night, that you might need some cheering up.'

'Ah, so you have heard of my misfortune.' I had long suspected that Charlotte's relationship with Mary was unusually close for mistress and maid.

'Yes, but in confidence of course, miss. And if you want to hear my thoughts, you're better off here than as a governess.'

I turned my head to look at her and Mary jumped back with the curling iron in her hand.

'Careful, miss, this thing is hot.'

I ignored her caution and asked, 'And why am I better off here?'

'You're a lady of quality. I could tell that the first day we met. But a governess, she's not fish or fowl. No one in a household ever likes the governess; and you'd be miserable, teaching some brat.' She said all this quickly and then lowered her eyes and added: 'miss.'

I looked at her in amazement of her effrontery, but after a pause laughed a quick bark, not unlike Charlotte's. Mary kept her eyes downcast but I could see a smile creep onto her face. I turned back toward the mirror and said, 'Well, get a move on girl. I mustn't be late for the ball.'

Inside the carriage on the way to the assembly rooms, Charlotte and Mrs Fitzhugh sat opposite me, both looking concerned.

'You look so pretty, my dear,' Mrs Fitzhugh said, for probably the third time that night. Charlotte nodded in agreement.

'Thank you, both, and I am in much improved spirits. Mary worked her wonders on me,' I said, looking steadily at Charlotte, who quickly assumed an attitude of nonchalance.

'I certainly hope we meet Mr Hickham to-night,' I said, wanting to move past my disappointment. 'What do you know of him, Mrs Fitzhugh?'

'As I said before, very little. I have met him and he is quite handsome and polite, paying me such little compliments as befits a more … mature lady like myself.' At this, Charlotte gave an impolite laugh—a snort really—which we ignored.

'Surely you have more details than that.'

She sighed, and said, 'He is in his late thirties but appears younger, about Charlotte's height, dark colouring, when no one is watching he looks languid, almost torporous, but when he is noticed becomes very affable. He looks very intently at the person to whom he is speaking, like … like …'

'Like Charlotte?' I supplied.

'Yes, that's it, just like Charlotte.'

And again we ignored a snort.

I shall not belabour the spectacle of yet another ball, except to say that the dancing was spirited, the gowns beautiful and the men charming, but in truth I did not notice any of this because I was too engaged trying to spot Mr Hickham. Perhaps my failure at securing a position had made me even more determined to apply myself as Charlotte's assistant.

But for most of the evening, my efforts were in vain. We soon found Mrs Ashby and her daughter, however, and I must admit her daughter's character left something to be desired, as did her diaphanous muslin.

'Miss House, I'm so happy you're here. Mama has told me all about you and I'm sure you will do everything you can to stop whoever is trying to ruin my chances with Mr Hickham.'

Charlotte took her regal tone with the effusive Miss Ashby. 'Of course, Miss Ashby. We shall do everything in our power to'—she moved closer to her and lowered her voice to a stage whisper—'stop these completely unfounded rumours.' As she said this she glanced sharply at Mrs Ashby who, after a moments hesitation, vigorously nodded.

Miss Ashby did not seem to comprehend the silent conversation taking place between my friend and her mother. She was a ripe and energetic young woman of rosy cheeks, blue eyes and warm auburn hair.

'She's fair to bursting out of that gown,' Mrs Fitzhugh said to me confidentially. 'Mind you, she is young and only taking advantage of that which nature so ...'

'Generously gave her,' I finished for her. We laughed and our laughter brought us to the attention of Charlotte.

'Forgive me, Miss Ashby, for being delinquent in introducing my friends, Mrs Fitzhugh and Miss Woodsen. They are as solicitous of protecting your honour as am I.'

'The more the merrier,' the young woman said, somewhat distracted by a young military man who was claiming her for the next dance. 'Pardon me, but Mr ... um'

'Henshaw, at your service,' the young man said.

'Silly me. Mr Henshaw has claimed this next dance.'

She was led off, leaving us with her mother.

'My daughter has high spirits, despite the trouble that afflicts us,' she said.

'She bears her burden well,' I said.

'She is young and foolish, but that is not a crime,' Mrs Ashby said.

'No, that is nature,' Charlotte admitted.

We remained with Mrs Ashby during the dance but found little of common interest with her. She spoke chiefly of her daughter and her matrimonial hopes with a calculating assessment of the agreements that might be made between the two families.

'She brings £500 in the three percents and upon the death of my cousin another £1,000, for as I may have told you my cousin is excessively fond of my sweet child. And my clever husband has also secured for her another £2,000 in the five percents, and then there is my mother's plate, which my father never cared for—men never understand the value of what they're eating on—which devolved to me thanks to my mother's agreement when she was wed. So all in all I think Mr Hickham cannot think that we bring nothing to the table. #

'Oh, but look how gracefully Sophia dances with that Mr Henshaw. He does cut a fine figure in his red coat. Of course, he's only with the militia and I doubt he'll afford a commission any time soon. Still, Sophia enjoys dancing with a man in uniform and I don't think there is any great harm in it.' #

Mrs Ashby continued in this fashion, little noticing or caring whether we paid attention. Then suddenly she gave a little cry. 'I think I see Mr Hickham yonder.'

I turned to see the man on whom Mrs Ashby had set her daughter's cap. He had a fine figure, taller than Charlotte with jet-black, thick hair and refined features atop a muscular physique that spoke of athletic pursuits. No little wonder at Mrs Ashby's excitement, I thought, £10,000 a year in his own right and the eldest son of a baron; she had a right to be enraptured at the thought of her daughter making such an alliance. #

He soon saw Mrs Ashby, aided by the semaphore of her handkerchief, and approached our group.

'My dear Mrs Ashby, how delightful to see you,' he said, with a sweep of his arm to accompany his bow. 'But where is the fair Miss Ashby?'

'You see her dancing to Highgate, Mr Hickham.' #

'Ah, of course, the spirited girl with the roses in her cheeks. And these ladies, why are they not dancing?'

'Pardon me, Mr Hickham. I should like you to meet my friends, Mrs ... um, Fitz ... hugh, Miss House and Miss Woodsen.'

'Mrs Um-Fitzhugh,' Mr Hickham cheekily said with his bow, 'and Miss House ... I've heard of you ... and Miss Woodsen. Delighted.'

'Mr Hickham, it is an honour,' Charlotte said.

'Nonsense, I am the one honoured here. Ah, the dance is ending, and as my dear Sophia has left me alone, would you do me the further honour of the next dance?'

Charlotte assented as Miss Ashby joined us.

'Frederick, I did not see you enter,' Miss Ashby cried, as she ran to him and claimed his arm.

'You were too busy enjoying yourself to notice me,' he said with mock hurt.

'Silly, that is your fault if you arrive so late, but dance with me now.'

'No, I have already claimed Miss House and she has kindly agreed. You, my dear, need some refreshment. You are flushed and could hardly sustain another dance.'

'I am rather knocked up,' she agreed. 'Mama, let's let Frederick have his dance while we find some negus.' #

Mr Hickham led Charlotte to dance while Mrs Fitzhugh and I remained.

'We are to be the wallflowers, then,' I said.

'I think you have no reason to fear,' Mrs Fitzhugh corrected me, and nodded in the direction of a man who approached us.

'Miss Woodsen, I hope I am not too late to claim this dance?' the man asked, whom I recognized but whose name I desperately could not recall.

'I am sure Jane would be delighted to dance, Mr Wallace,' Mrs Fitzhugh said. I stared at her in wonder, for it was the first time she had called me by my given name, and in gratitude for reminding me of the gentleman's name.

'Yes, of course, Mr Wallace, how kind of you to ask.'

Mr Wallace led me to the dancers and we took our positions at the far end of the line from Charlotte and Mr Hickham. Charlotte caught my eye and nodded to me as the dance began. I found Mr Wallace to be an able partner and light on his feet, impressive for a man with such a solid and muscular frame.

'You forgot me, Miss Woodsen,' Mr Wallace said just before we separated.

'I forgot your name, sir. I did not forget *you*,' I said as we rejoined.

He smiled. 'I am glad to have found you to-night,' Mr Wallace said. 'I have wanted to thank you for the aid you offered my cousin that night.'

'And how is Miss Williams? and Mrs Williams?' I asked before we separated again.

'She is well. They are well. Lucy is to marry Mr Tattersall after all.' Again we separated and again rejoined.

'I am happy to hear it,' I said, although I remembered well adding the notice to Charlotte's commonplace book.

'It is due to you and Miss House that the marriage is to take place.'

'She deserves all the credit, Mr Wallace. I was a mere player.'

'You caught her as she fell.'

'And you caught me.' We exchanged partners again and rejoined.

'It was my pleasure.'

'I enjoyed it too,' I said, amused at my sudden boldness. I thought my reply caught him off guard for he seemed to trip as we exchanged partners, coincidentally with the young man who had been the partner of Miss Ashby earlier.

'My apologies,' he said after he caught up. 'I was worried that you had left Bath.'

'I was unwell for a time but have recovered.'

'I was unsure where I might call.'

'I stay with Miss House.'

'Then I might call upon you?'

'Yes,' I said, quickly adding before another separation, 'No. 1 the Royal Crescent. That is the address.'

All too soon the dance ended. Mr Wallace made his good-bye and promised again to call. Charlotte collected me and we returned to Mrs Fitzhugh.

'Jane has reconnected with Mr Wallace,' Charlotte told Mrs Fitzhugh.

'He did not know where I lived,' I said. 'He wanted to call.'

'Your spirits certainly have improved.'

'There is nothing like the expectation of a man,' Mrs Fitzhugh added.

I noticed the archness of their tone and said, 'Yes, well, all right. And how did you enjoy your dance, Charlotte? Mr Hickham certainly shewed an interest in you.'

'He is an excellent partner,' she answered. 'Let us find a place to sit and I'll tell you of our conversation.'

We found seats and Charlotte started: 'He repeated that he knew of me and of my employment. "You are the court of last appeal," he said—I rather liked that—"but what need arises that involves you in my betrothal to Miss Ashby?"

'I told him that it was merely coincidence that we met and that I was surprised that we had not met earlier.

'"Oh, but I have heard you are a dangerous woman, Miss House," he said—I rather like that as well—"and it is not wise to make the acquaintance of dangerous women." Utterly charming and designed to put me off my guard, which I am embarrassed to say it did.'

'Did you get the impression that he is aware of the letters?' Mrs Fitzhugh asked.

'No, I am certain he is not, although I naturally did not broach the subject directly. He did give me to understand that he is quite aware and forgiving of Miss Ashby's ... outgoing nature.'

'Indeed!' I said, shocked.

'"Experience is the best teacher and I benefit from what she has already learned," he told me.'

'I cannot believe it,' I said. 'Mrs Ashby seemed so adamant in her daughter's defence. You were quite correct, Charlotte. Everybody lies.'

'Yes, Jane, everyone does.'

I sighed and said, 'Unfortunately we have learnt little to help Miss Ashby.'

Charlotte smiled and looked at me curiously. 'You still wish to help her, with what you now think of her?'

'You told Mrs Ashby that we would help regardless. Besides, from what you say, they are suited for one another, and yet you know that Mr Hickham would never consent to marriage were it publicly known.'

'Lord and Lady M_ would never countenance that,' Mrs Fitzhugh agreed.

'Quite,' Charlotte said. 'However, Jane, you are incorrect to say that I have learned little. I learnt quite a deal of the young lord's character. You will remember a moment of clumsiness during the dance?'

I had hoped no one had noticed Mr Wallace's clumsiness, but of course Charlotte would.

'Do not blame your young man. Mr Hickham tripped Mr Henshaw who bumped into Mr Wallace.'

'What?' I said. 'How uncouth!'

'On the contrary, it was brilliantly done. I am sure Mr Wallace and Mr Henshaw are both blaming their own clumsiness when it is Mr Hickham to blame. In fact, I don't know how he did it, for I did not see it, but the look of satisfaction on his face made his guilt clear.

'I fear Mr Hickham is a contradiction. He appears on the surface affable and charming but underneath I suspect he can be petty and vindictive over such a little slight. I fear he uses people for his own ends without consideration of their ... why are you both looking at me in that way?'

'I really must get some refreshment,' Mrs Fitzhugh said. 'Will you accompany me, Jane?'

'I should be happy to, Margaret,' I said, and allowed her to lead me away from the puzzled Charlotte. In fact the rest of the night we tried to avoid looking directly at Charlotte and from that point Mrs Fitzhugh and I were fast friends.

The Winslowes Are Found

'Get up, Jane. We have found them.' I awoke to my friend violently shaking me and I cried out.

'Oh for heaven's sake, Jane, it's me. Wake up. We have found the Winslowes and if we act, we may find the author of these letters.'

I got out of bed to find Charlotte and Mrs Fitzhugh already dressed and awaiting me. Mary gave me coffee, which I greedily drank.

'What time is it?' I asked after a reviving sip.

'It's a little gone four,' Charlotte said. I had been asleep merely an hour. 'Get her into these clothes, quickly Mary.'

'And why am I awake now? Oh my head, I think I had too much negus.'

'Yes you did, now into this sleeve, Jane.'

I shrugged them off and said, 'I demand to know what is going on!'

'I already told you, Jane. My little urchins have located the Winslowes and if we act, we may find out who is sending these letters and if possible, catch them in the act.'

'Oh,' I said, finally awakening. 'That is another matter entirely. You may dress me, Mary, if I might have another sip of coffee first.'

I was dressed while Charlotte related the events of the past hours. Shortly after our return from the ball, Donna and Charlie, the captains of our street Arabs, arrived at the servant's entrance loudly demanding to be taken to Charlotte.

'Luckily Mrs Hutton heeded my admonitions and they were brought to me. They had located the Winslowes here in Bath, living a stone's throw from us in the Circus, but under the mother's maiden name Hazelton.' #

'Extraordinary,' I said. 'Living under an assumed name. There is desperation there.' I could not help but think of the times I wished I could live under another name to escape my father's shame.

'Not quite as it seems,' Mrs Fitzhugh said. 'Mrs Winslowe and daughter stay with the family of her brother, Mr Hazelton, his wife and their daughter.'

'Oh,' I said, 'that explains it.' I was a little disappointed that the explanation was so pedestrian.

We were now walking downstairs. 'Very well, I understand all this, but why must we go in the middle of the night? Can we not visit them in the morning as civilised people?'

'We do not go to visit. We go to catch our prey. Hurry Jane!'

A few minutes walk brought us to the Circus where it intersects with Bennett Street and No. 18, the house at the corner. We three …

'Wait, there are four of us,' I said.

'Mary, what are you doing here?' Charlotte asked.

'I'm sorry, miss. I just followed you whilst putting a cloak on Miss Woodsen.'

'And left the house without a covering of your own, silly girl. Go back at once.'

'Quiet,' I hissed, 'the door just opened.' I motioned us back down Bennett Street out of sight of the young woman who had just exited the house.

'What if she comes down this street?' I asked Charlotte.

'She won't, but quick, into this doorway.'

We watched the young woman cross Bennett Street and continue south along the Circus. As soon as she was out of sight, Charlotte said, 'Mary, I want you to return home immediately and instruct Mrs Hutton to have something warm for us on our return. And we may have a guest.'

'How do you know where she will go?' Mrs Fitzhugh asked, as we quickly followed behind the woman who had left the house.

'Because the Ashbys stay in Gay Street. Yes, she has turned.'

We followed the young woman at a distance for at this quiet time of night our footsteps echoed loudly, but we need not have worried, for the singleness of her purpose did not dispose her to look back.

'Yes, this is the Ashby's address, No. 40. Down!' she commanded. 'We can surprise her on her return.' We hid in the stairwell of a basement entrance. Only Charlotte had a clear view. #

'What is she doing, Charlotte?' Mrs Fitzhugh asked.

'She is putting a letter under the door,' she said. 'She's coming back.'

The young lady approached us and despite our concealment it seemed impossible that she could not see us. I could not help but think we were a comical group. But the next few seconds shewed that the night was ill suited to comedy.

Charlotte suddenly stood upright and said, 'Miss Catherine Winslowe? My name is Charlotte House and you will come with us to explain yourself.'

A sharp cry and a low moan prepared me and I rushed to catch the young woman as she fainted. Fortunately she was very slender and with Mrs Fitzhugh's help we kept her upright. Apparently I improved with practice.

'This should do the trick,' Charlotte said, as she produced a vinaigrette and waved its pungent aroma under Miss Winslowe's nose. Its effect was immediate and the young woman regained her balance. #

'Who are you?' she asked. 'Why do you frighten me so?'

'Miss Winslowe, you have much to explain. We know you to be the author of poisonous letters directed at Miss Ashby.'

'Why do you wish them ill?' I asked.

'Ill? I do not. I only hope that another will not suffer as I have.' She gave another low moan and I readied myself to support her again. Charlotte opened the vinaigrette.

'No, there is no need,' she said, stopping Charlotte's hand.

'We will take you to your home,' Charlotte said.

'No, please do not. It would distress my mother.'

'Then we shall take you to our home and there you can answer our questions.'

It was a long trip back to our home. Even with our assistance, Miss Winslowe walked slowly and I ached with a desire to ask her further questions, but I knew that she needed rest and something warm in her before she could talk. And despite the knowledge that she threatened the happiness of another, I could not help but feel sympathy for the burden she seemed to carry.

Mary, Alice and Mrs Hutton all awaited us when we returned home.

'Mary, get some blankets for our guest; and Mrs Hutton,

some brandy all round,' Charlotte ordered. We brought Miss Winslowe into the drawing-room and soon had her wrapped in blankets while Alice stoked the fire already laid for us. Mrs Hutton returned with the brandy.

'This should warm you,' Mrs Fitzhugh told Miss Winslowe. After a swallow, the warmth came back to her cheeks and she nodded her thanks. Finally Charlotte thanked our helpers and closed the drawing-room doors after they left. We three sat, Charlotte directly across from our guest, and we drank our brandy, and I realized how cold I was despite our exertion helping Miss Winslowe.

'Now, Miss Winslowe, perhaps you will tell us what you meant, that you did not mean Miss Ashby ill.'

'It is for her sake that I wrote those letters, to keep her from danger.'

'Ah, I began to suspect as much,' Charlotte said. She leant back in her chair and steepled her fingers before her. 'And that danger is?'

'Mr Hickham.'

'And what has that man done that makes him a danger?' Charlotte asked in a very cool voice. Mrs Fitzhugh and I exchanged looks and I knew my eyes were as wide as hers.

'He is not a man. He is a monster.'

The sob in Miss Winslowe's throat stabbed at my heart. Mrs Fitzhugh started to rise to tend to her, but Charlotte's single raised finger stopped her.

'You are among friends, Miss Winslowe. Tell us what Mr Hickham has done to you.'

'He has used me and left me unsuitable for any other.' Her hand stole to her left breast. We all noticed her movement. All was silent in the room save the crackle of the fire and the distant ticking of the hall clock.

'Let us see, please,' Charlotte said, in that tone of command at which I had earlier laughed. Miss Winslowe slowly pushed back the blanket from her shoulder and then pulled back the edge of her bodice. I heard Mrs Fitzhugh gasp as we saw the angry red scar that started at her collar bone. Her hand continued around the edge of the bodice and we could see that scar continued diagonally across her upper chest. Her hand stopped.

'It continues,' she said softly.

'Margaret,' Charlotte said, dropping her raised finger. Mrs Fitzhugh rose and attended Miss Winslowe, returning the poor woman's hand to her lap and wrapping the blanket tight against her body.

After a minute, Charlotte continued her questioning. 'This was last year, when there was an understanding between yourself and Mr Hickham?'

'Yes.'

'Why did he ... assault you in this way?' Charlotte asked.

'He demanded things of me that I could not give him.'

'Was he very demanding?'

'You must understand that at first ... at first he was all charm. He could be funny and kind and warm, but one day, in the country, it was as if he tired of the game. I had seen it before, when he struck a servant with whom only minutes before he had been joking. And it was the same with me, he said he'd "paid his dues" and wanted his reward.'

'And he ... took it?'

'Yes.'

'And left you with that reminder.' She nodded.

'And then shortly thereafter your father died and you removed from Bath.'

'Yes. My mother and I returned this season with my uncle and aunt.'

'And then you read of Mr Hickham's betrothal to Miss Ashby.'

'Yes. I could not let another ...'

'Quite.'

'But why …' I stopped and looked at Charlotte to see if I might continue. She nodded and I added, 'Why defame Miss Ashby?'

'Because no one would believe me when Mr Hickham … defiled me.' She spoke the last with an understandable bitterness at odds with her previous calm demeanour. 'I am sure my father died from shame of it. I could not say anything that would make the world believe the truth of it. All I could hope is that Mr Hickham would not hurt another.'

'But you could not bring yourself to irreparably harm Miss Ashby. Is that why you sent the letters only to her and those closest to her—that the harm might be contained?' I asked.

Miss Winslowe nodded. 'I have no wish to harm Miss Ashby. I hoped that the Ashbys would end the engagement rather than risk scandal.'

Charlotte sighed. 'You should have considered Mrs Ashby's prospect of ten thousand a year. She would risk much.'

'But why did you not send letters to Mr Hickham?' I asked.

'But I did.'

'What!' Charlotte said. 'When was this?'

'When he returned to Bath two … three days ago now. I could not deliver it personally, so I sent it by post.'

'This is very grave. Mr Hickham we now know is a very dangerous man. Why did you take such a risk?'

'The Ashbys would not act. I knew that I could not impugn that man's honour, but that he might shrink from marrying someone whose own honour was in doubt.'

'I cannot fault your logic, but your action may have put you in great danger.'

'Surely Miss Winslowe did not sign her name to the letter,' I said.

'It is anonymous,' she confirmed.

'Mr Hickham is a man of cunning. What one person has

surmised, so may another, but this may play in our favour, if you will accept my help.'

'You will not … you will help me?'

'My dear, a great injury has been done you and a great injustice goes unpunished. I … we … must help you and see that Mr Hickham never harms another.'

WHEELS IN MOTION

Once she had recovered, we escorted Miss Winslowe home after securing a promise that she would deliver no further letters and would not venture from her home and would at all times be attended. We also retrieved the new letter she had delivered to the Ashbys. 'There's no need to continue stirring the pot,' Charlotte said.

We returned as the clock struck five and Mrs Fitzhugh retired claiming she was fagged by the night's events, but Charlotte and I remained awake, the result of the copious amounts of coffee that followed our brandy. We sat quietly in the drawing-room while the rest of the house continued the business of the new day.

'How did you know?' I asked.

'Eh? How did I know what?'

'That she would be delivering a letter to-night … last night.'

'Just a guess. Mr Hickham returns to Bath and there is a ball. It seemed reasonable those happenings might spur another letter. And when I further learned that Miss Winslowe had a cousin her age in attendance last night, it made it plain.'

'How so?'

Charlotte sighed. 'I had begun to suspect Miss Winslowe was the author but I was unsure how she stayed *au courant* because she was not out in society. Once I learnt of the cousin, I knew that she had seen Mr Hickham's return. And the proximity of her home to that of the Ashbys made it seem likely that she would attempt to place a letter that very night. Although I was unsure if we would catch Miss Winslowe or the cousin in the act.'

'And you knew all along that the letter writer did not wish Miss Ashby ill?'

'Almost from the first. There was the reluctance to write an actual accusation and the delivery to only those persons who would support Miss Ashby and her family.'

'Did you suspect Mr Hickham's villainy?'

'No, that came as a surprise. How could I have suspected him capable of such a crime? And he certainly gave me no indication that he knew anything of the matter, and yet we now know he was in receipt of a letter.'

I finally decided to broach the topic I had been avoiding since our return.

'You have a plan, Charlotte?'

She sighed heavily at my words and sank into her chair. 'God help me, Jane, I do not.'

'Do not deceive me. You have a plan.'

'I would move heaven and earth so that she may see some justice done. I had a thought, but it would be cruel hard.'

'You mean to reveal to Mr Hickham—if he remains unaware—that she is the author of the letters.'

She straightened and said, 'Jane, that is an abominable suggestion.'

'And yet you are thinking it.'

She sat silently for a full minute while she played with the correspondence on the side table and I listened to the downstairs help cleaning the entrance hall. Finally she answered, 'I am thinking it. How else can we hope to find some measure of justice unless we can prompt Mr Hickham to act openly against her? He has to be seen to act.'

'I agree.'

'Jane, you really do surprise me. You would risk her safety?'

'She risks it herself. She is not afraid. Could you not feel it? She saw what she must do to protect another and she did it as best she could figure. That took courage that I fear I could never summon.'

'You're right, of course. Not to the latter, but the former.' She smiled faintly. 'Oh, Jane, I am sorry that I have led you into this. It does not all end in marriage and happiness.'

'You have nothing to apologize for, Charlotte. This sad story brings it all into perspective, doesn't it? What are my sad tales in comparison to this? A man, a very rich and powerful man, takes what he wants and there is nothing to be done.'

Charlotte gave no reply and I saw that she was no longer listening to me and was instead looking at one of the papers she had taken from the side table and was smiling.

'Perhaps something can be done after all.' She stood and took the paper to her writing desk and made a mark with her pen and then brought the paper to me. It was the bill from the Assembly Room that listed the season's entertainment and I saw she had circled the next night's ball, a themed event.

'I'm sorry, Charlotte, but how does this help us?'

'We need the proper venue to persuade Mr Hickham to act without putting our client in danger and I think this fits the bill,' she said. Then the smile left her face. 'Unfortunately, I must ask you to summon that courage you so admire in Miss Winslowe.'

'Of course,' I said readily.

'Stout Jane,' she said, without a hint of a smile, which unnerved me. She pulled a bell rope to summon a servant and Mary soon arrived.

'Mary, please set our signal to summon my little helpers,' she said and then turned to me. 'Now it is time to put wheels in motion.'

❦

It tires me still to think of the preparations we undertook that day. Normally Charlotte abhors a themed ball—'It is impossible to tell the truth from the half-truth from the out-right lie when one has the cloak of incognito'—and so we had not planned to attend, and we further had to involve Miss Winslowe in our preparations. Luckily, that lady had the courage in her I had suspected.

I must admit my own resolve rose and fell throughout the day. I had readily agreed to Charlotte's plan—I could not put our client in danger—and I should be happy to say that my only doubts were that I might not acquit myself properly, but it would be nearer the mark to say that I was simply scared. I never thought I would explore the depth of my own courage in this way.

Charlotte never noticed or perhaps she chose to ignore my misgivings, but Mrs Fitzhugh did her best to comfort me while we waited for Miss Winslowe to meet us at the dress-makers.

'Charlotte would do it herself if she could.'

'And stick out like a mustard pot in a coal scuttle. She is much too tall. I know it is my lot.' #

'There would be no shame …'

I laughed. 'That is a lie. I cannot desert my friend or fail that wronged woman.'

'When first you met Charlotte, she told me, "There is a strength in Miss Woodsen."'

I smiled. 'Is that in any way supposed to make me feel better?'

'And yet you smiled.'

Mrs Fitzhugh's mention of my tragedy suddenly made me curious. I said, 'She told me that she and I were united in suf-fering a great sadness.'

Mrs Fitzhugh gave a little laugh. 'How like her not to include me in that select club.'

'I am sorry. I said too much.'

She shook her head. 'My husband's death was as great a tragedy to me as Charlotte's own. But his was a pedestrian death, not a romantic one. No matter.' Although intrigued by her statement, I could see the sadness in my friend's eyes and decided it would be best not to ask further questions. And shortly thereafter Charlotte and Miss Winslowe arrived and we were busy with our fittings.

Later that day, we three set off to see Mr King and acquaint him with his part to play. To say he was reluctant would be to understate the matter—'It would be my ruin!'—but he agreed that if our accusations were unfounded, no harm would ensue. He was also helpful in finding a little-used room that would be instrumental to our purpose and ensuring that an adequate place of concealment would be installed.

The next day came too soon and the dressmaker had encountered some difficulties, but Charlotte's motley band reported success.

'They have delivered all but two of the letters, and hope to find some way to secrete those to-day,' Charlotte said.

'And the effect?'

'A hit, a palpable hit. He has found a number of letters in a number of improbable places already. I hope he walks about in a rage.' #

'Yes,' I said, with a falter in my voice. 'Let us hope that anger gets the better of him.'

'He should be uncontrollable for my plan to succeed. If

my judgement of his personality proves correct, he will strike without regard to reason. And then we will have him.'

I confess I almost lost my nerve.

'Oh, I almost forgot. I asked Mr King to provide a stout footman to prevent any danger … and I have received word that he has just the man.' Charlotte said this last as an after-thought, but I could see from her reluctance to meet my gaze that she was uncomfortable. #

I answered, also not looking at her directly, 'That was kind of him. So everything is thought of.'

We Confront Mr Hickham

We sent our instructions to Miss Winslowe through the me-dium of the street urchins and advised her to be at the Upper Rooms early so that her arrival would not draw attention. Fortunately her costume was provided in the nick of time, as was ours, or our plans would have come to naught.

We left as soon as the costumes arrived so that we might have time to set the stage for the night's drama. But despite our early start, we found that many, anticipating the themed event, had already arrived. We prayed that Mr Hickham would follow his usual custom of arriving late.

Mr King met us and Mrs Fitzhugh left with him so that she might prepare our stage while Charlotte and I entered the ballroom. In my apprehension and preparations I had almost forgotten the effect of a masked ball and I took a fair start at the sight before me.

'Courage, Jane,' Charlotte whispered to me, perhaps think-ing I was uneasy about the dangers before me. But in truth I was taken aback by the spectacle. I had long become inured to the wonders of the ball, but a *bal masqué* was something truly different. The timid wine merchant from Bathwick becomes Robin the Hood, and his wife of many summers and children, incongruously, and fittingly, becomes his Maid Marian. The barrister, who with the thrust of his words and the flash of his briefs imagines himself Sir Barrister, now dons his suit of tin plate armour as Sir Gawain. And Charlotte House reveals her true nature as Jeanne d'Arc.

'That is a very noisy costume, Charlotte,' I said. 'Will it be appropriate for our later subterfuges?'

She shrugged. 'A single clasp releases it.'

'Do we not have a disagreement with France at present?'

She shrugged again. 'I like it.'

I laughed and she turned to look at me and smile. 'I'm glad I offer you some amusement. Look, there is Miss Winslowe.'

I looked in the direction indicated and saw Miss Winslowe dressed as an Egyptian princess. We joined her.

'Miss House?' she asked, taken aback by my friend's costume.

'It is, Miss Winslowe, and I thought I made it clear that you should remain hidden until called.'

'The gentleman is not yet here and it has been a long time since I've been out. And you provided me such a beautiful costume.'

'It is quite becoming,' I agreed. 'The lace of the headdress is exquisite.'

'And it has the distinction, thank God, of being unique—well almost unique, if we are to believe Mrs. La Fontaine,' Charlotte said. Her tone softened. 'I understand the strain you have been under, but we must time things to a nicety. Is this your cousin?' Charlotte asked, indicating the young woman standing beside Miss Winslowe.

'Oh, forgive my manners. Yes, this is Miss Hazelton. Betty, this is Miss House and Miss Woodsen.'

We curtseyed and then Charlotte gave Miss Hazelton an

approving look. 'You have been Miss Winslowe's spy, have you not?'

'Yes, Miss House. I have kept her informed on the conduct of that man and his intentions toward the unfortunate woman he has targeted.'

'Well, your job now is to shield Miss Winslowe. You have another cousin, Miss Winslowe?'

'Yes, Robert, Mr Hazelton. He remains by the entrance and will notify us when … when he arrives.'

'Very well, remain close to the tearoom. Hide there if you must.'

We left Miss Winslowe and her cousin and continued our search for some of the other players in the night's drama.

'Now where are the Ashbys?' Charlotte asked.

It was now my turn to spot them. 'I don't see them … no wait, Mrs Ashby is seated in the far corner, dressed as Sukey. Miss Ashby is no doubt already with a partner.' #

We manoeuvred through the crowd and joined Mrs Ashby.

'Mrs Asbhy, you are prepared?' Charlotte asked.

'Who! Oh, Miss House. Yes, I received your instructions. Are you sure you know the identity of …'

'I am sure of it.'

'But why do you need to reveal it in this *outré* fashion?'

'It is enough that you know it is necessary, Mrs Ashby, nothing more. You must leave as arranged as soon as you see Mr Hickham.'

'Yes, yes, anything to see my dear girl married to him.'

'Of course, Mrs Ashby, we want to see Mr Hickham gets his reward as well.'

That task done, we tried our best to remain unpartnered, an easier task for Charlotte. She looked so fierce as the Maid of Orléans that few men approached her. I hid in a corner until a man wearing a Domino costume approached. With his bow he quickly pulled aside his mask. #

'Mr Wallace,' I said, with a start.

'You are disappointed, Miss Woodsen?'

'No, I am delighted to see you. Only it is my feet, sir,' I said, pointing to my Persian slippers. 'The pain keeps me from dancing. It is the price I pay for my costume.'

'An exotic from the East. It is quite ... enchanting,' he said, his eyes exploring me.

'It is, perhaps, more daring than I would normally ... dare,' I said, and I blushed, both for my clumsy words and the truth of it. For our strategy to-night, I required a simple and bare costume. 'And so you see me here trying not to attract attention.'

'And in that effort you have failed miserably,' he said. I smiled at his pleasantry, somewhat nervously given the intensity of his scrutiny.

'Perhaps rather than dance I might join you here being inconspicuous.'

'Then you would be failing in your duty as a gentleman.'

He sighed. 'What am I to do? Fail in my duty as a gentleman or as a friend.' He sat down beside me.

We chatted of inconsequentials and through his charm I relaxed and almost forgot my duties that night. I was reminded of them, however when Charlotte returned.

'Pardon me, Mr Wallace, but might I steal Miss Woodsen from you?'

Mr Wallace was startled by the sight of Charlotte towering above him, dressed for battle. 'Miss House?'

'It is very rude of me, but there is an old friend here I had promised I would introduce to Miss Woodsen and she is leaving soon.'

'Of course, Miss House. I fear I am at fault for monopolizing her time.'

'I did not mind,' I said.

'Yes, but now you really must join me,' Charlotte said, her arm on mine.

'You will forgive me, Mr Wallace,' I said, giving him a backward glance as Charlotte pulled me away.

'Time to concentrate, Jane. I have already despatched Mrs Ashby. Mr Hickham has finally arrived.'

How Charlotte knew for certain it was Mr Hickham I was unsure, although perhaps she had foreknowledge of his costume. He was dressed as Harlequin, and although there were two others dressed similarly that night, they were no match for the presumptive baron. His size, the fit of his tights, the evil mirth of his mask and the size of his slapstick made him the object of every lady's eye. He had timed his entrance with the end of the dance and had attracted a crowd, but it was obvious his attention was elsewhere. And his arrogant detachment and swagger seemed to elevate interest in him rather than degrade it. We walked as close to him as we dared. #

Finally Miss Ashby, dressed as Judy, caught his attention and he walked toward her, his eyes still seeking another in the crowd. #

We saw him nod stiffly to her and speak to her, presumably asking her to dance. A man, who was standing next to Miss Ashby and who had presumably already asked the pleasure of her company, stepped forward and addressed him but then stept away under Mr Hickham's glare. He then proffered his arm and took Miss Ashby to the floor.

'I think we can assume that Mr Hickham is in a foul mood,' Charlotte said.

'I think he wants to rip someone's head clean off,' I agreed, as we watched the dance start. 'What was in those letters you sent?'

'Oh, I might have dispensed with Miss Winslowe's attacks on Miss Ashby for a direct assault on the young lord. What do we have now?' she asked after a sudden noise erupted from the floor. I looked and saw that the dancers had stopped and were looking at Mr Hickham, who stood still with a piece of paper in his hand. His slapstick had fallen to the floor, accounting for the sound.

Charlotte laughed what I can only describe as a cackle, and said, 'Oh, what brilliant children.'

Mr Hickham tore off his mask and threw it to the floor. His face was flushed, as he looked left and right. We saw Mr King step forward as planned to confront and delay Mr Hickham.

'Jane, we must hurry. Miss Winslowe has heard the commotion; you can see her by the tearoom. Now would be the perfect time. Yes, she has seen my signal.' Charlotte turned to me. 'We must go.'

We hurried out the room. I could hear Mr Hickham's voice cursing as we left and I wished to see and hear more, but I knew we must hurry. We had some difficulty exiting as the crowd pressed in, but soon found ourselves in the Small Octagon and then to the room Mr King had prepared. #

We opened the door and immediately heard Mrs Fitzhugh's voice. 'It has started?' she asked. 'Indeed it has,' I answered. We closed the door behind us and all was darkness until a candle was uncovered and we saw Mrs Fitzhugh step out from behind a screen. We ran to meet her and slipped behind the screen where Mrs Ashby was also waiting.

'What is going on?' Mrs Ashby cried.

'Madame,' Charlotte said in her voice that brooked no quarrel, 'be silent. All will shortly be revealed.'

Mrs Ashby's protestations subsided and I quickly shed the Persian slippers and exchanged them for ones matching Miss Winslowe's footwear. And Mrs Fitzhugh removed Charlotte's armour with the release of a single clasp. She then helped me as I struggled to put on the headdress and outer garments that were the double of Miss Winslowe's costume. Charlotte also produced another candle, lit it from the first and then lit two more candles in the room, only slightly relieving the gloom.

While we were engaged, the door opened and I heard Miss Winslowe say, 'He has seen me and is right behind me.' I stepped out from behind the screen while Charlotte shepherded Miss Winslowe behind it, and then doused her own light and Mrs Fitzhugh's candle.

'Who is that?' I heard Mrs Ashby ask from behind the screen, at least this time in a hushed tone. Mrs Fitzhugh quieted her.

I arranged the veil that should conceal my face and then the door opened again and Mr Hickham entered, his body framed against the light without. He softly closed the door behind him and as he did, I wondered, *Where is the footman? And Mr King?*

'Is it you, Catherine?' Mr Hickham asked softly with a coldness that drew me back.

'It is, Frederick,' Miss Winslowe answered for me from behind the screen.

Mr Hickham walked toward me, forcing me to take another step until my back was against the screen.

'Take another step and I scream,' she said, her tone also cold.

He stopped and drew himself up to his full height, and I felt very small.

'Why do you accuse me with your letters? You have nothing to fear from me, Catherine. '

'You are right, for you have taken everything from me already, my maidenhood, my father's life, but you have kindly left me a scar that reminds me every day of my foolishness.'

I heard a small gasp, hastily smothered, from behind me, but luckily Mr Hickham did not notice. I, however, saw him take a slow step toward me that went unnoticed behind the screen. And I was powerless to say anything for fear of betraying our imposture.

'Catherine, I am truly sorry for what has happened between us.' He took another step. 'Upon my honour as a gentleman, I wish that I could atone for what I have done.' Another step.

I heard an almost inaudible whisper behind me and then Miss Winslowe said, 'A real gentleman ... would not need to beat women ... to summon his manhood.'

Mr Hickham stopped again and said very quietly. 'You will pay for that, you little bitch.' Suddenly he lunged for me and I felt his hands around my throat. I fell backwards into the screen, which also fell. From behind the screen I heard Mrs Ashby cry out as if from far, far away.

And suddenly an aromatic sting brought me awake.

I realized I was on the floor being supported by Mrs Fitzhugh and I saw Charlotte before me holding a vinaigrette. 'Thank God!' she said.

I also saw Miss Winslowe kneeling before me and as I said, 'What happened?' she flung her arms around me and embraced me. 'Dear Miss Woodsen, I am so sorry.'

'You were unconscious, Jane,' Charlotte said in answer to my question, 'but only for a second.' She helped disentangle Miss Winslowe from me. 'She might still be wanting for breath, my dear.' Her words made me realize the pain about my neck where Mr Hickham's hands had choked me. Charlotte then brought Miss Winslowe to her feet and I looked back upon a room that now seemed filled with light and people.

I saw to my surprise Mr Hickham being restrained by a footman and ... a confused looking Mr Wallace. I also saw Mr King attending to Mrs Ashby, who had sustained a small cut to her forehead. 'Your actions reveal you, Mr Hickham,' Mr King said while staunching her wound. 'You are no longer welcome here and if I had any say in the matter, you should be run out of Bath altogether.'

'And you will never marry my daughter,' Mrs Ashby added.

'Pray God he will never hurt another,' Miss Winslowe said.

Mr Hickham said nothing to all this as he continued to struggle. Suddenly he broke free of the footman's grasp and then Mr Wallace's, who found himself holding a empty sleeve of the Harlequin costume. Mr Hickham seemed unsure of which direction to turn and then bolted toward the open door. Then I saw Charlotte step forward and place a foot before his path, over which Mr Hickham stumbled, almost falling to the ground.

I yelled, 'Stop him!'

He regained his balance and continued his run for the door but Mr Wallace had placed his hand on Mr Hickham's shoulder. That man turned sharply about and I saw his fist fly toward Mr Wallace's face. But Mr Wallace was prepared and bowed low, the fist flying over his head. Then he sprang up and his right fist knocked Mr Hickham's head to the side, followed by his body flying backward and then falling to the ground.

Mr Wallace appeared stunned at what had happened and stood motionless for a second, then with a little gasp he trapped his hand under his left arm.

More people entered the small room and Mr King directed: 'Take this gentleman away and show him the street.' The footmen who had just entered moved toward Mr Wallace, but Mr King said, 'No, the one on the floor.' The two footmen dragged Mr Hickham from the room.

'Could someone please help me to stand?' I asked in a voice lost amidst the confusion of the room. Mrs Fitzhugh heard me and tried to help but was unable. Then I felt Mr Wallace's left arm slip around my waist and together they brought me upright. I then saw the pain on Mr Wallace's face and noticed the colour had drained from it.

'Please, someone help Mr Wallace,' I said, this time loud enough to be heard. A gentleman I did not know rushed to support Mr Wallace, who staggered, and then Mr King came to Mr Wallace's aid. Charlotte moved to Mr Wallace and carefully examined his hand.

'He has broken his hand. Does anyone have spirits?'

A small flask was provided and Charlotte raised it to his lips. Immediately after swallowing, he said, 'Thank you. I can stand on my own now.'

Yet another person entered the room and I heard a man cry, 'Elizabeth! Is my wife here?'

'Oh, Mr Ashby,' Mrs Ashby cried, 'it is awful. The marriage is off. Please get me away from here.'

'I think we would all be better off if we left,' Charlotte said. 'Mr King, if you would see to Mr Wallace. I believe him to be staying with the Williamses.'

'Of course, Miss House,' he said with a tired sigh.

'I am so sorry about the attention this has caused.'

'We have done a job of it, have we not?' He shook his head. 'But do not let it trouble you. Exposing that man for a monster is its own reward.'

'I would prefer, of course, that my involvement were to remain unknown.'

'Naturally.'

'And I think for her own sake, Miss Winslowe would prefer …'

Mr King looked toward that lady, now accompanied by her cousins. 'Say no more. From what you tell me, she has suffered enough.'

'As has my poor Jane,' Charlotte said, coming to my side. 'Come Margaret, we shall take our fearless friend home and praise her until she blushes.'

Partial Justice

'I have sent a letter to Lord M_ informing him of his son's behaviour,' Mr King said.

'Have you? That is rather bold of you,' Charlotte said. I lay on the sopha, listening to them talk and feeling pains in my body that had developed overnight. Falling into the screen with Mr Hickham's body atop me had caused more injury than I had realized and I had spent the day recuperating. Mr King's visit found Charlotte and me in the drawing-room. A glass of port remained just out of my reach and I made a small sound of distress. #

Charlotte sighed and said, 'Honestly, Jane. You are not that knocked up.' She rose anyway and brought me the glass and returned to Mr King.

'As I was saying,' she said archly, 'that was a brave thing.'

'Yes, well, it was my duty. I couched it in the best terms of course, but it was an unpleasant task. The baron, I understand, is an old man and frail, but there is nothing that might stop his son's bad behaviour other than his father's displeasure. As the son of a baron, attaining justice will not be an easy thing, and unless Miss Winslowe or Miss Woodsen step forward ...' #

'I think Miss Winslowe has suffered enough and I think the notoriety—which I trust we will maintain—will considerably dampen Mr Hickham's appeal,' she said. 'As for Jane,' and here she looked at me, 'well, we cannot act freely or discreetly if we're always in court.'

I nodded my head in agreement to no little pain and took another sip.

'It is a partial justice at best,' said Mr King with a sigh.

'Partial justice is better than none. Miss Winslowe feels justly proud that she has stopped Miss Ashby from being Mr Hickham's victim. She no longer feels powerless, I think.'

I could see through half closed eyes Mr King nod, and then he said, 'I have looked in on your Mr Wallace, Miss Woodsen. Or perhaps I should say Doctor Wallace.'

I opened my eyes and said, 'I am happy that you have done so, sir, but he is not my ... wait, you said doctor?'

'Yes, formerly he travelled with Colonel William Davis and his regiment, although I think he and the colonel have parted ways.'

'I did not know he was a professional man,' I said, and then realized I actually knew very little of him 'How is he?'

'In pain and still a little confused—I did what I could to explain within the bounds of propriety—but happy that he could be of help. He asked of you and said that he would call when you are better.'

I sat up and said, 'If you see him next, you could say that I am better.'

Mr King gasped and I realized the scarf that concealed my neck had slipped. I quickly rearranged it.

'It's not as bad as it looks.'

'Now this is the real Jane, bravely bearing her injuries. They are rather gruesome, aren't they?' Charlotte asked, referring to the bruises about my neck.

'I should have had him beaten. I should have done it myself,' Mr King said with uncharacteristic vehemence.

'Mr King,' I said, 'you have acted very honourably and could not have acquitted yourself better.'

He stood and gave me a little bow. 'Thank you, Miss Woodsen. Well, I had best be off and see what else I can do to restore the smooth running of our society.'

Charlotte saw him out and returned to me. 'He is a very gallant man, our Mr King, and I think he feels a certain guilt in not seeing the true quality of Mr Hickham.'

'That is not his fault. Many were fooled by the man.'

Charlotte sat next to me on the sopha and took my hand. 'I have to tell you Jane that I also have some guilt in this matter.'

'How so?'

'I failed to ensure that you had adequate protection.'

'That is not your fault,' I said. 'In the rush of things ...'

'No, I knew as we left the ballroom that my plan had a flaw. Deciding at the last moment to use Mr King to delay Mr Hickham meant that there would be no footman. But I had to ensure that Mr Hickham would see Miss Winslowe leave the room and know that she was the author of the letters.'

'Ah,' I said, 'I rather noticed the footman's absence when Mr Hickham entered.'

'And yet you said nothing.'

'Well, *you* said nothing.'

I heard the door open and Mrs Fitzhugh entered. 'What is this *tête-à-tête?*' #

'Charlotte was just explaining how she risked my life,' I said.

'And Jane was just explaining how she let me do it.'

'As long as everyone is in agreement.'

'And how is Miss Winslowe?' Charlotte asked. Mrs Fitzhugh had gone to see how the other parties in the night's drama had fared.

'She seems in a fine mood. She said that it feels like a great weight has been lifted and that she can now continue her life.'

'And Mrs Ashby?' I asked.

'H'm, disappointed. On the one hand, she seems relieved to know that the letters did not reach a wider audience and that her daughter had escaped marriage to such a man.'

'And on the other, she's upset that a baron's son has slipped through her fingers,' Charlotte added.

Mrs Fitzhugh laughed. 'Precisely.'

'One cannot blame her. It is her job to see her daughter

married and now she must start again. Well, I am off; I must collect Mary and make my calls. Margaret, you will see to our invalid?'

'Of course.'

Charlotte left and Mrs Fitzhugh attended me, refilling my port and arranging pillows and generally filling my head with pleasantries, until she said, 'There's something I think I must tell you, Jane.'

'What is it?'

'Before I do, I must ask whether you are fond of Charlotte.'

'Why yes, very fond. Well, she can be ... Charlotte. She can be unkind and she does use people for her own ends. But then she can be very kind and I know she means well.' I paused and thought more about it before concluding, 'I think she is the very best friend I have ever known.'

'I had hoped as much. Even though I know her faults, she is as dear to me as if she were my own daughter and I am so happy you are friends.'

'This leads somewhere, does it not?'

'Your meeting with Mrs Danvers; it did not go well.'

With the excitement of the last few days I had almost forgotten. 'Yes?'

'I found this in the library.' She handed me the beginning of a letter that had been discarded because of a large blot of ink caused by a quill splitting. It said:

Mrs Danvers,

I am writing you to warn

I looked at her and said, 'She was writing to Mrs Danvers?'

'Yes, although from this one cannot say that she ever completed a letter or sent it.'

I could not help but recall the look on Mrs Danvers face.

'No, she most definitely sent it.' I handed the letter back to Mrs Fitzhugh.

'Of what do you think Charlotte accused me?'

'I do not know,' she said mournfully, looking down.

'Probably something pretty dreadful.'

'Oh no, I am sure it was … ' She looked up at me and caught my expression. 'Yes, it was probably something dreadful.'

'Stealing the plate? Pinching children?' I joked.

'You already knew!'

'I already saw the letter. She obviously left it out to be found. This is another of her little tableaux.'

'And you are not angry?'

'Why should I be angry? No less an authority than our Mary had already informed me that I should be miserable as a governess. Neither fish nor fowl, she said. Besides, where else can I find such excitement than at Charlotte's side? I have helped expose a future lord as a monster and helped a woman cruelly wronged obtain a measure of justice. And who knows what else I might do?'

'But you must confront Charlotte. I did not teach her to behave in this way.'

'Confront her? What on earth for? When did you find this?'

'This morning before I left.'

'Good, Charlotte has not been in the library, I think. Put it back where you found it. It will vex her more and more each day as I refuse to acknowledge it.' I smiled at the thought of it.

Mrs Fitzhugh looked at me strangely. 'You become more and more like her, you know,' she said and then left to return the letter.

After the door closed I relaxed and found my glass of port, which Mrs Fitzhugh left close at hand. I took a sip—my friend kept an excellent liquor cabinet—and closed my eyes and despite my aches I found myself exceedingly pleased and at home.

The Affair of the Reluctant Bachelor

*I*t was two weeks after our confrontation with Mr Hickham, while I was sitting with Charlotte and Mrs Fitzhugh, that Charlotte quietly said, 'Bored, bored, bored.' We ignored her, as it was not the first time we had heard this. Seeing that we ignored her, she continued, 'Are there no problems? Hasn't a curate been seen with an unchaperoned daughter? Isn't there a fishwife somewhere who wants her daughter to marry a duke?'

'You're being silly, Charlotte,' Mrs Fitzhugh said, not looking up from her correspondence.

'You urged Mrs Chandler not to pursue Mr Simpson for her daughter,' I said.

'Oh please, he cheats at cards to cover his debts, although I admit he is clever to have established his reputation of a nervous constitution. His constant fidgeting conceals the dexterity with which he marks cards. He will be found out all too soon.'

'We still have plenty to do,' I added. 'We go to a *soirée* this evening.' #

Charlotte gave a disgusted sound and I think I heard the word *'soirée'* muttered under her breath as if it were the most disgusting word in the language—or at least in French. I knew the relative inactivity chaffed her. For several days after that fateful night, Charlotte was busy doing what she could to see that Mr Hickham's disgrace was firmly established—'A word here, a word there, soon it spreads like the pox'—while attempting to conceal our rôle and that of Miss Winslow.

And soon enough her prediction came true and rumours about Mr Hickham, wildly distorted from the facts, circulated about the town. Callers to our home even related these rumours to Charlotte, who found herself in the position of defending Mr Hickham—'I cannot believe what you say, Mr Hickham seemed such an amiable fellow'—while able to fan the flames at the same time—'and I am sure the rumour that he struck a servant so savagely he almost died a monstrous calumny.'

I, of course, remained at home until the bruises about my neck faded, and I soon found myself wanting to rejoin society. I especially hoped I might have the society of Mr Wallace but apart from a few letters inquiring as to my health I had not seen nor heard of him since.

Charlotte also found herself increasingly restless once the rumours had established their own momentum. After she and our mutual friend had resumed their regular visits and entertainments, Charlotte declared again and again that she now found our routine tiresome.

'Your problem, Charlotte, is that our encounter with Mr Hickham has excited you. You crave adventure but all you find is the mundane, while I, for one, find some comfort from it.' I brought my hand to my neck hoping that I could draw some sympathy from her.

'Oh please, Jane, you have gone to the well one too many times.'

Mrs Fitzhugh gave a little laugh that confirmed my ploy had indeed outgrown its usefulness. I laughed as well and Charlotte at least smiled. Then came a knock at the door and the footman entered.

'A caller, Miss House,' Robert said, and handed her a card.

Charlotte lazily took the card from the proffered salver and glanced at it. 'What does he look like, Robert?'

He answered in his courtly way, 'I should not like to make a judgement on so brief a meeting, but he appears a refined young gentleman, Miss House.'

'H'm,' Charlotte said. 'Refined young men don't call this early in the day.'

'You say you're bored, my dear, let him in. We have already shed our morning dress and are prepared to meet the world,' Mrs Fitzhugh said. #

'Very well, Robert, let him in but be prepared to throw him out if he fails to amuse.' We stood to greet our visitor; Charlotte did so slowly.

Robert bowed, left and returned with our visitor. 'Mr Albert Worcester,' he announced before leaving us with the refined young gentleman. He was of slight build and moderate stature and dressed to the height of fashion, although he appeared a bit rumpled; and he carried a confused look about him that elicited a certain concern for his well being.

We curtseyed and spoke our names and he returned us each with a bow. As ever, Mrs Fitzhugh acted as a proper hostess and saw him to a chair.

'How is that spelled, Mr Worcester?' I asked, as I did not have the benefit of the card that Charlotte still held. #

'As in the shire, Miss ... Woodsen? Sorry, I'm so bad with names I practically forget my own sometimes. I depend on my man to remind me. I mean the name of the person I'm talking to, of course, not mine. No, a name goes in one ear and out the other, ha, ha.'

'Quite, Mr Worcester. And to what do we owe the pleasure of your visit?' Charlotte asked, which seemed to me a bit rude.

'Brass tacks, eh? No beating about the bush. Get to the

point, as the man says. Once more unto the what's it. It's a thing my man sometimes says.'

'Once more unto the breach, dear friends?' I offered. #

'That's it. But stay, do you know my man?'

'No Mr Worcester, we do not,' Charlotte said. 'We know nothing of him or you, other than you are a very wealthy young man from London, most likely Kensington, have travelled quite some distance to be here, have yet to take lodging and that you have recently discharged your valet, whom I believe to be the man to whom you refer.' #

Mr Worcester stared at her open mouthed.

'That is amazing,' he confirmed. 'How do you know this?'

Despite wanting to appear indifferent, Charlotte could not resist looking pleased. 'It is a simple matter. That you are wealthy is in evidence by your fashionable clothing that bespeaks a London tailor and your walking stick … which is seriously in danger from falling over and smashing a rather nice vase, due to its heavy gold knob.' Mrs Fitzhugh quietly laid the stick on the floor. 'That you do not have a valet at present is shown by your waistcoat, which is off by a button, evidence of a gentleman dressing himself. And your coat is stained by rain and as it hasn't rained here in days you have travelled a distance. And had you entered lodgings, those stains would have been erased by now.'

'Absolutely right. You're a magician!' He looked down at his waistcoat and I could see he weighed the propriety of fixing his buttons.

'No, I am merely observant.'

'And your surmise about Kensington?' I asked.

'When a young man from London suddenly appears on my doorstep I assume he has been sent by my brother Michael. I also, I admit, now recall his name.'

Mr Worcester nodded at this. 'Well this is fun. You

wouldn't know what I did with my pocket watch, would you? Can't find the silly thing anywhere.'

'No, Mr Worcester, I do not. And now if I might ask again the reason for your visit.'

'Well, as to that, I'm in a spot of bother. I've gone ahead and gotten myself engaged.'

'Congratulations,' Mrs Fitzhugh said.

'To two women, bit awkward.'

'Ah,' Charlotte said, rising, 'I am afraid I cannot help you and I hate to waste your time.'

'Charlotte, let him explain.'

'Yes, Charlotte, he looks so lost,' I agreed with Mrs Fitzhugh.

Charlotte looked levelly at Mr Worcester and I could tell that she could now see his despair as well. She sat and said, 'To have gotten engaged to one woman accidentally is perhaps understandable. To do it twice shows carelessness. How did this come about?'

'Charlotte, might we have some tea?' Mrs Fitzhugh asked. 'If as you say this young man has only just arrived after a long journey …'

'Please,' I begged.

Charlotte shrugged her shoulders and only began to call out Robert's name when he opened the door, having been ready no doubt to throw out our visitor.

'Some tea, Robert?'

'Yes, Miss House,' he answered and left. We waited for the tea, which arrived momentarily thanks to the prescience of Mrs Hutton. While Mrs Fitzhugh prepared our tea I noticed Mr Worcester make several attempts to fix his waistcoat only to give up in frustration. Once we were settled, Charlotte returned her attention to our guest and said: 'Now you will tell us how you came to be engaged to two women.'

'It all started with Evelyn Blankenship. You know her, of

course? No? Well she's a good sort if a trifle high minded, always saying stirring stuff about the rights of man and how we're all noble born, even the lowest among us. I can't see it myself and neither can her father, Sir Walter; they're always arguing about it. I stick up for her of course; you always have to back up an old chum, even if they're all wet.

'Did I mention she's pretty to look at, too? Or she would be if she weren't always telling you how you need to improve your mind. "Your mind is like clay, Bertie, soft formless clay. Someone needs to come along and make something of it." Some fellows like that sort of self-improvement, like my friend Blotto, that is Bartholomew, Bartholomew Cuthbertson. Says his mind's needing improving from day one and she's just the girl to do it. It takes all kinds to make a world, I always say.

'And I'm right because wouldn't you know it she thinks Blotto's mind—this is Mr Cuthbertson's mind—is soft and formless too, which is her way of expressing interest. And before you know it Blotto—Mr Cuthbertson, I mean—who previously was ignorant of the lowest among us, is now taking them soup and doing them various good works, or rather he's having a servant do it. He's completely smitten with her.

'But it will never work out because Blotto's the younger son and Lady Blankenship has got higher hopes for Evie—that is Miss Blankenship—and he has never said a word to Evelyn —that is Miss Blankenship …'

'If I might interrupt, Mr Worcester. You apparently maintain a social informality peculiar to your circle. You will not offend us if you refer to the participants in this matter as you would normally.'

'Oh, that's a relief and very liberal of you. Well, what was I saying? Oh yes, Mr Cuthbertson … well dash it all, there I go ignoring what you'd just said. *Blotto* … got it in two … has never said a word to *Evie* to jolly things along. Add to that he's got the face of a sad lobster and has never been good with the honeyed words and thus it may be quite some time before anyone applies for a special license.'

'Yes, Mr Worcester, but how does all this relate to your being engaged?' Charlotte asked, testily.

'Nearly there, Miss House. Now where was I? Yes, so Blotto follows Evelyn like a moonstruck cow, doing good works left and right but nothing comes of it because Lady Blankenship would never allow it and because Blotto refuses to plight the old troth because of the lobster aspect and that he considers himself unworthy of Evelyn.

'And that's when Evelyn has one of her brilliant ideas that the general public would consider a stinker but that she thinks a corker. She invites me to Dashwood Abbey, Blankenship's stately home, and announces between the soup and fish that we are engaged.'

'And what was the reasoning behind this,' Charlotte asked, this time with more interest.

'Stock in Worcester does not trade highly at the Abbey. On a previous visit, Sir Walter found me sitting fully clothed in the garden pond with a fowling piece and calling softly "Coo, coo … coo, coo," and since then he has considered me a lunatic, no less because the fowling piece shot through the lantern he held in his hands.' #

'I see, so in comparison to you …'

'Yes, that was Evelyn's cunning plan. She hopes to parade me before her parents, and threaten them with Worcester.'

'While at the same time making Blotto—Mr Cuthbertson—jealous.'

'Exactly, you have the *précis*. The flaw in her plan, of course, is that despite Sir Walter's low opinion of me, I am considered quite a catch by the mothers of the world.'

'Why would you agree to this plan, Mr Worcester?'

'She appealed to the principle by which all Worcester men live. You might even call it a code.'

'And that is?'

'Never let a chum down. I've known Evelyn for ages and when she looked into my eyes—did I mention she's pretty?—and asked for my help I couldn't say no.'

Charlotte leaned back in her contemplative attitude. She steepled her hands—no mean feat when sitting on a sopha—indicating she was intrigued by our guest's story.

'I admit I find your story absurd but you do seem to have acquitted yourself honourably. But this still leaves the matter of your other engagement. Who is the lady?'

'Miss Stephanie Stilton, Cheese Mite to her friends, because she's small you see, but she's trouble. Knowing her is like sitting next to a cannon that could go off at any second. She has red hair. Considered quite beautiful by those who don't know the danger she poses.'

'And is she another old friend?' Charlotte asked.

'Yes, although not mutual friends with Evie. Their tempers put them at odds with each other. And the Mite's an even older friend than Evie. She knew me before I was breeched.' #

'And how did you come to be engaged to Miss Stilton?' I asked, finding myself quite engaged in Mr Worcester's tale.

'Yes, were you similarly … manoeuvred?' Mrs Fitzhugh asked, obviously also finding the matter amusing.

'Not quite. I was visiting my Aunt Hermione, where Miss Stilton was also a guest. She's my aunt's niece on my uncle's side, well from his first marriage, which makes her related to me in some fashion I don't understand. Not my aunt, of course, she's obviously related to me, although you wouldn't think of it by looking at her. I think Stephanie is my uncle's first wife's sister's husband's …'

'The details are unnecessary, Mr Worcester,' Charlotte said. 'Pray continue.'

'Right-ho. So it was at my aunt's home in London and the Mite and I were in the garden, and there was a Moon and she got her hair tangled up in this tree thing and I had to help her free herself and she had to tilt her head back like this and I had to lean forward like this to help her and somehow or other I kissed her. I don't know how it happened; I know it was improper. I mentioned there was a Moon, didn't I?

'Well who should come by right at that time but Aunt Hermione and she said, "Albert!" in that voice that shatters glass and frightens small children and horses and I said the first thing that popped into my head.'

By this time even Charlotte was smiling when she asked, 'And that was?'

'I said, "It's all right, we're engaged."'

We all now laughed heartily at poor Mr Worcester's expense, who blinked sheepishly at our amusement.

'I say, it may be funny to you, but I find myself in rather a pickle.'

'My ... our apologies, Mr Worcester,' Charlotte said, 'but surely Miss Stilton does not hold you to this.'

'She bally well does. She was in a cross mood because of her own romantic difficulties, you see.'

'Ah, another rival for her affections?'

'Old Potty, known him for years, thick as a brick wall, and about as big. He's mad about the Mite, but she won't return his affections because he's too afraid to ask Aunt Hermione for the living she has floating around.'

'He would take orders?' she asked. It was now obvious Mr Worcester interested her strangely.

'Already has. He's a sort of under curate, toiling away in obscurity. Cheese Mite always says he has the stuff for it, but is kept in check by his vicar, jealous of Potty's natural aptitude. Don't see it myself. I'm not judged particularly bright, but Potty could give lessons to the village idiot. Good sort, though. Leant me a shilling when that was all he had in the world. Shows he's full of Christian charity, which is probably useful for a vicar.' #

'Presumably so,' Charlotte said. 'I take it then that Miss Stilton wants to goad Mr—excuse me, what is the gentleman's actual name?'

'Let me think … Clarence Potterwhistle. No, that's not right. Potterthwaite. That's it.'

'Then Miss Stilton wants to use your proposal to goad Mr Potterthwaite into asking your Aunt Hermione for the living.'

'You've hit the nail on the head, Miss House. Potty's terrified of the old maternal relative. Fact is, everyone's frightened of her. She pulls off the *grande dame* act as to the manor born. And the truth is you don't have to go very far back to catch the distinct aroma of salted cod from the family fortune.'

'How interesting that these two women should have hatched such similar schemes.'

'Happens all the time, actually.'

'And how does your aunt view your engagement?'

'She approves wholeheartedly. She's been trying to unite Worcester and Stilton for ages.'

'A heady mixture indeed, and now, I have to ask, why do you come to me?'

'You were correct, I do know your brother … sorry, 'bout to say … asked me not to call him that … your brother Michael. He said you could help me avert the calamity.'

'You have a nickname for him as well? Your lips are sealed? Never mind, what is the calamity?'

'Aunt Hermione has removed to Bath and I've come to join her at Deerfield Park. She has also invited Miss Stilton's family. And I just got word before I left that Sir Walter and family will be joining the party as well. The whole lot of them in Bath cheek by jowl and for once I don't have my man to tell me what to do.' #

'I see the difficulty. There will be unpleasantness when it

is discovered that you … wait, how does the absence of your valet affect the matter?'

Her question stopped his litany of woes and he fixed on his face a worshipful expression before continuing. 'It will probably sound odd to you, but I depend on him for these situations.'

'These situations? You often find yourself accidentally engaged to two women?'

'No, no, of course not; two is unusual.'

'You amaze me, Mr Worcester. Perhaps you should tell us why you don't have the services of your valet.'

'Owing to a disagreement over purple waistcoats, I'm afraid. We can't see eye to eye on the matter and regrettably I had to let him go. Can't be dictated to by one's valet after all.'

We all noticed that Mr Worcester looked very sad and Mrs Fitzhugh laid her arm on his.

'Extraordinary,' Charlotte said. 'And your man would advise you what to do whenever you found yourself accidentally engaged?'

'Yes, he has a great mind, you see. No problem is in- something.'

'Insurmountable?'

'That's it. I feel rather lost without him.'

'And what is this worthy's name?'

'Oh, Cheevers. So you see, Miss House, I have no one to tell me what to do and your brother suggested you might act as my guide.'

Charlotte laughed. 'I would be happy to be your Cheevers, Mr Worcester.'

A PLAN OF ACTION

'You amaze me more and more, Charlotte,' I said after our guest had left.

'And why is that my dear?' she asked with her pleasantly condescending smile, rather than the withering one she uses on dowager countesses.

'I was certain you would tell Robert to send Mr Worcester packing.'

'I too am intrigued,' Mrs Fitzhugh added.

'It is a lark, I admit, but I thought it might be pleasant to address ourselves to a problem of little import.'

I sniffed and said, 'It is a matter of great import to Mr Worcester. In the matter of Miss Stilton, he might face a breach of promise.' #

'I misspoke then—a matter of little complexity. After all, I should be able to match the talents of Mr Worcester's valet. I think I want to know a little more about our client and the other actors. Jane, will you join me?'

We left Mrs Fitzhugh in the study to finish her correspondence and entered the library. Charlotte turned to the shelves to find the volume she needed.

'Jane, find my London commonplace books to see what there is of Mr Worcester—start two years previous—and I shall see what I can find of Sir Walter in Debrett's.' #

Luckily more of Charlotte's library had arrived to supplement her travelling books and I found the London books for 'W' and leafed through until I found the time period. Rather than interrupt Charlotte with each discovery pertaining to Mr Worcester, I added them to the journal I now kept relating to our employment. Charlotte, of course, merely remembered whatever she read, but I had not that facility. I often wondered aloud how troublesome it would be to retain so much knowledge, but she always said when information no longer was useful she promptly forgot it. I found difficulty believing her statement and asked her to give me an example of knowledge she no longer found useful. She countered that she could not because she had forgotten any examples. I countered that she could not cite an example because knowledge never becomes useless. She merely looked at me, blinked twice and said, 'I'm sorry, what were we talking about?'

'Jane, have you found anything? And what is that smile about?'

'Sorry, yes,' I said, and looked at my notes. 'You have several clippings about Mr Worcester but apart from one notation—"mostly harmless"—you appear to have given him little thought. I find two engagement notices—one in fact to Miss Stilton, and he has appeared several times before a magistrate for assault and drunken behaviour.'

'Hidden depths, indeed.'

'Not quite as it seems, Charlotte. These incidents appear to involve the bad blood between Oxford and Cambridge.' #

'Oh that! I suppose we cannot hold that against Mr Worcester. Were you to go back a few years earlier you might find my brother involved in similar affairs of honour.'

'And what of Sir Walter?' I asked.

'He is a baronet in Surrey of great wealth and unsavoury reputation, whose family has been supplying gunpowder to the Navy for generations. He has two daughters, of whom Miss Blankenship is the eldest. I do recall now that his daughter is outspoken and has caused him no little trouble.' #

'We should also find what there is of Mr Worcester's aunt and Mr Stilton.'

'No need, I know of Mrs Walthorpe, the aunt: a tyrant of an old lady but not genuinely unkind. And as for Miss Stilton's father, he stands for parliament and should he ever be successful will doubtless experience a long and meaningless career. His daughter is also considered quite beautiful and spirited. For a man of little distinction, Mr Worcester seems fond of women of some notoriety.'

'What is our plan of action?'

'Our first step is to ensure the interested parties remain unaware of Mr Worcester's competing claims, and to do that we need to be on hand.'

I was sceptical. 'How will we do that?'

'Isn't it obvious? Some time has already passed since Mr Worcester found himself engaged, and yet the families remain unaware. Undoubtedly some part of the delay may be attributed to preparation for their remove to Bath. But I think we may find there are other reasons for the delay. Come, we must collect our friend and call on Mrs Walthorpe. And it might be a good idea to have Alice prepare what you will need for a visit.'

Fortune smiled on us for we found Mrs Walthorpe very eager to welcome Charlotte. Despite a rather severe aspect, she did not seem quite the forbidding creature Mr Worcester had described and offered us refreshment to prolong our visit.

'My dear Miss House, how is your brother? I do not see enough of him and he is just the sort of young man of consequence with whom Albert should be seen.'

'My brother is well and often speaks of you and your nephew in glowing terms. He asked especially that I should call on you once he heard that you would visit Bath. I apologize for the timing of our visit. I did not know that you had only recently arrived and you've barely had time to settle.'

'Your concern does you credit, Miss House, and I am very happy to meet you. I have heard so much of you from your brother. Such a polite young man. And he has always complimented you as a young woman of sense and perspicacity. If only my Albert ... but where is he? He was to arrive to-day from London. We are planning such a party, Miss House. Mr Stilton, whom your brother has no doubt informed you stands for Parliament, is here with his wife and daughter, a charming young woman who ... well, never mind about that, you will know shortly. And Sir Walter Blankenship and his family are to join us. He does me a very great honour in attending. Together our families have been very instrumental to the defence of our nation.'

Salted cod and gunpowder are both equally important to the Navy, I thought, as Mrs Walthorpe continued, expounding further on the importance of her guests. She directed no remarks to me or Mrs Fitzhugh and I saw my friend's eyes droop as Mrs Walthorpe's words extolling her guests washed over us. Distantly I heard a knock and a door open.

'Albert!' she suddenly exclaimed in a voice that brought us out of our somnolence. I suddenly realized Mr Worcester was standing before us. He seemed to be swaying slightly, either from the impact of his aunt's voice, which he had accurately described, or else from his surprise upon seeing us.

'Where have you been?' his aunt demanded.

Mrs Fitzhugh and I stood to join Charlotte and our action reminded Mrs Walthorpe of her duty.

'Miss House, Mrs Fitzhugh, Miss Woodsen,' she said, as we curtseyed in turn, 'may I present my nephew, Mr Albert Worcester.'

Mr Worcester bowed and then stared at us and several times opened his mouth to speak but no words escaped his lips.

'Say something Albert!'

Charlotte, however, spoke before Mr Worcester. 'It is very good to meet you for the first time, Mr Worcester.'

'How do you do?' he asked woodenly.

'It is so nice to meet you Mr Worcester,' I added. Mrs Fitzhugh nodded her head slowly in confirmation.

'Surely you must be tired if you have just arrived, Mr Worcester,' Charlotte said.

'You look quite done in, Mr Worcester,' Mrs Fitzhugh agreed.

'Hmph!' Mrs Walthorpe said. 'You do look unpresentable. Beach!' Her shout induced Mr Worcester to sway again but also produced the butler. 'Take my nephew away and get him cleaned up.' And then her tone softened. 'Albert, get something to eat. You do look a little peaked.'

After he left she returned her attention to Charlotte and even seemed dimly aware of my presence and that of my friend.

'My apologies. He has only arrived from London and no doubt he has much on his mind.'

Upon Mrs Walthorpe's statement, Charlotte gave Mrs Fitzhugh a look and a nod.

'And why would that be?' Mrs Fitzhugh said, her eye on Charlotte as she asked her question. Charlotte nodded her approval.

'Why ... I do not know whether I should say at this time. I have made several announcements in the past that have not ...'

'I thought I recognized that look; Mr Worcester is engaged!' Charlotte said with a practiced enthusiasm.

'Er, yes, to Miss Stilton.'

'*Oh,*' Charlotte said, and then cast her eyes downward.

Mrs Walthorpe waited for Charlotte to expand on her comment. Then she looked inquiringly at me and all I could do was offer a pleasant smile as I began to understand Charlotte's plan. Finally our hostess asked, 'Is there something wrong, Miss House?'

'No, it is not my place.'

'Please, your brother calls you a young lady of discernment. Is there something that concerns you?'

'No, please, it is only ...'

'Yes?'

'I seem to recall from something my brother mentioned. Was not your nephew previously engaged to Miss Stilton?'

Mrs Walthorpe looked uncomfortably about the room and then picked at an imaginary defect upon her sleeve.

'Some time ago, yes, it was then a young man's fancy. I assure you this proposal is far more ...'

'Serious?'

Mrs Walthorpe nodded. 'Then I am sure there is no need for concern and I fear any opinions you might hear from me would be presumptuous,' Charlotte said brightly. 'After all, I'm sure Mr Worcester has no reputation as an imprudent young man.'

Mrs Walthorpe stopped nodding and coughed suddenly and repeatedly. Mrs Fitzhugh quickly refreshed our hostess's cup and offered it to her. She gratefully swallowed and after composing herself she said, 'Perhaps Miss House, you will treat news of my nephew's engagement as a private matter. It might be premature to ...'

'Of course Mrs Walthorpe. You may rely on the discretion of my friends as well. I think we're all aware of the delicacy of announcing an engagement.'

Mrs Fitzhugh nodded her agreement and said, 'Oh absolutely. It is so embarrassing to announce an engagement one day and be forced to retract that news the next.'

I added, 'Young love can be so impetuous.'

Mrs Walthorpe now seemed to comprehend fully the existence of myself and Mrs Fitzhugh and she nodded pleasantly to us. 'How very fortunate is your visit,' she said. 'I was about to ...' She left her remark unfinished.

'It is always a pleasure to visit Deerfield Park. I remember visiting the Pembertons here. You will be here for the season?' Charlotte asked.

'Yes, perhaps you—and your friends—would care to stay and join our party. I would welcome your counsel … I mean company.'

Charlotte looked at us and we nodded our agreement. Part one of our plan of action seemed to be progressing.

DEERFIELD PARK

We quickly established ourselves at Deerfield Park. Charlotte sent back our carriage with directions to return with what we needed for a short visit, and I was despatched to find Mr Worcester and inform him that we would remain to help. Directed by the butler Beach, I walked down to the lake in search of Mr Worcester. I took my time doing so because despite the season and the lateness of the day it was very pleasant and the grounds beautiful. I stopped at the bridge at the end of the lake and looked back at the house, its honey-coloured stone now bathed in a warm golden light. Some ducks skimmed over the water and the quiet and the country air made it hard to believe we were only just outside Bath. But the sun edged closer to the horizon and I began to chill. I was about to return to the house when I heard a 'Psst!' #

I looked around and saw no one and called out 'Who's there?'

'Are you alone, Miss Woodsen?' I heard Mr Worcester ask.

My eyes widened, but I said, 'I am, sir.'

Mr Worcester stept out from behind one of the columns that held the roof of the stone bridge.

'Why are you hiding?'

'Don't want to run into Aunt Hermione, or Beach, or the

Stiltons.' He looked warily about and then approached me when he saw that I was alone.

'Why not?'

'My aunt will certainly want to discuss announcing the engagement. I've held her off because of our travel but she'll want to inform everyone in Bath.'

'Do not fear, Mr Worcester. Charlotte has persuaded your aunt to delay an announcement, given your history of ... impetuosity.'

'Who's Charlotte?'

'Miss House,' I supplied. Mr Worcester's relaxed form of address was obviously having its influence on me.

'Oh. Oh! I see! That's very clever. She has sown doubt. I suppose I do have a reputation for hasty engagements that come to naught. Ha, ha.' His shoulders, which had been around his ears, relaxed. He turned toward the stone railing and looked out over the water. 'Ducks, jolly nice things, ducks. That is a load off my mind. Wait a tick, what about the Stiltons? And the Blankenships!' His shoulders shot up again.

'One thing at a time, Mr Worcester. I am to take you back to the house where we might discuss our strategy. I am sure Miss House has already devised a method to ... deal with the other parties.'

'Yes,' he said, nodding vigorously. 'Don't keep me in the dark. It was a rum thing coming into the drawing-room and seeing you three with my aunt.'

He looked so miserable that I put my hand on his shoulder. There was something about Mr Worcester, like a sad little puppy that can't find its toy, that brought out my concern. 'There, there,' I said. His shoulders relaxed again. 'I'm sorry we didn't have a chance to inform you. Miss House wanted to call on your aunt before the Blankenships arrived and so we wasted not a moment.' I patted his shoulder.

He turned toward me. 'You're awfully kind, Miss Woodsen.'

I noticed he had nice soulful brown eyes, no doubt my reason for thinking of a puppy. Most men of my acquaintance, because of their status in society and their dominance over the fair sex, are too proud to admit they need a helpmate. But some men want, nay require, a woman's hand to guide them through life. I was about to express my thoughts on the matter when I heard ...

'Jane!'

I looked about and saw Charlotte standing at the end of the bridge. I removed my hand from Mr Worcester's shoulder.

'Where have you been? I see you've found Mr Worcester. We need him in conference immediately before I encounter the Stiltons. If you would be so kind as to return to the house, sir, we will join you momentarily.'

'Right-ho,' he said and walked away.

'Jane, what were you doing?' Charlotte asked as soon as he was out of earshot.

'I ... I don't know. He looked so lost and forlorn.'

'He is our client, Jane,' she said, looking at me very sternly. I stared back at her in something of a daze. Then Charlotte's look relaxed and she clasped me about the shoulders and we started walking after Mr Worcester.

'Oh Jane, I have seen this before. You are susceptible to lost men. It is nothing to be ashamed of but definitely something to be guarded against. I dare say another ten seconds and I would have had a third proposal to deal with.'

'Nonsense!' I said. 'I only felt compassion for the dear ... for Mr Worcester.'

'Of course,' she said, although I think she still worried of my susceptibility to Mr Worcester's charms. 'Now we have found a strategy to silence Mr Worcester's aunt, at least temporarily. We must do the same for the Stiltons.'

'Can we not simply convince them as well that it would be imprudent to announce the engagement?'

'Yes, but the situation is different for the mother of a bride. Her desire to publish an announcement is much stronger than that of the bridegroom's aunt. She must think that publication will more tightly bind Mr Worcester to his promise. And so I think for the Stiltons, we must add another argument to delay the announcement.'

'And what would that be?'

'I have no idea. Come. Let's catch up with Mr Worcester. If we do not hurry we will be rushed to dress for dinner.'

☙

Despite Charlotte's worry, we made it back with enough time to hold a brief conference with Mr Worcester and Mrs Fitzhugh and then to dress and be ready by the dinner gong. We joined the rest of the party assembled in the drawing-room and although Mrs Walthorpe had only arrived days before and was renting the house, she greeted us as the *grande dame* of the manor, as Mr Worcester had described. She quickly sorted us—a relatively easy task with the Blankenships not yet arrived—and we entered the dining room. #

Deerfield Park was certainly the grandest home I'd ever visited and the dining room was magnificently set, even for such a small party. The girandole on the table, decorated with chasing nymphs, was a positive fire hazard and I could not guess the number of candles it held. And the light from the girandole and the light from the chandeliers reflected manifold off the plate and cutlery on the table and the shining parquetry floor beneath. #

I found myself sitting beside Miss Stilton and across from Mrs Fitzhugh, while Charlotte found herself immediately next Mr Stilton and across from Mr Worcester. Mrs Stilton had Mrs Walthorpe's other ear.

'So, Miss Woodsen, you are a friend of Bertie?' Miss Stilton asked in what seemed a frosty voice. 'I thought I knew all his friends.' She was very pretty and had exceedingly red hair, a turned up nose and skin like pink marble, but she was even shorter than myself.

'No, Miss Stilton, the relationship is more tenuous. I am a friend of Miss House, whose brother is a friend of Mr Worcester's and is known to Mrs Walthorpe.'

'Oh, you know Squiddy?' she asked in a completely different tone that suddenly seemed to claim me as friend.

'Squiddy?'

'Michael. *Mistah* House. He's so respectable now, but I know a few friends who called him Squiddy in his day. I, of course, tease him mercilessly about it.'

'Whatever for? I mean why Squiddy?'

'Tentacles, m'dear, tentacles.' She made little wriggling motions with her fingers.

'Stephanie!' I heard her mother hiss.

'Sorry mother.' She turned toward me conspiratorially. 'If you know Squiddy, you must be all right.'

Apparently the very rich were quite different from my own very provincial experience. Charlotte and Mrs Fitzhugh did not seem disconcerted from the knowing ways of Mr Worcester and Miss Stilton, but I found it difficult to behave accordingly. I decided not to deny an acquaintance with Charlotte's brother, as it seemed to put me in Miss Stilton's confidence. To avoid further conversation, I paid attention to my beef consommé. I next heard Charlotte addressing our hostess.

'Mrs Walthorpe, when do Sir Walter and his family arrive?'

'To-morrow, Miss House. And I have planned a shooting party.'

Mr Worcester rose and reached for a serving dish. 'Excuse

me Aunt Hermione, is this not Gaston's *Mignonette de poulet petit Duc?'* he asked. #

'Pardon my nephew's interruption, my dear,' Mrs Walthorpe said with a smile and then turned to her nephew with a frosty look. 'It is indeed, Albert.'

'You asked Gaston to cook your favourite nephew his favourite dish?'

For a second a smile flickered on her lips but then melted away. 'I did nothing of the sort. I asked my *chef de cuisine* to prepare his signature dish, and I might remind you that you are my only nephew.' #

Mr Worcester endured his aunt's frosty stare and then returned his attention to the fowl, attacking it with a trencherman's appetite. #

'Do you shoot, Mr Worcester?' Charlotte asked.

'Eh? Quite a bit when I was younger, but I'm afraid I've lost my interest,' he answered jocularly between mouthfuls. I scarcely recognized him as the diffident young man I had met on the bridge.

'A young man should be well versed in firearms, Mr Worcester,' Mr Stilton said. 'With horsemanship, it is an essential skill for life in the country.'

'You are not comfortable on a horse, my dear,' his wife said.

'I do agree with you, Mr Stilton, that a gentleman should shoot. To his credit however, I suspect Mr Worcester is very capable on the dance floor,' Charlotte said.

'I am comfortable on a horse. It is the horse which is not comfortable with me,' Mr Stilton muttered. From his girth and deportment I could well understand the horse's attitude.

'I believe I have that reputation, Miss House,' Mr Worcester replied.

'I also wager that a fashionable man such as yourself is familiar with the waltz.' #

I realized now that Charlotte's strategy—keeping the conversation moving from topic to topic to discourage talk of the betrothal while lowering Mr Worcester's opinion with the Stiltons—stood some chance of success.

'The waltz is considered quite scandalous,' I said, pretending to have first-hand knowledge of it. I only recently heard of it from Mrs Fitzhugh as some sort of continental thing of which she did not approve. 'So much touching.'

'Albert, I hope you have not sunk so far,' his aunt said.

'Touching what?' Mr Stilton asked, now reaching for the fish.

'Stephanie, you have not danced this waltz?' Mrs Stilton asked.

'In the Viennese fashion, the gentleman may put his hand on his partner's shoulder, or around her waist,' Mrs Fitzhugh provided, happy to impart her knowledge. 'It is in ¾ time.'

'Why shouldn't I, Mama?'

'Jolly fun the wortz,' Mr Worcester said, mangling the unfamiliar word.

Charlotte's skilful campaign of character assassination was a perfect complement to the dinner, from the *Mignonette de poulet petit Duc* to the *Sylphides à la crème d'écrevisses* to the *Diablotins* and finally the fruit. In my mind, I tallied the sins of which Mr Worcester stood accused: a bad shot, a bad horseman—no wait, that was Mr Stilton—a libertine and during the dessert it was revealed he was an indifferent player of whist and an abuser of animals (his story of the goose though amusing did not put him in a good light). I was surprised at how nobly he suffered these accusations upon his character. True, we had warned him of our strategy but nevertheless he shewed considerable fortitude.

At times I feared Charlotte would arouse in Mrs Walthorpe a natural defence of her nephew, but Charlotte always first gained her co-operation. 'I understand from my brother that you are fond of whist, Mrs Walthorpe.' And from there she discovered that Mrs Walthorpe and Mrs Stilton were often partners and also discovered that Mr Worcester's appreciation of the game was mild at best, he being more fond of *vingt-et-un*. #

After dinner, we retired to the drawing-room while the men remained for brandy in the dining room, although Mrs Walthorpe also provided us an excellent port.

'Your nephew seems a charming young man, Mrs Walthorpe,' Mrs Fitzhugh offered after we had settled.

'Hmph.'

'I don't know when I've known a more delightful gentleman. His stories were so ...' I stopped when I saw a pained look on Mrs Stilton's face.

'That was funny about the goose,' Miss Stilton said, smiling. 'Seems a shame he had to ...' she did not continue but instead made a wringing motion with her hands.

Mrs Stilton sighed but then roused herself. 'I'm sure his high-spirited ways will quiet once he is married.'

Mrs Fitzhugh agreed with her. 'No doubt Miss Stilton will influence him to take a more ... sober tone.'

Mrs Walthorpe and Mrs Stilton both quickly looked at Miss Stilton who still seemed to be thinking of the fate of the goose, and then both those women looked at each other and simultaneously took a sip—perhaps more than a sip—of port.

Charlotte then gave me a look and quickly put a finger to her lips. She did the same with Mrs Fitzhugh and I realized she wanted us to halt our campaign and let time do its work. We remained mostly silent, drinking port, until the gentlemen rejoined us.

Mr Worcester had apparently been telling a story to Mr Stilton. 'And then I said, "Why not one for the goat as well?" Ha, ha. No, it was a sheep wasn't it? Still the same though.'

'No Mr Worcester, it is not,' Mr Stilton said. He sat beside his wife and as he did so they exchanged looks of long suffering.

Mr Worcester remained standing and Charlotte rose to join him. I noticed that Miss Stilton observed this.

'You appear in good spirits, Mr Worcester,' I heard Charlotte say.

'Thank you, I am feeling rather braced.'

'It is in stark contrast to your earlier mood.'

'The Worcester spirit always rallies at the sound of the dinner gong. There's something about dressing for the soup and fish that calms the nerves and after enjoying Gaston's godlike gifts, the world seems a less forbidding place.'

'There is no other reason?'

'No. None at all. No other reason.'

'I see. I must apologize, sir, for painting you in an unfavourable light before your aunt and the Stiltons,' Charlotte said quietly. I noticed Miss Stilton straining to hear their conversation.

'No need to apologize. Even with her obligatory regard for her sister's son, my aunt has always regarded me as a blot on the family escutcheon.' #

'I can tell she cares for a you a great deal.'

'Whatever can Bertie and Miss House be whispering?' Miss Stilton asked loudly.

'Stephanie, I would appreciate your not bellowing,' her father said, reaching for the brandy he had brought from the dining room.

'I was only complimenting Mr Worcester on his courageous political opinion, contrary as it is to the ruling party,' Charlotte said.

Suddenly Mr Stilton was choking and his wife was attending him by slapping him on the back.

'Kindly stop hitting me,' he said finally after his coughing fit subsided. He mopped his brow with his handkerchief, lumbered to his feet and said, 'Mr Worcester, do I understand that you are in favour of _?'

Mr Worcester stood there frozen, his mouth agape.

'Bertie's never had a political opinion in his entire life, courageous or otherwise,' Miss Stilton said.

'Quiet, Stephanie!'

Mr Worcester finally offered, 'I might have said it was a good idea.'

Sensing that Mr Worcester's opinion was not yet fully formed, Mr Stilton decided to take a more politic tone.

'My boy, you're surely not aware of the ramifications of the policy you are suggesting. It would be most disruptive to me … I mean the party … were it known …' He mopped his brow again. 'Mrs Walthorpe, if I could borrow your nephew for a moment?'

'Please, Mr Stilton,' she said and waved him away. It was clear she was startled at the turn of events. 'Imagine Albert having a political opinion!'

Mr Stilton led Mr Worcester away. The conversation among our reduced party was somewhat strained after this and soon Mrs Walthorpe announced that she was still tired after her journey from London. After inviting us to remain, she and Mrs Stilton retired, although I noticed they maintained a whispered conversation as they left.

'Well played, Miss House,' Miss Stilton said after they had left.

'Come again?' Charlotte asked sweetly.

'Why are you interfering in my engagement with Bertie?'

Charlotte took her seat and said, 'Very well, we shall speak plainly and put our cards on the table.'

Miss Stilton sat opposite her. She remained silent a few seconds and then asked, 'You're not in love with Bertie are you?'

'No, I am not.'

'Well that's all right then. I didn't think you were—Bertie is an acquired taste—but then what is your interest?'

'It coincides with yours, actually. I want to see you happy with ... heavens, I've forgotten his name.'

'Mr Potterthwaite,' Mrs Fitzhugh supplied.

'Thank you, Margaret.'

'How do you know about Potty?'

'Mr Worcester has told us all,' Charlotte said.

'Oh! Why would he ... oh I see! He doesn't have Cheevers around to tell him what to do and he has turned to you. Squiddy's mentioned you. Says you're something of a matchmaker.'

'Who?'

'Your brother,' I said.

'Really! Extraordinary!' The information appeared to delight Charlotte and caused her to remain silent.

'It was not very nice your holding Mr Worcester to a hasty proposal,' Mrs Fitzhugh said in the void left by Charlotte.

'Well, if you know everything, then you know I just ... I really want to marry Clarence. He's just too afraid of Mrs Walthorpe to ask her for the living she holds and on the few occasions they have met, he has failed to impress her.' #

'Yes, but what you don't know is that Mr Worcester is already engaged to Evelyn Blankenship,' Charlotte said, recovered from the amazement of her brother's nickname.

It was now Miss Stilton's turn to be amazed. 'Gosh, he really does live the life, doesn't he? When was this?'

'A week before he proposed to you.'

'Evelyn Blankenship? I know Bertie is mentally negligible but that seems beyond the pale even for him. She is pretty, of course, so his attraction is understandable, but what she might see in him ...'

She stopped when she saw my cross look.

'He is a good sort and quite fine in his way. After all,

we were engaged before as a sort of lark. Thank goodness Cheevers sorted that out. But wait, if as you say you want to see me happy with Clarence ...'

Charlotte nodded and said, 'You may continue with your stratagem of screwing Mr Potterthwaite's courage to the sticking point. We must, however, prevent your parents or Mr Worcester's aunt from openly talking about your engagement when the Blankenships arrive.' #

'Oh I see. Why didn't you say this before?'

'We only met at dinner, my dear,' Mrs Fitzhugh said.

'Yes, I suppose there wasn't time. So all that during dinner, you were trying to ... what exactly?'

Charlotte sighed. 'It was a complicated game of sowing doubt with your parents, to discourage them from making a public announcement about the engagement.'

'I don't think there's any danger of that now. In fact, I may be hard pressed to resist their entreaties to reject Bertie post haste.'

'I said it was a complicated game.'

'It would certainly simplify matters were you not engaged to Mr Worcester,' I said.

'You'll forgive me if I still consider Bertie in play,' Miss Stilton said to me, and then rose. 'I'd best return to my parents and repair the damage. I'll bid you good night.'

After she had left, Mrs Fitzhugh yawned and then said, 'You were in excellent form to-night Charlotte. Do not stay up too late.' She also bid us good night and left.

Charlotte seemed quite pleased with our friend's praise. I almost hated asking, 'And how do we forestall the Blankenships to-morrow?'

Her smile left her face and she said, 'I begin to appreciate Cheever's skills, Jane. I may be hard pressed to match the talents of a valet.'

We remained in the drawing-room another hour and formed our strategy for the morrow.

A SHOOTING PARTY

The day dawned slowly over Deerfield Park. A light fog that hung over the grounds was slowly being dispersed by the weak autumn sun. I looked out my bedroom window and could see the servants leaving the house to supply the tents and tables for our shooting party. I could see their breath steaming as they laboured to carry the baskets and cases containing the plate and glassware for our refreshments, and I hoped I would not be too cold during the shooting party. #

I met Charlotte and Mrs Fitzhugh for a simple breakfast. We were up before the others and used the time to acquaint Mrs Fitzhugh of our plans.

While we were in conference, Miss Stilton arrived. 'I thought I would be first down. Doubtless you are conspiring before the Blankenships arrive.'

'Doubtless,' I said, somewhat irritably. The woman's abuse of poor Mr Worcester annoyed me.

'You look forward to the party, Miss Stilton?' Mrs Fitzhugh asked.

'Yes, it should be quite fun. My father fancies himself a country gentleman and will no doubt be blazing about. I suggest you remain behind him for until he manages to shoot himself, it is the safest place to be. Yes, the possibilities for excitement at this party seem endless.'

Mrs Fitzhugh gave a weak smile. 'I shall take your advice.'

Miss Stilton helped herself to breakfast while we resumed our conference.

'The Blankenships are due to arrive when, Margaret?' Charlotte asked.

'I believe Mrs Walthorpe said about ten o'clock. They arrived in Bath yesterday to see to their house there before joining us to-day.'

'We are to have a late start to our shoot then.'

Mrs Fitzhugh laughed, 'From Miss Stilton's statement I do not believe it will be a serious hunt. It certainly will not be the gentleman with his hunting dog and a servant or two to flush the coverts, with perhaps a loaf a bread and some cheese produced from a pocket for luncheon.' #

'I certainly hope it won't be,' I said. 'I hope for sandwiches and cake and a proper tea.'

Charlotte said, 'From the activities of the servants I think we have little to fear.'

At this time we heard a respectful cough from the doorway and saw a footman trying to attract attention.

'Miss Stilton, there is a gentleman just arrived who would speak with you, a Mr Potterthwaite.'

Miss Stilton made a high-pitched squeak of excitement that I thought unbecoming and rapidly left the room with the footman.

'Whatever can that be about?' Mrs Fitzhugh mused. 'An addition to our party?'

We soon heard raised voices belonging to Mr and Mrs Stilton and their daughter. A few minutes later all three Stiltons, preceded by Mrs Walthorpe, entered the room.

'I must apologize for my daughter inviting Mr Potterthwaite,' Mrs Stilton said, speaking to Mrs Walthorpe.

'There is no need,' Mrs Walthorpe said with only a hint of displeasure. 'Any friend of your daughter is welcome here.'

'Our hostess bears it well,' Mrs Fitzhugh whispered to us as we rose to greet our arrivals. 'An unplanned for guest is such an impertinence.'

'She clearly wants this match for her nephew,' Charlotte said.

Mrs Walthorpe turned her attention to us. 'My friends, our party has a new member. A Mr Potterthwaite, a friend of Miss Stilton, will be joining us shortly.'

'He is a ... presentable young man. A curate, and his father is an old friend,' Mrs Stilton said, trying to put the imposition in a good light. 'Oh, here he is.'

We turned as the footman entered the room followed by a very large, young man who paused uncertainly in the doorway. He was well over six feet with unruly black hair and a baffled expression on an overlong face. He was more curate than any two I had ever met. The footman cleared his throat and motioned to the young man to enter.

'Oh do come in Mr Potterthwaite!' Mrs Walthorpe said in a commanding tone. Her voice broke his hesitation and he entered. The footman, perhaps now feeling his duty superfluous, quietly said, 'Mr Clarence Potterthwaite,' and left.

The requisite introductions were made and Mr Potterthwaite was made to sit down. He was ill at ease, and as he sat his long arms and elbows knocked over a vase that luckily did not fall to the floor, thanks to Charlotte's quick action.

'Sorry, sorry!' he said, shooting to his feet. His legs shoved back his chair that nearly fell over, stopped by Mrs Fitzhugh. My friend brought back his chair, placed her hand on his shoulder and guided him to his seat. She also discreetly moved a small picture frame from beyond the reach of his elbows.

'I am so happy to have you here, sir,' Mrs Walthorpe said, this time in a more modulated tone. 'I had not the anticipation of your coming ... but you are welcome all the same.'

'Thank you, ma'am. I am sorry to be a bother.'

Mrs Walthorpe graciously dismissed his concern.

'You are a curate sir?' I asked him.

He nodded and said, 'I serve the parish of Stanton Green.'

'Why I know it very well,' Mrs Walthorpe said. 'And I know your vicar quite well.'

'Yes ma'am, he has spoken of you often.'

'You now seem familiar to me, young man. Have we met before?'

'On occasion, ma'am.'

Having made that connexion, Mrs Walthorpe now engaged him in some pleasant conversation that put him at ease. I could see that Miss Stilton appeared relieved that her surprise was meeting with approval.

'So that is Miss Stilton's intended,' Mrs Fitzhugh whispered to us.

'He seems a nice enough fellow, if a bit clumsy,' Charlotte said. 'You will notice Miss Stilton?'

'Yes,' I said, 'she was quite pleased at his arrival. She must care for him.'

'You had doubts, Jane?' Mrs Fitzhugh asked.

'I do not ... I did not like her because of her behaviour toward Mr Worcester.'

'We can excuse her, I think,' Charlotte said. 'She is in love and that makes her do stupid things, but there was no real evil in it.'

I was about to provide a noncommittal answer when I heard Mr Potterthwaite exclaim, 'Worcester!' followed by the crash of his chair. I looked and saw Mr Potterthwaite erect and appearing even larger than before. His hands were clenching and unclenching slowly. I also saw Mr Worcester standing uncertainly in the doorway, as Mr Potterthwaite had done a few minutes earlier.

'Oh, hullo Potty,' Mr Worcester said weakly. 'Fancy seeing you here.'

'Albert!' Mrs Walthorpe said with a voice that commanded attention, including Mr Potterthwaite's. Despite the pleasant conversation he had been enjoying with her, he still quaked at the sound of her raised voice, even when not directed at him.

'You certainly took your time this morning,' his aunt said. 'The Blankenships will be arriving shortly.'

'May I have a word with you privately, Worcester,' Mr Potterthwaite said, a little more quietly.

'Actually, I'd hoped to have a little something in the way of toast and jam and … and maybe a boiled egg, or …' #

'Mrs Walthorpe, please excuse me, but I must have a word with Mr Worcester,' Mr Potterthwaite said with a bow to our hostess.

'Yes, well if you must, but you'll find little to recommend from conversation with my nephew.'

Mr Potterthwaite led Mr Worcester by the arm and took him from the room.

'I was unaware Mr Potterthwaite knew Albert,' Mrs Walthorpe said. 'He seems a nice young man, Miss Stilton.'

Miss Stilton quickly nodded her agreement and said, 'He's done amazingly well at Stanton Green organizing fetes and such, but he's so constrained what he can do there as just a curate.'

Mrs Walthorpe admitted that a curate worked under limitations but that the Reverend Herbert would no doubt be at a loss without him, and then turned her attention to the elder Stiltons.

Miss Stilton, upset that she had failed to further promote Mr Potterthwaite's charms, then joined our group. 'Miss House, I did not expect Clarence would come. He had seemed in such fear of Mrs Walthorpe when I gave him my earlier ultimatum.'

'What ultimatum was that?'

'I told him that if he did not love me enough to ask Mrs Walthorpe for the living, that I might as well marry Bertie.'

I thought of Mr Potterthwaite's behaviour and gasped, 'You don't think … he does not plan to harm Mr Worcester?'

'I very much fear he does.'

'But he is a curate!' Mrs Fitzhugh said.

'While at Oxford he was known as the Pugnacious Padre, both for his skill at the pugilistic arts and for his promotion of abolition.'

'I see,' Charlotte said. 'Jane, Margaret, perhaps you can remind Mr Potterthwaite of the strictures of his office. I must remain here to await the Blankenships.'

We agreed and made our apologies to our hostess and left the room. Fortunately we found the footman who had introduced Mr Potterthwaite. We asked him if he had seen the gentlemen, and he directed us to the north lawn. We hurried outside and looked in vain for any sign of Mr Potterthwaite and Mr Worcester.

'Stupid girl indeed!' I said. 'Her scheming and manipulation may see Mr Worcester injured.'

'I agree she is a silly girl but I doubt Mr Potterthwaite would be so reckless … wait, do you hear something?'

Distantly I heard, 'Get down from there, you blasted Worcester!'

'Yes, I believe it comes from that direction.'

We ran toward an opening in the wall that defined the north lawn. On the other side of the wall we found Mr Potterthwaite standing beneath an oak tree, throwing stones into its branches. He heard our approach and turned.

'Mr Potterthwaite!' I said.

My cry made him start and then turn, with perhaps another invective upon his lips, but when he saw us, he said, 'Ladies, forgive me, I don't remember your names.'

We introduced ourselves again and then he said, 'Pardon my manners. I should introduce Mr Worcester. But then you must already be acquainted.' He looked upward and threw another stone into the tree. There we saw Mr Worcester clinging tightly to a branch—a very high branch.

'Good morning,' he said.

'Good morning, sir,' I answered. He appeared unharmed and my anxiety was relieved.

'You are very high up. Should you not come down?'

'No, I'm quite comfortable, excellent view from here. Look, I can see them arranging the marquee for our shoot.' He pointed in the direction of the shoot but his attitude provided an easy target for Mr Potterthwaite, who struck his outstretched arm with a stone. He cried out and temporarily lost his grasp on the branch and slipped, but he managed to secure his hold. #

'I really must insist you come down. I am sure Mr Potterthwaite means you no harm—well, no real harm.'

'I do not wish to disagree with you, Miss Woodsen, but my agenda with Mr Worcester closely parallels that of Moses's agenda with the Midianites and I am almost certain smiting comes under the heading of harm.' #

'But surely a man of the cloth —'

'I am only a curate—an under curate really—and as such I am not yet set in my ways.' He then stooped to find another stone.

My friend appealed to him, 'Miss Stilton would certainly disapprove of your harming Mr Worcester.'

'As I have already lost her to Mr Worcester I can suffer her disapprobation.'

'It will cause her considerable distress.'

'Which the passage of time will undoubtedly heal.'

'Come, Mr Potterthwaite, all is not lost,' I said. 'Do you not recall the pleasant conversation you had with Mrs Walthorpe before Mr Worcester's arrival?'

My words checked his swing and his stone easily missed. 'Yes?'

'Does she seem the tyrant you feared to ask for a living?'

'No, she seemed very ... say, you seem to know a lot about all this.'

'Mr Worcester came to me for help … came to Miss House that is, for help,' I amended when I saw Mrs Fitzhugh's raised eyebrow. 'We are familiar with and sympathetic to your plight.'

'You know that I would marry Miss Stilton?'

'Yes, and we know that she requires that you ask Mrs Walthorpe for the living that she controls. But she would never grant you this if you harm her nephew.'

'Is that true, Worcester?' he shouted upwards.

'Let me think for a second, Potty. Of course I think better on *terra firma*. I'd come down and ponder it if you promise to lay off the smiting.' #

''Fraid I could not promise that in all honesty, Bertie.'

'Right-ho. Decent of you to warn me. Well as to your question, Aunt Hermione's always considered me something of a sickly branch on the family tree. Ha! Rather apt metaphor, don't you think? But yes, I suppose the ties that bind would lead one to conclude that she would look poorly on any physical harm coming to her favourite nephew.' #

Mr Potterthwaite looked back to us. 'You really think I could ask Mrs Walthorpe for the living?'

'Perhaps not immediately,' my friend said, 'but over the course of this weekend. She does not seem ill disposed toward you and a persistent campaign of solicitude might find her very receptive. I might be able to supply you with those little delicate compliments which are always acceptable to ladies.' #

'That would be very kind, Mrs Fitzhugh. I'm not very good at that sort of thing. Perhaps we could walk a bit and you might give me some examples.'

My friend and Mr Potterthwaite left, leaving me standing under the tree.

'I think it is safe to come down now, Mr Worcester.'

'I doubt it will be safe, but I will come down.'

I watched as he made his way down and wondered how

he ever found his way up the tree, as the lowest branch was considerably above his height. He was forced to drop to the ground from the lowest branch and fortunately only injured his dignity.

'Thank you, Miss Woodsen. I began to plan my life in that tree.'

'Like St. Simeon Stylites.' #

'Pardon?'

'A holy man who lived atop a pillar during the time of the Emperor Theodosius.'

'You're remarkably well informed. Lived on a pillar, eh? I wonder how many engagements he was fleeing.'

'We should return to the house. I must dress for the party.'

'Quite right, Miss Woodsen, although I might ask you to precede me. I'm afraid I've split my breeches.'

A pheasant rose from its covert followed by the crack of a gun and then a shouted 'Blast!'

'You're holding it all wrong, Papa,' Miss Blankenship said. I had heard this conversation or variants of it many times now since the start of the shoot.

The sun had now risen high enough to have completely cleared away the fog and was warm enough that I was quite comfortable. I shielded my eyes from the sun to observe the shooting party. Sir Walter, who had arrived with his family shortly after Mr Worcester and I had returned to the house, was standing with Mr Stilton some distance from us, attended by the gamekeeper. We ladies, save for Miss Blankenship who stood beside her father, were seated some distance away.

'Leave your father alone, dear, you're only making it worse,' Lady Blankenship said.

'But his elbows are too high!' his daughter protested with a backward glance to her mother. The young lady was as beautiful as Mr Worcester had described. Her hair was a warm brown worn rather long that melted into the golden oak leaf pattern of her spencer. She was tall, not as tall as Charlotte perhaps, but she certainly shared my friend's posture. Her dark, practically black eyes, made her appear quite imperious, and were the only visible trait that linked her with her short, stout father.

'Crack!'

'Damn!'

'Mr Stilton, please.' I heard his wife say in the repeat of another conversation I had heard many times now.

'Sorry, Mrs Stilton,' he replied.

'It is obviously defective sir,' said Mr Potterthwaite, who attended Mr Stilton.

'Eh, what's that?'

'It is defective. I saw you leading that bird remarkably well. You could only have missed were it defective.'

'How very perceptive of you, my boy.'

Mr Potterthwaite bowed to Mr Stilton and then shot a look back at Mrs Fitzhugh, seated next to me, who gave him a smile of approval in return.

'Crack!'

'Blast!'

'Papa, elbows down,' Miss Blankenship said.

'Mr Potterthwaite, might you inspect my piece?' Sir Walter asked, ignoring his daughter.

'There is nothing wrong with it, sir. Your shoulder is too high and your head is too bent and you're squinting,' his daughter said. I had to agree with her assessment.

'I would be happy to, sir,' Mr Potterthwaite said, delighted to be thought of as a perceptive young man. 'As they are a matched set, they may both suffer from the same defect,'

'How very thoughtful Mr Potterthwaite is, Mrs Walthorpe,' I heard Mrs Fitzhugh say quietly to our hostess. I turned to look and noticed now that Mrs Walthorpe bore an irritable expression that seemed directed at the large curate—or under curate.

'What is that?' she asked, curtly.

'He seeks to console your guests and finds them excuses for their poor aim.'

'Oh, is that what he's doing?'

'Most assuredly. To his obviously educated eye he must know there is nothing wrong with those very handsome fowling pieces. They belonged to your late husband, I presume?'

'Yes they did. I ... how clever of you to notice Mr Potterthwaite's solicitousness toward my guests.'

'Danger averted,' I heard in my ear, and I turned to Charlotte.

'Margaret is very skilful,' I agreed. 'I worried that Mr Potterthwaite had gone too far in his criticism.'

'And what do you think of Miss Blankenship's criticism of her father's shooting?'

'Accurate, although I think the principal reason he has failed to down any birds is that he closes his eyes before he fires. He is quite gun shy.'

Charlotte laughed. 'You are correct. Have you ever fired a weapon?'

'Yes, several times. We are country folk and my father had no sons, so he often included my sister and me in his manly pursuits, over the objections of my mother.' I smiled at the recollection and I realized this was the first time since his death that I had thought of our happy times together. Nevertheless, I dared not think too much of him lest I be undone by grief, so I asked Charlotte, 'Did you have an opportunity to speak to the Blankenships privately?'

'No, their late arrival made that impossible. In fact, you

remind me that I should take some steps in that direction. Come, see if you can follow my lead as I sow some mischief.'

'Mr Worcester, why do you not join the shoot?' Charlotte asked in a loud voice.

'As I said at dinner, I have lost my interest in shooting,' he said with a glance at Sir Walter. He sat some distance from us, playing with the gamekeeper's dogs that, because of the failure of the men to fell any birds, were otherwise unoccupied.

Sir Walter, overhearing our conversation, said 'Ha!' but did not further elaborate.

Charlotte gave me a little nod and I said, 'Oh Mr Worcester, please won't you give it a try.'

'Go ahead Bertie,' Miss Stilton urged. 'You can't do any worse than father.'

Finally he agreed and Mrs Walthorpe's gamekeeper provided him a weapon and then signalled to his game flushers. Half a minute later two pheasants streaked into the air and Mr Worcester brought them both down.

'Well done ... I mean lucky shot Worcester,' Mr Potterthwaite said.

Mr Worcester gave his weapon to the gamekeeper and tried to look nonchalant but I could tell he was proud of his shot. I could also see that Mr Stilton and Sir Walter resented his skill.

'Did you know he could do that?' I whispered to Charlotte.

'Yes, I remembered Michael saying that Mr Worcester was a good shot.'

'Your form is very good, Mr Worcester,' Miss Blankenship said, 'but you might do better to drop your left elbow more.'

'It would be hard to do better than hit two birds with one shot,' Miss Stilton said. There seemed to be a mutual antagonism between the two ladies.

'It was pure luck,' Mr Potterthwaite said.

'Often happens to beginners,' Sir Walter said.

'Still there is always room for improvement,' Miss Blankenship said, addressing Miss Stilton.

'Perhaps you should try again, Bertie,' Miss Stilton said, looking up at Miss Blankenship, undaunted by her imperious glare.

Mr Worcester agreed and was given another weapon and again we waited for a bird. The wait, however, was nearer a minute and came from the opposite direction. He had to quickly change his focus and track the bird and was about to fire when Charlotte said sharply, 'Elbow down, Mr Worcester!'

He fired wide of his mark and the bird streaked safely away and then we heard from the direction of the game flushers, 'You've shot me, you idiot.'

'I told you he was a menace!' Sir Walter said.

Hearing the voice, Miss Blankenship gave a muffled cry and raised her hand to her mouth. We then saw one of the flushers stand up and declare loudly, 'Worcester, you great big fool, you've gone and shot me.'

The other flushers, the gamekeeper and the rest of the shooting party rushed to the man. He was dark haired and handsome in a man about town sort of way that was at odds with his current rough dress. A small trickle of blood ran down the side of his face from his temple. The gamekeeper took out a handkerchief and wiped the wound clean.

'It's just the one pellet,' he said, and quickly produced a jack knife and dug it out, accompanied by a wail from the injured man. 'Now apologize to the gentleman.'

'I certainly will not.'

'Is that you, Blotto?' Mr Worcester asked, his face betraying his amazement.

'Course it is. What do you think you're doing shooting the help?'

'Sorry, old man. Didn't know it was you. What are you doing here anyway?'

'Albert, you know this man?' Mrs Walthorpe asked.

'Yes, it's Blotto. Mr Cuthbertson. You know him too.'

She looked more closely at him and said, 'He does resemble Mr Cuthbertson. Whatever are you doing here?'

'Oh, you know, this and that. Bertie invited me.'

'Albert, is this true?'

'Well ... ' he looked at Charlotte who nodded, and said 'yes.'

'I would kindly ask that if you invite your friends to my house you might inform me. What I don't understand is why you are flushing birds?'

Mr Cuthbertson looked at Miss Blankenship for help.

'I ... I asked him to,' Miss Blankenship said uncertainly.

'Not your idiotic campaign again, Evelyn,' her father said.

She bridled at this and replied with no trace of uncertainty, 'It is not idiotic, sir. I merely asked Mr Cuthbertson to research for me some of the occupations of the lower ... I mean those who actually work ...'

'God help me, you might as well be French!' He turned to our hostess, 'Please forgive my daughter her foolishness, Mrs Walthorpe.'

'I cannot pretend to understand what has happened, but it is of little consequence.' She called a footman and told him, 'Charles, please take Mr Cuthbertson to the house and have someone see to his wound, and then settle him in whatever room Mrs Cook thinks would be best. Thank you. Now Sir Walter, why don't we break for some refreshment? And Albert, please give that gun to Mr Bates; you've bagged your limit for the day.'

'So that is Mr Cuthbertson,' I said. 'He does not look at all like a sad lobster.' The shooting had stopped after the incident and we were all taking tea under the marquee.

Mrs Fitzhugh said, 'I think Mr Worcester was referring to his moustaches. They are somewhat ... delicate. And were he to frown ...'

We laughed at the thought of his thin moustache downward cast like the whiskers of a sad lobster. I hoped I could remove the image from my mind before I met the gentleman again.

'You've done quite well with Mr Potterthwaite, Margaret,' Charlotte told our friend over tea.

'Yes,' I agreed, 'he seems to be getting on quite well with Mrs Walthorpe. What do you think of his chances for success, were he to ask her for the living?' We could see the gentleman talking quite animatedly with our hostess. In fact he was so animated that he upset his cup, luckily only staining his clothing and not our hostess's.

'I think his chances are quite good, assuming he does not spill anything further,' Mrs Fitzhugh said. Then she added, 'Poor Mr Worcester, however,' and nodded in that man's direction. I saw him slumped forward in his chair, his chin supported in his bridged hands, with an expression of suffering on his face.

'Yes, poor Mr Worcester,' I agreed.

'Oh please, will you two stop saying that,' Charlotte said. 'It was very mean to alarm him like that.'

'But it produced the proper effect, Margaret. Sir Walter now holds him in even lower contempt than before.'

'It was also very irresponsible. Suppose he had more seriously wounded Mr Cuthbertson? You acted rashly and did not stop to consider the consequences beyond that it furthered your interests.'

I marvelled at this conversation and the effect Mrs Fitzhugh's words had on Charlotte. I had never seen her chastened before and I suddenly recognized the nature of their relationship.

'Yes, ma'am. I will do better in future,' Charlotte said meekly.

'You were her governess!'

'What? Oh, of course, Jane.'

'I thought you were a family friend.'

'She is,' Charlotte said. 'She is a very old—well long time—and dear family friend. But she was my governess first. My only governess and my only teacher because my father respected her abilities so.'

'And because you threw fits whenever he thought of replacing me with another instructor who better matched your needs.'

'You always seemed capable of instructing me.'

'Ha!' she said with a laugh like Charlotte's. 'One minute a question about anatomy, another something about Lysander's strategy at Notium and then a question about polyphonic motets. And I knew nothing of these matters.' #

'And yet you answered them.'

'In due course, yes. I would always say, "I'll explain later." Luckily your father kept an excellent library. Although I always knew you used that library to ask me the questions in the first place.'

Charlotte now smiled in a way I had never seen before, a smile of simple happiness, untinged with any design or purpose. It frankly unnerved me. I coughed and said, 'Perhaps we should do something to improve Mr Worcester's spirits.'

My words broke the spell and Charlotte returned to her more familiar self. 'Mr Worcester's spirits are not my immediate concern. We have certainly improved the situation where Mr Potterthwaite is concerned, but now we must turn our attention to Mr Cuthbertson. His entrance to our party was hardly auspicious and certainly did not improve him in his standing with Sir Walter.'

I could not help but smile at remembering the tumult caused by his appearance, but my reverie was interrupted by the approach of Mr Worcester.

'Mr Worcester, please join us,' Mrs Fitzhugh said.

'Thank you ladies, I think I have worn out my welcome with the Stiltons and the Blankenships.'

'I apologize that my outcry caused you to shoot wide,' Charlotte said, 'but it was all in a good cause.'

'Yes, what cause was that exactly? "The make Worcester look like an idiot cause?"'

'Precisely. You have fallen even further in the estimation of Mr Stilton and Sir Walter. They can hardly countenance the idea of you as a son in law.'

'What! Hey, that's right. Do you think they'll want to issue the old *nolle prosequi?*' #

'That is my hope. With luck, we may have disentangled you from your obligations.'

'That's fine, but it still leaves Stephanie and Evie in the soup. What they see in two fatheads like Potty and Blotto are beyond me, but still, love is blind as the man said, and I'd like to see them holding the bluebird in the end.'

Charlotte laughed and said, 'How very curious is your speech, Mr Worcester, but I understand your meaning. I too would like to see the couples united. And with your help, I believe we can make that happen, although it might entail no little risk to your person. We must stir the pot with the aim of bringing it to a boil.'

STIRRING THE POT

'Oh, excuse me, Mr Potterthwaite, I did not know you were here,' I lied, after I entered the library and began the campaign Charlotte had outlined. He stood quickly, failing for once to produce any damage.

'Miss Woodsen, I could leave.'

'No, sir, that is not necessary. I will leave. I was looking for Mr Worcester, for I wanted to wish him happiness.' And I made to leave for the door.

'Happiness for what?'

I stopped and said, 'Why, for his engagement to Miss Stilton. She has decided after all to hold him to his promise in light of your refusal ... why, you look unwell. What have I said?'

He had sat down and was holding his head in his hands and rocking back and forth.

'I have lost her!' he said with a groan. I ran to his side and knelt beside his chair.

'But surely you have only yourself to blame? I do not believe Mr Worcester loves Miss Stilton. In fact he told me that he finds her ... socially inferior ... but that he will nevertheless stand by his promise of marriage.'

'That fiend! And I worship the very ground she walks on, while he is not fit to touch the hem of her dress.'

'Well, I'm sorry that I cannot comprehend your dilemma. My understanding from Miss Stilton is that she would readily accept your offer were you to simply ask Mrs Walthorpe for the living.'

'But I am not yet finished offering her delicate compliments.'

'The time for delicate compliments is over, sir.'

He groaned again. I began to find my position and the retelling of his tale somewhat tedious, but I resisted the urge to hurry him along. Finally he said, 'You do not know the fear she inspires in me. She reminds me of my own Aunt Agatha, a fearsome woman who … no, I cannot even repeat it.'

I stood and asked him, 'Did Daniel lose his courage in the lion's den? Did Shadrach, Meshach or even Abednego quail in the fiery furnace? No they did not, for they had their faith to support them, as you have the image of Miss Stilton to support you.' #

'Yes, you're right, Miss Woodsen.'

'I saw Mrs Walthorpe in the drawing-room talking with my friend Charlotte. Mrs Walthorpe seemed in a most amiable and receptive mood to me. Why, I recollect that I heard her speaking quite highly of you. Were I you I would speak with her immediately.'

'You really think I should?'

'Yes, I do, although you might not want to mention your intentions toward Miss Stilton. And it might be as well if you ask Mrs Walthorpe for the living while Charlotte is there. As a matter of fact, she would make an excellent witness were you to commit an agreement to paper.'

Next I searched for Mr Cuthbertson, whom I found in the arboretum. He had changed clothes and did not seem the worse for his accident, save that he wore a bandage about his head, concealed under a green turban that I thought an affectation. 'Good day, Mr Cuthbertson.'

'Oh, hullo. You are …'

'I am Miss Woodsen. Pardon me, I know we have not been introduced, but I wanted to see if you were feeling better.'

'That is kind of you, but do not fear for me. It was nothing. It takes more than a dratted Worcester to take me down.'

'You are not fond of Mr Worcester? He seems a charming man.'

'Ha! He is a snake.'

'Really? He claims you are old friends.'

'Friends! Would a friend steal the woman you love? Would he try to kill you?'

'The woman you love? Who is that? I beg your pardon, it is an impertinence to ask.'

'No, I don't mind. In fact, I want ... I need to tell someone and it might be easier with ... no, it would not be proper.'

I nodded my understanding and waited, hoping his need to speak would outweigh his reticence. I was quickly rewarded.

'I love Evelyn,' he said quickly and then looked about guiltily. 'There, I have said it.'

'Oh, I believed you indifferent to her.'

'Indifferent!' He leapt up. 'I worship her. What makes you think I am indifferent to her?'

'I am sorry, I had not noticed love in your eyes when you looked at her, unlike her expression ... no, it is not my place to tell,' I said with a coy glance out the drawing-room window, where Miss Blankenship stood, as I had ascertained before entering the room. He looked out the window as well and then back to me, and then to her again before returning to me.

'She has said something to you?'

I nodded. 'I noticed her alarm when you were wounded. I could tell she cares about you deeply. After you left, I sought to comfort her and I asked her about you. She said that while friends, you had never given her reason to believe that you held a true affection for her.'

'Oh, agony!' he cried and threw back his head, making the points of his moustaches point downward. He paced about the room and then returned to me, his face now downcast and I had to resist the image in my mind of a bereft lobster.

'Have you never spoken of this with her?'

'I dared not, for I am not worthy of her love.'

'Well, I hate to be blunt, Mr Cuthbertson, but if that is your attitude then it is perhaps best that she marry Mr Worcester.'

'What? I thought you sympathetic.'

'I can hardly take sides, sir. I do not know you or Miss Blankenship and have only recently met Mr Worcester. But I do know that harmony in marriage requires a union of equals. Naturally a man can make claim to strength, position, wealth and knowledge. I do not question this, but none of these matter if the man does not believe himself equal to his wife.'

'Worcester is not the equal of Evelyn. In a million years he could never hope to be.'

'But *he* believes himself to be or else he would not have sought her hand, Mr Cuthbertson. I am sorry; I have upset you.'

'No, no, you tell me things I should hear. Do you think me worthy of her?'

I sighed. 'It does not matter what I think. If you are worthy of her, go to her and ask her hand.'

'Yes, I most certainly shall.'

I allowed a few seconds to pass silently before I said, 'When?'

'Directly.'

'She is presently standing outside this room, quite alone. Look, she sees us and is waving.' I lowered my voice. 'Go to her now.' I may have placed my hand behind his back and given him a little shove, but I will not swear to it.

He left the room without a word and half a minute later I saw him on the other side of the windows.

A COMPLICATION

I left the arboretum, not wishing to intrude on the happiness taking place outside, and went in search of my friends, but after a half hour with no luck went to the drawing-room, which was now empty save for Mrs Fitzhugh.

'You have done it, Jane?' she asked as I entered.

'Yes, I left Mr Cuthbertson proposing to Miss Blankenship and with luck Mr Potterthwaite has already asked Mrs Walthorpe for the living.'

'That is wonderful. Mr Worcester can now be at ease.'

'Yes,' I said doubtfully, 'and yet … but here is Charlotte.'

I caught her attention as she walked by the drawing-room and she joined us.

'At last I find you,' she said laughing. 'And before you ask, Mr Potterthwaite has the living. He has it in writing, with myself as a witness.'

'He was not afraid?' I asked.

'Hardly! I don't know what you said to buck him up so, Jane. He found us here in the drawing-room, asked politely to have a word and made an excellent argument why he deserved the living. He had obviously practiced his speech many times, lacking only the nerve to deliver it. I must say he has hidden depths that should serve him well as a vicar. He appealed to her vanity, used her friendship with his vicar and told her of his plans for a benevolent society.' #

'And he did not break or upset anything?' Mrs Fitzhugh asked.

'Nothing other than a figurine of the Infant Samuel that I managed to conceal.' #

Mrs Fitzhugh was about to say something when we heard the sound of someone running. Through the open door we saw Mr Worcester fly by. I would have called out to him to join us but he was already gone.

'Why is he running?'

'No doubt he wishes to avoid either Mr Potterthwaite or Mr Cuthbertson, Margaret. As we warned him, our plan to goad those gentleman implied some risk to his person.'

We heard sounds again and this time we saw Mr Potterthwaite running in the direction taken by Mr Worcester.

'Apparently it was Mr Potterthwaite he was fleeing. Well, let us now address the endgame. You are aware of the remaining difficulties Jane?'

'Yes, I think so. Mr Potterthwaite must still ask Mr Stilton for permission to marry his daughter and as you said before, Mrs Stilton will still favour Mr Worcester over Mr Potterthwaite, even with a living.'

'And we still have done nothing to improve Sir Walter's opinion of Mr Cuthbertson,' Mrs Fitzhugh added.

Charlotte nodded and said, 'And although Mr Worcester's various proposals should soon be returned, it would still be impolitic were the various parents to be aware of the ... various proposals. Neither do we want the ladies to inform their parents of their actual intent until we have laid the groundwork ...'

A head looked into the library and Mr Cuthbertson asked, 'Have you ladies seen Worcester?'

Charlotte pointed in the opposite direction taken by Mr Worcester and Mr Potterthwaite, adding that she believed Mr Worcester was headed to the stables. Our visitor nodded, said his thanks and ran off.

'... laid the groundwork that will ensure their parents agree to the unions. Luckily I was able to make Mr Potterthwaite understand that applying immediately to Mr Stilton would not be prudent.'

'I am afraid I did not find opportunity to make the same entreaty to my charge,' I said.

'Excuse me, Mrs Fitzhugh, have you seen Mr Worcester? I have some news for him,' Miss Blankenship asked, whom I now saw standing at the drawing-room door.

'I believe he said he planned to ... uh ... he was going to ...'

'Walk the maze,' I supplied.

'Really? The last time he went in a maze he was lost for days.'

'Charlotte gave him a clue to navigate it,' Mrs Fitzhugh said with a forced smile.

'Uh … yes,' Charlotte said, 'always take the … second opening on the left, but not your left, the maze's left relative to the entrance. That will lead you to the centre of the maze. And to find the entrance from the centre, always take the second right. You should have no difficulty in finding him.'

'You're sure? I shouldn't want to be lost looking for him.'

'Quite sure. I have made a study of mazes—the Deerfield Park maze is quite famous—and have even written a monograph on the subject.' #

'Oh, how clever. And you're sure he's in the maze?'

'Positive,' I said.

'Thank you, sorry to disturb you. Miss House, Miss Woodsen.'

After she left us Charlotte gave us both a nod. 'That was very cunning of you. I may have to rescue her before dinner, however.'

'It should keep her from speaking prematurely to her parents,' I said. 'And I think that leaves us with only one player unaware of our strategy.'

'Yes, and unless Miss Stilton happens along in the next few seconds, I think you might undertake finding her and informing her of the continuing need for discretion.'

Miss Stilton did not appear and so I went in search of her. Directed by a maid, I found her at the lake feeding the ducks, or rather making large balls of moistened compressed bread and hurling them at unsuspecting fowl.

'Oh, hullo,' she said with a scowl as she aimed at a sleeping duck that had escaped her efforts so far. Fortunately for the duck in question, the bread ball crumbled in flight and spread crumbs over a large area, attracting the ducks that had earlier fled.

'Stupid ducks,' she said.

'Miss Stilton, are you all right?' I asked, concerned about her mood.

'Oh yes, everything's fine, apparently Potty's talked to Bertie's aunt and she has granted him the living. He just told me and dashed off.'

'Oh, that is good news,' I said brightly.

'No it isn't. I was being sarcastic. Inspired by this, I fear Potty will go to my father and ask for my hand and that is the last thing that I want.'

I was nonplussed. I had been prepared to persuade Miss Stilton of the very course of action she was now advocating.

'You mean you don't want to marry Mr Potterthwaite?'

'Of course I do, you ninny. That's all I've ever wanted. But even with the living … I fear it won't be enough. My parents may still object to Clarence.'

'You could defy them.'

'I could, but Clarence wouldn't. He has too much honour about him.'

She threw another ball of bread at the ducks but her heart wasn't in it.

'I do not wish to be rude, Miss Woodsen, but what are you doing here?'

'Oddly enough, I wanted to ask that you keep Mr Potterthwaite from asking your father for his permission to marry. My friend Miss House hopes she might find some way to improve his chances of success, but it would be best not to act prematurely.'

'Well, it's too late. He's probably gone and done it.'

'No, when last I saw him, or rather heard him, he was still hoping to smite Mr Worcester, whom he had again chased up a tree. And if you will help me rescue Mr Worcester, perhaps I can help ensure that Mr Potterthwaite not speak to your father.'

'H'm, you interest me strangely. Very well, I suppose I owe it anyway to Bertie to rescue him.'

We left the pond and made our way back to the north lawn where as expected we found the two gentlemen in question, but I was also surprised to find Miss Blankenship, who apparently had not made it to the maze, and Mr Cuthbertson. The three of them were looking upward at Mr Worcester, who had sought refuge in the very same tree as before.

'You mean you really don't love Evie?' Mr Cuthbertson asked of Mr Worcester.

'Of course I don't, you fathead. I know she adores you and always has.'

At these words Miss Blankenship and Mr Cuthbertson looked tenderly at each other.

'And you really don't want to marry Stephanie?' Mr Potterthwaite asked. 'You're not just saying that to escape being smitten … uh, smited?'

'Yes, I don't … I mean no I'm not. It was just a thing we did to make you brace Aunt Hermione about the living. Starts with a "p." Ploy, that's the word.'

Mr Worcester's words still left Mr Potterthwaite looking confused. 'Look the Mite's a terrific girl, but … oh, hullo young blot on my horizon,' Mr Worcester said, presumably addressing this last to my companion.

'Up a tree again, Bertie? Remember that summer when we were children …'

I whispered to her, 'Perhaps it would be as best not to share childhood reminiscences with Mr Potterthwaite in attendance.'

She shot a glance at her intended, who wore a scowl appropriate for dealing with Midianites, and nodded.

'Serves you right, you blasted Worcester,' she shouted instead. 'It's all your fault for … for …'

'For offering your help unasked,' I supplied. 'Miss Stilton did not ask you to propose'—I heard a gasp from Miss Blankenship—'and your presumption that Mr Potterthwaite lacked the nerve to ask his aunt for the living was unwarranted. True, your actions were those of a … a … '

'A *preux chevalier?*' Mr Worcester suggested. #

'Uh, yes if you like … the action of a *preux chevalier* on behalf of Miss Stilton and Mr Potterthwaite …'

'Please, call me Potty, everyone does.'

'Don't you dare call me Cheese Mite!'

'Bertie, old man, is that what you did for Evie? You sacrificed … well, that's not quite the right word,' he said nervously after a glare from his intended, 'you pretended to be engaged thinking I lacked the nerve to declare my love for my darling Evelyn?'

'Uh, yes.'

'What a silly ass,' Mr Cuthbertson said.

I spoke. 'Perhaps Mr Worcester could come down now, Mr Cuthbertson? Without fear of bodily harm?'

'Of course, Miss Woodsen. And please call me Blotto.'

Miss Blankenship then gave me a glare that did not encourage me so to do.

'And you, Mr Potterthwaite, will not harm Mr Worcester?' I asked.

'So Stephanie never had any intention of marrying Worcester?' he asked in return.

'No!' I and Miss Stilton said in unison.

'Then I have no quarrel with him,' Mr Potterthwaite said.

'I think you can come down now, Mr Worcester,' I said. 'Gentlemen, if you might assist him?'

While the men helped him down, I heard a terse exchange behind me.

'I assume we both had the same idea, Miss Stilton.'

'Yes. How did you do it?'

'I simply announced it at dinner. Father nearly choked. And you?'

'I, uh, tricked him into it, in front of his aunt.'

'Well played.'

'And you.'

I relaxed after hearing this, although my estimation of Miss Stilton fell further. Although the two ladies remained cool to one another, at least they were civil.

Aided by the two suitors, Mr Worcester was able to return to earth without any damage to his self or wardrobe. After he was down, Mr Potterthwaite said, 'You caused an awful lot of trouble sticking your nose in like that, Bertie.' He offered his hand and they shook.

'Imagine me being afraid to propose to Evie,' Mr Cuthbertson added, also offering his hand, which Mr Worcester also shook.

I smiled at the sight of the two men, who moments before had wished Mr Worcester ill, now clasping him to their bosoms as a true, if somewhat addled friend. Good feelings abounded as Mr Worcester congratulated the parties on their successes until Miss Stilton said, 'But we still have the problem of our parents.'

'What's that?' Mr Potterthwaite asked.

'Dearest one, I might have been premature in saying that my parents would have no objection to you if you could obtain the living from Bertie's aunt.'

I heard a sigh from Miss Blankenship as well. 'I fear Mama and Papa will also question my wisdom in choosing a younger son as the man I wish to marry.'

The gloom this cast on our group affected me so strongly

that I unwisely said, 'Do not worry so! My friend Charlotte, Miss House, is the smartest person I have ever met. She has no doubt already used her considerable talents to find some way to overcome these objections.'

Alas, my efforts to improve their spirits were only slightly successful. I was, however, able to confirm that all parties would delay any representation to their parents. We returned to the house a subdued group, the lengthening shadows and increasing cold doing little to lift our spirits.

Our party separated, the ladies and the gentlemen exchanging doomed glances before returning to their various rooms, while Mr Worcester spoke with a servant who had caught his attention.

I hurried to find Charlotte and Mrs Fitzhugh, which proved difficult until a maid informed me they were in the conservatory, a part of the house I had not yet visited. I found them there, Charlotte sitting at the pianoforte, listlessly playing the Bach that was her favourite distraction, while Mrs Fitzhugh unravelled some handiwork that apparently displeased her. They both looked up at my arrival.

'You have found her? Charlotte asked.

'Yes I have. What is more I have reconciled all parties with the rôle Mr Worcester has played.' I related the story at length, hoping to delay what I feared would be disappointing news from my friends.

'At least we no longer need worry about keeping the couples in the dark,' Mrs Fitzhugh said.

'Yes, it was skilfully done, Jane. I only wish I had as much success.'

'You have thought of nothing that might persuade the parents to accept Mr Potterthwaite and Mr Cuthbertson as acceptable suitors?'

'Margaret and I have thought long and hard on it but we …'

The sound of either someone clearing his throat or a mournful mountain goat appreciating its view interrupted her. Suspecting the former I turned and beheld a servant who had silently entered the room. I recognized him as the servant with whom Mr Worcester had been in conversation.

'Pardon me, but perhaps I may be of assistance,' the servant said. I realized now that he was dressed as a valet and appeared to be about forty years of age. His manner and bearing were impeccable and although not of great height he seemed tall of stature nevertheless. A look of keen intelligence shone from his eyes; a look that seemed to say that he knew all that troubled us.

'Who are you and why do you think ...'

'Hush, Margaret,' Charlotte said. 'I think we are in the presence of Mr Worcester's valet, Cheevers.' She gave him a nod, which he acknowledged.

'I am Miss House, and these are my friends, Mrs Fitzhugh and Miss Woodsen.'

'I apologize for intruding, ma'am, but I thought it best to relieve your worries at the earliest convenience. When I saw this young lady hurrying to meet you I thought to speak to you before any precipitate action might render a satisfactory outcome difficult.'

'Do I understand then that you have some means by which we could ... persuade the families to accept the gentlemen of whom we were earlier speaking?'

'Quite so, ma'am.'

'And those means are?'

Cheevers cleared his throat a second time, again suggesting the sound of a contemplative ruminant, and said, 'I am not at liberty to disclose that to you. I can only provide to the gentlemen sufficient information that will persuade, as you put it, the fathers in question to embrace their future sons.'

'Embrace?'

'Yes, ma'am.'

'It's that good?'

'Mr Worcester would pronounce it a corker.'

'Very good. You will provide that information to the gentlemen directly?'

'I will do so now. And may I say how skilfully you have managed this affair to date. I am only sorry that owing to my disagreement with Mr Worcester, I have been negligent, but that difficulty is now behind us.'

'Ah, he has succumbed to your opinion as to purple waistcoats?'

'One does not wish to say.'

'Well, well, I wondered if he had earlier seemed in better spirits. I suspect he had just received word from you of your return. But though I thank you for your kind words, Cheevers, I have proved incapable of finding any resolution.'

What might have been a smile played across his face briefly to be replaced by his emotionless mask. 'I was privy to information you were not, ma'am.' He nodded again and left, his tread almost inaudible and the closing of the door behind him but a whisper.

'So that was Cheevers,' I said. 'One does feel in the presence of a superior mind.'

'A remarkable man,' Mrs Fitzhugh said, apparently eager to reverse her previous outrage at what she thought was his effrontery. 'I can well understand Mr Worcester valuing his services.'

Charlotte remained silent.

'What is it, Charlotte?'

'I would like to know what secret he possesses. It is the only way I can retire with some dignity from this matter.'

'Nonsense, dear, you have done very well.'

I agreed with my friend. 'Cheevers said as much.'

Charlotte may have been prepared to say more but we

heard the chimes of a clock reminding us that it was time to prepare for dinner and we hurried to our rooms.

An Almost Perfect Conclusion

'I do not know what can be keeping them,' Mrs Walthorpe said for the third time. 'It is most unusual that they should all be late.' Charlotte, Mrs Fitzhugh and I had been sitting with her for nearly half an hour, waiting for the other guests to arrive. It was understandable that she should be so upset by this breach of decorum and I felt somewhat guilty that our actions presumably were responsible for the delay.

Our hostess smiled nervously at us, looked to the clock again, made an attempt at further conversation, looked back to the clock and started when she saw the door to the drawing-room silently open. Cheevers entered, bowed to her after her acknowledgement, and silently glided to her side and whispered into her ear some information that made her ask, 'How sick is he?' Cheevers' murmured words could not reach us but it was obvious what news he brought. Mrs Walthorpe took no effort to conceal her irritation. Cheevers left us as quietly as he entered.

'I must apologize for my nephew,' she said, with a wincing smile. 'That was his valet … I don't know when he arrived … apparently Albert is unwell and cannot join us.'

We voiced our concern for Mr Worcester. 'Perhaps he is still troubled by the wounding of Mr Cuthbertson,' I offered.

'Yes,' she said, turning the word into two or three syllables.

The door opened again, this time quite audibly, and the measured tread of a footman made a stark contrast to Cheevers' quiet glide. Again our hostess received whispered information that this time she found to her liking. After the footman left, she again addressed us.

'I am so sorry. They will soon arrive. Apparently there were some matters that Mr Stilton and Sir Walter needed to discuss. They are both highly influential men, you know, very important to the defence of the realm.'

'Please do not worry on our account,' Mrs Fitzhugh said. 'I shall appreciate my dinner all the more.'

Mrs Walthorpe said nothing to this but in the silence I heard someone's stomach protest at the delay.

Before another protest could be offered, our hostess said, 'I do not know what delays the other young gentlemen, or Miss Blankenship or …'

The opening of the door and the entrance of all the missing guests interrupted her litany. Not too surprisingly, the younger guests seemed in a happy mood while the parents appeared quite glum. Mr Stilton and Sir Walter appeared especially unhappy and exchanged nervous, guilty looks. It fell to their wives to make excuses for their tardiness.

'I cannot apologize enough. A family matter of some … it was a surprise,' Mrs Stilton began while Lady Blankenship said, 'We've learned some disturbing … well, not disturbing …'—she gave a quick glance to Mr Cuthbertson—'happy news …' Both mothers stopped and looked at one another.

Mrs Walthorpe seemed to understand that extraordinary developments had delayed her guests and that the matter should not be addressed while food grew colder. She quickly ordered us and we entered the dining room.

Conversation was plentiful at my end of the table, with Mr Potterthwaite and Mr Cuthbertson proving themselves very voluble young men now that their concerns for their happiness were removed. Mrs Walthorpe, I noticed, observed the easy familiarity between Miss Stilton and the large curate, who happily knocked over glasses with little more than a cheerful 'beg pardon.' The Blankenships meanwhile ruefully observed their future son tell a story about a performing dog that had Miss Blankenship uncharacteristically giggling with abandon.

'Miss Stilton,' Mrs Walthorpe said, 'I am sorry to inform you that my nephew will not be joining us for dinner.'

That lady looked round and said, 'What, Bertie's not here?'

'No, he is unwell.'

'Oh, that is too bad. I'm sure a night's rest will set him right.'

'That man's a menace,' Sir Walter said, temporarily forgetting in which direction lay his allegiances.

'Bertie's not that bad,' Mr Cuthbertson said rather boldly to his prospective father, smiling broadly and giving the appearance of a happy lobster.

'He nearly killed you.'

'Water under the bridge, Sir Walter. Forgive and forget.'

'Here, here, sir,' Mr Potterthwaite said with enthusiasm. 'Here's to Bertie.' He raised his soupspoon in a toast, miraculously not spilling its contents.

Miss Stilton and Miss Blankenship agreed enthusiastically and wished their best to Mr Worcester as well. Mrs Walthorpe looked puzzled but pleased at her nephew's newfound popularity.

'I am glad you think so highly of him,' she said.

'It takes a man of character to know when to retire from the field,' Mr Cuthbertson said.

Mr Potterthwaite was about to say something in response to this when Charlotte abruptly said, 'I hope it was nothing unpleasant that delayed you to dinner Lady Blankenship.'

'No, Miss House, not at all.'

'Quite the opposite in fact,' Mr Cuthbertson said.

'Please sir, perhaps this is not the best time,' Lady Blankenship said, looking to her husband.

'Indeed sir, I must agree ... I think it best ...' For once Sir Walter did not appear so sure of himself. Mr Cuthbertson coughed and said something under his breath that I did not quite catch, that sounded oddly like 'bunny has a cold.' The effect of these words caused Sir Walter's face to blanch and kept him silent. I also noticed that Mr Stilton appeared quite shaken by the odd phrase as well.

'Why I disagree, this is a proper time,' Mr Cuthbertson said, rising to his feet. 'I am surrounded by good company'— he raised his wine glass and nodded pleasantly to Miss Stilton and Mr Potterthwaite, and then looked to Miss Blankenship who smiled and returned his nod—'and so I announce that I have asked Evelyn to marry me and she has agreed.'

My friends and I congratulated the happy couple. Even Mrs Walthorpe smiled politely, although she was clearly puzzled by the suitability of the match.

After Mr Cuthbertson sat, Mr Potterthwaite stood, nearly colliding with a footman placing a plate of pheasant. I heard ineffectual protestations come from Mrs Stilton and a hurried 'Hush, Mama' come from Miss Stilton. Ignoring all this, Mr Potterthwaite said, 'Well, as we're all having such a good time, I'd like to say that Miss Stilton has also agreed to be my wife.'

Mrs Stilton let out a small cry of despair. Mr Stilton buried his head in his hands. And Mrs Walthorpe dropped her knife.

'You,' Mrs Walthorpe said, 'you wish to marry Miss Stilton? But I thought ...' She looked at the Stiltons who would not meet her eyes. Then she looked at Miss Stilton. 'I thought there was an understanding that Albert ...'

'Oh that. Bertie asked if he might withdraw his kind offer and then Mr Potterthwaite asked me and I said yes.'

Mrs Walthorpe said nothing for a moment and then put

her hand to her forehead. 'I knew the minute that man arrived it would be trouble,' she said.

'Excuse me,' Sir Walter said, no longer unsure of himself and rising to his feet in anger. 'Do I understand that Mr Worcester had engaged himself to you?' addressing Miss Stilton.

'Papa, please don't cause trouble,' Miss Blankenship said.

'Trouble? I cause trouble? I hardly think I can be accused of causing trouble when it is this Worcester who is engaged both to my daughter and this … this …'

'Sir Walter!' Mr Cuthbertson said loudly.

'What!'

'Dunny-on-the-Wold!' Mr Cuthbertson said it clearly this time and the effect it had on Sir Walter was immediate. He sat and took a handkerchief to his face. Mr Stilton also looked distraught. And then I noticed Charlotte, who was smiling happily to herself, and nodding and enjoying the spectacle as if it were a play.

Perhaps startled at the effect of his words, Mr Cuthbertson sat and said to our hostess, 'Please forgive my outburst. It was inexcusable.' She gave him a little nod, which I thought quite gracious of her. He then turned to his future father-in-law. 'Please sir, I offer my apology to you as well. It was painful for me to have to say that and hope I shall never need utter those words again, but it would be as well if you could accept that which has happened.'

Sir Walter looked at Mr Cuthbertson and it was as if it were the first time he had ever really looked at him. He smiled weakly and said, 'Thank you, my boy.'

During this whole scene, Mr Potterthwaite had remained standing and Mrs Fitzhugh said, 'May I congratulate you and Miss Stilton.'

'Yes, good show Potty,' Mr Cuthbertson said.

Charlotte and I also offered our best wishes. Mrs

Walthorpe's graciousness could not extend that far and I could not blame her.

'I am feeling a little unwell myself,' she said. 'Please enjoy …' She let her words trail away and left us although I heard her tell a footman to locate her nephew and bring him to her.

Sir Walter then stood and announced that he too suffered from the rigours of the day and left, accompanied by his wife, his daughter and Mr Cuthbertson, who solicitously looked after his future father-in-law.

The Stiltons made a show of continuing the meal but Mr Stilton soon complained that the food had grown too cold for his digestion and left with his wife. Mr Potterthwaite rose to leave as well but Miss Stilton was still eating her pheasant. He whispered to her and she said, 'But I'm hungry.' Another whisper from him convinced her to leave as well, leaving my friends and me alone in the dining room.

'That went well,' I said, and burst out laughing. My friends joined in my laughter.

A STOUT DRAINPIPE

We finished our meal in a happy mood. Buoyed by the uniting of two couples, Charlotte was in an expansive mood and told us several funny stories that had the footmen struggling to keep from laughing. Mrs Fitzhugh, to my surprise, began to tell stories about youthful indiscretions—not hers, mind you—although Charlotte kept rolling her eyes when she denied her involvement. The wine poured by the attentive footmen fuelled our merriment and I began to realize how servants learned the information that we later learnt from them. Fortunately I kept my head as I suspect did Charlotte, despite her performance as a raconteur. I later had evidence that

Charlotte was in control when she interrupted a particularly risqué story Mrs Fitzhugh had begun.

Many hours after the meal had begun, we finally quitted the dining room, much to the relief I am sure of the servants. I am afraid that freed by the constraints of a hostess or other guests, we had treated the dining room as Liberty Hall and done just what we pleased. We eschewed the drawing-room and instead went up to our bedrooms, Charlotte and Mrs Fitzhugh sharing the rather grand Clock Room, while I went to my small room commensurate with a lady's companion. As we negotiated the stairs to our rooms, we passed several servants who appeared to be on a mission. #

I soon saw the purpose of their mission when I opened the door to my bedroom and saw it was now made even smaller.

'Mr Worcester!' I exclaimed, when I saw him revealed by the room's candle already lit.

'Please, Miss Woodsen, if you might lower your voice?' he pleaded. 'And if you might close the door behind you?'

I did as he asked even though the situation seemed to perilously parallel one of Mrs Fitzhugh's tales.

'What are you doing in my room, sir?'

'I am trying to remain one step ahead of the servants my aunt has set on my trail,' he said in a whisper.

'Oh,' I said, feeling guilty that in all our joy over the successful uniting of the two couples that we had quite forgotten our client. 'I am sorry. Your aunt must be frightfully upset.'

'You have said a mouthful, my dear Miss Woodsen, and rather accurately. My Aunt Hermione can be quite frightful when upset. I happened to overhear, while secreted behind a large vase, my aunt give instructions to the servants that they should find me, and it may have been my imagination but I would swear that the words "skin him alive" were bandied about.'

I kept the smile from my face as I said, 'I am sure you are mistaken.'

'That may be, but still caution is usually called for in …'

He was interrupted by a knock at the door and the voice of a maid asking, 'Miss Woodsen? Is everything all right? There's been a report of a … burglar.'

The effect of this on poor Mr Worcester made me feel for him as never before. He looked frantically about the room for some place of concealment, but my small room offered little opportunity. I suddenly realized his only hope would be a bold move on my part. I grabbed him by the arm and pulled him to the door, which he immediately resisted, but remembering my first meeting with Charlotte, I looked him steadily in the eye and instead of pulling him I led him to the right of the door like a mother would her child and he obediently followed.

I heard his small gasp as I flung open the door, which as it opened to the right concealed him.

'A burglar!' I said in alarm.

'Yes, miss,' the maid said in reply, somewhat startled by my cry and the rapid opening of the door. She looked over my shoulder and could easily see that my spare room contained no one. Fortunately the opened door almost met the wardrobe, hiding Mr Worcester from view.

Inspired by my success with Mr Worcester, I reached out to grab the shoulder of the maid and draw her into the room, but she instinctively drew back.

'Are you sure?' I asked, releasing her shoulder and stepping out into the hallway, looking left and right with alarm.

'It's … I'm not sure. One of the guests heard a noise and Mrs Walthorpe wanted us to …'

'Do you wish to check my room?' I asked, adding more panic to my voice, and placing my hand behind her back, pushing her toward the open door. As before she resisted.

'No, miss. I'm sure it's nothing. I am sorry to have bothered you.'

I thanked her and retreated to my room after first giving the hallway another theatrical inspection for her benefit. Upon re-entering my bedroom and closing the door, Mr Worcester began to pour out his thanks.

'That was very quick thinking. I cannot thank you enough. My plan was to escape down the drainpipe outside my room but there wasn't time before all these blasted servants began pouring out of the woodwork. Again, I thank you again and again.'

'You are very kind, Mr Worcester. But would it not be best to adopt a firm policy with your aunt? Tell her that you have achieved man's estate and that your choices are your own?' #

He looked at me with a wild surprise upon his face and said, 'Why ever would I do that?'

He was about to say further when he was again interrupted by a knock at the door and ran immediately to his place of concealment. However this time I heard Charlotte's voice ask, 'Jane, are you there?'

I opened the door and saw my friend and behind her Mr Worcester's valet.

'Come inside quick,' I said, bidding them enter and quickly closed the door.

'Cheevers!' Mr Worcester exclaimed once they had entered.

His manservant replied with a nod and said, 'It would be best to remain quiet, sir.'

'Of course, of course, of course. Have you thought of a way out of all this? Is that why you are here?'

The valet appeared somewhat downcast as he replied, 'Alas sir, we are unable to restore you to your aunt's good graces, however Miss House has found another means by which you might exit the house.'

Mr Worcester looked at my friend, who said, 'It is why

we came here and chance has united us. I recalled there is a drainpipe immediately outside your window, Jane.'

'A stout drainpipe?' Mr Worcester enquired.

'Serviceable.'

Mr Worcester leapt to the window and lifted the sash.

'That?' he asked, his voice somewhat muffled as his head was outside the window. 'Doesn't seem very stout.'

'I am afraid sir, that under the circumstances …'

And yet again there came a knock at the door, but this time I heard the forceful voice of Mrs Walthorpe ask, 'Miss Woodsen, may I come in?'

In a flash Mr Worcester was out the window. Charlotte quickly lowered the sash and Cheevers was already in the corner vacated by his employer.

Charlotte indicated I should open the door just as I heard a distant cry and the sound of a body falling to the ground.

I opened the door and saw Mrs Walthorpe in the company of the maid from earlier.

'Oh, Miss Woodsen, Miss House.' She looked into the small room and seemed disappointed.

'Please come in,' I said. 'Are you still looking for that burglar?'

Mrs Walthorpe, however, remained outside in the hallway, and said, 'What? Oh, no. The burglar was all in the imagination of this silly girl,' she said, indicating the maid, who looked down at the floor. 'I was actually looking for Cheevers, Albert's manservant. This girl said she thought she saw him in this hallway.'

'I passed him myself,' Charlotte volunteered. 'He seemed to be searching for Mr Worcester.'

'Oh, and did you notice in which direction he travelled?'

'He said that he would be returning to Mr Worcester's room to pack for his master.'

'Did he? Well, I must detain you no longer. Good night.'

We would have bid her good night in return but she left abruptly with the maid in tow. I closed the door.

'Pardon me,' Cheevers said as he went to the window, opened it and looked outside. He brought his head back inside, closed the window and turned to us with a smile so faint it might be a trick of the light.

'Mr Worcester is unharmed?' I asked.

'That I cannot say, but I see no sign of him below, miss. Thank you for your concern and may I thank you also for the assistance you have leant Mr Worcester.' He bowed to each of us.

'You're very welcome,' Charlotte said, 'although you may now find it difficult to pack your master's things.'

'I had already taken the liberty of packing and dropping Mr Worcester's belongings out the window. Now with your permission I shall withdraw and ...'

But Charlotte stayed him by placing her hand upon his shoulder, an intimacy people of their stations would not normally share.

'Before you leave, I must ask if "Dunny-on-the-Wold" is the secret with which you commanded Sir Walter and Mr Stilton to agree to their daughter's unions?'

She took her hand from his shoulder. The shadow of a smile again ran across his face—'It would not be wise for me to say, ma'am'—and was gone.

Charlotte also displayed her quick, tight smile. 'Ah, perhaps I should have asked whether you are aware that Dunny-on-the-Wold is a notoriously "rotten borough?"* My brother Michael has had occasion to mention it to me. It has but one occupant, a very elderly man if I recall.' #

'Perhaps I do recall your brother mentioning the borough, on the occasion of his dining at Mr Worcester's home. Although I might correct you in saying that it contained but one *constituent,* the man you mentioned who at 92 may be considered elderly, *and* his comparatively younger wife, aged 81.'

'Well it is a small world. Yes, I recall asking my brother what should happen to the borough should that very elderly man die. And do you know what he told me?'

'No, ma'am.'

'He said it would be abolished and it would lose its representation.'

'On that I might reassure you, for I have heard that the population of the borough in question has increased, despite rumours as to the passing of the gentleman to whom you refer.'

'That is good news indeed then for Mr Stilton, for I believe that is the constituency for which he stands. So the population has increased, you say?'

'Yes, I believe the town now boasts five and twenty, owing no doubt to the fecundity of its residents. And by a rare coincidence, the new residents are employed by the company owned by Sir Walter.'

At this a slow, full smile spread over Charlotte's face.

'No doubt. Thank you, Cheevers. You now have my permission to leave, although I might add before you go that our interests will not always run parallel. Mr Worcester is after all, a young gentleman in possession of a large fortune and if there were *ever* a young man in want of a sensible wife …'

'Quite so, Miss House. I look forward to our next meeting.' With that, Cheevers left, the door behind him closing with nary a sound.

☙

We announced our intention to leave Deerfield Park the next day. To her credit, our hostess pleaded that we should remain despite the ruination of her plans to see her nephew married.

'My dear Mrs Walthorpe, we really should be going home. I am terribly sorry that your hopes for your nephew have gone awry.'

'Thank you, Miss House, but I suspect Miss Stilton would not have made a suitable match for Albert. She is a trifle … high spirited. And I am actually more hopeful than ever that Albert might find a suitable wife.'

'Really, why is that?' Mrs Fitzhugh asked.

'Upon questioning my guests, I have ascertained that Albert was engaged to both Miss Blankenship and Miss Stilton. Surely being engaged to two women shows he is not averse to the prospect of marriage. Perhaps next time … if only I could separate him from that man of his.'

'Cheevers?'

'Yes, Miss House. That man has kept Albert a bachelor for far too long. It is in his own best interest after all that Albert remains unmarried. Oh well, it is too much to hope for. Thank you again for remaining here. And my best wishes to your brother.'

I looked back from the coach as we left Deerfield Park and saw the house lit brightly by the winter sun. We heard the crack of firearms as the men again attempted to do the pheasant population no good.

'I'm looking forward to going home,' I said.

'You did not enjoy your stay?' Mrs Fitzhugh asked.

'It seemed a complicated business and overlong to my taste,' I said. 'I prefer the simplicity of the city to the subterfuges of a country house.'

'Well said, Jane,' Charlotte said.

'In fact, I think I am quite through with Mr Worcester.'

'Oh, no, there I think you are wrong. I do not think *we* are done with Mr Worcester. But for now, I must agree with you; it will be good to be home.'

* Editor's note: A 'rotten borough' was a parliamentary constituency that maintained its two representatives to the House of Commons despite its population having fallen precipitately, sometimes in contrast with a considerably larger nearby city. Old Sarum near Salisbury, with its three houses and seven voters, is the classic example of a rotten borough.

A 'pocket borough' is a borough completely under the control of one person or interest. Pocket boroughs were so common that sometimes members of parliament were referred to as 'Mr So-and-So elected on Lord This-and-That's interest.'

In this affair, Dunny-on-the-Wold went from being a rotten borough to a pocket borough, under the control of Sir Walter. The 1832 Reform Act abolished 56 rotten and 130 pocket boroughs and added 41 boroughs to more equally represent population and industrial centres.

The Bride Who Wasn't There

'Take a look at this man, Charlotte,' I said as I looked out the window of our drawing-room. It was a particularly cold rainy day and I had hopes it might turn to snow if only to relieve the monotony of a week of rain. I had noticed not for the first time a man, bowed down by the wet and cold, walking in front of our home with an indecisive step. At times he seemed on the verge of approaching our door but then would stop, seize his hat upon his head and retreat down the street, only to return a minute later and repeat his actions. 'I think this man is suffering from a great burden.'

Charlotte stopped her incessant tinkering with her Bach fugue, which I admit was partly the reason I called her to the window. As I had learned, Charlotte was not only a gifted musician but also a determined one. Since our return from Deerfield Park, she had applied herself to recreating a missing page of her incomplete score. Mrs Fitzhugh and I initially approved of this, for it meant a relief from Charlotte's usual complaints of boredom, but after a week of hearing the same notes played over and over, each iteration only slightly different from the previous, I now welcomed any break in her routine.

'What man, Jane?' She joined my side just as the man had moved out of view.

'He has turned away again but he should return shortly.'

To her credit Charlotte remained at my side to wait, softly whistling the same notes she had played on the pianoforte. Then the man returned and again made toward our door, but turned around and walked away. This time, however, he stopped after a few steps, his back to us, his head down, drenched to the bone, the very picture of despair.

Charlotte stopped her whistling and went into the hallway and called for Mary, Robert being out on errands. She did not wait for Mary, however, but immediately went to our front door, opened it and called out to the man. Peering out through the window, I could see Charlotte step outside despite the rain and walk toward the man. I left to join my friend and found Mary walking down from the floor above to see what was the matter.

'Mary, there's a gentleman outside who looks as if he's had a shock and he's quite wet. I think Miss House will bring him in. If you would please fetch some towels and then ask Mrs Hutton to provide something warm?'

Mary ran to do as I asked and I went to join Charlotte, stopping to grab an umbrella before stepping outside.

I found Charlotte pleading with the man.

'Please, sir, won't you come inside.'

'She's gone!' he cried. 'I don't know how it happened. She stepped in but she didn't come out!'

'You may tell us all about it inside. I am Miss House, and this is Miss Woodsen,' she said, as she noticed me trying to shield us from the rain. 'We may be able to help.'

'You are really Miss House?' he asked, finally turning to us.

Charlotte nodded, the action releasing a shower from the water that had already collected on her hair.

The man, who I could now see appeared about thirty years of age with dark black curls peeking out from under his hat, bowed in return, which added to the shower as water from the brim poured onto my friend. Charlotte endured it without notice, however, and again pleaded with the man to come inside.

'I came to see you without hope that anyone had the power to solve this mystery. Might I come inside and plead for your help?' he asked, apparently unaware this had been our design all along.

'Yes, come inside sir,' Charlotte pleaded. This time he appeared to understand and Charlotte and I shepherded him inside just as Mary arrived with the towels. When she saw how soaked Charlotte appeared, however, she exclaimed that she would fetch more.

Once inside the man said to Charlotte, 'The man from the register office said I should come here at once. He said you could help but I could not believe him.'

'Mr Houston was correct. I can help you, but first we must get you dry and give you something warm to drink.'

By this time Mrs Fitzhugh had come downstairs from her room where she had been resting from a cold and she and Mary saw to the comfort of the man. They removed his hat and coat and gave those items to Alice that they might be dried. Charlotte excused herself that she might see to her wet clothes. Then Mrs Hutton arrived, who objected to the delicacy with which the towels were applied and vigorously dried the man's hair, leaving him looking even more dazed but decidedly drier. Finally we led him to the drawing-room just as hot coffee and brandy arrived.

Our visitor was taking his first sip as Charlotte returned, somehow miraculously in dry clothing.

'Now sir, your name if you please?' she asked him after he had fortified himself with the coffee and brandy.

He smiled weakly and said, 'Mr Hogarth Simms.'

'And as I have said, I am Miss House, and these are my friends, Mrs Fitzhugh and Miss Woodsen.' The man gave each of us another weak smile and then looked at the others in the room. Following his gaze, Charlotte looked round at the servants who remained in attendance, interest plainly written on their faces. 'Thank you, Mrs Hutton, Mary, Alice.'

Clearly Mary and Alice wanted to remain but Mrs Hutton herded them out of the drawing-room; however, even she gave a backward glance before she closed the door behind her.

'Mr Simms, earlier you said, "She's gone!" To whom were your referring?'

The man's anguished look immediately returned. 'My wife-to-be, Mrs Violet Brown. She left for the register office but never arrived. I have lost her. She stepped in but she never stept out.'

Charlotte raised an eyebrow at this and then glanced at me. She made a gesture to me that I interpreted as meaning I should employ my journal and record our visitor's narrative. Luckily it was close to hand and I rose to obtain it and returned without I think Mr Simms ever noticing. His gaze remaining fixed on Charlotte, who asked, 'Please, perhaps you could start at the beginning. Your troubles began this morning?'

Mr Simms nodded at this. 'Yes, this morning. We were to be married at the register office. I had arranged for a chair to take her to the register office while I followed ... on foot ... I am not a wealthy man, Miss House.' He looked at her enquiringly and she said softly, 'Please continue. Where did you engage the chairmen?' #

Encouraged by this he continued his story. 'From their station on Northgate Street. I directed them to Barton Buildings where Mrs Brown resides at her boarding house. We left there at ten o'clock, only I was forced to return to my residence on Miles's Buildings as I had left the ring I was to give to my beloved. After I retrieved it, I made my way but was further delayed by an altercation on the street. A young boy apparently had picked a man's pocket and was running away from the man and his friends. The boy knocked me down in his flight and I was further trampled by his pursuers.' #

'Whence that bruise on your head?' Charlotte asked.

'What bruise? Ow!' he cried once he examined his head. 'Yes, I must have received it when I fell.'

'Where did this incident occur?'

'Oh, on George Street, just a short distance from my lodgings.' #

'I see. And the men who trampled you, they stopped to help?'

'Yes they did, all of them except the man whose pocket was picked, and they were very apologetic but brusque as they wished to continue the chase.'

'And how long afterward did you notice your pocket had been picked?'

Mr Simms appeared startled by Charlotte's question. 'How did you know that?'

'It is an old trick. Please continue.'

'I had progressed down Milsom Street, almost to Quiet Street, when I thought to ensure I still carried Violet's ring—I felt quite a fool for having forgotten it earlier. That is when I discovered it still safe, but found my purse missing. I returned to where I had been knocked down but could not find it, and then it occurred to me that it had been stolen. I followed in the direction the men had fled but I saw no sign of them.' #

'Doubtless they ran in a different direction once you were out of sight.'

'Er ... yes, that is exactly what happened. I asked passersby if they had seen the men flee and I learned they had indeed taken another direction. But by then they were already out of sight. And I was already out of my mind for without my purse I could pay neither the registrar nor the chairmen. And I was already late.'

Mr Simms's recitation was agitating him afresh and Mrs Fitzhugh said, 'Calm yourself, sir. This was not your fault.'

'Indeed it was not,' I added.

'Please continue,' Charlotte said, upset both by our interruptions and our visitor's distress. 'You resumed your journey to the register office.'

He nodded. 'I decided I must not delay longer. It would be cruel to keep Violet waiting, so I ran as fast as I could to the Guildhall.' After these words, grief seemed to take hold of Mr Simms. He looked down to his hands and we heard great wracking sobs and watched his body convulse with anguish. As usual, my tender heart would have me rush to the poor man, but I remained seated, somehow aware I would interrupt Charlotte's questioning. And I was correct, for she continued: 'And did you find her already delivered to the register office?'

'What?' Mr Simms asked in a strangled voice. He looked up to reveal his tear-stained face.

'Was Mrs Brown awaiting your arrival?'

'No, I thought I said, she never stept out the chair.'

'The chair you found waiting for you at the Guildhall? For it must have arrived before you.'

Confusion was evident on the poor man's face. 'No, it arrived at almost the same time as I.'

'Despite your being delayed and the chairmen leaving before you, everyone arrived at the same time?' Charlotte asked.

'Yes, but that is unimportant. When they lowered the chair and opened the door, my Violet did not exit but another woman entirely!'

Mrs Fitzhugh and I gasped, but Charlotte displayed no surprise, not even the lifting of an eyebrow.

'Describe this woman,' she commanded. 'Does she resemble Mrs Brown?'

'Not at all! My Violet has warm lustrous brown hair and her eyes, oh her eyes are a deep violet and thus her name.'

'Yes, Mr Simms, I'm sure she is lovely, but my question is whether the woman who emerged from the chair resembles Mrs Brown in general?'

Mr Simms stopped his praise and said, 'Oh! I suppose she resembled Violet as much as any woman of moderate height with long brown hair.'

'And were they dressed similarly?'

'Yes, I suppose they were. Violet wore a dark blue Spencer with a golden coloured dress and this lady wore a light blue Spencer with a cream dress. But Violet wore a cap and this lady a bonnet.'

'Do you have this woman's name?'

'I … I believe her name was Mrs … Mulberry?'

'You are not certain?' I asked.

'No. There was much confusion. I cried out to the chairmen, "Where is Violet?" But they did not understand. I told them the woman who emerged from the chair was not Violet and at the same time the woman demanded to know why she had been brought here.'

'How did the chairmen explain that the woman who emerged was not the woman who had entered?' Charlotte asked.

'As I just said, they did not explain it. They insisted the woman they delivered was the woman who entered their chair. I asked them whether they remembered me helping Violet inside and they said "of course," but they insisted this Mrs Mulberry, or whatever her name, was Violet. I called them liars and all the while this woman was angrily accusing the chairmen of abducting her. Then the chairmen insisted they be paid for delivering her.'

I found Mr Simms's story more and more amazing and I

noticed from her open mouthed look Mrs Fitzhugh did as well. 'What did you do?' I asked him.

'I did not know what to do. I demanded they produce Violet. I even looked inside the chair although obviously there could not have been room for another. I grabbed the woman by the hand and pleaded with her to tell me where I might find Violet but she knew nothing. I do not know why they lied to me. Eventually all our accusations brought the attention of many onlookers and the registrar emerged from his office to ask what was the matter. I pleaded with him and he took matters in hand. As the woman still wanted to go home he told the chairmen to take her there and he advised me that I should seek your advice.'

He said this last with such a pitiable look that Mrs Fitzhugh and I put our arms around the poor man and I suspect that even Charlotte felt the impulse to comfort him as well, but as ever she kept her mind to the aspects of his story that most interested her.

'Surely the chairmen must have observed her leave the chair and this other women enter. Either that or they are lying.' I said.

'They claim they never saw her leave or Mrs Mulberry enter. They came straight from her home to the register office.'

'And yet they arrived at the same time as you despite your delay,' Charlotte said and then spoke no more for several seconds until she suddenly said. 'We must act immediately, Mr Simms. We must go to Northgate Street. Jane, are you up for travelling in this weather?'

'What? You can't be serious.'

'I am Jane. Would you deny this man our help? Alice! Alice! Send the boy for the carriage. Margaret, you will remain behind? I would not subject you to this weather and I had expected a few callers this morning. Good. Mr Simms you will take us where you engaged the chair.'

During all this Alice had entered and left to despatch the boy. Mrs Hutton entered and Charlotte ordered her to ready Mr Simms's coat posthaste and Mary entered informing me that we had a caller and announced Mr Wallace's name.

'Who's this?' Charlotte cried. 'Ah, thus your reluctance, Jane. Bring him in, Mary, so we may make our apologies.'

'But I … if I could …' I did not know what to say. Mr Wallace had called several times in the past week but always at odds with our schedule. I had yesterday sent him a letter informing him that to-day might be suitable for a visit and now here he was, entering our drawing-room.

'Pardon me, have I come at a bad time?' he asked. He stood uncertainly in the doorway and I noticed he still held his hand stiffly. I looked to him and then to Charlotte and then to Mr Simms.

'This gentleman is in need of our help,' I said to Mr Wallace with a definite air of frustration.

'Well Mr Wallace, you have certainly picked the wrong day to visit,' Charlotte said with her annoying indifference.

'Perhaps Mr Wallace might accompany you,' Mrs Fitzhugh said.

'That is a perfect idea,' I said.

'What!' Charlotte cried.

'After all, it would be a more proper arrangement,' Mrs Fitzhugh said.

I looked to Mr Wallace with I am sure a pleading look.

'I … uh … would be happy to join you. I'm sorry, what is going on?'

It was now Mrs Fitzhugh's turn to order us about, telling me to acquaint Mr Wallace with our new client's plight and telling Charlotte that Mr Wallace would accompany us. I set about my task while hearing in the background Charlotte's objections to Mrs Fitzhugh's plans.

'I am sorry to spring this on you, Mr Wallace,' I said after

I explained the tragedy that had befallen Mr Simms. 'I had thought with the weather my time would be my own.'

'No, it is all right. But I'm afraid I don't understand what is going on.'

I sighed. 'But I've told you! Mr Simms's intended ...'

'No, I understand all that. I don't know what your friend ... Miss House ... how is she involved in this? This is a matter for ... well I'm not sure who ...' #

'Precisely! You will not change your mind? You will come?'

He nodded, the look of confusion on his face changing to a smile at my pleading.

'I have been informed that you have picked the right day to visit after all, Mr Wallace,' Charlotte said with a look of ill humour.

He gave her a little bow. 'I hope I will not be an inconvenience, Miss House.'

'Yes, well ... ah, the carriage is here, and here comes Mrs Hutton with your coat, Mr Simms. Let us see if we can find what has happened to the future Mrs Simms.'

A MEETING WITH THE CHAIRMEN

'I am sorry that we are meeting under ... maybe you are not comfortable ... I should not have ...' I faltered, unsure what to say to Mr Wallace who looked out the window of the carriage. He and Mr Simms sat opposite us with Charlotte on my right. Mr Simms sat staring vacantly while Charlotte was busily engaged looking out the windows and humming her maddening tune.

Mr Wallace gave me a weak smile. 'I admit I did not anticipate this, Miss Woodsen.'

Charlotte gave a little sniff that I ignored.

'But I am happy to be of service,' he said, perhaps prompted to counter Charlotte's displeasure. His smile brightened.

'We are here,' Mr Simms observed.

We had arrived at the chairmen's station on Northgate Street and found it occupied by two chairs and a cluster of men who sought shelter from the rain in the lee of a building. Mr Simms sprang from our carriage and ran toward the men while Mr Wallace helped us down and then held an umbrella to shelter us.

'It is not them!' Mr Simms cried as he returned to us. 'These are not the men.'

'Calm yourself sir. Let us see if these men know the men you engaged,' Charlotte told him. She walked toward the men who straightened as she approached.

'Excuse me; we seek the men whom this man earlier engaged. Are they about?'

'What, Old Joe and Tom? Aye, they are,' a young man said, 'but they have a fare. Perhaps we can be of service.' The other waiting chairmen eagerly agreed and surged forward and I noticed that Mr Wallace unconsciously moved to Charlotte's side.

'No, it is Old Joe then I need speak with,' Charlotte said decisively, and ignoring Mr Wallace's gallant gesture, she stepped forward and away from his protection. 'They are the only other men who work this spot?'

The men retreated apart from the young man who continued to address Charlotte.

'Yes, just them.'

Charlotte thanked the young man and quickly pressed a small coin in his hand that just as quickly disappeared into his pocket.

'Perhaps we should wait in the carriage. Mr Simms please, you'll only grow wetter,' she said to the man who walked the street looking for the return of Old Joe, but finally she convinced him to return to the carriage.

'Tell us how you met Mrs Brown, sir,' I asked Mr Simms, hoping to distract his attention.

'Oh, I met her in Bournemouth. Her husband died … two years previous I think it was, at sea on his return from America where he had business.'

'And how did you come to Bath?' Charlotte asked.

'She has … family here. I am sorry that I am not more coherent,' he said with a sob.

'Steady on,' Mr Wallace said, clumsily patting Mr Simms's shoulder. 'I'm sure Miss House will see through this mystery,' he added uncertainly.

Charlotte gave him a grateful nod at these words that was interrupted by Mr Simms saying: 'They have returned!' He sprang out the carriage and again we followed. Mr Simms was already in heated conversation with the men, even as they lowered their empty chair to the ground.

'We told you before, the lady what got out was the lady what got in!' the man I presumed to be Old Joe said to Mr Simms.

'Please forgive my friend's excitement,' Charlotte told Old Joe, a wizened fellow whom one would have thought incapable of his duties. She stepped close to the man, Mr Wallace sheltering her with an umbrella. 'If you would be so kind as to answer my questions, you will be amply rewarded.'

Charlotte's remark riveted Old Joe's attention, who politely tipped his hat. 'Anything I might do for you ma'am, ask away.'

'Good, you obviously remember this man and the woman he put in your chair.'

'Yes I do. Nervous fella and in a hurry, but they all are in weather like this.'

'And did you stop anywhere between here and the register office?'

'No, we went there straight away.'

'And yet you arrived there late?'

'Who says we were late?'

'Let me rephrase that: you arrived there at the same time as this man.'

'Yes, I guess we did.'

'Did nothing delay you? There was not a disturbance or commotion?'

'How did you know that? But it was nothing, just the usual trouble with too many chairs on the street and we had to help some lads making a delivery. They'd made a mess of it and was blocking the street.'

'So there were many chairs on the street? Where was this?'

'Queen Street and Trim.'

'So you left your chair?'

'Only for a moment, we moved some boxes that had fallen off a cart—there were others who helped us.'

'Other chairmen?' Charlotte asked.

'Other chairmen, yeah.'

'Did you recognize them?' she asked again.

'Course I recognized them. Don't I know everyone who works in Bath?' He turned to his partner. 'You tell this nice lady if I don't know everyone who carries a chair in Bath.'

His partner, a much younger man wearing an ill fitting livery, agreed with that fatalism the young use in confirming the pronouncements of their elders.

'Old Joe knows everyone in Bath,' he agreed.

'Everyone in Bath that carries a chair, I said. I don't claim to know everyone in Bath.'

Charlotte sighed, obviously finding the process of procuring information from Old Joe quite tedious.

'Could you give me the names of these other chairmen?' she asked.

'Sure I could. Tell them who they was, Tom,' he said, addressing the younger man.

'I have no idea, ma'am. I don't know 'em, but then I'm new,' Tom said.

'But I thought you said you know everyone!' Charlotte said with noticeable irritation to Old Joe.

'I said I know everyone that carries a chair and if I can see them, I can recognize them,' he said, but he made this statement shifting uneasily on his feet, embarrassed by his admission.

'Old Joe can't see so good, ma'am,' Tom offered. 'That's why I'm in front. He can see fine close up, but not so good far away.'

'But I know these streets like the back of my hand,' Old Joe said as proof of his worthiness.

'Aye, he does and he's still strong, stronger than me,' Tom said in support of his partner.

Charlotte sighed and then asked of Tom, 'Can you describe the men who helped?'

'No, ma'am, they was men, weren't they? One thing, though, they weren't very strong and they weren't much help, even though it was they who said we should help the delivery men. Me and Old Joe did most of the work, and they were on their way before we had everything picked up.'

At this information, Charlotte's face lit up and for several seconds she was silent. Then she began to walk around the chair the men had deposited. She seemed to be inspecting it. Finally she asked, 'Their chair, was it alike to yours?'

Tom decided a second, then said, 'Aye, it was. But there are many chairs like this in the city.'

'Thank you, you've been very helpful,' Charlotte said and swiftly produced coins for Old Joe and Tom, an act that caught Mr Simms's eye. I could not help think he was weighing what he now owed my friend for he seemed for a second to have forgotten his grief.

We prepared to leave when Charlotte asked of the men, 'Oh, do you remember to what house this delivery was destined?' Charlotte asked.

'No I don't,' Tom replied after a glance to his partner. 'The cart had spilled below the arch, right in the middle.'

'Ah, then at the very corner of Queen and Trim,' Charlotte said. 'Thank you again. And should I need call on your services, what number is your chair?'

Tom looked confused but answered. 'I don't rightly know, but just ask for …'

'Number Twelve,' Old Joe said. 'That's been the number of this chair this past ten years.'

Charlotte again thanked the chairmen.

'That is all you need ask?' I asked my friend.

'I think it is enough. Come, let us go to Queen Street.'

Charlotte swept us back to the carriage with her usual energy, although by now I wished we were back home. My friend and I had taken the precaution of wearing country shoes but still my feet were wet and I was cold, which Mr Wallace noticed as he helped me into the carriage.

'Your hand is freezing,' he said to me as we settled into the carriage, which was already in motion, Charlotte having told our driver to proceed to Queen Street but a short distance away.

'Thank you, I know,' I said. He made to remove his coat and give it to me but I stopped his generous but unnecessary act.

'You and Mr Simms are sitting on the carriage's rugs. If you would kindly hand one to me.' He did and I quickly bundled myself just as the carriage slowed for Queen Street.

'I will get out,' Charlotte said. 'Jane, you've made yourself too comfortable. Mr Wallace, if you would accompany me?'

Mr Simms also made to leave but Charlotte stopped him.

'Please sir, remain with my friend and give her your address and that of Mrs Brown and also a detailed description of Mrs Brown ... kindly omitting any subjective impressions.'

I was surprised to be left behind but also grateful to remain sheltered. I obtained the information Charlotte had asked and entered it my journal, although it was clear Mr Simms would have preferred to accompany Charlotte. He watched intently as Charlotte inspected the buildings with Mr Wallace attending her by holding the umbrella over her head. I also saw them walk to the door of a house and knock and ask questions of the person who answered. After five minutes they returned, Charlotte giving instructions to our driver to return us home.

'What did you discover?'

But Charlotte shook her head and said, 'Nothing I'm afraid. We will return home. You look chilled to the bone, Jane.'

'Then you have found nothing that will help me?' Mr Simms asked her.

'At the moment, no, but I have high hopes that this mystery will be solved.'

We returned to Number 1 a downcast lot. Mr Wallace said nothing; Mr Simms occasionally asked Charlotte if there were any hope; and Charlotte reassured Mr Simms, although in fact she did not offer much hope. I grew colder, disheartened that for once Charlotte seemed to be at a loss.

At the house, Charlotte sent Mr Simms on his way with assurances that she would work tirelessly on his behalf. He left even more dejected than when he arrived, crushed no doubt by my friend being unable to help him.

'How very sad that we were not able to help,' I said after he had left. 'But we can still entertain you, Mr Wallace.'

'I'm afraid Mr Wallace must go,' Charlotte said with sudden decisiveness at odds with her previous pessimism.

'Remember, remain close but do not be spotted,' she said to that gentleman.

'I will do my best.'

'With any luck you will be relieved by my agents and you may report back to me.'

'What? Where are you going?'

'I'm sorry Miss Woodsen, he may already be out of sight.' He took my hand, squeezed it awkwardly for he must use his left hand, and was out the door before I could say anything to prevent his leaving.

'A very useful man,' Charlotte said.

'You! What have you done?'

'Oh you're back. What did you ... what's going on here?' Mrs Fitzhugh asked as she came down the stairs.

'Charlotte made Mr Wallace leave!'

'I did nothing of the sort! Well, no I guess in all fairness I did. He is in my employ, Jane. He is following Mr Simms.'

'What!'

'Jane, don't shout!' Mrs Fitzhugh said. 'You're both soaked. Alice! Get more towels and then you two tell me what is going on.' She commanded us into the drawing-room and we sat.

Charlotte bore a superior smile and said, 'I'm sorry Jane, but I needed your Mr Wallace to follow Mr Simms. All is not as it seems.'

'I don't understand. What is not as it seems?'

'This whole outrageous story. It seems designed to draw attention to itself. If the purpose is to abduct Mrs Brown, why not take her in a more quiet manner? And you will notice how readily Mr Simms adopted any of my embellishments such as the theft of his purse and also his desire to avoid the information that he and the chairmen arrived at the Guildhall at the same time.'

'Then you doubt she was ... abducted.'

'Yes, I think it unlikely.'

'What do you think happened Charlotte?' Mrs Fitzhugh asked, but Alice returning with more towels prevented Charlotte's reply, followed afterward with Robert bringing a tray.

'At first I was confused,' she finally said after we were wrapped in towels and drinking coffee. 'But once the chairmen said that they were delayed at Trim Street and left the chair it made sense. I had already considered two possibilities: that Mrs Brown and Mrs Mulberry switched chairs, or that the chairmen had switched chairs. After our conversation with Old Joe and Tom, I knew it was the latter.'

'You mean they are accomplices?'

'Those two worthies? No, they are at best unwitting accomplices. As confirmed by young Tom, their chair is of a type that's rather common. They are numbered by the Bath Corporation and it may be some time … or until I inform them … before they are aware their chair now bears the number sixteen.' #

'Instead of twelve? But how would they not notice … oh I see. Yes, I suppose it is quite simple. Well not simple …'

'I am afraid I remain puzzled by this,' Mrs Fitzhugh said. I awaited Charlotte offering her explanation, but instead she indicated that I should relay our investigation and surmises to our friend.

I told her of our conversation with Old Joe and Tom and then attempted to recreate what happened at Queen and Trim streets. #

'Both chairs arrived at Trim Street, only to find it blocked by a cart that had spilled its contents. Both sets of chairmen deposited their chairs and … and Tom said the others left while Tom and Old Joe were still assisting with the deliverymen, who must also have been accomplices. But this makes no sense, why should not Mrs Brown have simply … oh, they would have noticed the chair was empty by its weight. So the other chairmen simply took Old Joe and Tom's chair.'

'Very good, Jane. I am glad we have come to the same conclusions. My only question remains whether Mr Simms has been fooled or is attempting to fool us.'

Mrs Fitzhugh smiled. 'Ah, that explains the message I gave to your little urchins.'

'They've been?'

'Yes, I gave them the message you left me as you were leaving.'

Charlotte turned to me: 'You see, Jane, I wanted the children to keep Mr Simms under observation, but until they could be put in place, I needed your Mr Wallace.'

'Of course,' I said, feeling stupid that I had not understood immediately and of my anger at Charlotte for sending him away.

'The three of us could hardly have hoped to follow Mr Simms discreetly,' she further added.

'Is that why you did not include me when you investigated at Trim Street? You wished to ask Mr Wallace's assistance.'

Charlotte nodded. 'Yes, I needed you to keep Mr Simms occupied in the carriage while I asked Mr Wallace this favour. I must say his ready understanding impressed me. But now we must change into dry clothes and await developments.'

Mr Simms's Destination

Time dragged heavily as I waited for Mr Wallace. I glanced nervously at the clock on the mantel and saw that it had gone seven. I had worried all during dinner that we had not yet heard from Mr Wallace and now we sat in the drawing-room afterward and still he had not returned.

'Suppose he is hurt!' I said.

'Unlikely,' Charlotte said.

'He does not have full use of his hand.'

'He seemed to use it quite well helping you into the carriage.'

'Your Mr Wallace seems very capable, Jane,' Mrs Fitzhugh said, no doubt tiring of my exchange with Charlotte. 'I'm sure his appearance would discourage anyone from ...'

'What is wrong with his appearance?'

'Oh Jane, if you're going to be like this every time ... now see, a carriage is arriving,' Charlotte said as she looked out the window. I also arose and looked out and saw the lights of a carriage. It was stopped before our home and I saw the driver jump down and hurry to the door and open it. He extended a hand and I saw Mr Wallace reach out for support.

Charlotte also saw this, which caused her to call out for Robert to open the front door. I hurried out the room followed close behind by Mrs Fitzhugh. Robert was already out the door helping the driver extricate Mr Wallace from the carriage. We watched as the three men approached.

'You are injured,' I cried.

'Now, now, it's not as bad as it looks. Oh, bloody hell!' he cried out as he negotiated our front door step. 'Excuse me!'

Robert rushed to Mr Wallace and supported him and with the driver's aid they helped him into the house.

'It is a turned ankle, nothing more,' he said, after the driver had been dismissed and Mr Wallace was settled into a chair in the study with his left leg propped high.

'Thank you,' he said to Mrs Fitzhugh who under his instruction was wrapping a wet cloth tightly around his swollen ankle. I was reminded that Mr Wallace was actually Doctor Wallace, although he had never represented himself as such. 'Thank you!' he said with extra vigour after a final tight wrap.

'Mr Wallace, I apologize that I have sent you in harm's way,' Charlotte said, with a quick, contrite glance to me.

'Nonsense, it is nothing but a turned ankle,' I said, touched by my friend's embarrassment.

'Oh well then, if it's nothing but a turned ankle then I should best be going,' Mr Wallace said with mock hurt and he made a play at standing followed by a real cry.

'You are all being ridiculous,' Mrs Fitzhugh said. 'What he really needs is stronger help,' handing him a glass she had filled from a decanter she procured from somewhere.

He sniffed the brown liquid and smiled, took a sip and sighed and then downed the remainder.

'Oh Mrs Fitzhugh, you have provided the best medicine,' he said.

'Now tell us what happened,' I commanded, eager to know how he came to be injured.

'I followed your Mr Simms as you asked, Miss House. He walked quickly and I rushed to keep up but it seemed every time I did he would glance back.'

'And did he return to his home?' Charlotte asked.

'No, he did not. He made some small purchases and also stopped for food and drink. Finally he went across Pulteney Bridge and came to a house on Argyle Street. Actually it was a small shop, a milliner's, and he entered and remained. He must be in the rooms above the shop.' #

'He remains there?'

'Yes.'

'But he might leave while you are gone,' I said.

'Thankfully one of your "agents" found me. A small boy tugged my coat and asked if I were Mr Wallace and he remains, or one of a number of other small boys I assume, will keep a watch over the house. How they found me is a mystery.'

'Not too deep a one. After you left the children arrived to report back to me on the other errand I had given them. I then despatched them to look for you and one of them obviously thought to watch Pulteney Bridge. I shall have to reward him well. Did you catch the boy's name?'

'Peter it was, although I have already rewarded him.'

'That was very kind of you, Mr Wallace.'

'But you still haven't said how you came to be injured,' I said.

'Oh, that. When Peter tugged at my coat I had walked back to get a better look at the upper room of the house and I was craning my neck back. He pulled me off balance and I tripped over the kerb.'

I laughed and felt instantly sorry for it for he coloured quite red.

'And yet you still rewarded Peter,' Mrs Fitzhugh said. 'You are a man of character, sir.'

'I am a man who is too clumsy for his own good. I remained as long as I could but after a while I knew I could not follow Mr Simms were he to leave, and so I have returned. And now Miss House, what does all this mean?'

Charlotte recounted to him all that we had surmised about the switch of the chairs, which left Mr Wallace astounded.

'Well I'll be blowed. That's a pretty piece of reasoning, Miss House. But this Simms, what are we to think of him?'

Charlotte sighed and said, 'I am … I do not wish to advance theories before I have all the particulars.'

'Oh come Charlotte,' I said, 'we will not hold it against you if you guess wrong. Your surmises are better than most people's facts.'

'Yes, out with it Charlotte,' Mrs Fitzhugh said with the voice of a governess commanding her charge to recite her lines.

'Very well, here are the possibilities. One, it is possible there is no Mrs Brown. After all, Violet Brown? What an absurd name! But if she does not exist, I am afraid I am clueless as to Mr Simms's game. Two, Mr Simms has done away with her, but then why ask my assistance? Or three, and this is most likely, Mr Simms and Mrs Brown together have staged this disappearance.'

We looked at her with amazement. That Mrs Brown should be party to her own abduction seemed preposterous.

'What about the simpler explanation that Mrs Brown has left Mr Simms at the altar?' Mr Wallace asked, with ready nods from myself and Mrs Fitzhugh.

'No, we have left simple behind. With the knowledge that he neither proceeded to his home or that of Mrs Brown and the knowledge I have received from my agents …'

'What knowledge is that?' he asked.

'The knowledge that no one will own to the picking of Mr Simm's pocket.'

Mrs Fitzhugh nodded as if she understood and I realized the benefit she had from long acquaintance with Charlotte's methods.

'Forgive me, how can you know that?' Mr Wallace finally asked.

'The children are very well acquainted with the criminal element—they *are* the criminal element—and know who works the street where Mr Simms claims to have been robbed. I can assure you no one picked Mr Simms's pocket.'

'Then his story …' I said, unsure what to say next.

'He needed an excuse for his late appearance at the register office. Undoubtedly because he was involved in the switch. He may even have been one of the delivery-men.'

'But this is all senseless,' I continued to protest. 'Why would he do this?'

'Again, I should not care to theorize and appear less than brilliant when my theories prove groundless. Let us move to practicalities. Mr Wallace, you are too injured to move. Perhaps a night of rest will see you recovered but I think it best if you spend that night here. You are agreed Margaret? I need not ask you Jane.'

And so it was decided that Mr Wallace should stay and a room was made ready for him. Mrs Fitzhugh also deduced that he must be hungry.

'Starving, in fact. Following people works up an appetite.'

'Jane, you might ask Mrs Hutton to make some Sandwiches—I think our dinner roast should suffice,' Mrs Fitzhugh ordered. 'And he must have it here, to avoid moving him further.'

Charlotte agreed and added, 'And I must return to our library; I think I have an unfinished port and a treatise on the transit of Venus that I must finish. Good night, Mr Wallace. Perhaps Mrs Fitzhugh you shall remain here … to lend propriety?' #

'Oh, but I have not yet recovered from my cold,' she said with a forced cough. 'I had best go where it is … warmer.' My friends left us with many backward glances.

'And so we are alone together,' he said at last after a long silence. Perhaps like me he felt at a loss, for it was very improper for us to be alone, but as this was our first real chance to talk since the events at the masked ball, I would not waste the opportunity.

'Yes. I am sorry for your poor ankle.'

'It is a mark of honour. Actually it is a mark of stupidity, but now that I reflect upon it, it has led to being our alone together.'

'Ah, you had planned this.'

He smiled. 'Never in a million years. And I had not dreamed that this was Miss House's … hobby.'

'Oh, you dismiss it as a hobby?'

'No, please do not misunderstand me. I am at a loss what to call it. And *you*, you are part of it.'

I nodded. 'I am. I am proud of it,' daring him to object but not wanting him to do so.

He said nothing, which was perhaps his wisest course. He shifted uncomfortably in his chair.

'Your ankle, it is worse?'

'Your friend may have wrapped it a little too tightly. I cannot complain, though. I have done as much for others and it were best tight, but I am afraid it has gone dry.' He said the last with a little grunt.

'Let me rewrap it. No, I insist.' I moved my chair to help with the task. Mrs Fitzhugh had wrapped the ankle quite expertly with a neat knot that I hoped I could duplicate. But a touch of the now dry bandages proved they were already quite warm.

'Ow!'

'I am sorry; it is a tight knot. You say have done this for others?'

'Yes.'

'When?'

He sighed. 'I have done this for the soldiers of the regiment.'

'Are you a surgeon or a doctor?' I asked, reluctant to ask and find that he was not a gentleman, which I had presumed. And then I realized it would make no difference to me, who as a lady's companion could make no great claim to status. #

'I am a doctor, but in ... in the field some of the niceties are lost and even a doctor must get his hands dirty. The distinctions are lost and I have learned much from the surgeons that accompany the regiment. But even a poor doctor knows how to wrap an ankle.'

I removed the last of the wrapping, soaked it in the cold water and wrung it dry.

'Best to leave it a little wet.'

I complied and reapplied it. As the wet cloth touched his skin he sighed and said, 'That feels nice.'

I lowered my head a little to hide the flush that I feared would unmask me.

'Tighter, please,' he said. 'Don't be afraid.'

I murmured something and wrapped his ankle tighter, unnerved at the sounds he made and yet somehow pleased that my actions were responsible. I finished the wrapping with Mrs Fitzhugh's careful knot.

'Thank you. A nice compromise.'

Robert chose this time to bring Mr Wallace's Sandwiches, hardly waiting after his knock before entering. He found me with my hands still touching Mr Wallace's leg, but apart from a slight smile on his lips, he made no comment.

'Would the gentleman care for something extra in his coffee?'

'That would be very much appreciated, Robert is it?'

'Yes sir. Would you care for anything, ma'am?'

'No thank you.' Robert bowed and was about to leave.

'Please Robert, would you stay. Uh ... Mr Wallace may need some help.'

Mr Wallace looked at me upon my words, then Robert looked at Mr Wallace and finally Robert looked at me.

'I am sorry, miss, but I must arrange to have the chair from the lumber room brought down for Mr Wallace. But if you would rather someone should stay ...'

'No, please see to the chair. But I may call if ... if Mr Wallace requires assistance.'

'Certainly,' he said, and looked from me to Mr Wallace. 'I shall remain vigilant should you call,' and left the room. The door closing behind him left an uncomfortable silence in the room.

'You are afraid to be alone with me.'

I was about to deny it but instead I said, 'Yes. My friends

have abandoned me. They leave me here with you. Even Robert seems to be in on the game. And it's not proper.'

'Then you fear that I will not behave as a gentleman ought.' He straightened in his chair and again the movement made him pronounce his discomfort. 'I can assure you that in my present state my options are limited.'

'You keep getting injured when you're around me.'

'You're right. I must stop visiting you if I wish to remain well, but I think it would be a far less interesting life.' He laughed and the sound broke the tension. 'Now Miss Woodsen, as much as I am enamoured of you and as much as you are concerned about my behaviour, I am still a very hungry man with a plate of Sandwiches just out of reach. So perhaps you might do me the great favour of handing me something to eat.'

Just then I found myself liking Mr Wallace very much. A moment had passed where I felt uncomfortable and I cursed and thanked my friends for placing me in this situation. I knew that they believed that nothing improper would ensue from our being together and in this their judgement was correct. But I had begun to doubt my own restraint and I think sensing that, Mr Wallace wished to assure me that I had no reason to doubt his conduct and to remind me that I had no reason to doubt mine.

We talked about a great many things after this, my love of adventure and of reading and the countryside. And he told me of his time with the regiment, although he was very guarded, only telling me funny stories and nothing of the horrors of war and certainly avoiding anything that made it sound romantic or brave. Finally he yawned, not Charlotte's stage yawn, but one with a deep desire for sleep, caused from the rigours of his day and the something extra in his coffee.

'I am so sorry, it is the hour and not the company. Perhaps I should be off to bed.'

'Of course, I have kept you up.' I called for Robert. The door opened almost immediately.

'We should get Mr Wallace to bed, Robert.'

'Very well, miss.' He eyed our solidly built visitor and added, 'I shall fetch help.'

He left us and a few seconds later I could hear him leave the house. I was confused by this but Mr Wallace solved the mystery.

'He means to carry me upstairs in a chair and has gone to find some strong fellows. I apologize, Miss House, for the trouble I cause.'

He had addressed my friend who now entered the study, followed by Mrs Fitzhugh. I wondered where they had been that they were so ready to join us.

'It is no trouble, sir. I only hope the strong fellows I heard you mention are not too far into their cups.'

'I believe Robert had engaged them as soon as we knew Mr Wallace was to stay. Doubtless he advised them to remain upright,' Mrs Fitzhugh supplied.

We now heard the voices of several men proceed from the back of the house, which prompted Charlotte and me to step into the hallway. Presently Robert produced two strong young men who, confronted by their betters, shyly looked down at the ground.

'Oh well done, Robert. These two fine lads look strong enough. Thank you kindly for your assistance, sirs,' she said, addressing the last to the two men. As always, Charlotte could put people of any class at ease.

Robert then directed the men to follow him upstairs. A few minutes later they returned with Robert directing from behind.

'Easy, to your left. Mind the wall!' he told them as they brought the device down the stairs. I had no idea the household maintained one of these chairs meant to bring invalids directly from the baths and straight to their room.

The men brought the chair to the hallway and lowered it without incident. Without the weight of an occupant, it was a relatively easy task. But now they prepared to move Mr Wallace from the study to the chair. They helped him to stand although it was now evident that his leg could not bear weight without considerable pain.

'Please pardon my outbursts. I ... Ow! ... I am most dreadfully ... Damme that hurts!' He said this last comment on the occasion of his foot hitting the doorway.

'Please mind the gentleman,' Robert advised.

'Not their fault Robert,' Mr Wallace said charitably, as they eased him into the chair. 'Thank you,' he said after he sat.

'Up with him now, lads,' Robert ordered.

They took either ends of the poles supporting the chair and walked with their burden to the stairs. What seemed easy coming down with an empty chair, however, now looked more daunting going up. Fortunately they were very strong young men and under Robert's guidance successfully negotiated the stairs. They brought Mr Wallace to the third floor and with a great deal of puffing and heaving and not a few more oaths, we watched him helped into his room.

'Goodnight, Miss House, Mrs Fitzhugh, Miss Woodsen,' he said, while still upright.

'Goodnight, Mr Wallace,' we three said almost in unison.

The two men deposited Mr Wallace on his bed after which Robert rewarded them and obtained their promise to help on the morrow.

Robert informed us that he would help prepare Mr Wallace for bed and ordered Alice to see our helpers out the house. Looking around, I realized that our journey had also attracted the attention of both Alice, Mary and Mrs Hutton, although once my glance caught the attention of our housekeeper she promptly chased Mary and Alice downstairs before herself descending.

'My opinion of your Mr Wallace has completely changed, Jane,' Charlotte said to me. 'I find him vastly entertaining.'

MR SIMMS'S CONFESSION

The next morning as I walked downstairs for breakfast I heard Charlotte speaking in the library. As the door was open, I looked inside and saw Charlotte talking to a small boy I recognized as one of the urchins in her employ.

'You are quite sure, Charlie?'

'Yes, miss. The milliner and his wife, two servants, Mr Simms and another woman.'

'And this other woman?'

'Donna didn't see much, just a woman looking out a window. She had brown hair and ... well, Donna said she looked sad.'

'Thank you Charlie. Mrs Hutton has some Sandwiches you may take to the others. Standing watch is hungry work. Now off with you, and alert the others as I asked.'

Charlie left hurriedly after giving me a tip of an imaginary hat like a proper gentleman.

'You have news?'

'H'm? Yes, Jane. I think we know the location of the missing Mrs Brown. Perhaps after you have breakfasted, we can pay her a visit.'

'I will be ready in a few minutes,' I assured her, and hurried to find something quick to eat. I found Mrs Fitzhugh and Mr Wallace already finished. At this I was surprised, for I had anticipated that I should be made aware of Mr Wallace's descent down our stairs, and how he had effected this without the hullabaloo of the previous night was a wonder.

'Good morning, sir. I am very surprised to find you here before me. I had thought I might attend to your … expedition down the stairs.'

'I am sorry to have robbed you of the entertainment, but my ankle is much improved and with Robert's help and this stick I was able to descend without the aid of a chair and two stout lads,' he said with a smile and a bow.

'Well, how disappointing, but I suppose I must take some solace that you are well. As I suspect are you Margaret,' I said, turning to my friend.

'I am feeling well. I think I am recovered from my cold.'

'Do I understand there are developments regarding Mr Simms?' Mr Wallace asked.

'Yes, Charlotte thinks Mrs Brown has been found in the house where you followed Mr Simms. We shall go there directly after I have had something to eat.'

'Oh ho! The plot thickens. Perhaps she is being held against her will?' #

'No, that cannot be. I subscribe to Charlotte's opinion—outlandish as it is—that both Mr Simms and Mrs Brown hatched this plot. You think differently?'

'I may be indulging in a flair for the dramatic I did not know I possessed. I hope you will apprise me of further developments.'

'But … you are leaving?' I asked, knowing full well the necessity of his departure.

Mrs Fitzhugh coughed and said, 'Jane, it would hardly be proper for Mr Wallace to remain in a household of three women.'

'Yes, of course, I know.'

'I've sent a message to my sister, asking if I might yet again recuperate in her home. No doubt I will be gone when you return from your investigations.'

'Jane, are you ready to leave yet?' Charlotte asked upon

entering the dining room. 'The carriage has arrived. Oh, Margaret you are looking well. Will you accompany us?'

'Yes, I think I am up to it. But give Jane a moment further to eat something. And have you eaten anything or are you as usual too excited?'

Charlotte raised a dismissive eyebrow at our friend's comment. I quickly ate some toast and a boiled egg and burned my mouth on coffee.

'I'm ready,' I said, losing a few crumbs as I spoke. 'I hope you will recover soon, Mr Wallace, and I will tell you how we fare.'

'You will be cautious. If Mr Simms is holding the woman against her will …'

'Don't worry, sir,' Charlotte said, 'I think Mr Simms will prove tractable. And now we must leave.'

Which we did in our carriage, under fair and cold skies, yesterday's rain a memory but for the muddy streets. The streets were busy and the driver proceeded slowly. Charlotte was annoyed by our progress.

'It will take as much time as it takes, Charlotte,' Mrs Fitzhugh said.

'Yes, you have the house under observation. And if we arrive in a tumult, it would draw attention,' I said.

Charlotte relaxed a little at this.

'Why don't you tell Margaret of Charlie's report?'

'Yes, what draws us out?'

Charlotte considered this and said, 'Very well, the news is that in addition to the normal complement of the house and Mr Simms, the children have observed a woman, who matches our description of Mrs Brown.'

'Oh, but can they be sure? May she not be some relative or a visitor?'

'It is entirely possible, but I certainly hope it is her for I do not wish additional players in our drama.'

Despite our slow progress, it did not take long before we were crossing Pulteney Bridge. Charlotte had the driver stop immediately after the crossing and we exited after giving the driver instructions to wait for us. We walked the remaining distance to the house and here we stood out a little for it was still too early for fashionable women to be shopping. It was a time for shopkeepers and costermongers and fishwives to be about but fortunately we attracted little attention, except for two children, a boy and girl, who approached us. I recognized the girl as Donna who immediately gave Charlotte her report. #

'They're still in there, miss. And one of us's watching in back, too.'

'Good,' Charlotte said. 'And the others have arrived?'

'They're here, but you can't see 'em. If you cry out, we'll know.'

Charlotte nodded and motioned for the children to leave. In seconds it was if they had disappeared. Charlotte then led us to the milliner's shop where Mr Simms had led Mr Wallace.

'Jane, would you be so kind as to wait here—precisely here—while we go inside the shop.'

Surprised at the unexpectedness of her request, all I did was nod while Charlotte and Mrs Fitzhugh entered the shop. A bell tinkled as they opened the door and through the window I could see a man at the counter put down his mug, obviously finishing his breakfast. He put the mug under the counter and awaited his customers. I could dimly hear Mrs Fitzhugh exchange a pleasantry with the man while Charlotte seemed to be busy examining the wares. She passed out of view and I wanted to move to observe her but remembered her 'precisely here.'

After a few minutes of waiting, I became bored and spent my time trying to spot the children who had us under observation when the door behind me opened. I turned to see Mr Simms.

'Mr Simms!' I said in surprise.

He stopped short, his mouth open but without speaking a word. I heard the door bell tinkle again and my friends stepped out.

'Ah, Mr Simms, just the man I was hoping to see for I have a few questions. If you might invite us inside I think we can see a prompt conclusion to this affair.'

'Oh, Miss House. I was just stepping out … it is not convenient …'

'Mr Simms, I know all. Now take us upstairs and introduce us to the woman I see looking down at us from above.'

I looked up at her words and indeed saw a woman looking down at us, who stepped back from the window at my glance. How Charlotte knew she had been observing us was unknowable.

Mr Simms's whole body fell at Charlotte's words. His resignation was obvious. He turned and opened the door behind him and bade us enter. I gave one last look back to the street for any sign of the children.

We entered and climbed the stairs to the first floor where we met a maid who took our coats while Mr Simms waited. The maid's duty done, he shewed us to a small sitting room where we saw a woman standing by the window from where she had observed us. She appeared several years older than Mr Simms but still comely.

'Mrs Brown, I presume?' Charlotte asked.

The woman looked to Mr Simms, who sighed and said, 'She knows all, Violet.'

The woman's expression turned to horror and she cried, 'You will expose us!'

'I shall do nothing of the kind, unless you fail to divulge all the particulars of your deception. I do not appreciate being used,' Charlotte said, her voice tinged with menace, but then her tone softened somewhat and she added, 'unless it is for the purpose of some noble cause.'

Mr Simms rushed to her side. 'I assure you it is a noble cause, no less than freedom from a man who would see my Violet again under his control and me dead, I am sure.'

'Very well, Mr Simms, perhaps you should tell me about this man.'

The Story of Edward Gascoigne

Mr Simms had us sit and then related the story. 'His name is Edward Gascoigne and as his name would suggest, his family is from France, although they have lived in England a very long time. He is a younger son but he inherited his family's fortune upon the death of his older brother.

'My Violet was a young girl of sixteen when she met Gascoigne in Dorset. He was … one and thirty?' He looked to her for confirmation, which prompted her to speak. #

'He was very handsome and I thought him kind. He paid me every attention even though he was far above me. I came from a large and poor family and I was the youngest of four sisters. My prospects for marriage seemed bleak, but he proposed and we were married.'

Charlotte said, 'Ah, then Brown is an alias?'

'Yes, after what happened … I could not go about with that name.'

She turned away after saying this and Mr Simms said, 'Let me tell it.'

'No, just give me a moment.'

We waited until she was composed and then she continued.

'It was a workable marriage at first. I did not love him, but

I appreciated what he had done for me and my family. He raised me up in society, taught me manners and refinements, even hired tutors for me. He praised me in every way and I would repay him for all this, but I could not repay him in the way he wanted most, a son.

'I had two sons ... stillborn. The second time, I nearly died. Sometimes I think I did die. Our marriage did die. His manner changed toward me and I could not bear the thought that I was unable to repay his kindness to my family and me. We kept separate beds, but he visited me when we ... when we would try ...

'But it would not happen, and our lives separated but for this one duty. Then one day he left to see to his interests in America and his ship was lost. After a year's absence, I mourned him as a widow. And my grief was made worse by the thought I could not have left him a son to carry his name. And without a son, his property descended to a cousin who, though generous to me, made it clear I was not wanted. He had a finer distinction of class than Edward.

'So I left and found a small house and did well for myself. But Edward's cousin was unwise and speculated and he lost the house and property, for the entail had ended with Edward's death and the fortune, the house and the land were his to ruin. #

'The years passed and then three years ago I was surprised when Edward appeared at my house. He had taken so long to return to England and the hardships he had endured left him a changed man, a very bitter man. He had returned home to find his fortune and his wife gone. The only thought he had was to restore his family and he demanded we resume as man and wife.

'But he frightened me so. He was no longer a man I could admire and when he demanded ... I hit him, with something, I don't know with what and he fell dead again, or at least I thought him dead. And in my panic, I left the house and him lying dead. I travelled to Bournemouth and took another name.' #

At this she looked to Mr Simms and squeezed his hand. He continued the story.

'We met and fell in love. It is as simple as that. But I am poor and I knew I could not support Violet as she ought. However, she had the house and some unclaimed property and we decided that I should travel to Dorchester and see if I could conclude her affairs there. #

'But then I learned that Gascoigne did not die that day and that he was determined to find Violet. My own efforts on her behalf further alerted him and I returned to Bournemouth. However I worried that my actions might lead him to Violet and so we decided to come here and marry as soon as possible —however we were not quick enough. Gascoigne came here and began his search for her, but then we thought of a way that we might send him away.'

'Yes,' Charlotte said, 'and your plan involved me. Thank you for your consideration.'

He looked down at his feet. 'I am sorry, but I have heard something of your reputation. We thought if we could have you on our side it would help convince him that Violet had left me as she had left him. And it need be something extraordinary to call attention to her disappearance.'

'Ah, you see Jane the need for my meddling to remain unknown. Soon I should be forced to adopt disguises if I hope to remain effective.'

'Well you were certainly convincing, Mr Simms,' Mrs Fitzhugh said. 'I consider myself an able judge of character and yet you deceived me.'

'Do not judge yourself too harshly, Margaret,' Charlotte said. 'I think Mr Simms has a great deal of experience playing to an audience.'

'I do, Miss House, and yet it appears I was unable to deceive you.'

'You took direction a little too well. I assume you have worked on the stage?'

'I have done, yes. And I am sorry to have deceived you, but it was worth it to free Violet of that man.'

'Now on to practical matters,' Charlotte continued. 'I assume you have left a false trail? Where has Mrs Brown—I think Margaret we shall continue to call her that—supposedly gone?'

'I have left instructions for any correspondence to be forwarded to me in Cardiff,' Mrs Brown said. #

'And there the trail would run cold?'

She shook her head. 'My sister is there. She should take rooms there in my name and will leave further instructions for mail to be forwarded again.'

'Oh, well done,' Charlotte said. 'Now as to the switch. You paid some chairmen to make the switch?'

It was now Mr Simms's turn to shake his head. 'No, as I said I am too poor for that. I am afraid I am not a principled man. Upon my arriving in a new city, I find it worthwhile to make friends with chairmen and carriage drivers. It has in the past provided me useful information, not always for good purpose.'

'As it has for me,' Charlotte said. 'So you had befriended them and spun them the same tale.'

'Yes, I convinced them to help by telling them the tale. No money changed hands.'

'And the woman in the chair, what was her name?' Mrs Fitzhugh asked.

I made to look through my notebook for the information but Charlotte supplied, 'Mrs Mulberry I think it was.'

'She was their fare and not an accomplice. It was a necessary part of the plan, you see,' Mr Simms said.

'Yes, the chairmen you tricked would have noticed an empty box. And from my own researches, I know that you were not accosted by pickpockets.'

'What about the bruise?' Mrs Fitzhugh asked.

He opened his mouth to answer but Charlotte spoke first. 'You were one of the delivery-men.'

'What does that have to do with it?' I asked.

Again Mr Simms was to answer when Charlotte said, 'You were in a hurry to beat the chairmen to their destination. You fell in your pursuit.'

'It might be as well to let Mr Simms tell his own story, Charlotte,' Mrs Fitzhugh chided her.

'I do apologize. Please, what were you to say, Mr Simms?'

'Uh, you are correct. I fell in my rush. I made up the story of the pickpockets to justify my injury and delay.'

Charlotte smiled at his words and Mrs Fitzhugh rolled her eyes.

'What are you to do with us, Miss House?' Mrs Brown asked quietly, interrupting Charlotte's satisfaction.

My friend looked at her steadily but she held Charlotte's gaze. I wondered at my friend's dilemma and hoped that she would not let her pride stand in the way.

'Do? I will not do anything. I will not aid you in your deception nor will I expose you.'

'Don't be horrid, Charlotte,' Mrs Fitzhugh said.

'I am not being horrid; I am only being practical. It is obvious that my reputation is too well known and I do not wish to spread it further by involving myself in this matter.'

'Please Charlotte, you must see for yourself the danger they face,' I pleaded with my friend.

'No, I do not Jane. Should I believe their word that this Gascoigne exists? And if he does, should I believe their characterization of him? I simply do not wish myself further embroiled. If what you say is true, then I hope for your success but I cannot act on your behalf based on your say so.'

At this, the look on Charlotte's face hardened and I could see it would do no good to argue with her. Mrs Brown also saw Charlotte's determination and knew it would do no good to plead further and we lapsed into embarrassed silence. Fortunately our mutual friend found words to cover our silence. 'What are your plans?' Mrs Fitzhugh asked.

Mr Simms coughed and said, 'I was able to realize enough from Violet's property to book passage to America and there we should start afresh.'

'That will be hard, to travel to a new world and start over.'

Mrs Brown spoke. 'We realize this. But with an ocean between us and Edward, we can be man and wife without question.'

'When are you to leave?' I asked.

'I am to leave to-day for Bristol,' she said.

'I will follow in two weeks,' he said. 'Until then, I am to act the part of a man abandoned by his love. I … Miss House, I am sorry that we … that I thought to involve you. I fear my fondness for the melodramatic led me astray.'

At last some softness stole over Charlotte's features.

'I am certain you can act the part of the abandoned lover, Mr Simms. Good day to you then and my best wishes on your happiness,' Charlotte said and turned to leave. The suddenness of her departure surprised us and we hastily made our goodbyes as well and hurried to follow our friend. We found her on the street. She made a quick wave of her hand and we could see half a dozen children scurry away like rats.

'Charlotte, do you not think …'

'Margaret, I do not wish to discuss it further. I spoke the truth; my reputation will be my undoing. Involving myself in this shall only add to it and for what—a mystery that is no mystery?'

'Is it rather not that you loathe to aid them because by doing so you must admit to being taken in by their deception?'

'Let us return home,' Charlotte said, ignoring our friend.

A Visit from Edward Gascoigne

A week has passed since we left Mr Simms and Mrs Brown, and what a difference a week makes. The disappearance of Mrs Brown has become widely known and has been the topic of conversation everywhere. Already several callers have asked Charlotte her opinion of the mystery, and she has been obliged to pretend she knows nothing of the matter and so she has had to hear the details of it presented to her again and again. I begin to suspect that Charlotte would rather admit to being baffled by the mystery than be forced to admit she is unaware of it. But she will have her pride.

A bad feeling has also persisted between my friends. They do not openly discuss it but I think Charlotte was hurt by Mrs Fitzhugh's accusation that Charlotte will not help the lovers because she would hate to pretend that she was deceived. Nevertheless she remains true to her promise not to expose their deception and so must make this pretence that she has remained ignorant of this news.

Mrs Fitzhugh, however, I know has been the source of so much of the speculation surrounding the disappearance of Mrs Brown and has done her best to hint that woman must be fleeing a pursuer. Were it not that I hate to see my friends at odds I would have to say I find it amusing.

I found myself the attention of Mr Wallace, who after a day of rest, became a frequent visitor to Number 1. Of course Charlotte made a great deal of his visits and the disruption of our routine, but I sensed that she did not very greatly mind his visits. His efforts on her behalf deserved at least her forbearance. And at least with him she could talk openly of the matter.

And it was during such a visit that we were reminded of the disappearing bride when Robert came into the drawing-room with a card for Charlotte.

'What is it, Robert?'

'A caller, ma'am.'

'One that you obviously do not care …' Charlotte stopped as she read the name on the card. 'Please, bring him in.'

Mr Wallace stood and said, 'Perhaps I should take my leave.'

'Please, it would be best if you remained,' Charlotte said with a forced smile.

Robert returned and said, 'Mr Edward Gascoigne.'

Mrs Fitzhugh and I stood at this revelation and we greeted our visitor with our mouths open for his appearance surprised us. Mrs Brown had described him as handsome and he was indeed a magnificent wreck of a man. He was not tall, although he would probably be taller could he stand straight, but his left leg was bent horribly. His shoulders seemed to brush either side of the doorway and he eclipsed Robert as he entered. At one time his face was undoubtedly fair, with a strong nose and chin and coal black eyes, but now all that one could see was the cruel scar that went across his dark, tanned face. Despite his savage appearance, he was dressed as a gentleman, if somewhat shabbily, and his bow to us was that of a man addressing his equals.

'Have I the honour of addressing Miss House?' he said in a strangled whisper.

'You do sir,' Charlotte said, stepping forward in contrast to my fearful backward step.

'It has come to my attention that you may know something of the disappearance of a Mrs Brown, whom I knew as my wife, Violet Gascoigne.' He said the last with some difficulty, his voice becoming even more of a whisper.

'I know nothing of her disappearance, sir. A man came to me asking my help in finding his missing bride-to-be. I told him I had no idea where she might be and that it was hardly my concern. I … I did not want to give him my opinion that she had reconsidered his offer and left him standing. If he chuses to believe her disappearance a mystery, well that is his solace.'

'Liar,' he said, still in a whisper but louder.

Mr Wallace stepped forward at this and said angrily, 'You will leave immediately, sir.' He put his hand on Mr Gascoigne's arm but it was like putting a hand on a statue and expecting it to move.

'Please Mr Wallace, allow him to speak. You were calling me a liar, were you not?'

'I was. You know something more. I have made enquiries. You're something of a busybody and … and you're my only hope.' His voice faltered as suddenly the man began coughing, the coughs shaking his whole body and forcing him further bent over. He took a handkerchief and tried to stifle his coughs to no avail.

'Mr Wallace, please help him to a chair,' Charlotte said.

My friend helped our visitor to a chair and Mrs Fitzhugh hurriedly prepared a drink and offered it to him, which he greedily drank.

'Thank you,' he whispered after he drank, the glass falling from his hand.

'It is consumption,' Mr Wallace said, looking pointedly at the crimson stained handkerchief Mr Gascoigne held. He quickly put his handkerchief into his pocket. #

'I apologize for …'

'There is no need sir, and I wish that I could tell you what you wish, but I know nothing,' Charlotte said.

'Tell me that she is well … and happy. Tell me that much and I shall leave.'

Charlotte's face remained calm. I caught her eye and looked at her questioningly. She shook her head at me and then addressed him. 'I can tell you no such thing.'

'She fears me, I know. When last we met … my life has been hard and the only thought that sustained me was my love of her. I thought of her day and night during my suffering and I only wanted her to … Oh, I scared her. I know that now. Look at what I have become. I am enough to frighten anyone. Please Miss House, for the love of God, tell me where she is!' He said this in his loudest voice yet but for all that it still seemed the sound of a man underwater fighting for his life. He looked at us each, his eyes bright and fierce.

I looked at my friends. Mr Wallace shewed his sympathy for the man and I saw Mrs Fitzhugh look away with grief. But Charlotte kept her resolve.

'I am heartfully sorry, Mr Gascoigne. I know nothing of this matter. Are you better now? Would you like something else?'

The man's head hung low now and he said, 'No. Nothing. Please sir, if you would help me to stand? I will go.'

Mr Wallace raised the man to his feet and we crowded round him, save for Charlotte who kept her distance.

'Miss House, one last thing. As I said, I have made my enquiries and I know you to be a honourable woman. There is something I have for … Mrs Brown.' He took a small bag from a pocket and laid it on a table with the distinct chink of coin. 'Would you see that she gets this?'

At this, I thought Charlotte's reserve had at last broken. She approached him and stood quite close, her arm resting on his shoulder, her other hand also beginning to reach for him, but then it fell and she stepped back and she looked at him steadily and said, 'I have told you, I do not know where she is. I could not give it to her.'

'Then give it to the poor, for all I care,' he said, with the irritation of his arrival. He stood as tall as he could and removed Mr Wallace's arm, gently but firmly, and walked to the door and left.

We heard Robert attend to him and then the front door opened. We all hurried to the window and peered out and saw him walk down the street on his tortured legs. I blinked away my tears. And then I heard Charlotte laugh and say, 'Well, that was quite a performance.'

We turned and looked at her. She was counting the coins. 'I'm glad he's not out too much for that last gambit. Why are you looking at me like that?'

'Charlotte, I should think you would feel some sympathy.'

'On the contrary, Margaret, I have every sympathy. Mr Gascoigne shewed a cunning that I envy. And the purse was a nice touch. As was this.'

With a flourish she produced a white cloth stained red.

'His handkerchief!' I cried. 'Charlotte, how could you?'

But she ignored me. 'Mr Wallace, would you please inspect this?' She held it out and he walked slowly to her, loathe to take the cloth from her.

'Why it's … it's not blood. I think it's ink.'

Charlotte snatched the cloth back and waved it in the air and then with a flash it was gone again.

'A nice little souvenir, I think,' she said.

'He was lying,' I said with a gasp.

'Oh, not all of it. His dark skin speaks of a long time at sea. There was a hint of a tattoo on the side of his neck. I saw other scars on the back of his hands and his fingers were callused. The scar on his face was real as was his leg, although I noticed as he walked away his limp was not as pronounced. He did not lie; his life was hard. But the dramatic whisper and the cough, while well done and certainly indicative of consumption, were staged to elicit our sympathy.'

At this we fell silent, ashamed that we were so easily fooled.

'Please, do not feel bad. Compassion and feeling may sometimes outweigh wisdom.'

'I would have told him what he wanted,' Mr Wallace said.

'As would I,' agreed Mrs Fitzhugh. I merely nodded in agreement.

Charlotte smiled, that annoyingly superior smile that I had to admit was her due. She said, 'And yet you didn't. I think we have a good working understanding, wouldn't you agree Mr Wallace?'

He looked at her with uncertainty, and then said, 'Yes, a very good understanding ... we have.'

'And now if you'll excuse me, I must see that Mr Simms receives this. It is a small amount, but I'm sure it will be appreciated.' With that she prepared to leave the room but then stopped.

'I may also visit the Lower Rooms and belatedly make known my opinion on the disappearance of Mrs Brown.'

'What? Why have you changed your opinion, Charlotte?' Mrs Fitzhugh asked.

Charlotte took a moment before admitting, 'I was wrong. That man may be one of the most dangerous I have met. I cannot let my pride stand in the way of doing what is right and I will do what I can to throw him off the scent. Will you come with me, Margaret?'

'With pleasure,' our friend replied, and with that they both left the room. 'You may wish to come as well Mr Wallace, for I cannot leave you alone here with Jane,' Charlotte shouted at us from the hall.

As I heard the sound of her tread upon the stairs, I turned to my friend and said, 'She definitely likes you. And there are not many she truly likes.'

'I do not know whether to be honoured or alarmed,' he said.

'Oh both!' I said. 'Definitely both.'

The Affair of Brotherly Love

he clock in the hallway caught my attention in that fleeting way that clocks sometimes do. Most of the time they do their job of measuring out the seconds, minutes and hours of our lives unnoticed save when there is an anticipated engagement and are then consulted with regularity. Sometimes they remind one of the remaining hours until dawn during a troubled night. But occasionally they simply remind one of the passage of time, not a specific period mind you, but just the simple unfolding of one day into the next and the sense that things are as they always should be.

The realization that my life was as it should be came to me a few days after the New Year, sitting with Mrs Fitzhugh in the drawing-room, we both attending to our duties. My good friend was busy with her embroidery while I was writing in my new journal the details concerning the happiness that Charlotte had brought to Mrs Suthers after her daughter had been unmasked as the mysterious Rajput Singh. The foreign names in the affair had me puzzled and I had scattered about me various atlases so that I might have some hope of spelling the place names correctly.

My new journal was the result of a conversation I had with Charlotte some weeks earlier when I was chronicling a previous affair. She asked me what I was about, surrounded by a similar collection of her commonplace books and the notes I was writing. I told her that her commonplace books contained all the notes and trivia and news that often precipitated her involvement in some matter but that they did not contain a precise enumeration of the steps she had taken in obtaining happiness for those she helped. I said I was undertaking the job of committing these steps to paper so that they might prove as an *aide-mémoire*. #

In a reprise of an earlier conversation, which apparently she had managed to forget, she replied that she had her memory as her guide in these affairs and could recall that which was needed, while I responded that I had not that facility and benefited from writing down the particulars. She then made some cutting observation that I would benefit from improving my mind. In my early association with her the remark would have stung, but I had learned that my friend's remarks are not to be a true judge of her opinions.

Thus I was not surprised that for a present Charlotte gave me several handsome bound journals that I might not have 'heaps of paper littering the floor whenever I was about my business.' I was surprised, however, when I discovered a key among my presents.

'What is this?' I asked that Christmas morning.

'Come with me and I'll show you, Jane.' Charlotte led me to the library and shewed me a large strongbox that somehow I had overlooked; a mystery for the delivery of such a massive object should not have gone unnoticed.

'How long has this been here?'

'For as long as I have been in this house and for as long as you've been here. You should improve your powers of observations as well as your memory, my dear. May I have the key?'

I gave it to her and she opened the sturdy lock that secured it and raised the top. I looked inside and found a few papers that I recognized as deeds, correspondence and a few keep-sakes, but not such an amount as required so large a box.

'You might consign your writing to the box as needed. This is the only other key—Michael has the copy—and I give it to you for safekeeping although I may need it from time to time to retrieve my own items.'

She handed me the key and as I took it I realized the reason she did not keep a journal of her involvement in these affairs: should these matters become public it could ruin many lives and expose my friend's occupation.

As I was thinking this I bent down to inspect the box more closely. 'Odd, that the lock of this box, which you say has been in this house for as long as you've been here, is remark-ably unscratched.'

'Yes, well I am fastidious in my habits.'

I recalled all this as I sat with my pen motionless in my hand and I heard the ticking of the hallway clock. I closed my eyes and I heard my friend beside me humming a Scots air as she knitted and casting my mind further I could hear Charlotte in the library as she moved a chair and upstairs I could hear Alice's unmistakable laugh. I could not help but recall the other time when the sound of the clock had fo-cussed my thoughts so intently, when Miss Winslow related the depravity of Mr Hickham.

'It is your home now, Jane. You are a fixture in her life, and in mine, and we could not do without you.'

I opened my eyes at my friend's voice and felt tears sting the corner of my eyes.

'How did you know what I was thinking?' I asked, my voice betraying my emotion.

'Charlotte is not the only person in this house capable of observation. You are sitting with your pen poised above the journal Charlotte gave you and listening to the sounds of the house with your eyes closed and a slight smile. We have had a delightful season and yet there is that optimism mixed with melancholy that starts the New Year. And I suspect you miss your sister.'

Her words produced a guilty start. To be honest, I had banished thoughts of my sister since her letter informing me that our Aunt Edith had proposed that she adopt Elinor. Of course I loved my Aunt Edith and could hope for no more happy home for Elinor, but I hated to contemplate the dissolution of my family. With my father and mother gone and Elinor to take the name Simonds, I would be the last Woodsen of my immediate family.

'Yes,' I lied, 'she has been much on my mind.'

'Perhaps I might speak to Charlotte about arranging for your sister to visit us.'

I thanked her for the proposal, ashamed I had not thought of the possibility of Elinor visiting Bath. Admittedly it would be an imposition were I, who existed solely on her charity, to ask Charlotte such a favour, but the thought at least should have occurred to me. I felt my old life slipping away. Even the sad memory of that horrible season one year ago, as we watched my father's fortunes quickly crumble, seemed distant. How quickly life can change for the better, I thought, but how important it is not to forget what came before.

Thankfully Robert informing us that we had a visitor— 'Mr Charles Dundas'—interrupted these musings. His announcement produced both Charlotte, who had apparently overheard this information, and then our visitor. #

Mr Dundas proved to be a pleasant man of at least fifty years, who bowed to us smartly and then took Charlotte's hand. I looked to Mrs Fitzhugh for some clarification only to see the gentleman now making the same gesture to her. It was obvious that he was an old friend.

'My dear Margaret, looking lovely as ever,' I heard him say very solicitously, and I was surprised to see her blush. Clearly he was a man of some affability and forwardness to be addressing my friend by her first name, especially as he was married, as evidenced by my friend's inquiry.

'And how is Anne? And Janet? I had sent a letter in June, but ...'

'My dear wife was unwell this summer but has recovered. I must chide her for neglecting her friends. And Janet is as lovely as ever, and quite the favourite at every ball.' As he said this, his eyes were upon me.

'Charles, may I introduce our friend Miss Woodsen,' Mrs Fitzhugh said, obviously still in a flush from his attentions.

Charlotte added, 'Jane, Mr Dundas is an old family friend. He and my father had mutual political interests, interests he now shares with my brother.'

'It is a pleasure to meet you Miss Woodsen. You must be the particular friend Michael has mentioned. I am very pleased to know that Charlotte has a fast friend.'

'Thank you kindly, sir,' I replied, unsure what to say to this charming man. He was clearly a favourite with Charlotte and Mrs Fitzhugh and I suddenly felt like an outsider, and minutes before I had felt such a fixture in my friends' lives.

But Mr Dundas would have none of this. He sensed my reticence and for the next few minutes he employed his considerable charm on me, asking me about my family, noticing my discomfort and immediately changing to my observations about Bath and Charlotte and how did I like the weather and was the dancing pleasurable and did I notice the fashions that women were wearing? I did not notice this whole time that we had progressed to sitting and drinking tea, so captivated was I by Mr Dundas's attentions.

My surprise at finding myself so swept along by Mr Dundas must have been evident to my friends.

'You have made another conquest, Charles,' Mrs Fitzhugh

said. 'Beware this man Jane, he is a politician and a lawyer and a businessman. He most certainly cannot be trusted.'

'Oh, I know your name!' I said. 'You are Mr Dundas of the canal company. I remember from the clippings.'

He gave a slight nod at this. 'It is gratifying to be recognized. And so Charlotte, you maintain your interest in the company?'

'Of course, I like to see what you are doing with our money.'

'Er, yes. Actually that is partly the reason for my visit. Which is principally to visit two lovely—now three lovely ladies—but also to ask your assistance for a friend. You have perhaps heard the calamity that has befallen Mr George Haversham?'

Charlotte sank back in her chair to think a moment and said, 'Yes, something about a realignment of the canal and a map. But how can I help with this? I am not without my charms and wit, but …'

'Please Charlotte, I am well aware from Michael of your divertissements. And I remember the little girl who puzzled out the mystery of my lame horse. You have an acute understanding of human nature that may be of use in a delicate matter …'

As he said this, his eyes flicked toward me.

'Do not concern yourself about Jane. She is an active player in these divertissements as you call them and is the soul of discretion.'

I felt uncomfortable being described as such, not necessarily trusting my discretion quite as much as Charlotte, but I nodded my head in agreement.

Mr Dundas then looked at me directly and smiled. 'I had thought as much. Please, all of you, treat what I am about to say in the strictest confidence. Mr Haversham is something of a *protégé* of mine. He has been an active investor in the Kennet and Avon and has been procuring some of the land needed for the canal. As you know, not all the investors have been as forthcoming with their funds as you and your brother. We sometimes … lack the funds to buy what is immediately needed. Instead George has been buying it and selling it to the company, for a tidy profit.'

'He is a land speculator then,' Charlotte said.

'Yes, but he is a honourable man and agrees to prices that we have already negotiated. But recently a change to the route has been considered because of water supply concerns and a map showing that route has been recently made public, somewhat prematurely. The news will all but bankrupt George, and it has already bankrupted him mentally and physically.'

'This is all very sad, but I hardly see how I might help.'

'I come to you at the behest of Mr Haversham's intended, Miss Streetham. She has reason to believe that George's younger brother, Edward, is the source of the information. She asked me how her suspicions could be confirmed. Understand that she does not wish to accuse Edward without cause. George's health is precarious enough without knowledge that his own brother's actions have led to his downfall. Understandably this news has already played havoc with their wedding plans. Any accusations she might make may doom their union.'

'I see. Perhaps then I can be of some service. Please ask her to call on …'

'I am afraid you must call on her in Bradford-on-Avon.'

'What! Why must I call on her if she is asking me for help?'

'She and her mother remain with George. They are seeing to his care. As I said, he is … he is utterly devastated by the … worried that he …'

'They fear for his life by his own hand?'

'Yes. That is the truth of it. George has always been upright in all his dealings. He is, as you say a land speculator, and a shrewd businessman, but he is as honest as they come. His ruin affects many others, including the canal company, and he feels that burden more than most would.'

'Then perhaps confirmation that his brother is the cause of all his woes would only further devastate him.'

'I am sure it will. But if Edward is the cause ... he gambles and drinks and is too fond of the worst sort of women and has caused his brother hardship after hardship. I will not be surprised to discover he is the culprit. If George recovers, he must be made aware of his brother's iniquity. Please Charlotte, I ask this for Miss Streetham and I ask this for myself.'

'But have you any proof that Edward stole this map?'

Mr Dundas shook his head. 'I'm afraid that is the puzzle of the whole thing. The map was never stolen. In fact it remains in a locked room.'

BRADFORD-ON-AVON

The trip from Bath to Bradford was accomplished easily in Mr Dundas's landau, he remaining in Bath to attend to canal business. He also told us we might stay at Mr Haversham's house there, where Miss Streetham and her mother remained to see to the poor man's health. #

The wet weather of previous weeks had given way to clear and cold and our journey took only a few hours. Mrs Fitzhugh and Charlotte used the time to tell me stories about Mr Dundas that confirmed my instant liking of the man. Charlotte, however, remained doubtful what help she might offer Miss Streetham.

'If the younger brother is responsible, how am I to prove it? And what good will come of it?'

'Surely it is a matter of justice,' I responded.

'Justice! That is a weighty responsibility.'

'You have undertaken it before.'

'Yes, when I thought I might have some hope of success. Here success will only bring more unhappiness.'

'Then why do it?' But my question solicited no response from Charlotte.

'It is the locked room,' Mrs Fitzhugh said, her comment surprising me. Usually when Charlotte and I dispute she merely watches us with amusement and detachment.

'You are correct as always, Margaret.'

'She cannot ignore the challenge of how the map could be stolen and yet remain in a locked room.'

'But you forget the other possibility—the real reason I travel to Bradford.'

'And what is that?' I asked.

'The possibility that the younger brother is blameless, which if I can prove it should at least reassure the lady that her future brother-in-law is not the villain she imagines.'

Her comment had me puzzled. 'You think it possible the brother is blameless?'

'I neither think one way nor the other. It is merely a possibility and the only good outcome I can see.'

Her words silenced me, for I felt foolish in not entertaining the possibility that the gentleman might be innocent; the story as presented had seemed so plausible. Suddenly the words 'weighty responsibility' struck home and I realized that I must be as guarded as my friend and approach these matters with an open mind.

So it was in silence that the journey continued. I thought Mrs Fitzhugh also lost in thought and then realized she had merely gone to sleep despite the rocking of the carriage. But before long we arrived in Bradford and climbed St. Margaret's Hill and found the house that Mr Haversham had rented. #

Our arrival was keenly anticipated, for we saw a maid observe our arrival, and she was quickly joined by a young lady

I guessed to be Miss Streetham, followed almost immediately by an older woman I similarly guessed to be her mother.

'Miss House, is it?' the young lady enquired as we emerged from the carriage, correctly judging which of us was Charlotte.

'Yes, Miss Streetham?' Charlotte returned, 'And these are my friends, Miss Woodsen and Mrs Fitzhugh. It was kind of you to meet us directly.'

To her credit, Charlotte was all warmth, not a hint showing of her misgivings or judgement as to the appropriateness of introductions done on the street.

'Beryl, allow our visitors to step inside. Please forgive my daughter, but her only concern is for her young man.' Mrs Streetham hustled us inside, calling out to maids and footmen to see to our belongings and insisting we refresh ourselves after our journey. She clearly did not shirk from ordering about Mr Haversham's household.

Once we were seated in the small drawing-room and I had my journal ready, Mrs Fitzhugh asked in a soft voice, 'And how is Mr Haversham?'

'He is improving,' Miss Streetham said, although her downcast eyes and the slow shake of Mrs Streetham's head belied this.

'I shall need to speak with him, if this matter is ...' Charlotte began, but was interrupted by Miss Streetham.

'No, not now. It would kill him,' she said sharply, giving lie to her former statement. And then realizing the implications of what she had said, her head sunk further and I heard her small sob.

Mrs Fitzhugh made as if to rush to the poor woman's side but to my surprise Charlotte was there first, putting her arm around her shoulders and squeezing her tight and saying, 'Then I shall speak to him when he is better. Don't concern yourself, Miss Streetham. We are only here to help.'

Charlotte will always surprise me, I thought. She can seem so detached and yet is capable of great warmth, when she chuses. But having known her long enough, I also suspected that Charlotte's actions might be attributable to her need to keep the woman calm enough for questioning, a suspicion that was quickly confirmed.

'But if I am to help, I need to know more. Can you compose yourself enough to answer some questions?'

Miss Streetham nodded and then looked directly at Charlotte. 'Please, ask your questions.'

Charlotte said 'Good!' and resumed her seat. 'Mr Dundas has led me to believe that you suspect Mr Edward Haversham had stolen the map, which has proven detrimental to his brother's business. Why would you think this?'

'I found Mr Edward in his brother's office days before this unfortunate event. I am sure he saw the map and I think he stole it. No, I am sure he stole it.'

'You have little love for your future brother?' Mrs Fitzhugh asked.

'He is a cad of the worst sort,' she said fiercely, little trace left of her tears. 'Where Mr Haversham is decent and honourable, Mr Edward is profligate and untrustworthy. He is constantly mired in gambling debts and entreating his brother to rescue him, which George has done again and again. No, I have little love for him, nor I suspect has he much love for me. He knows my opinion of him.'

'To return to the map,' Charlotte said, with a pointed look at our mutual friend for her interruption. 'Do you say you saw him take it? Did he leave with it?'

'No, he did not. But who else could have stolen it? Only Mr Haversham and his partner Mr Clarke were even aware of its existence.'

'And yourself?'

'No, not at the time. Let me explain. George … Mr Haversham … and his partner had been absent from Bradford for some time, but they were expected to return in a day or two. I visited his office that I might bring some letters that had been sent to this house by mistake. You see my mother and I were visiting here and were staying at the Swan. Then George was called away and I thought to visit his office when I could … just that I might be of use.' #

Mrs Streetham said, 'Mr Haversham's office boy is … he is the crippled son of one of the workers on the canal. George took it upon himself to employ the boy, but he is challenged in what he can do.'

'Yes, so I visited the office on occasion to see what help I might offer,' Miss Streetham said.

'Excuse me,' Charlotte said. 'Where is this office?'

'On St Margaret Street, nearer the canal.'

'Please continue.'

'I visited the office that day and saw Mr Edward waiting in his brother's office. The office boy, being familiar with him for all the times he had visited George, had let him in. And when I confronted him, Mr Edward that is, he was very upset and fled shortly after.'

'But he did not have the map? He could have secreted it upon his person?'

She smiled and said, 'I suppose he might have, but it is a very large map. I do not think he had it. And …'

She stopped, obviously unsure what she should next say.

'And?' Charlotte prompted.

'George arrived only a few minutes after Edward had left. He had returned early and visited his office that morning and then called at the Swan, and learning he had missed me, he hurried to his office.'

'I see,' Charlotte said. 'And Mr Haversham did not notice the absence of the map?'

She looked down at the floor and said in a small voice, 'No, he did not. In fact, he rather called attention to it being there.'

Her words hung in the air. I made a small noise of surprise at this, whence Charlotte shot me a glance as if to say keep quiet.

'What did he say?' she prompted, when Miss Streetham said nothing further.

'He ... he said he should put it away for safekeeping. That is when I learned of the map and its significance.'

'What?' I cried. 'If it was the map then surely you have no reason to suspect ...'

'Hush, Jane,' Charlotte said calmly. 'Please continue, Miss Streetham. What did Mr Haversham do with the map?'

'I watched him unroll it, fold it and put it in the strongbox.'

At this even Mrs Fitzhugh voiced her amazement, which Charlotte chose to ignore.

'And yet you still suspect the brother?'

'Yes, if you had seen him, the guilt was there upon his face. And this is a man who has admitted his every crime with a face that has never shown guilt or remorse. But this time, I know he understood the severity of what he had done.'

'Or was about to do,' Charlotte said. 'You must think then that he later stole into Mr Haversham's office, opened the strongbox and left with the map.'

'Yes, that is what must have happened.'

'Then it would be a simple matter to look into the strong-box and ...'

The look of distress on her face made it clear that it would not be a simple matter.

Charlotte sighed. 'Yes, you do not want to burden Mr Haversham with the knowledge that his brother is the instrument of his downfall. Nor do you want him to think badly of you if you wrongly accuse his brother. Yes, it is a pretty puzzle all round.'

She sat back and lightly drummed her fingertips together. 'Very well, we have a plan of action. One, I must inspect the office and see whether the map remains locked away. And two, I must meet this brother and learn for myself whether he is capable of so terrible an act. And finally, I must question Mr Haversham when he is able.'

Unfortunately we were unable to begin our investigation immediately. Mrs Fitzhugh calmly reminded Charlotte that it had been several hours since our last meal and that even though our travel had been swift and pleasant, she would benefit from a short respite and refreshment.

In this she found a ready ally in me, and Mrs Streetham also insisted that we should be the better for some food. Clearly Charlotte and Miss Streetham wished no delay, but our compromise was that they should continue to converse while Mrs Fitzhugh and I had a hasty luncheon. I took the time to observe the demeanour of the servants employed by Mr Haversham, thinking their qualities might reflect on their employer and that Charlotte might be too engrossed with the young lady to notice.

And I formed a favourable impression of the land speculator based on the solicitude of the servants. Obviously they did not know the reason for our visit but they sensed that we were well-wishers and several times professed their concern for their master. I also gained the impression that they too had little love for Edward Haversham, comparing their master's behaviour to that of his brother. Mrs Streetham very properly admonished the servants for being so free with their opinions, but I could tell she was impressed that they shewed such concern for her future son-in-law. I also was impressed by their devotion when I realized that these servants probably had only known their master a short time, as they were presumably secured for his recent tenancy in Bradford.

Finally we were ready for a visit to Mr Haversham's office. Mr Dundas's landau was sent for and Charlotte, Miss Streetham and I set off for St Margaret's Street. I could not help but wonder if the town would have been my home had I been able to secure the position with Mrs Danvers. I found it charming overall but it paled beside Bath and was secretly happy Charlotte had intervened.

We were quickly at the offices. We knocked and were met by the boy, Kenneth, who brought us inside to meet Mr Clarke, the partner. The offices were an untidy affair and not at all the image of a successful business. It had been a shop previously, with one room separated from the rest of the lower floor by leaded glass double doors. It obviously served as their office and was bestrewn with charts and maps and drawings tacked to the walls or laid out on a large table. Mr Clarke led us into the office that contained only two chairs. Miss Streetham took one of the chairs while Charlotte and I remained standing.

'I am sorry I'm unable to offer better accommodations,' Mr Clarke said. 'As you can see we are crowded here. This is just one of several offices we have along the canal.'

'You are a busy concern, sir,' I said.

'We are indeed,' he said, displaying a twitch at the corner of his mouth that betrayed his worries.

'Surely news of the new canal route must be devastating to your interests,' Charlotte said, which I thought unnecessarily direct. She was surveying the office as she said her remark, making a slow circuit, her long fingers lightly brushing the cabinets and the table that held the many scattered maps and technical drawings. At one point she stopped to pick up a wadded ball of paper and place it in a overfilled box that was obviously used for refuse.

'We shall weather the storm,' he said, a twitch again betraying his emotions, as did the hand he put on the back of one of the chairs to steady himself.

Charlotte stopped her circuit at the doors and bent down to peer at the lock. 'A Bramah lock?' #

Mr Clarke left his place by the chair to join Charlotte. I took advantage of this to take the remaining chair and then produced my notebook and pencil stub from my reticule. I made a note of the lock with the thought of asking later the significance of her observation.

'Yes, I suggested we install the lock.'

'Of course,' Charlotte said. 'When was this?'

'About two months previous.'

'And who has the keys to the office?'

'Only myself and Mr Haversham.'

Charlotte nodded at this information and continued her inspection of the office, stopping at a large roll top desk, next to which on the floor sat a strongbox.

'Miss Streetham, this is the office where you discovered Mr Edward awaiting his brother?' She asked this question while crouched low in a rather undignified position in order to more closely inspect the box.

'Yes, Miss House. He was inside, sitting in one of these chairs, when I came into the outer office. He tried to appear nonchalant but I am certain he was … I am certain he was up to no good.'

'Then the door was not locked?' Charlotte asked, standing and then turning to Mr Clarke for elucidation.

But Miss Streetham replied, 'No, for George had returned that morning and had been in the office earlier and then left for an errand.'

Mr Clarke coughed and said, 'I am afraid he had not yet learnt the habit of locking these doors whenever he stept out.'

'Do you think it possible Mr Edward had taken the map with him when he left the office?'

'The maps in question are rather large, Miss House,' Mr Clarke said, 'similar to these you see here.' He waved his hand at the large maps in the office, some that were at least six by six feet and printed on heavy paper.

Charlotte moved closer to inspect the maps and the table below.

'Maps? More than one?' she asked him.

'At least three are relevant to the new route.'

She peered more closely at the table and asked, 'Do you create the maps here?'

'Oh no, we use the maps and refer to them and may make notations, but they are created by the canal company.'

'I see. And was the boy here?' She asked this of Miss Streetham.

'Yes.'

'But he allowed Mr Edward to sit in this office,' Charlotte said, leaving the wisdom of that decision apparent.

'Kenneth is a simple boy, Miss House,' Mr Clarke said. 'If the office had been locked ...' He did not continue, not wishing, I think, to accuse Mr Haversham of neglect before Miss Streetham.

'I should like to talk to the boy,' Charlotte said.

This did not sit well with Mr Clarke. 'I said he is a simple boy. It is not necessary to berate him for ...'

'I do not wish to berate him for anything. Miss Streetham, you have a friendship with the boy? Would you ask him to come here?'

She seemed doubtful, but she left the room and returned with the boy, about twelve years of age I guessed, although his simple face made him appear even younger. He walked with a limp caused by his twisted foot.

'Kenneth!' Charlotte said with a bright smile on her face. 'Please young man, sit yourself down.' She directed the boy to the seat Miss Streetham had vacated. 'You can be of considerable help to me by answering a few questions. Can you do that?'

The boy nodded, a smile on his face from Charlotte's kind manner.

'Yes, miss.'

'Good lad. Now do you remember the day that Mr Haversham ...'

'Mr George,' Miss Streetham interjected.

'Yes, the day Mr George returned early from travelling. Miss Streetham was here and found Mr Edward waiting in the office.'

The boy's expression made it clear he did not remember.

'Mr George gave you a penny when he returned, do you remember that?'

This was information of which I was unaware, obviously divulged to Charlotte from her private conversation with Miss Streetham. The boy now remembered the day in question. He nodded enthusiastically.

'Good,' Charlotte said. 'Now you remember Mr Edward visiting the office that day? You let him inside and he went into the office to wait for his brother?'

'Yes, he said it was all right.'

'Of course it was, Kenneth. You did the right thing.'

'Mr Edward is very kind, like Mr George.'

Charlotte looked to Miss Streetham, who answered the unspoken question, 'Edward is ... he does have an easy manner with children.'

Charlotte turned her attention back to the boy. 'Now Kenneth, do you remember if Mr Edward did anything while waiting in the office? Did he just sit in a chair and wait?'

The boy shook his head no, which excited our attention.

'What was he doing in the office, boy?' Mr Clarke asked.

The boy shrank back from him and Charlotte turned to look at us with a scowl. We shrank back from her and she then turned back to the boy with I am sure her most pleasing smile. Charlotte too had an easy manner with children. I saw her relax back into her chair and the boy's attitude also relaxed.

'Oh, Kenneth, how stupid of me; I asked you two things at once. Why don't you tell me what Mr Edward did.'

'Don't know. I wasn't here.'

Guessing our reactions, Charlotte quickly lifted a finger to forestall any outbursts of surprise from us.

'Oh, I guess I am wrong. I thought you had let Mr Edward in?'

'Yes'm,' he said, 'but he gave me a penny too and sent me to buy him a sweet. And one for me.'

Charlotte could not control our surprise at this, nor did she try. The boy did not seem to feel it directed to him and instead smiled, as if he had done a conjuring trick. Charlotte opened her reticule and gave the boy a coin.

'Here you are, Kenneth, for being a clever boy. You may buy yourself a sweet whenever you like. Now run along.'

The boy took the coin, bobbed his head in thanks and flew from the room. Once he had left, she turned to us and said, 'So now we know that with the boy gone Edward had ample opportunity to remove the map. But we must have proof that the map has been taken. Mr Clarke, would you open the strongbox?'

Mr Clarke looked surprised at this request. 'But I do not have the key. We were to have another made, but at present only Mr Haversham has a key.'

'H'm, that is most annoying. Until we can confirm that the map was stolen …'

'It most certainly was not stolen, Miss House,' the partner assured us. 'I talked to George later that day and he told me he locked the map in this strongbox, which as you can see remains unopened. Let me speak frankly—and I regret what harm this might cause you, Miss Streetham—there can be no good in looking into this matter. What is done is done. We speculated and we lost.'

'You are remarkably philosophic, sir,' I said. Privately I

wondered whether Mr Clarke's losses were as severe as Mr Haversham's.

'We are in business, ma'am. Business is risk. Now I don't wish to be rude, but this reversal of fortune does not mean I have leisure for conversation. Far from it, in fact.'

'Of course, Mr Clarke,' Charlotte said. 'I appreciate your taking the time to talk to us. We shall see ourselves out then.'

But she stopped our departure to ask one further question. 'Mr Clarke, can you remember whether the door to the office was locked the next day?'

He hesitated but a moment before answering. 'Yes, I remember unlocking the door the following morning.'

We made our goodbyes again and left, although as she was leaving, she caught the attention of Kenneth and bade him step outside the office.

'Kenneth, is it your job to keep the office neat and tidy?' she asked him.

He nodded uncertainly.

'Do you throw out the trash every day?'

He nodded. 'Then you haven't done a very good job of it. I saw a box filled with trash in the office. Why don't you empty it now?'

The boy eyes widened. He ran back into the office and emerged a few seconds later with the box.

'Let us follow him,' Charlotte said.

We were puzzled but followed and found the boy behind the building where he put all the paper into a large box, presumably to be later given to the rag and bone man.

'Thank you, Kenneth. Here, have some more sweets,' she said, and gave another coin to the boy, who took it and ran away.

'What was that all about?' I asked. 'Was it really necessary to chide the boy?'

'Oh, Jane, he is not harmed. Sweets will soothe any unpleasantness. And now we are done here, I think.'

'Have you come to any conclusions, Miss House?' Miss Streetham asked.

'Oh, it is too early for that. But I have made some observations that may prove useful. What I need now is to talk to Mr Edward Haversham, and if you can arrange that Miss Streetham, perhaps some conclusions may be in the offing.'

☞

We returned to Mr Haversham's house with the short winter day long gone. Advised by Miss Streetham, Charlotte despatched messages to Mr Edward, hoping that she might find him in Bath, prevailing on his friends, or in Bradford at any of the inns he frequented. The difficulty being that as his circumstances rose but mostly fell, his lodgings became increasingly casual, making it difficult for a communication to reach him.

'I fear it may be some time before we hear from him,' Miss Streetham warned us. 'If any of his ventures are successful, usually proceeds from a card game, then he indulges in luxury. But George has also told me of some of the more squalid hiding holes in which he has found Edward. He is so forgiving of Edward and almost seems to envy him at times.'

'That is an unusual comment,' I said. We were seated at dinner, which had been delayed by some further distress afflicting Mr Haversham, necessitating a call from an apothecary who supplied a sleeping draught. It had been very distressing to hear the moans of the poor man wafting from the upper floors, until sleep found him and brought a measure of peace to the household. #

'George, Mr Haversham'—and here her eyes flicked upwards as she thought of the tortured man—'he has always had a reputation of being most punctilious. Edward has ... described him in more colourful terms. George took on responsibility early upon the death of his father and I think looks on his brother almost as a son.'

'It does him great credit, I am sure,' Mrs Fitzhugh said. 'But I think from your comment that perhaps he chafes at such rectitude.'

She smiled and said, 'I know as much from what he has said. I told him once that I ... cared deeply for him because he was serious and dependable. And he replied that he wished just once he would do the wrong thing just to surprise me.'

'And has he?' Charlotte asked.

'What?'

'Done the wrong thing? Just to surprise you.'

'No, never,' she said, and we could see by her smile she considered his steadfastness a virtue, and not perhaps a tiresome predictability.

'Clearly you are made for each other,' Charlotte said.

At this, Mrs Streetham said. 'George Haversham is the ideal son in law. And my Beryl is his perfect helpmeet.'

We three did not demur to this assessment, although we did exchange a knowing glance. I knew that my friends were thinking that Mr Haversham might no longer be the ideal son-in-law. Obviously his financial prospects were sufficiently bleak as to unseat his reason. And yet Mrs Streetham had maintained her delusion that all would be well.

Until now, that is. After her pronouncement, she said nothing further and for the rest of the meal sat pensively. Her daughter too seemed subdued and it was in dull spirits that those two ladies retired early.

Without their company, Charlotte, Mrs Fitzhugh and I had freedom to discuss our opinions on the matter.

'I fear that Mr Haversham may be too devastated by his

financial setback to …' Mrs Fitzhugh said in hushed tones, voicing the thought we already shared.

'Yes,' I agreed, 'I fear this too.'

'But it is immaterial to the matter of the theft of the map and the identification of the culprit. Jane, what is your assessment of the matter?'

'Well, as much as the character of the brother makes it seem likely he is the culprit, we don't really have any evidence of his guilt. We don't even know whether the map is missing from the strongbox.'

'How is it that you have not determined that?' Mrs Fitzhugh asked. 'You visited the office.'

Charlotte sighed and said, 'There is only one key to the strongbox and it is, or was, upon Mr Haversham's person. And as Miss Streetham will not allow us to speak with him or even see him …'

'Oh, but I have seen him,' our friend said.

'What?' Charlotte asked. 'Have you spoken to him?'

'No, and if you had seen him, you would understand why. He moans and mutters to himself, oblivious to those around him. He is quite pitiable and it is no wonder that Miss Streetham would keep him from you.'

'But how then did you come to see him?'

Our friend looked slightly away from Charlotte before answering, 'Perhaps it is my manner and my offer to help in his care, rather than speak of questioning him.'

'Oh, very well done, Margaret. Did you come to see any keys?'

She looked directly at Charlotte at this and said, 'Yes, there are keys on a ring by his bedside.'

'And do you think Mr Haversham shall require any ministering to-night?'

'If not, I could propose the need for such and could again offer my help.'

'Excellent. Then we might visit the office again to-morrow and ascertain whether the map is in fact missing.'

THE YOUNGER BROTHER

Despite the success of Mrs Fitzhugh's mission, we were unable to leave immediately for the office the next morning as we were paid an early visit by Mr Edward Haversham.

Because of our planned excursion, Charlotte, Mrs Fitzhugh and I were able to receive him without delay. There was understandably some awkwardness in our meeting as Mrs Streetham and her daughter made introductions.

'I am sorry for my early arrival, but the letter I received did request "my most prompt attendance," and so you see me here now,' he said, with a slight smile indicating his amusement at the commanding tone of Charlotte's letter.

'Your prompt attendance is appreciated sir,' Charlotte said after a moment's hesitation, a hesitation she used to survey our caller. He was tall and languid, affecting an air of detached amusement. His hair was dark and unruly and spoke of reckless youth, although I thought it already receding. His eyes were a warm brown that further added to his relaxed manner, and I could see that in Miss Streetham's eyes his insouciance would raise objection. I too found his manner offensive, considering the seriousness of the situation, although I admit my views were prejudiced by that knowledge of him I had.

'There is no change for the worse with my brother, I hope?' he asked suddenly, any hint of amusement gone from his manner.

'No Edward, George remains fevered and prostrate with grief,' Miss Streetham said, the accusation in her tone very clear.

He could not meet her gaze or even mine and instead

turned to Charlotte, who said, 'I am sorry to not have better news, sir, but perhaps we could have more hope of alleviating your brother's suffering if we had a better idea the cause of it.'

Miss Streetham gave a small sound at this, not quite a gasp but definitely a sound of puzzlement. I too was confused by my friend's statement.

'I thought the cause of his distress was obvious—his financial interests,' he said.

'Yes, sir, that is certainly the cause of it, but the severity of it, that is another matter. It would help if I knew something of your brother's character. Miss Streetham, of course, sings his praises but I cannot expect her to be impartial. I know from experience, however, that a sibling's appraisal can be far more revealing.'

'Of my brother I can only tell you that he is … there is no more honest and forthright fellow in all England. His honour is unimpeachable.'

'Yes,' Charlotte said, lingering on the sibilance. 'That sounds more like an accusation. His forthrightness and honour sound at odds with the reports of your own character.'

'The reports that say I am a scoundrel and a disgrace to our family name? Yes, I am afraid all that is true.'

'Then I would have every reason to believe that you stole the map from your brother's office, the map showing the realignment of the canal, and then sold it.'

'Good, finally I am openly accused! And finally I can deny it. I did not sell that map, not that I wouldn't put it past me. But I didn't and I am sorry that for once my brother's business acumen has failed him.' He turned to Miss Streetham. 'I am very sorry for the trouble that has befallen George and that it should have affected you as well, Miss Streetham, heartfully sorry.'

He looked at her with what I thought genuine sorrow. She looked for a moment as if she might accept his words, but finally she spat out, 'I don't believe you!' before rushing from the room. I thought her words affected him, but he might merely be dissembling.

During this small drama Charlotte was silent, seeming to weigh what she had heard and finding something amiss, although I had heard nothing more obvious than what might be an outright lie. She now returned her attention to our guest who still looked in the direction taken by the emotional woman.

'Do you deny being in your brother's office?'

'No, I was there on the day to which I am sure you are referring. I saw Miss Streetham arrive and I hastily left. She has no taste for me you see, and George was not there so there seemed no reason to remain.'

'And can you explain your presence?'

'Oh yes, I was there to beg for money from George, who would most certainly have given it to me.'

'And you did not take the map?'

'This verges on being tiresome, Miss House. The map was there when I left.'

'But you knew of the map before your visit?'

This was a question for which Mr Haversham seemed unprepared.

'I … yes, in a way. I met George in Bath a few days previous. He was obviously upset and had confided to me that … certain changes needed to be made in the alignment. He said he had bet wrong and lost and I … I uncharitably compared his bets to mine.'

'And did you know that news of the re-alignment might be beneficial to some while disastrous to others?'

At this he would not meet Charlotte's eyes upon his answer. 'Yes, I knew that. You must understand, Miss House, that I might have acted upon this information had I been able. I'm no longer as young as I pretend, as your friend's observation of my hairline will attest. Like my brother, my vanity is important. Already my eyes are weak and my prospects bleak as a younger son who has not chosen the clergy, the military or God forbid some trade. But the fact of the matter is that you see me as destitute to-day as I was before this whole sorry business. I have not benefited one jot. Indeed I am even further fallen in Miss Streetham's estimation, something I would not have thought possible. Now have I answered your questions?'

'Yes. Thank you, sir. I believe you to have been as forthright as it is in your power to be.'

He smiled at her last remark, bowed and left us.

'He is certainly honest about his villainy,' Mrs Fitzhugh said. 'I suppose that must count for something.'

'That cannot excuse him,' I said, 'and he must certainly be the person who took the map. Don't you agree, Charlotte?'

'I think we must immediately leave for the offices of Haversham and Clarke and look inside that strongbox.'

Mrs Fitzhugh, Charlotte and I left immediately for the office by foot, the weather remaining pleasant. Miss Streetham remained behind simply because we left without her, Charlotte explaining that she felt that lady had been too upset over her meeting with Mr Edward.

I took the opportunity to ask the question that had puzzled me the day before.

'What is the significance of the Bramah lock?' I asked Charlotte.

'Oh, it is advertised as impervious to a pick lock. Unless a copy of the key were made, it should be impossible to enter the office without visibly damaging the lock or door. I am afraid that is another factor making it unlikely that Mr. Edward could have returned later that day to steal the map, although as we have no proof what day the map was taken, it is possible Mr Haversham had left it unlocked some subsequent day.'

'Is it very far?' Mrs Fitzhugh interjected as we walked down St. Margaret's Street.

'No,' Charlotte said, 'simply too far to appear at our best upon our arrival. You know how flushed Jane can appear after exertion.'

I wished to object at this but it was true that I easily flushed and instead said, 'Would it not be better were Miss Streetham to accompany us? Mr Clarke might not be as amenable without her presence.'

'Let us hope that our innate ... reasonableness will prevail, for I do not wish her presence.'

'But why not?' I asked.

'Her anger at the brother is distracting. Let us leave it at that.'

She walked slightly ahead of us, ending our conversation, and we soon arrived at the office. Kenneth the office boy greeted us to the sounds of men arguing. To our surprise, we found Mr Dundas in a heated argument with Mr Clarke.

'You will show me the map, sir, immediately.'

'As I have told you, and that woman yesterday, I do not have a key to the strongbox and I object to your accusations. When Mr Haversham is recovered ...'

'Excuse me, gentleman, I think I can solve your difficulties,' Charlotte said, stepping forward and presenting the key.

Both men turned to look at her, unaware until her announcement of our arrival.

'Charlotte, what is that?' asked Mr Dundas.

'It is, thanks to some light-fingered work by Margaret, the key to the strongbox. I suggest we open it and determine once and for all whether the map is contained therein.'

'I ... uh ... well this is ... without Mr Haversham's knowledge ...' Mr Clarke said, sputtering his words very guiltily to my mind.

'Excellent work, my dear Margaret,' Mr Dundas said, taking the key from Charlotte. 'Who knows how long George will be afflicted? Don't you want to clear the accusations against you?'

Great emotion worked upon the face of Mr Clarke but finally he settled for a look of resignation. 'Yes,' he finally agreed. 'Let it be done.'

We hurried into Mr Haversham's inner office, although I remained just outside the glass doors, for it was very crowded. I had to stand on tiptoe to look over Mrs Fitzhugh shoulder while Mr Dundas crouched down to operate the lock.

'Hmph!' he said with the exertion as he kneeled in front of the box. He inserted the key and with some difficulty opened the padlock and slipped it from the hasp. He opened the heavy lid with the aid of Mr Clarke. The strongbox was about half full, the bottom filled with bundled letters, deeds and other business matters but on top of it all were several large sheets folded in octavo.

Mr Dundas stood, again with the aid of Mr Clarke, and they took the maps to a desk and unfolded them. Once revealed Mr Dundas exclaimed, 'It is the map!'

'I told you it would be there,' Mr Clarke exulted.

'May I see?' Charlotte asked. Mr Dundas stepped aside so that Charlotte might stand before it and then read out, '"Revised K&A Canal route through Devizes." Is this then the cause of so much hardship for Mr Haversham?'

'It is,' Mr Dundas confirmed. 'He bought land along the old route with his own money previously, predicting a good investment'—he ran his finger along the map, squinting at it and muttered about his missing glasses—'but I had sent him this revision, unaware of his ... gamble. If he had had more time, he might have recouped some of his investment. Not much perhaps, but maybe enough to save him from ruin.'

I noticed Charlotte stiffen slightly and then hurriedly reach down and refold the map. She gave the map back to Mr Clarke and said, 'I suppose you might as well return this to the strongbox, although now that the horse has bolted ...'

Mr Clarke, appearing relieved, reached to take the map from Charlotte, who hesitated ever so slightly before relinquishing it. This interaction was shielded from Mr Dundas by Charlotte's back.

'Still I shall return it as George intended,' he said and returned it to the box, locked it and then returned the key to Charlotte. 'I trust you shall return this to George.'

Charlotte nodded and accepted the key. The transaction prodded Mr Dundas.

'Mr Clarke, I fear I owe you an apology for I ...'

'There is no need, Mr Dundas. This has been a trying time for us all and you were only acting in the good faith of the canal company. But if you will excuse me, I have a great deal of work now that I have not the benefit of my partner.'

He summarily ushered us out of the office, Mr Dundas appearing very contrite and far from his affable self. Mrs Fitzhugh moved to console him once we were outside.

'Mr Dundas, I am surprised to find you here,' Mrs Fitzhugh said, 'but it is pleasurable nonetheless.'

He smiled at this. 'And a pleasure for me too. My arrival would not have been a surprise were you to have waited for the afternoon post, when you would have found a letter informing you of my arrival.'

'And of what does Mr Clarke stand accused?' I asked.

Mr Dundas walked away from the office, trailed by three women. He was clearly uncomfortable.

'It is enough that I was incorrect in my suspicion,' he said.

'Hah!' cried Charlotte. 'It is not enough. I assume there is some suspicion as to his involvement in this affair, presumably relating to his losses ... or his gains?'

Mr Dundas sighed and said, 'Very well, Charlotte. As you have already guessed ... there are rumours that Mr Clarke was not as hurt from the disclosure as his partner, and I thought he might have released the map to third parties who acted on his behalf, well in advance. But as the map was there ... well I cannot account for the premature news. However at least we now know Edward is blameless in all this. Come, we must hasten to tell Miss Streetham.'

MR HAVERSHAM RECOVERS

We returned to Mr Haversham's home to find great rejoicing. That gentleman had awakened from the deep sleep induced the previous night by the sleeping draught and had announced himself hungry.

'He is still very tired, of course, but he had a thin gruel and seems much the better for it,' Mrs Streetham announced. Her daughter and the housekeeper remained with Mr Haversham.

'Should he have no difficulty keeping that down, I hope we may bring him something more substantial.'

'I would like to help if I could, Mrs Streetham,' our friend offered. Charlotte looked at Mrs Fitzhugh with a knowing smile, assured that the key would be returned without anyone the wiser.

'That would be very kind of you. You have a very reassuring presence, Mrs Fitzhugh. I can tell you have a knowledge of troubled times.'

The two ladies retreated from the drawing-room to discuss what best to bring Mr Haversham.

'This is good news,' Mr Dundas said to us after their departure. 'George is a dear friend and he and that young woman deserve some happiness.'

'Is there any hope that Mr Haversham's fortunes may survive this calamity?' I asked.

'There is always hope, I suppose,' he said after a moment's thought. 'George has a reputation for honesty and integrity uncommon in our day. There are those who would take advantage of that; and there are those who would stand by him.'

'Has he no reserves?' Charlotte asked. 'What did his father leave him?'

'Very little, I am afraid. He has land, of course, but its income is negligible for his father did not manage it wisely. No, his wealth derives from his business acumen, which up to now never failed him. But at least his father instilled in his sons a love of geography and maps that George has maintained.'

We continued to talk of the matter; Mr Dundas seemed to delight in offering explanations for the mystery of the map and Charlotte seemed equally to enjoy dismissing them. It was obvious this man's influence on the young Charlotte— promoting her active mind with fancies that she might dissect and examine.

During our conversation, we had continuing reports of improvements. Mrs Fitzhugh confirmed that Mr Haversham had tolerated coddled eggs and some weak tea. This news prompted Charlotte to despatch a message to Edward Haversham.

'It is his right to know his brother has improved,' Charlotte said. 'We now have proof after all that the map was never taken.'

Mr Dundas could not deny this and so the message was sent and later that day the younger brother returned.

'This is joyous news,' he told Miss Streetham upon his greeting her.

'Oh Edward, how I have wronged you. My sin is unforgiveable,' she said in earnest, pleading tones, addressing him now as the brother she once again hoped he might be.

'No, no, you could not wrong me for I have been the worst sort of brother and the worst sort of friend. George has always treated me better than he should and I have only repaid his kindness by asking for more. I promise you, Beryl, if I may be so bold to call you Beryl, I promise you that I shall help my brother ... and his wife ... and I ... I am sure that happy day will come for you both ...'

The man could not continue and I saw that Mr Edward Haversham had turned that corner in his life that leads to wisdom and redemption. Miss Streetham held his hand and it almost seemed as if he wanted to draw it away—in shame for how he had lived his life—but she held it all the more firmly.

In all my life I have never witnessed a more touching scene and I looked to my friend Charlotte with the expectation that even she would be moved by this expression of love and forgiveness. However the look of her face was one of amazement and epiphany, to be replaced by her swift smile when once she discovered my gaze.

All the rest of the day we heard continued good reports of Mr Haversham and after our dinner we learned that he wondered at the many unfamiliar voices he heard issuing from downstairs. He was informed of our presence and assistance and over the objections of his caregivers asked that he might thank us for our troubles.

Mrs Streetham led Charlotte, Mrs Fitzhugh and me to his room, where we found him sitting upright. His resemblance to his brother was remarkable, save for the influence of the years between them and the suffering he had endured. His hairline had further receded and I suspect before his troubles he might have carried more weight than his brother, but otherwise they were identical.

'Beryl and her dear mother have told me that you have sought to clear my brother's name, and I thank you,' he said. We wisely did not offer to correct his interpretation of our visit.

'I am so ashamed that my ... illness gave rise to any speculation that my brother would do such a thing.'

Mrs Streetham, however, coughed and said, 'But Edward's conduct in past has ...'

'No!' Mr Haversham said, and in his excitement he raised himself from his pillow. 'You do not know him. You do not know the strength he has!'

But this act robbed him of his strength and he collapsed back to his bed. I thought we might have overtaxed the man and was about to suggest we leave when Charlotte said, 'We are happy that we could act on your behalf to defend your brother when you were indisposed.'

'You are very kind. I am also told you are friends of Uncle Charles—that is Mr Dundas ...' he stopped and looked at us quizzically, his eyes squinting as if to see us better.

'Perhaps you would benefit from your glasses?' Charlotte offered.

'Mr Haversham does not wear glasses,' Miss Streetham said, who apparently had entered the room while we were in conversation.

Charlotte took several steps closer to Mr Haversham and peered more closely at the man.

'No, I believe you do. Do you keep them in this table?'

He smiled weakly. 'Yes, if you would be so kind.'

Charlotte opened the drawer of a table next to the bed and produced the glasses, which he donned.

'I am sorry at my little deception, Beryl.'

'But why did you think it necessary, George?'

His pause at answering allowed Mrs Fitzhugh to say, 'Men are as vain as women, my dear.'

For some reason, perhaps simply the strain of the past days, this remark caused Miss Streetham, and then her mother, to laugh with abandon, which also caused Mr Haversham to smile. We left the room shortly thereafter, leaving mother, daughter and future son to enjoy their happiness in private.

In the drawing-room, Mr Dundas prepared to leave us.

'Thank you again, Charlotte, and my dear Margaret and my newest friend Miss Woodsen.'

'Please sir, it would be an honour were you to call me Jane,' I offered, surprised and yet not that this man had so inspired such a want of intimacy.

'Careful, Jane, for you shall soon be calling him Uncle Charles,' Charlotte said.

'That is a certainty,' Mr Edward Haversham confirmed. 'Come sir, I will leave with you that we might allow this household some rest.'

'If you could remain behind a moment, Mr Haversham, I should be grateful,' Charlotte said.

Mr Dundas raised a questioning eyebrow that Charlotte answered with a nod. I could not fathom Charlotte's desire to speak with Mr Haversham and I could not understand how Mr Dundas could be any the wiser, but he seemed satisfied to leave matters with her. He bid us good night again and left.

'Please, Mr Haversham, will you sit with us?' Charlotte said as a command. Most people encountering Charlotte's imperious tone for the first time would have instantly complied, but he smiled warily before he casually took a seat.

'You have questions for me?' he asked with an insolence that recalled my earlier suspicions of him.

'Yes, I would appreciate knowing for how long you have been in love with Miss Streetham.'

I gasped at this and looked to Mrs Fitzhugh, but she simply nodded her head. 'Well it was rather obvious, Jane,' she said.

'I remember you now,' Mr Haversham said, 'but I don't

think we've ever met. Uncle Charles had told me of a little girl that he said was a wicked reasoner. Very well, I own up to it. I have loved her since the moment I met her.'

'You have gone to lengths to hide it from her.'

'I would not have her know for the world. She is for George as should be plain for anyone to see,' he said emphatically.

'Have no fear; we will keep this knowledge to ourselves. But in return, I want to know how you stole the map.'

It was now Mrs Fitzhugh's turn to gasp.

'Oh really, I thought you had done your best to clear my name?'

'There is no use in denying it. Perhaps it would be easier if you merely confirm my belief that you stole the map by the simple expedient of wadding it up and putting it in the wastebasket and letting the boy Kenneth throw it out with the trash.'

He opened his mouth as if to again object and then thought better of it. Finally he said, 'I suppose there is no use in denying it. You are correct in your belief.'

'But we found the map and Mr Haversham, that is Mr George Haversham, confirmed the map remained in his office after this man had left,' I objected.

'Yes, the copy remained in his office, but the original escaped in the trash,' Charlotte said, as if the concept were a simple matter.

'Copy? What copy?'

Charlotte ignored my question and instead addressed Mr Haversham: 'How did you become aware of the copy?'

But Mr Haversham refused to say anything in response. Rather than confront him again, Charlotte addressed my question.

'There had to be a copy, Jane. It is a fact that information about the map had circulated and yet we found the map in the strongbox. *Quod erat demonstrandum.* And I sincerely doubt that Mr Edward Haversham could create a copy of such a large and detailed map in the time allotted, so I must surmise your brother created the map. I found marks on the table below the map and many of the tools needed to create a duplicate.' #

'Damn you then, yes he created that copy and yes he confessed it to me!' Mr Haversham said loudly.

'Please, lower your voice or your brother's one instance of dishonesty will be discovered,' Charlotte commanded.

'You will not speak of this?'

'No, I have no desire so to do. But I would know of your brother's intentions.'

'It was Mr Clarke who led George astray. His plan was to release a copy of the map, but altered to suggest a different route. It would be shown to just a few individuals under the pretence of a theft. It would allow Mr Clarke and George enough time to buy and sell enough property that when the real map was made public ... well they might escape ruin.'

'I completely underestimated Mr Clarke's inventiveness. Yes it was a brilliant move. Those speculators who acted on information from a stolen map could hardly then cry foul. But still, how did you come to know of the plan?'

And now I saw shame on Mr Haversham's face. 'My brother thought I would ... he thought I might know someone ...'

'Ah, he thought you might either know someone who would "steal" the map or ... or did he also ask you to do this for him?'

'Oh God help him, he did. I have always resented and revered my brother for the man he was, and to see him reduced to this ... I pleaded with him not to turn his back on those principles that had governed his life, but he only felt anger that I would not help him, after all the times he had rescued me.'

'And so you did steal the map, only you stole the original and what … you sold it?'

'No!' and again he said this too loudly before continuing more softly. 'I could not sell it. I could not profit from it. I did it to keep my brother from temptation, to keep him worthy of the love of …'

And at this he cried, without guile or concern for propriety. And finally I saw a look of compassion on my friend's face. When finally Mr Haversham collected himself, she said, 'You have done well for your brother. Your timing may have been ill advised, but I suppose 'twere well it were done quickly.' #

'You will not speak a word of this?' he asked.

'You have my word, sir,' Charlotte said, and Mrs Fitzhugh and I also agreed to silence.

'Thank you, thank you. Then I will leave you and return to my wicked ways.'

'Oh Mr Haversham, I think those days are behind you,' I said.

'Yes, you are meant for better things, like aiding your brother,' Mrs Fitzhugh said. 'From what I understand, he will need every assistance.'

He then left us and we three friends gratefully took our seats again, now aided by the port we had denied ourselves after dinner.

'How long have you known the solution to this matter?' I asked Charlotte and then felt stupid. 'Oh of course, since you had Kenneth throw out the trash.'

'Well certainly that is how I knew how the theft was effected, but it was not until I realized that Mr George Haversham wore glasses that I felt confident enough to directly accuse Mr Edward.'

'How does that matter?' Mrs Fitzhugh asked.

'Must I explain this? Very well, you both found baffling the fact that the map was found still in the strongbox when in fact that explained almost all, whereas my chief puzzlement was Mr Haversham stating that map remained in the office after the brother had left. He should have seen that he held the copy, but once I knew of his nearsightedness and his vanity, it all became clear. In retrospect, I should have suspected this after Mr Edward complained of his weak eyes, as it may be a shared family trait.'

'I still don't … oh, he did not wish to wear his glasses before Miss Streetham and thus could not tell that he held the copy and not the original,' I said. 'You might say you observed that he could not see.'

'Oh, nicely put Jane. Nicely put.'

The Affair of the Code Duello

our Mr Wallace is here, Jane,' Charlotte observed from the window overlooking the street. I did not even look up from my journal at her words, having learned it was best not to respond to her …

'And he is accompanied by a lovely young woman.'

At this I stood up and would have rushed to her side, only I heard through the open drawing-room door the knocker on the front door and then the steady tread of Robert walking to open it.

I looked to Charlotte, who merely shrugged and offered no explanation of it, and then to Mrs Fitzhugh, who smiled mischievously at me. My friends came to my side and we heard Mr Wallace's voice in conversation with Robert. After a few moments, Robert came to stand outside the drawing-room door and announced, 'Mr Wallace has arrived, Miss House,' and he offered the salver that held Mr Wallace's calling card. Charlotte took the card, reversed it and we saw the note: 'Urgent I talk to you, Miss House, on behalf of a friend.'

'Very good, Robert. Please show Mr Wallace and his friend in.' Robert nodded and left and I thought the man's measured tread infuriatingly slow. *Who could this woman be that he called friend?*

Robert then returned and announced our guests as 'Mr Wallace and Miss Deirdre Bassett.'

We exchanged our greetings, I perhaps with less than my usual *sang-froid* for I was both struck by the beauty of our visitor, still apparent despite her obvious unease, and her hand upon the arm of *my* Mr Wallace. She was several inches shorter than Charlotte, which still left her several inches above me, with jet black hair and a fine complection not marred by her cheeks bright from the wintry air. I guessed her to be of my age, but her beauty and her obvious wealth from the fineness of her dress, made her seem to be my senior. #

'Thank you Miss House for seeing me,' Mr Wallace began uncertainly. 'It is a matter of some urgency you see for this woman's … well, I don't know how the matter stands, but might he be your betrothed?' he asked of his companion. After a moment's hesitation she shook her head no. 'Then I come on behalf of a Mr Jenkins, a friend of mine.' Those last words he addressed to us.

You will understand how relieved I felt at those words. *Of course, Mr Wallace's friend is Mr Jenkins, to whom this woman may or may not be betrothed.* I looked at Mr Wallace, who gave me back a weak smile. He seemed unusually perturbed.

'You obviously have a difficult tale to tell,' Charlotte said. 'Please, let us sit while you tell it.'

We took our seats, Miss Bassett clearly thankful of my friend's suggestion. I also took the opportunity to retrieve my journal.

'Thank you, Miss House, and it is more appropriate that *I* thank you, for I have importuned on Mr Wallace to bring me here, also on behalf of Mr Jenkins.'

'It does not matter who thanks me. Tell me of your distress and how I may help.'

'I come because Mr Jenkins, a man I know, is now party

to a duel because he defended my … well, it is embarrassing to say.' #

Miss Bassett turned her head away while making her admission, an act that only made her seem prettier. I then noticed that Charlotte, in reaction to Miss Bassett's statement, bore a numbed expression so curiously unlike her normal self. I also noticed Mrs Fitzhugh looking to our friend. The silence began to hang uneasily and so I asked, 'He defended your honour?'

My question broke Charlotte's reverie, who looked sharply at me. She obviously wished me to hold my tongue and at this I was relieved, for her irritation was preferable to her numb look.

Miss Bassett now answered my question. 'No, not my honour, but my …' and would not continue.

'He defended her beauty,' Mr Wallace supplied.

'What? He challenged someone to a duel over her beauty?' I asked, again incurring a sharp glance from Charlotte.

'No, he was challenged for insulting the gentleman who … well it's all rather silly … no, not silly for it has come to this, but the provocation is … it is complicated,' Mr Wallace said.

Charlotte remarked, 'Do tell. And while you're at it, tell me how you are involved, Mr Wallace.'

He rubbed his jaw before answering. 'Actually, I think I may be one of the seconds. I am uncertain at this moment.'

'This is a muddled affair. Were you present at the exchange that precipitated the challenge?'

'Yes, in a sense. This morning I was with friends at a coffee-house, one of those friends being Mr Jenkins, whom I know through the regiment, but not well. He has only recently arrived in Bath from Bristol. He had instigated the trip to the coffeehouse, claiming its virtues … of which there were few readily apparent to my eye. But that is beside the point. He became rather voluble as to the charms of Miss Bassett, whom

I had never met, although his description of her beauty, could never do …' He faltered after noticing my gaze, which I fear may have been intense.

'Oh, where was I?' he then said. 'Yes, it was all rather odd for normally Mr Jenkins is a quiet sort of man, not given to calling attention to himself. But here he was, loudly praising Miss Bassett's … appearance, when the gentleman sitting at a nearby table observed that Mr Jenkins certainly must be exaggerating. To which Mr Jenkins added further encomiums to which this gentleman said, "Surely not," or words to that effect, which led Mr Jenkins to expound further.'

'And then a challenge was issued?'

'No, not at that time.'

'Then when, Mr Wallace?' Charlotte asked.

'It happened that Mr Jenkins knew that Miss Bassett should be shopping; and he suggested to us that if we might proceed to Bath Street we could observe her and this gentleman would be forced to admit that she is "the most beautiful woman that anyone had ever seen."' #

'And what would induce him, and you, to follow, other than a natural desire to see "the most beautiful woman anyone had ever seen?"'

Mr Wallace looked uncomfortably at Miss Bassett before answering, 'Well, some money was at stake.'

'Ah, I thought as much.'

'They were very modest wagers, Mr Jenkins betting that we would agree as to his claim. It was all in fun, and all we had to do to collect was disagree. I could not say there was any animosity, and the five of us, that is myself, Mr Jenkins, his friend Mr Purcell, the gentleman who objected—that is, Mr Sunderland—and his friend Mr … oh, I forget his name but I do not imagine it important. We left the coffeehouse and proceeded to Bath Street.

'It was sometime, however, before Miss Bassett's arrival

and as you know it is quite cold to-day and to warm ourselves—well several of us had flasks that were exchanged.'

'So, now money and drink are involved. Please advance to the point that you observe Miss Bassett.'

'Very well. He, Mr Jenkins, spotted Miss Bassett walking with her servant and called her to our attention.' He paused.

'And the outcome of the various wagers?'

'Um, some paid him and some didn't.' Mr Wallace would not meet my eye as he said this.

'I see,' Charlotte said. 'And I assume one who did not pay was this Mr Sunderland?'

'Yes, he agreed that Miss Bassett was very pretty but not the most beautiful woman he had ever seen, although he admitted himself at a disadvantage at making such a judgement for being across the street. To which Mr Jenkins proposed they cross the street and he would introduce Mr Sunderland to Miss Bassett.'

'What, you then all accosted Miss Bassett on the street?'

'No, just Mr Jenkins and Mr Sunderland crossed the street.'

'Perhaps I might continue the tale, Miss House?' Miss Bassett offered.

'Please.'

'I saw these gentlemen across the street, or rather I heard their raised voices, and I recognized Mr Jenkins, whom I know and who has called upon me at my house and with whom, from time to time, I have danced.'

'But Mr Wallace thought your relationship close enough that he thought you betrothed,' I said.

'Yes, surely there must be more than a few dances?' Mrs Fitzhugh also observed.

As Charlotte did not shush us, our questions must have been pertinent.

'Yes, well, he did ask me to marry, about two months ago, but I begged time to consider.'

'I think many would consider two months a great deal of time. What is the cause of your reticence?' Charlotte asked.

'It is ... well it seems ridiculous to say this now, but I thought he lacked ... I did not think his ardour sufficient. As Mr Wallace has already described him, Mr Jenkins is a quiet man, not much given to making his feelings known. But obviously I now have ample proof of his regard for me and ... oh, I feel so horrible for saying this, but the differences in our stations no longer seems ...'

'Ah, I see. Mr Jenkins is not a gentleman?'

'He is a merchant, an importer of spirits and is very successful in that, but no, he has no property even though he could well afford it. But more than that, he is a man of numbers and calculations. I do not mean to say that he is cold or uncaring, merely that his cautious ways do not excite ... my interest.'

'But to return to your narrative,' I urged. 'Mr Jenkins and Mr Sunderland were to cross the street.'

Fortunately my prompting did not rouse my friend's ire. 'Quite right, Jane. Please continue.'

'Mr Jenkins approached with Mr Sunderland and I was introduced to him. He seemed a good sort of gentleman—very handsome and dashing—but as I had further shopping I could not tarry long and soon made to leave, but as I was going I heard loud arguing from these gentleman and then Mr Sunderland shouted, "Are you calling me a liar, sir?" and then Mr Jenkins shouted, even louder, "Yes, I am, sir. I am calling you a liar if you fail to admit Miss Bassett is" ... well, what Mr Wallace said earlier.'

'That you are the most beautiful woman, &c.?' Charlotte asked, to which Miss Bassett nodded in agreement, with what I had to concede appeared honest embarrassment.

Mr Wallace continued the story: 'I ran across the street, for I saw the path these gentleman were taking, but I heard the word "satisfaction" and knew I was too late. Then our comrades joined us, with Mr Sunderland's friend … ah, I have it now, Mr Arkwright … defending his friend and Mr Purcell defending Mr Jenkins.'

'But you did not defend Mr Jenkins?'

Mr Wallace guiltily nodded. 'I do not count myself a particular friend of Mr Jenkins and the matter … I beg your pardon Miss Bassett, but I thought the matter rather stupid. And it was made even more pointless as neither gentleman could agree what was the original offence, but finally it was agreed that calling Mr Sunderland a liar was paramount to not admitting Miss Bassett the most beautiful woman he had ever seen.'

By now I must admit to being tired of that phrase.

'And how did you find yourself being a second?' Mrs Fitzhugh asked Mr Wallace.

'I am afraid by virtue of being in the wrong place at the wrong time, and I am not his immediate second and I sincerely hope that I might escape this duty altogether should Mr Jenkins's brother be available. It is not a welcome duty for I do not approve of men so foolishly risking their lives, not when men already die in battle, but as I was of Mr Jenkins's party and I do owe him a service …'

'I see,' Charlotte said. 'You do not care for him?'

Mr Wallace looked at Miss Bassett. 'I hardly know him, but I think him a good man and my only negative impression of him results from this unwise action. He is … as Miss Bassett has described him … a deliberate thoughtful man who …' Mr Wallace stopped, obviously loathe to speak badly of someone, and then added, 'He *also* does not excite my interest.'

'And to return to his proposal, Miss Bassett? Do his actions to-day overcome your reluctance?'

'I would be lying were I to say I am unmoved. That a man

would fight a duel … it raises him in my estimation. I am frightfully ashamed to admit it. But regardless of my esteem, I could not stand to see anyone come to harm over me.'

Charlotte paused to evaluate this and then said, 'I like your honesty, Miss Bassett, and it is understandable that you now view Mr Jenkins in a new light. But I fear I may not be in a position to be of much help. A woman can hardly interfere in such matters.'

'I had thought of that, Miss House,' Mr Wallace said. 'And I thought I might be your intermediary.'

'You would do this? You would heed my beck and call?'

He nodded and she said, 'You surprise me, sir. Very well then, I will have to direct you from the comfort of my armchair. Can I assume you tried to persuade Mr Jenkins to offer his apology to Mr Sunderland?'

'Yes I have, but my words fall on deaf ears. He will only say, "She is the most beautiful woman in the world" and that he would not have it said … you spoke, Miss Woodsen?'

'No, pardon me,' I said, embarrassed that my groan was so audible. 'Please continue.'

'But that is all I have to say. He cannot be persuaded. But at the very least Mr Sunderland agreed to delay an actual challenge until to-morrow.'

'Ah, well done. That gives us some time to persuade Mr Sunderland to forgive the affront, but my memory of him is that his honour is easily wounded and he has fought a duel … or duels … before. Still one must try.'

'I agree and so I go later to-day to meet with him and his second. But as you say, he appeared quick to find insult.'

'Good, you anticipate me. And I would also have you appeal again to Mr Jenkins, perhaps with the information that Miss Bassett would not have him enter this duel. And then you must report back to me every particular.'

After Mr Wallace, Miss Bassett and her maid departed, Charlotte and I went to the library to consult her commonplace books, but not before I had a whispered conversation with Mrs Fitzhugh as we were leaving the drawing-room.

'What was the matter with Charlotte?'

'What can you mean, Jane?'

I made an exasperated sound and said, 'You know very well what I mean. I saw you look to her, as did I. She was very upset at the news of the duel.'

Mrs Fitzhugh sighed, and said, 'Dear Jane, you must know by now that Charlotte has a secret past that troubles her and that she wishes it to remain secret, even from you.' But the look in my friend's eyes made me think that it was not her wish that I should remain uninformed.

'I have suspected ...' I began to say, and then stopped for if I were truthful I would admit I had suspected nothing. Of course I knew Charlotte to be moody and at times secretive, but I had assumed it was part of the persona that she wished to present. Perhaps my own woes and concerns precluded me from observing the woes of those around me, even those I held in great esteem.

'No, it cannot be that you are unaware.' Mrs Fitzhugh said, interpreting my confusion correctly. 'I am surprised at your ignorance. Well, you know Charlotte's methods. Apply that which you have learned, Jane.'

I left her then and hurried to the library to join Charlotte already surrounded by her commonplace books.

'Take these Jane and see what you might find of Mr Jenkins,' she said, handing me two books. I took the books and used the opportunity to inspect more closely my friend's demeanour.

'There is something the matter, Jane?' she asked upon observing my inspection.

The low winter sun through the library windows cast shadows upon her face, making her appear quite careworn. But she also wore her look of irritation that did not invite further inquiry and so I lied.

'No, nothing more than the thought that distasteful as it is, a woman, such as Miss Bassett, could not help but feel moved that a man would risk his life to defend her beauty.'

'Tchah! I could not disagree more. It is an act of arrant stupidity. You would be advised to follow your Mr Wallace's example. He knows something of the waste of men's lives.'

'Oh assuredly, Charlotte,' I agreed in haste.

'Now find what you can of Mr Jenkins,' she commanded.

But half an hour of mutual search proved fruitless. 'I see nothing here of Mr Jenkins,' I said in exasperation.

At my words, Charlotte looked up and said. 'Neither do I, but I did not have high hopes. My network does not extend to Bristol spirit importers. But of Mr Sunderland I find a little. I have met him before, of course, and have danced with him … I have recorded he is very good … but I think the card room holds more attraction for him than the ballroom. And if my memory is correct, he has fought two duels, but in each case apparently honour was satisfied after a single exchange and no injuries were sustained. My information is supplemented by rumour and … ah, here is information supplied by Uncle Charles, that is Mr Dundas.' Her finger traced words in her book. 'He recounted to me: "He's accomplished at cards but it's balanced by a need to bet on anything, including things beyond his control. So he might walk away from the table richer and foolishly lose it on whether it rains or not."'

'Has he a fortune?'

'He is the second son of a prominent Newbury family but

beyond this I know nothing. A distressingly incomplete record, in fact, that I think requires remediation.'

I shook my head. 'If you propose a visit to the Assembly rooms or the Pump Room or any of our myriad sources of gossip, I remind you that I am engaged at our mantua maker to-day.' #

'Which is why I shall travel there with Margaret. You may take Mary with you.'

The Mantua Maker

Mary and I slowly walked down the street, our lack of progress owing principally to my musings on the strange affair before us and the secret that I now knew Charlotte kept from me. My mind whirled as I thought of all those peculiarities of my friend and how they might be assembled to give a picture of that secret. Chief among her mysteries, of course, was her reluctance to show interest in any man, but I dismissed her reluctance to her being in no desire to marry. She was still young ...

And then it occurred to me that I did not actually know my benefactress's age. The topic had never arisen, or rather on those occasions on which it did, there was never a resolution to our conversation. Charlotte might be as young as maybe a year or two older than myself or ...

And then again I was struck, but this time by the memory of my first meeting Charlotte. I was near seventeen and not yet out, the delay attributable to my father's poor financial health, he wanting to delay the necessity of providing for my dowry as long as possible. When I met Miss House, she had obviously been out for several years and seemed far older than myself, although that impression might have been influenced by the telescope of youth, which magnified differences in ages. #

I began to wonder then just how old Charlotte might be and I bore in mind her accomplishments. She certainly had a knowledge of the world including politics, science and the arts that would be difficult to amass by the age of five and twenty. Might she then be seven and twenty? Many would think her a spinster at that age.

That thought made me laugh. *Charlotte a spinster!* #

'Miss? Is there something wrong?'

Mary's question made me realize I had stopped in the street in amazement. 'What? No, I was suddenly struck by the most outrageous thought.'

'Perhaps it would be as best if we finished crossing the street, miss. My feet are getting wet.'

At this mention a passing cart splashed icy water at our feet. 'A good point, Mary.'

We hurriedly crossed to the other side of the street and continued on our way. The interruption, however, made my mind return to the plight of Mr Jenkins.

'What do you think of duelling?' I asked Mary. It was unusual to ask a servant's opinion on such a matter, I admit, but I had formed a good understanding with Mary.

'Miss? What?'

'Men fighting duels. What is your opinion?'

'I don't know that I've thought of it much. It's something gentlemen do and I don't know of anyone ... Mr Wallace isn't in a duel is he?' she asked in alarm. Now it was she who paused our step.

'No, of course not ... no I ask merely your opinion. Come, you are more than any lady's maid. You are Miss House's maid and you have seen and heard more and are privy to more than any maid in Bath ... perhaps to more than you should be privy, I dare say. And I would have your opinion.'

My thought in asking Mary her opinion was also motivated by Charlotte's odd appearance when she learned of the duel. I hoped that Mary might hold some information as to my friend's distress. I urged her to continue walking so that our conversation would attract less attention.

'I suppose I don't understand it, miss. Why don't they just go at it hammer 'n' tong? That's how men solve their problems, i'n'it, so I don't see why gentlemen shouldn't do the same.' #

'That might leave unsightly injury.'

'Better than getting killed.'

'Yes, there is that. You don't find it … romantic then?'

'La! Romantic! Wait, you're sure Mr Wallace …'

'No, of course not. I would not countenance …'

And then the thought struck me that I would in no way ever wish to see Mr Wallace risk his life for something so … foolish. I felt chagrin that I might see in the actions of Mr Jenkins anything noble or romantic.

'You're very wise, Mary.'

'Me? Oh now I see you've had me on, miss. Here we are!' she said as we arrived. I decided that my questioning of Mary would have to conclude after my appointment.

We entered and Mary was led away to join the servants of the house whilst I was led to the drawing-room and was treated to tea and a warm fire while I awaited Mrs La Fontaine. I was early for my appointment, for one did not wish to keep that woman waiting; and naturally she liked to keep her customers waiting so that she might preserve her reputation of desirability.

Until now, I had never engaged the noted mantua-maker, having attempted to repair and adapt what few clothes I retained, hoping to cover what flaws I could not repair with ribbons or whatever scraps I might beg of Charlotte or Mrs Fitzhugh. And I had even tried, with Mary's help, to create something entirely new but I had not the flair nor skill for it and my friends finally reasoned with me that I should have new clothes expertly made.

I had been to Mrs La Fontaine's establishment the week before with my friends, but now that I was alone I was quite apprehensive of my reception. And so I sat drinking the indifferent tea, my mind still on the precipitate actions of Mr Jenkins. Although my talk with Mary had made me see reason, I still could not help but think that he must love Miss Bassett to take such a risk and that his actions did warrant some change in her appreciation of him.

I was surprised then when Mrs La Fontaine flew into the room with her assistant.

'Oh Miss House, please forgive me for forcing you … But where is Miss House?' she asked upon realizing I was alone.

'It is only me to-day, Mrs La Fontaine.'

'And who exactly are you?'

'I am Miss House's friend … *her particular friend*, Miss Woodsen.'

She looked at me in that way you do when you find an unfamiliar offering at dinner—you don't know if you've ever eaten it before and you suspect you're not going to like it.

'Ah yes, I remember now, the short girl. Well, any friend of Miss House deserves my utmost attention.' Her assistant spoke in a whisper to her employer.

'Oh yes, it is time for your fitting. Please come through to the next room.'

I obliged and found the three dresses we had contracted for awaiting me.

'Oh, these are lovelier than I could have ever imagined. The quality of the work is superb,' I gushed, and my praise had its effect.

'I am glad you like them Miss Watson.'

I smiled and bore the error, thinking it was a small price to pay to gain her good graces.

'You had good taste in selecting these. They are quite fashionable in London. You are returning there?'

Here I knew not what to say. I had presumed on my hostess for far too long and I knew that eventually Charlotte and Mrs Fitzhugh would return to London and I was unsure if I was to join them. I had no reason to think that Charlotte would not wish me to accompany her; surely she would not have insisted on buying me these dresses otherwise. But she had never specifically said that I was to come and so naturally I worried. #

'Yes,' I said, preferring to believe that Charlotte believed the matter already settled.

'Then you will look grand in these and the lines will perhaps convey an impression of height.' I smiled at this, thinking I might have been paid a compliment or a criticism or both.

'You are Miss House's particular friend, are you not?' Mrs La Fontaine asked, apparently having forgot my earlier statement.

'Yes, I have that honour.'

'H'm, then we must take special pains to make these dresses truly outstanding. Perhaps a contrasting colour here, do you think?' she said in an aside to her assistant. Soon they were in heavy conversation, the assistant never quite speaking above a whisper while Mrs La Fontaine only agreed to her own opinions, rejecting the asked for opinions of her assistant.

I was left standing there on the little footstool feeling both ignored and yet the centre of attention. To draw attention to my existence, I asked, 'Mrs La Fontaine, are you acquainted by any chance with a Mr Sunderland?'

'Sunderland, Sunderland? Why the name is familiar, but I can't recall …'

Again her assistant whispered something.

'Ah, thank you Julia. That is the man indeed. Yes, Miss Wilson, I do recall him now, if he be … pardon me, but you do have the full confidence of your friend, do you not?'

I recalled the number of confidences shared by Mrs La Fontaine and Charlotte while I sat nearby, apparently invisible to the dress maker.

'I do.'

'Well, I believe Mr Sunderland is that gentleman Miss Caroline Chivington has repeatedly rejected as a suitor.'

'Oh, and has she given reason for her rejection?' At this Mrs La Fontaine shushed away her assistant and leaned closer to me.

'Well, Miss Chivington is a very well mannered young woman … a bit of a bore frankly. She follows all the niceties of dress and appearance and manner and never does anything remotely outrageous or interesting. What Mr Sunderland can find fascinating about her is a mystery, but I always say there is someone for every taste.

'But Mr Sunderland is another matter. He is chivalrous and gallant and charming and *dangerous.*' She said this last word with a special emphasis.

'For you know he has a reputation for constantly duelling that has made him … infamous. He seeks out any offence to his honour and has such a manner that urges his … I may say his victim for that is the truth of the matter … he urges his victim to give satisfaction and then cruelly despatches him.'

I forbore mentioning Charlotte's information that he had only fought two duels without injury, and instead asked, 'And is that the reason for Miss Chivington's refusal?'

'I have heard this, but she might have better reason to refuse him.'

'Which is?' I prompted.

'Mr Sunderland's finances may not bear scrutiny,' she replied.

'I thought him a wealthy man.'

'He maintains that appearance but I have it from Mr Arbuthnot the tailor that Mr Sunderland's tardiness in paying his bills may require an action. I have it further from Mr Arbuthnot that there has been a very recent financial calamity resulting from speculation in the canal company. I am sure a young woman such as yourself does not know of these things but I myself barely escaped a loss of my canal stock. An older woman such as myself must take care, even if Mr La Fontaine had so carefully provided for me.'

I was surprised at this last, having always assumed Mr La Fontaine was an invention, like that of our housekeeper's husband. I also thought it possible that not all Mrs La Fontaine's information could be considered reliable. #

'Do you have any idea why Mr Sunderland is so quick to take offence?'

'None whatsoever, unless it be ... oh my, I don't know if I should say.'

I said nothing, assured that Mrs La Fontaine could not long withhold gossip and to no surprise I was proved correct.

'Well, as you are Miss House's particular friend I can tell you that I have heard that the timing of Mr Sunderland's birth was not propitious as it happened not long after the death of his father, who died of a long ... a very long, illness. A wasting disease, I believe.'

I would have asked for clarification but Mrs La Fontaine was informed of the arrival of another customer and as my fittings were done I had to leave, but with information I thought my friends would appreciate.

MR WALLACE REPORTS

'No, I am afraid Mr Jenkins remains adamant. Nothing I could say would deter him and if as expected Mr Sunderland demands satisfaction to-morrow, he will accept the challenge.' And then Mr Wallace gave us a wry smile and amended, 'Unless of course it is Mr Jenkins who demands satisfaction and challenges Mr Sunderland. Apparently he believes the failure to call Miss Bassett ... to acknowledge her beauty ... the more serious offence.' #

This was disappointing but not unexpected news from Mr Wallace, who had returned to us after communicating with both parties. He had most recently met with Mr Jenkins after earlier talking to Mr Sunderland and he met with us after dinner. We were now seated with him in the drawing-room, where he drank coffee and brandy to warm himself after his travels.

'Tell us what you know of him, Mr Wallace. Miss Bassett said he is not a gentleman,' Charlotte said.

'I suppose not, but he's certainly wealthy enough from importing rum. He has considerable contracts with the army and navy. An army may march on its stomach, but rum and gin keeps it happy. I've had conversations with him about preserving food.'

'Preserving food?' Mrs Fitzhugh asked.

'Yes, it's appalling what the men eat in the field or sailors on long voyages. They say Napoleon will pay 12,000 francs to whoever can find a way to keep food from spoiling, and I think His Majesty should do the same. Mr Jenkins pursues the same goal and it's a noble one, regardless if it might also make him even wealthier.' #

'And your opinion of him?' Charlotte asked.

'Well, something of a cold fish,' he said, but then stopped himself. 'No, that's not fair. He's really just awkward and uncertain about everything except business and so he says little. I wouldn't want to be stuck in a coach with him for a long trip, but he acts as a gentleman ought; I'll not gainsay it.'

'Where did you speak to him?'

'At his home in the Circus,' he said while refreshing his coffee and helping himself from the plate of biscuits he'd requested.

'And in attendance were?'

'Mr Jenkins, his friend Mr Purcell and myself.'

'Ah, his brother is not yet come?'

'No, a message was sent but as his brother is in Liverpool he is not likely to save me from my unwanted duty.'

'How did Mr Jenkins seem?'

'Very much like his usual self. He appeared to be going over his books with Mr Purcell. Mr Jenkins arrived here only Tuesday from Bristol, Mr Purcell having arrived earlier.'

'So he did not seem like a man putting his affairs in order.'

'Oh, I see what you mean. No, he seemed his regular sober self.'

'Which is at odds with his demeanour this morning, when he challenged Mr Sunderland?'

'Yes, that's true. It *was* very uncharacteristic of him. He normally keeps his opinions to himself. I suppose his admiration of Miss Bassett got the better of him.'

'Perhaps. Now what precisely did you say to attempt to dissuade him?'

'I said it would be throwing his life away. I asked him if he'd ever even fired a pistol … he not being a gentleman, I thought it unlikely.'

'And?'

'He had never fired a pistol and he thought my question … he thought I was questioning his right to challenge Sunderland, which was not my thought. Actually that does bring to mind one peculiarity of Jenkins. He doesn't quite know his place; and there is a slight resentment of those superior to him. I don't in any way suggest he has revolutionary ideas. I think it is just that he is too busy making money to obey decorum.'

'Ah, thank you Mr Wallace, that is quite helpful. Now, what do you make of his friend, Mr Purcell?'

'Nothing. He is an assistant; I hardly noticed him.'

'That is unfortunate. I had hoped for better from you.' I thought this unfair to Mr Wallace, as did Mrs Fitzhugh, who said, 'Charlotte, I think Mr Wallace has performed admirably.'

Charlotte dismissed us both with her casual disdain and then asked Mr Wallace, 'H'm, can you say at least whether you think this man is loyal to his employer?'

Mr Wallace paused for a second to examine this thought and also to help himself to another biscuit.

'Yes, I think that might be a reasonable way to describe him, a loyal assistant, from the little I saw of the man.'

'And you earlier met Mr Sunderland and his seconds?'

'Ah, now there's an entirely different story. Sunderland's a fine looking sort of gentleman and very affable. He very graciously greeted me. I met him at his home in Queens Street where I found him with his second. I implored him to forgive Jenkins his unfortunate choice of words and reminded him that as a gentleman, he could safely ignore the affront with no stain upon his honour. I also told him that Jenkins had never even fired a pistol before and would probably tremble so much he couldn't even hold it properly.'

'And what did he say?'

'Well, as to the first, he said that as Mr Jenkins had chosen to insult a gentleman he supposed it fair to do him the courtesy of treating him as such, and as to the second, he said that if Mr Jenkins were in no fit state to hold a pistol, he would of course hold fire, and that Mr Jenkins need merely apologize to prevent the duel, but that otherwise he expected to meet him at Claverton Downs.' #

'And as to his mood?'

'As I said, he was very affable and friendly and did not appear concerned as to the outcome.'

For a few seconds Charlotte said nothing before offering, 'It is odd that both men seem unconcerned about the prospects of a duel.'

'Not odd in Sunderland's case,' Mr Wallace replied. 'He proudly shewed me his duelling pistols and said that as he has survived two previous duels he supposed he should survive a third. I suppose his optimism is understandable, especially if the parties agree that honour is satisfied after the first exchange. And that is the damnable thing about duelling. Men think their chances good because rarely is a shot placed in the first exchange and often the parties agree to end it there. But I've seen it end far worse, with someone injured or dead. It would be a fine thing if we could stop this madness.' #

He sat back in his chair after he made this statement and held his cup with both hands as if to wring what warmth he could from it.

'I fear stopping it may not be in our power,' Charlotte said. 'Men can be so bound up in their honour they forget the injuries they inflict may extend beyond themselves.'

She said this with a sadness that made me look at her and again I saw that numbness of her face that I now knew indicated grief, but she quickly recovered her composure to continue her questioning.

'You earlier mentioned Claverton Downs. Is that where he proposes to have this duel?'

'What?' Mr Wallace said with a start after falling into a reverie of his own. 'Yes, although of course it's up to Mr Jenkins as the challenged party to chuse, but that's where this sort of thing is usually done. I suppose I'll have to give him the lay of the land, he not being acquainted with the area.'

'And when do you think this will be?'

'They will probably meet Monday, although it could be as early as Sunday.'

'Sunday? That seems an unsuitable day,' I said.

'It's not unknown, my dear,' Mrs Fitzhugh said. 'I remember quite a few duels fought on a Sunday.'

'Certainly common enough,' Mr Wallace agreed, although his words were difficult to understand as he said them while eating another biscuit. 'You know most people are at church and thus the duel avoids attention.'

'You certainly are very hungry, Mr Wallace. Did no one offer you any refreshment?' Charlotte enquired.

Mr Wallace answered this with a sour look. 'No, they didn't. All I was offered was some very poor port by Mr Sunderland.'

'Then we must find you something to eat before you faint from hunger. It can be your payment for a job well done, which praise I hope satisfies your two admirers.'

MISS CHIVINGTON'S COMPLAINT

The next day found us calling on Miss Chivington at an hour far too early to be considered social, but Charlotte wanted to meet with her before Miss Chivington began her own round of calls. And the information I had provided Charlotte from Mrs La Fontaine convinced her of the importance of meeting with Miss Chivington. Charlotte and I left on this task while Mrs Fitzhugh ran her own errands.

Fortunately we found Miss Chivington at home and the card Charlotte handed the footman resulted in an audience.

'Thank you for seeing me, Miss Chivington.'

'You are very welcome, Miss House. It has been sometime since we last met and I am happy to renew our acquaintance.'

'You were just out when we last met, I think,' Charlotte said, which caused me to wonder again how old she might be. 'I am happy to see how pretty you've become.'

Miss Chivington blushed prettily at Charlotte's praise. 'You are too kind, Miss House. Now, your card said I might help you?'

Charlotte nodded at this and said, 'Yes, I think you are acquainted with a Mr Sunderland?'

'I … I am well acquainted with Mr Sunderland.'

'Are you aware that he is to fight a duel?'

'Oh, when is he not involved in some such stupidity?' She said this with sudden emotion and stood and turned away from us, and for a second it seemed she would leave us, only to slowly return to her seat. 'You will forgive me. Mr Sunderland vexes me greatly.'

After a pause, Charlotte said softly, 'Some would not consider two duels excessive. Some would only think he is a man of honour.'

'Only two fought, but how many times has he narrowly escaped it only by the intervention of wiser heads? And all to defend imagined slights upon his honour.'

Charlotte used the opportunity to join her on the sopha and take her hand.

'No, Miss Chivington, his honour, while an excuse for his umbrage, was not the original cause of this duel. He refused to acknowledge the claims of another man that a certain Miss Bassett is the most beautiful woman there ever was. And I believe he was unable to acknowledge it because he believes another deserves that description.'

Miss Chivington gasped at this. 'This is intolerable! That I should in any way be the cause of this!'

'Your feelings do you credit. But what of your feelings for Mr Sunderland?'

'Why, I have known him all my life. He is a good friend to my family. He is a ...'

'You fail to describe the most salient feelings. What do you feel for him?'

'I ... this is improper, is it not?'

'Please Miss Chivington, do not hold your tongue. Time is of the essence. What are your feelings for him?'

'I would love him, Miss House, were it not for his obstinacy and pride that makes him do unwise things.' She said this with her head held high and with the full force of an earnest declaration, her face betraying her conflicting emotions of love and disapproval. I could have no doubt as to her feelings.

'Have you told him this?'

'Yes, on the several occasions on which he has asked me to marry. And he very recently asked me again, to which I said no for the same reasons.'

'What day was this?'

'Only two days before.'

'What? He proposes to you on Thursday and on Friday he becomes embroiled in a duel?' I asked.

'Oh, do you think he was so upset over my refusal?'

An approving look from Charlotte informed me my question was not inopportune.

'It might seem that way, Miss Chivington,' Charlotte said. 'But you cannot blame yourself.'

'Perhaps if I had ...'

'Stop! You must not think that! His decisions are his own.'

'Oh, I wish he had never returned to Bath!' she cried.

I saw that information surprised Charlotte. 'I was unaware he had been absent. When did he return?'

She replied, 'This Tuesday he arrived from Bristol. He had the most difficult time of it, for his own barouche was unavailable and he travelled by coach, only to have it be damaged in some way and unable to continue the journey.'

'Perhaps that put him in a foul mood and contributed to his taking offence at Mr Jenkins,' I suggested.

'No, he spoke of it laughingly. I admit I was surprised at his attitude and thought it indicated he had taken a more generous view. He even seemed ... I admit I was surprised by the calm with which he took my refusal.'

And a little hurt, I thought ungraciously. She thought she had the power of refusal, but then he refused to be unduly upset. I could see that she was revisiting her last encounter with Mr Sunderland and found myself interested in that as well.

'What did he say, exactly, in response to your refusal?' I asked.

'He merely smiled and said as that was my decision, he would abide by it, and that ... he said he hoped I should never regret it. Oh what have I done!' She clasped her hand to her mouth to cover her emotion and said behind it, 'He will throw his life away!'

'Calm yourself!' I cried, but I also feared this interpretation. I looked to Charlotte for support but I saw her gazing fixedly beyond us and I knew that she was lost in her calculations, undoubtedly also convinced that Mr Sunderland planned to offer himself up in the duel.

'Charlotte,' I said softly. My voice instantly brought her back to the matter at hand and she said, 'Miss Chivington, take heart. It may not be as bleak as you suppose.'

'But I had hoped I might sway him. Now I have gone too far, for I do love him. I know that I complained of his honour and pride, but I failed to mention his compassion and integrity.'

We did our best to console her but I fear we left her in a miserable state, and I confessed my fears to Charlotte as we walked back through the cold streets, our breath clouding as we spoke.

'Your words to Miss Chivington were kind, but I think Mr Sunderland's parting words indicate he may not defend himself in this duel.'

'That may certainly be a valid interpretation, but you may also recall Mr Wallace's testimony that Mr Sunderland did not appear unduly disturbed ... affable was his term I recall.'

'Perhaps he has assumed a certain ... fatalism.'

'Perhaps ... or his parting words were simply a last attempt to elicit sympathy and instil guilt.'

I thought of this possibility as we walked. Perhaps my romanticism *had* got the better of me. Unfortunately my pondering made me oblivious of the cold until my pattens slipped on the now frozen, muddy street, and I would have fallen had not Charlotte caught me. #

'It is getting cold,' I said unnecessarily.

'Yes, I should be happy to be home with our fire and tea, but wait, here is Margaret.'

We had neared the Upper Rooms and found our friend waving at us from across the street and we waited for her to join us.

'It is getting cold,' she told us as she approached us. Her nose and cheeks were bright from her exertion and the weather.

'So Jane informs me. How did your errands go?' Charlotte asked while urging us to continue homeward. Charlotte offered her arm to our friend and then to me and then we three began walking.

'Very successfully. It is as you suspected, Mr Sunderland's

fortunes are diminished, although I have learned that they may improve, and I have further rumours of the untimeliness of his birth.'

'Ah, so those were your errands,' I needlessly added.

'Yes Jane, I sent Margaret to … elicit information from a few selected shopkeepers. It is amazing what a woman *d'un certain âge* and charm can accomplish.' #

Mrs Fitzhugh smiled coquettishly and nodded her head. 'Your turn will come someday, Charlotte, mark my words.'

'I look forward to it. Now what did you learn?'

'Ah, his accounts at his tailor have long gone unpaid but as yet there have been no complaints for it is suspected that he might soon inherit Langton Hall, his family estate.'

'How is that? I thought he was the younger son.'

Mrs Fitzhugh answered, 'He is, but his brother has contracted the same wasting disease that afflicted their father and there is speculation he will soon die. Apparently our Mr Sunderland, George is his given name, little resembles his father or brother. That, and the timing of his birth, gave rise to the speculation that he may not be legitimate.'

'That speculation might end or prove moot once he has inherited,' I said.

'Oh, and I believe he has also economized by the sale of his barouche,' Mrs Fitzhugh added. #

Charlotte remarked, 'Has he? This is all very interesting.'

But I could not understand her thoughts. 'But how? Each discovery seems to contradict. He might be so despondent over his finances and the rejection of his proposal that he plans to offer no defence in the duel, or he might be facing a much better financial future following the tragedy of his brother dying in the same manner as his father.'

'You must learn to think of the whole, Jane,' Charlotte said, chiding me. 'Oh, don't worry, it may come to you yet. But here we are home and not a moment too soon for I am freezing. Let's warm ourselves and wait for Mr Wallace to tell us of the challenge.'

THE GAUNTLET IS THROWN

'As expected, the challenge was delivered at noon and immediately answered. Mr Jenkins has chosen pistols. As he does not own duelling pistols, Mr Sunderland has graciously offered him the use of one of his.'

'How kind of him,' I said.

'And when is it to happen?' Mrs Fitzhugh asked.

'Monday at dawn at Claverton Downs,' he said, resignedly. 'I was able to wring that concession from them, to provide them another day for reflection ... and perhaps for Miss House to find a solution to this problem?'

'I am afraid I have no idea how to avoid this, Mr Wallace. I can only hope that it will end with neither man injured.'

She said this while taking her tea, her whole attention seeming to be on her enjoyment of the warmth of the room, the pleasure of her company and the quality of the brew she sipped. In fact since our return, Charlotte seemed to have dismissed the whole affair as a *fait accompli*. Mrs Fitzhugh and I had discussed little else while Charlotte only offered noncommittal sounds as we awaited Mr Wallace's arrival. Her seeming indifference began to grate on me. #

'Out with it, Charlotte,' I said, 'you know something about this that is not apparent to us.'

She opened her mouth to speak and then stopped. I could almost hear her unspoken words—'When is that not true?'—but obviously thought better of it. Instead she said, 'You know I am loathe to offer a theory, but in this instance, I will say it. I believe this duel to be an invention of Mr Jenkins and Mr Sunderland, and I predict that on Monday both men will fire wide, into the ground, or perhaps not even at all after a reconciliation. In fact, I would not be surprised if the extra day Mr Wallace has skilfully provided will be credited as the reason for the reconciliation.' #

We looked at her in amazement and she smiled back at us with satisfaction. Infuriating woman!

'What!' Mr Wallace cried. 'I cannot credit it. Perhaps Mr Jenkins might stoop to such a tactic, for he is not a gentleman, but surely Mr Sunderland ...'

'For that same reasoning, it is most likely Mr Sunderland whose plan this is,' answered Charlotte, 'for it is not likely that Mr Jenkins should know the forms of duelling.'

'But to what ends?' Mrs Fitzhugh asked, as equally alarmed as Mr Wallace. 'How do they profit from this?'

In a flash, I saw it all. I comprehended the whole, or at least a major portion of it. 'Mr Jenkins proves his ardour for Miss Bassett!'

'Very good Jane. Yes, he proves to her the lengths he will go to win her favour. You heard her opinion of him improve, did you not? And Mr Jenkins also has the benefit of improving his station, although whether that was part of his calculations ... no, surely Mr Sunderland used it in his argument.'

'I am afraid I do not understand,' I said.

But Mr Wallace cleared his throat and said, 'Perhaps I can explain?' Charlotte nodded and he continued, 'If Mr Jenkins finds himself in a duel with a gentleman, he is elevated, if ever so slightly, to that status. Mr Sunderland could have refused to be insulted, but he chose to challenge. And if nothing else, it certainly makes Mr Jenkins a more interesting man. But I still do not see your reasoning, Miss House. How do you know this to be true?'

Charlotte rose and moved behind her chair, placing her hands upon its back. I had noticed my friend had a disposition to walk when expounding her brilliance.

'You would have me reveal all my mysteries and expose my reasoning as mere pedestrian good sense? Very well, let us examine some of the absurd coincidences: First, two men who appear unacquainted, of differing stations, find themselves in a duel. But are they unacquainted? They both arrive in Bath on Tuesday by coach, a coach delayed by several hours. Could it be that they become acquainted on that coach?

'Second, Mr Sunderland proposes and is rejected on Thursday and on Friday is insulted by Mr Jenkins. Third, Mr Jenkins, normally a quiet man by Mr Wallace's description, loudly boasts of Miss Bassett's virtue at a coffeehouse he has insisted they visit, where Mr Sunderland awaits. And finally, rather than issue a challenge on Friday, they wait until Saturday and delay until Monday, giving them opportunity to say that tempers have cooled.'

'But they resisted my ...' Mr Wallace began and then stopped.

'They perhaps offered token resistance to your suggestion of delaying the duel until Monday?'

'I suppose it might be construed that way, Miss House,' he admitted.

Mrs Fitzhugh, who had been quiet and obviously thinking of the implications of Charlotte's theory, now objected. 'I will grant you that Mr Jenkins might benefit from this duel, but how will Mr Sunderland benefit? Did you not say Miss ... oh, what is her name ... Miss Chivington despaired of his behaviour? She cannot look kindly on his challenge.'

'I admit his goals to be more difficult to fathom, but I suggest they include both money and an excuse. Remember, he can claim he was forced into this duel because he could not allow another woman to be claimed fairer than Miss Chivington. Oh, she might call such action "intolerable," but on consideration, I think it cannot fail to impress. And then when he either fires wide or, even more likely as I think on it, forgives Mr Jenkins his accusation, I think he will rise in her opinion. Why, he may even claim his duelling days are over; especially if as suspected he inherits his father's estate and becomes the squire of the county.'

For a half minute, we digested this, then Mrs Fitzhugh asked, 'You also mentioned money.'

'Yes, as to the motivation for that, you yourself provided the information. His excuse that his barouche was unavailable is exposed as a lie, as you discovered he had sold it. And you also tell us of his outstanding bills and Mr Wallace remarked of his indifferent port. So I think it possible that Mr Jenkins will pay Mr Sunderland for the privilege of duelling with him—or rather of not duelling with him.'

'That is outrageous!' Mr Wallace said.

'What, more outrageous than the stupidity of duelling?' Charlotte countered.

'Yes,' he said after a moment's reflection, but then smiled. 'I concede your point, but … wait, I have been used in this, haven't I?'

Charlotte laughed. 'I very much fear you have been used. I don't know whether Mr Jenkins's loyal assistant or Mr Sunderland's close friend are party to this, but I think they also wanted a man of unimpeachable character to be witness to the proceedings, and so they conspired to include you in the party.'

I noticed Mr Wallace straighten as he was described as a man of unimpeachable character. 'I think much of this drama has been staged for your benefit. They hope that you will tell of their determination to duel and also of their coming to their good senses. Mr Sunderland especially hopes that you will speak of his Damascus moment when he realizes the futility of duelling. Why, he may even ask you to represent his changed opinion to Miss Chivington.' #

'That I will not do!'

'Why not?' I asked. 'You called duelling an insanity. And these men will not actually fight. In fact, they will show themselves reasonable, compassionate men by refusing to fight.'

'Yes, but it is not honourable, and I will not be used in this way. And I shall say so.'

'That is of course your prerogative,' Charlotte said, 'but consider that this is my theory and that I may be incorrect in some of my suppositions or even all. And if you publicly denounce them and I am incorrect, *you* may find yourself answering a challenge.'

At this Mr Wallace smiled but before he could say anything, Charlotte continued. 'But as a favour to me, I would ask that you continue to act as Mr Jenkins's second. It would reassure me that someone on whom I can depend is there should my suppositions prove wrong.'

He laughed and said, 'Well then, Miss House, you may depend on me … if as you say, you have supposed wrong.'

Charlotte invited Mr Wallace to dine with us, for which he was grateful. He told us of the various preparations he had undertaken for the duel, although he now admitted to chagrin if it were all to prove a deception. He had found a surgeon, a friend, to attend to the participants should there be injuries—'I had thought it odd that they had given no thought to this but now I see how suspicious is the oversight'—and he had also arranged carriages to take his party to the duelling ground.

Over dinner, however, we forgot the drama of Mr Jenkins and Mr Sunderland and instead talked of everything and anything other than younger sons and compromising letters and ill-conceived marriages. Mr Wallace told of his childhood adventures when he fancied himself a pirate and how he had taken his drawing-room from the Spanish forces represented by his older brother and younger sister.

Charlotte confessed she had done much the same with her

brother Michael, and I offered stories of running far too wild as an Indian of the American forest. We all laughed and I felt especially happy that my friends esteemed my Mr Wallace. It was with reluctance that we bid him farewell at the door.

'I must go, for the snow has started,' he said, and I looked out our front door and saw that indeed snow was softly falling. My friends stood with me by the front door and we all bade him be careful on his walk home.

That night as I prepared for bed, I thought of what had happened. Despite my unfounded misgivings as to London, I had come to feel at home with Charlotte and dear Mrs Fitzhugh, but now my thoughts also included notions of a life with Mr Wallace. It was madness to think it, of course, for my fortune consisted of what few clothes I had, soon to be supplemented by three dresses, and the £100 a year left me by our uncle, which amount I shared with my sister.

Mr Wallace might return to the regiment, especially as hostilities with France had resumed, but until then, he was of limited means. But I did not relish the idea of him in harm's way. Whatever his decision, however, a separation between us seemed inevitable, for he would either leave Bath—the city having a surfeit of doctors—or for the regiment.

And I would surely … and then a stab of panic as I thought of my future. Would I return to London with Charlotte? If she did not intend for me to travel with her, then she would have urged me to seek employment, I reasoned. After all, had I the recommendation of Charlotte House I could certainly find a position.

As I pulled aside the covers and slipped into bed, I resolved to ask Charlotte to-morrow if I were to accompany her and despite my worries, fell quickly asleep.

❦

'Jane, wake up!' Mrs Fitzhugh said. I opened my eyes not to the dawn but the pitch black of night and the feeling I had only been asleep an hour.

'What time is it?'

'It is just gone three. But you must wake now! The duel is to-day.'

I looked at my friend with alarm for I had surely not slept a whole day. More likely it was that she was mistaken as to the day; perhaps she suffered from a confusion of the womb that befalls women of a certain age. I recalled my Aunt Jennings, who would swear it was day when it was night and hot when it was cold.

'The duel is Monday and this is surely Sunday,' I said, after taking her hand in mine and stroking it in a calming fashion.

But she snatched back her hand and said, 'No, it is to-day. Your Mr Wallace has sent us a note. Come downstairs as soon as you're able.'

She left the room taking with her the candle, and so I stumbled in the dark to find my dressing gown. After cursing my barked shin I escaped my bedroom and ran downstairs. I found the drawing-room occupied by Charlotte and Mrs Fitzhugh, similarly clad in dressing gowns, addressing Robert, who failed to conceal a yawn.

'Have the carriage readied and find the horses however you must,' she commanded. He bustled out and she turned to me.

'Mr Wallace has surprised us with this information,' she said, handing me a note.

Miss House,

I am sorry for this late information, but I have only just learned that Mr Jenkins and Mr Sunderland have decided to hold their 'contest' to-morrow. I must hurry and inform my friend of this change and see to our carriage. I fear this change has some bearing on your theory for I cannot see the reason for it. But I shall know the truth of it in a few scant hours at dawn.

> *Your servant,*
> *John Wallace*

I looked to Charlotte and now noticed her worry. 'When was this delivered?'

'Not long ago, a quarter of an hour previous perhaps,' she said, but then with one of her quick smiles that left no trace, 'and delivered by one of our own emissaries. Mr Wallace has learned how to contact and use them.'

'And what can it mean? How do you explain this change of plans?' I asked. Mrs Fitzhugh laid her hand on my arm and I realized then that Charlotte had no explanation.

'I think it best if we endeavour to arrive at Claverton Downs before the two parties,' Charlotte said, ignoring my question. 'I am sorry; I should ask before assuming you will join me in a mad dash to witness a duel.'

'Of course I will come,' I said, 'you know you need not ask.'

'Stout Jane. Where would I be without you at my side? But then we must prepare for a cold ride and a long wait in the snow. And I think you will need to bring your country shoes.'

PISTOLS AT DAWN

'It is remarkably cold,' I said through my clenched but chattering teeth. Our footsteps were muffled as we walked through the soft snow that covered the withered grass. We were quite alone, our carriage having deposited us and left us further down the road. The slight hiss of the falling snow contrarily made the empty downs seem preternaturally quiet, adding to the sense of isolation.

'Nonsense, Jane,' Charlotte said, but her red cheeks, blue lips and … could it be that for once her impeccable posture was disfigured into a hunched attitude? … betrayed her true feelings. 'Well, perhaps it is cold, but it does no good to complain of it.'

We were walking to the place where Mr Wallace had earlier explained the principals would be meeting. We were well ahead of the appointed time, owing to Robert's success at quickly obtaining the horses for our carriage and Charlotte's worry that we might arrive too late. She had the driver send the carriage at mad speed along the road, the frozen ruts jostling us so that I felt a little ill and gladly exchanged the interior of the carriage for the crisp air.

However a mere few minutes walking had chilled me to the bone, while Charlotte struggled in the pre-dawn light to find us the place of concealment Mr Wallace had suggested.

'Why must they meet at dawn?'

'I believe you know the answer. To attract the least attention, although I believe they are also eager to limit the possibility of injury by firing in the indistinct light.'

'Not shooting each other at all would be the surest way of limiting the possibility of injury.'

'Oh, so you no longer find the prospect of duelling so romantic.'

'I can find nothing of romance at this hour of the morning. And why did they need to come so far?'

'Jane, you did not have to come.'

'Of course I did, I … I thought I heard a sound.'

'Quick, behind this tree,' Charlotte commanded.

We soon heard and then saw a carriage arrive and drive

unsteadily onto the down, and presently emerged several men who were hard to distinguish in the dim light.

'I think they might be Mr Jenkins's party. Yes, I see Mr Wallace!'

'Hush Jane, or they will discover us. In fact, they *will* discover us if we remain here. We need a better covert.' Charlotte led us to the safety of a thicker screen of trees, and we must have been easily spotted but for the fact the men were engaged in surveying the ground directly before them. Once we were safely concealed, we could observe their actions more easily. We also took the opportunity to wrap tightly our mufflers about our faces, throw a rug from the carriage about us and stand with an arm behind each other's back.

'What are they doing?' I asked Charlotte, slightly improved by the warmth of the rug and the closeness of our bodies.

'I believe they are ascertaining the boundaries of the duelling square. Ah, and I think Mr Wallace is pointing where the sun will rise. I believe by good fortune we have found the spot Mr Wallace had suggested.' #

I could now see two of the men walking stiffly across the ground, for the purposes of marking out the distance of twenty paces.

'It seems premature until Mr Sunderland arrives,' I said.

'I believe a good general wants to know the lay of the land before his opponent's arrival. Mr Wallace knows this and would give his champion any fair advantage, although that is perhaps an inappropriate term to use in this situation.'

'You continue in your belief this is a ruse? You seemed worried earlier.'

'I confess this rush had me concerned but I have since thought of several reasons why it might have been necessary and besides, we have no options.'

'Well then, not that I am complaining, but why are we here if we can do nothing?'

'Please keep your voice down, Jane,' she commanded in a voice that I thought louder than my own. Then in a softer voice, she said, 'It is often instructive to see how my theories and suppositions fare against actual events. And perhaps if I sense I am wrong we might … Ah, that must be Mr Jenkins. He is pulling from his flask. Oh, that is an unwise thing to do. But now your Mr Wallace intervenes and has put a stop to it. I must say he impresses me more and more. And I think it increasingly obvious he knows far more of duelling than he would allow. What is that?'

Another carriage arrived and this time it delivered Mr Sunderland's party. I had to guess the tallest individual to be Mr Sunderland, based on Mr Wallace's description. But he was so heavily protected from the cold by a thick muffler that I saw little of his face.

The light was growing stronger now and I could identify most of the participants as the two principals and their seconds, but I could not imagine the purpose of the smallest gentleman, who arrived with Mr Sunderland.

'Who would the small man be, Charlotte?'

'What? Oh most likely an impartial third party to announce the call to fire. I believe we are still missing Mr Wallace's friend, the surgeon.'

The men were now making their greetings and the principals were offering hands, which I briefly hoped meant a reconciliation, but apparently it was merely the meeting of equals bent upon their mutual destruction. It struck me quite forcibly how foolish this was, despite my earlier admiration.

After the introductions were completed, both parties surveyed the down and after some conversation, the duelling square was properly laid out with planted sticks marking the corners. Apparently the principals would stand so that neither would be staring directly at the rising sun, or so I assumed from the two men walking to the two opposite sides of the square and from the seconds pointing where the sun would rise … in fact had begun to rise. More handshakes were exchanged after this; a very proper and civilized way of killing each other to be sure.

Now the men reassembled by the carriage and again flasks were produced, but Mr Wallace was able to dissuade the principals from partaking. Much stamping of feet and slapping of arms was also involved, and I wished I might do the same but for the fear of calling attention to us.

Another ten minutes passed and the sun was high enough now to send long shadows across the down. Finally another carriage arrived bearing two men who again were greeted by all with a good deal of attendant handshakes and bows and again offered flasks.

I began to wish, guiltily, that they might begin. After all, I did not wish to be one of the casualties by succumbing to the cold. Apparently the same thought occurred to the men, and with some more pleasantries and bowing and shaking of hands they walked out to the duelling square.

I noticed that Mr Wallace carried a box, which I took to be the case for the pistols, which surmise proved correct when the box was opened and examined by all the seconds.

The weapons were also exchanged and all this took some time. I imagined some of the conversation included praise of the quality of the weapons. Finally, the process began of loading the weapons and at this stage Mr Sunderland left his group to stand with his arm resting on a tree for support. His head was bent down and I saw him drink from a flask.

'Mr Sunderland seems very unsettled,' I said, 'but perhaps he is acting the reluctant duellist to give credit to his change of heart.'

Charlotte replied, 'Then he is certainly a gifted actor, and we must give Mr Jenkins credit as well, for he also walks about in a daze, and they are both too fond of their flasks.'

I looked to Mr Jenkins after Charlotte said this and saw that he did seem distressed, holding his hand to his heart and appearing to be in some pain. To my eye, he looked as someone experiencing remorse as to what was to happen shortly.

And then I heard the short man yell, 'Gentleman, if I may have your attention?'

The party assembled in the middle of the duelling square. After that first loud remark I could not hear any conversation, but I knew the duel was about to begin from the serious aspect of the proceedings and finally the stiff bows Mr Jenkins and Mr Sunderland exchanged.

The brace of pistols was presented and the two men chose their weapons. The short man then commanded them to take their positions, which they did, a mere twelve paces apart, and then turned to face one another, but with their pistols pointed at the ground. The short man then raised his hand.

'They will fire wide,' Charlotte said, almost as a prayer.

The short man dropped his hand and yelled 'Fire!' upon which the two men raised their weapons ... and pointedly fired at one another almost in unison. On the open down, with the softly falling snow, the sound was not as devastating as I had expected, but the sight of the two men falling backward has surely scarred itself upon my memory.

Mr Jenkins seemed merely to fall backward, his arms flung wide, while Mr Sunderland's hands flew toward his head, releasing his hold of his pistol, which went flying, as did the length of his muffler.

Despite our distance, I could see the look of horror on the faces of the men gathered as if I were one of their party. Mr Wallace was the most distressed of all and I saw him looking to our place of concealment. It was then that I noticed my friend standing next to me and I saw on her face a similar look of horror. I stood to join her and that movement broke her stillness and she began to run to the duelling ground.

My Particular Friend

As it made no sense to remain behind after Charlotte had revealed herself, I rushed to join her but her run slowed to a fast walk after a few steps. I saw her wrap her muffler tighter about her face, which I imitated. Mr Wallace, seeing us emerge from the copse, took a few steps toward us, but then thought better of it, turned back and rushed to Mr Jenkins. We soon stood but a slight distance away from Mr Wallace and the principal second Mr Purcell.

I saw Mr Wallace struggle with Mr Jenkins's greatcoat and also saw Mr Jenkins move his hand over his heart as I had seen him do earlier.

'He is alive!' I cried. Both my cry and Mr Jenkins sitting upright in the snow so completely surprised Mr Wallace that he stumbled and fell back into the snow.

Mine was not the only outcry and it would be improper were I to repeat some of what was uttered, but I completely understood the emotion that produced those remarks. Mr Jenkins was now standing, although helped by Mr Purcell, and Mr Wallace had returned to trying to find his wound. I saw him reach inside the greatcoat, palm down as if to check for blood, but when he withdrew his hand he held ... the silver flask from which Mr Jenkins had earlier been drinking, but now its shape was contorted by the impact of a bullet.

'My God, Jenkins, you're lucky to be alive,' Mr Purcell said.

Mr Wallace continued searching for any injury, ripping away at his clothing with a penknife. I should have looked away, but my curiosity would not allow it. Finally Mr Jenkins's chest was revealed to show angry red flesh, but clearly not pierced by a bullet.

I looked to my friend and expected to see the same surprise on her face, but instead I only saw a vast smile.

'Come Jane, let's see how Mr Sunderland has fared,' she said to me quietly, and led me to the other group. We found

Mr Arkwright, the surgeon and the short man hovering over the supine form of Mr Sunderland, but we also heard that gentleman's voice saying, 'Help me up, please.'

As he stood, his face, no longer concealed by a muffler, shewed a terrible red line of burned flesh across his left cheek. Mr Sunderland raised his hand to touch it but the surgeon stopped him and examined the wound. I shuddered to think of Mr Jenkins's bullet so nearly killing him.

But I did not wonder long before I felt Charlotte's hand upon my arm.

'We must leave before questions are asked,' she said softly but forcefully. I would have liked to stay and marvel at the Providence that had spared these men but I followed my friend, who made directly for the road. Despite her haste, however, she stopped to bend down and retrieve something from the ground. As I passed the spot where she had knelt, I saw the case that had held the duelling pistols, its remaining contents—a powder flask, ramrod and cleaning supplies— spilled on the ground where they had fallen during the excitement.

Once past the carriages we were soon out of the sight of the party. I marvelled that neither our presence nor departure had been remarked upon. We then made our way to the road and walked perhaps a quarter mile until we found our carriage waiting to take us home.

Explanations

Upon our return, Charlotte immediately despatched five messages. Two of the messages were sent to Miss Bassett and Miss Chivington, two to Mr Jenkins and Mr Sunderland and the last to Mr Wallace.

Of course, we also had to inform Mrs Fitzhugh of all that

had happened, but only after a substantial meal and hot drink. I was telling her of the moment when both men fired and then flew backward. The gasp she produced informed me as to my skill at telling tales.

'I was horrified at what had happened, and so was Charlotte. She even stood and gave away our concealment.'

'That was unwise,' Mrs Fitzhugh said, looking at Charlotte.

'I admit I was momentarily alarmed,' Charlotte said, 'and my reaction was made more severe by the thought that my reasoning had proved faulty. Fortunately it was not, merely my appreciation for the extent that the gentlemen would go was insufficient.'

'But surely your reasoning was at fault,' I said. 'They neither fired dumb nor announced a reconciliation. Instead they took aim at one another and only a kind Providence ...'

'Oh, please Jane, it was nothing of the sort. It was all staged so skilfully that even I was deceived, and I must credit Mr Sunderland's ingenuity. He may now retire from the field honourably, and with the scar to prove how far he has gone to defend his good name.'

'You mean Mr Sunderland deliberately shot Mr Jenkins where he was protected by his flask and Mr Jenkins ...' but I could not complete my statement for it sounded hopelessly impossible.

'Don't be facetious, Jane, no one could be so good a shot with a pistol, and surely Mr Jenkins is not so good a shot as to merely graze Mr Sunderland's cheek. I think you will find the solution here.' #

She stood and with a look of absolute triumph reached her hand into a pocket and ...

'Oh, they are in the other pocket,' she said, sheepishly. She then reached into her other pocket and extending her hand produced three small balls upon it.

'Those are pistol balls?' Mrs Fitzhugh asked.

'Yes, I …'

'You took those from the ground as we were leaving,' I said.

Charlotte looked annoyed at my interruption and perhaps her failure at producing the desired dramatic effect, and said, 'Just so. And these are the proof of their subterfuge.' She said the last with some drama.

'They look like ordinary pistol balls,' Mrs Fitzhugh said.

'Then take them, Margaret.'

She took the balls from Charlotte and weighed them in her hands. 'They are curiously light,' she remarked and then handed them to me. The balls were indeed very light.

'Of what are these made?' I asked.

'I think they are made of dried clay and then wrapped in lead leaf. See where I have scraped one?'

I examined them and saw that one indeed displayed a dark brown colour underneath a thin lead covering.

'Oh, I see,' I said.

'I do not understand,' Mrs Fitzhugh said.

'These balls are harmless,' Charlotte explained. 'They have not been fired and will turn to powder once … uh, fired.' She smiled at the double meanings of the word.

'But how could they hope to maintain this deception? Surely the seconds …' I said, about to accuse the seconds of complicity, but then remembered that Charlotte had earlier suggested their involvement.

'Yes, Mr Sunderland's second is surely a party to this, although Mr Purcell need not be so. Mr Arkwright loaded the pistols and affirmed everything was proper and Mr Purcell may have took him at his word. The balls look realistic enough to have fooled anyone who had not handled them.' #

'But how was this accomplished? If the balls are harmless, how can you explain their injuries?' Mrs Fitzhugh asked, understandably confused. As she asked her question, however, my mind raced as I thought of the earlier proceedings.

'It was prepared in advance. Mr Sunderland's face was quite concealed by his muffler. A hot poker?' I suggested.

'That is my thought,' Charlotte confirmed. 'It would take some nerve and likely the cooperation of Mr Arkwright to produce the desired effect, although I suspect that the effect produced was more severe than the one desired. And you will recall Mr Jenkins walking about stiffly? I think he must have received a sharp blow in advance to have produced that amount of bruising. They must have been in great pain all the while … ah ha! which might explain their fondness for their flasks.'

☙

The rest of that day we had hoped for a call from Mr Wallace to inform us of the outcome of the morning's events, but he never visited. However the next day we received our first two callers.

Charlotte made them acquainted: 'Miss Bassett, may I introduce Miss Chivington. Miss Bassett is the friend of Mr Jenkins, who …'

'I now have the honour to be his betrothed,' Miss Bassett said, her eyes downcast in modesty.

'Ah, I see. Well then, Miss Chivington is the friend of …'

'I … I also have entered into a promise of marriage, to Mr Sunderland,' that lady said.

Charlotte gave them both her quick grimace of a smile. 'Then felicitations to you both. Please, let us all sit and you may tell of the changed opinions that have led you to this happy state.'

We all sat; Mrs Fitzhugh and I shared the sopha a little apart from Charlotte and the two women. I felt, I think we both felt, as if we were watching a play. By unspoken agreement, we remained quiet, content to let Charlotte act alone.

But both women also remained silent and so Charlotte prompted them.

'Miss Chivington, your new opinion puzzles me most. I had thought you quite hardened to Mr Sunderland.'

She played with the linen she held in her hand for a moment before answering. 'He has forever foresworn duelling, Miss House, and he is heartily sorry for the injury he has caused Mr Jenkins. I think him to be a changed man.'

'I presume then you have called on him.'

'Immediately after receiving your letter. I saw him, so horribly marked upon his face and it was as you said, Miss House. He could not call Miss … he could not agree with the claim that precipitated the duel, for he thought …'

'There is no need to further elaborate,' Charlotte said. 'But what assures you he is a new man?'

'From his words. He said that almost killing a man and almost dying himself have impressed on him the stupidity of his actions. He actually called it stupidity. And he said that were a man to take a wife, he must assume new responsibilities, especially now that he is to be the master of Langton Hall.'

'Oh, I am sorry to hear of the death of his older brother. When did this news reach him?'

'Just Saturday. He is to leave to-morrow for home, for he must console his mother.'

'And now to you, Miss Bassett. May I assume Mr Jenkins has convinced you of his ardour?'

'You shame me, Miss House, but I deserve your scorn. Yes, how can I refuse a man who would risk all for me?'

'Well perhaps not quite all,' she said, and then shewed them the pistol balls. She explained their purpose, and Mrs Fitzhugh and I watched as the two women shewed confusion, surprise and then outrage. I must have shown some surprise as well, for I did not anticipate Charlotte revealing to them the subterfuge.

'How dare they attempt this callous trick!' Miss Chivington exclaimed.

'Calm yourself, my dear,' Charlotte said, 'and you too, Miss Bassett,' she amended upon seeing her about to speak. 'Let us please consider the motivations of these two men and see if their actions can be considered honourable.'

Good luck with that, I thought.

'We begin with Mr Sunderland. You had repeatedly refused him, so he thought he must find a way to prove his love for you and retire from the relentless defence of his honour. By appearing to have nearly killed his opponent and almost dying himself, he can show the world—*as you had just stated*—that he has the integrity of a gentleman, and by foreswearing duelling forever, he can now claim wisdom as well. And do not forget that he was also willing to endure the pain of a red hot poker applied to his face.'

She said this last with such drama that Miss Chivington put her hand to her mouth.

'And now we turn to Miss Bassett, who now realizes her love for Mr Jenkins, stripped of any prejudice against his birth or his station. A man who has shown his passion for her—for he must be passionate to have endured the beating that explains the bruises upon his chest. You have both rejected honourable men, who have gone to this extreme to prove their worthiness.'

Neither woman agreed to this assessment, but they both seemed to be weighing her words. Finally Miss Chivington said, 'But why tell us this?'

'Because you were deceived and I think a marriage should not begin with a lie. You deserve to know what your future husbands will do for you, and what they will *not* do for you.

I would urge you, however, to keep secret your knowledge of their subterfuge. Allow them the satisfaction of their guile and cunning; men's opinions of themselves are such fragile things. Someday you may chuse to tell them you know, perhaps someday when that knowledge may be to your advantage.'

The two women left us rather subdued, and I confronted Charlotte about revealing all.

'Why Charlotte, why would you risk their happiness?'

'Better to risk it now than learn of it later.'

'But how will they learn of it? You will not speak of it, I am sure, and if you suspect me …'

'I suspect no one. But fundamentally, I do not wish them to be deceived. If their love can win out over their pride, then there shall be a marriage. It is for them to decide. And besides, *you* did not object.'

I would argue it further but then it was announced that Mr Wallace had arrived. He came in and immediately Mrs Fitzhugh and I plied him with questions as to the particulars of the previous morning.

'Mr Sunderland was the most grievously injured. I've never seen a bullet leave a mark like that; it looked more like someone had laid a hot poker upon his face. And Mr Jenkins has broken a rib. I'm afraid this has put paid to your theory, Miss House.'

It was then that Charlotte again produced the bullets—she was getting quite good at the dramatic reveal—and explained what had really happened. Again I watched the display of confusion, surprise and then outrage, and it was all Charlotte could do to stop him from running into the street and damning the two at the top of his lungs.

'Please sir, if you will not comport yourself as a gentleman ought …'

'You accuse me of not acting as a gentleman, and yet you condone this outrage.'

'I do not condone it, but it is done and no harm has resulted.'

'No harm! Mr Jenkins has a broken rib and Mr Sunderland has been horribly scarred.'

'Then let that be their lesson, sir. Would you deny them their happiness?'

That question stopped his tirade for a moment. 'You would put it on me?'

'Since you seem to be the arbiter of decency and correct behaviour, yes.'

'They did what they did for love, Mr Wallace,' I said. 'Surely towards that end, much can be forgiven.'

He looked at me surprised, so focused was he on his argument with Charlotte.

'After all, you withdrew your objection when you thought they were to shoot wide,' Mrs Fitzhugh reminded him.

'I merely postponed my objections when I was reminded it was all theory, but now that I have proof of their deception I am unwilling to forgive,' he said, but the force of his words had abated.

'Please Mr Wallace, you hold it in your hands to deny happiness to two couples,' Charlotte said, ignoring her own efforts toward that end.

He looked at us in turn and saw three pairs of eyes pleading with him.

'Oh, damn it, this is most unfair. You outnumber me.'

And thus we knew we had engaged his silence, a silence that was soon to be tested for Robert announced the arrival of Mr Jenkins and Mr Sunderland.

The two gentlemen just announced eyed each other warily. Were it not for the evidence of the clay bullets, I should have thought the duel real enough, for they played perfectly the parts of two men who had recently contested each other.

'Miss House? What is the meaning of this?' Mr Sunderland asked my friend without the courtesy of exchanging greetings.

'It will be evident shortly, Mr Sunderland,' Charlotte said, with the hauteur of nobility allowing the peasants to petition their betters. 'Thank you for coming.'

'Do I know you, madame?' Mr Jenkins asked, 'you look familiar to me.' But he fortunately knew his manners. 'Forgive me the impertinence,' he said, offered a good bow, and then added, 'allow me to introduce myself …'

'We are familiar with you, Mr Jenkins,' Charlotte said, and then introduced each of us. 'And you are already friends with Mr Wallace.'

After Charlotte bid everyone sit, she said, 'Perhaps I should explain, Mr Jenkins, that Miss Bassett had asked my help in preventing the duel you have just fought with Mr Sunderland.'

'And may I ask, who are you to meddle in such matters? I do not believe we are acquainted, other than through our mutual acquaintance in Mr Wallace.'

'Who I am does not matter, for I was unable to find any way to prevent your duel, and it further does not matter, for that duel was a farce.'

I prepared myself for the inevitable outrage of such a statement. I admit that this affair had taxed my patience and I little wanted to again endure the cycle of confusion, surprise and anger. I wanted to shout, 'We have the clay bullets. All is revealed. We know you laid a poker across your face. We know you took a beating to pretend you'd been shot. We know you met on the coach from Bristol. We know the women you love have repeatedly rejected your proposals!'

But instead I waited, with a frown on my lips, as Charlotte produced the bullets and explained their significance and Mr Wallace, unable to restrain himself, denounced the men as scoundrels. I sat silent during all this until Mr Jenkins, during the midst of his response to Mr Wallace, suddenly said to me, 'You were there, on the downs! And you as well.' The last was addressed to Charlotte.

The accusation surprised me and I did not know whether to confirm or deny. I looked to Charlotte.

'Yes, Mr Jenkins, that is how we know what had happened yesterday. We have kept a very close eye on your activities and you might think on that.'

'You threaten us with exposure?' Mr Sunderland asked, fear now overriding his anger.

'I do, if you do not treat your future wives with the respect they deserve, and I caution you especially, Mr Sunderland, if you do not forever foreswear duelling.'

This demand he had not expected and both he and Mr Jenkins clamoured for an explanation.

'If you will be quiet, I will explain,' she said softly but firmly, and then stood to address them. The weak winter sun caught the side of her face and the light, combined with her height and manner, commanded their attention. After the men had subsided, she continued: 'I understand the reasons for what you did. You both wanted to sway the women you loved and for that reason, I am willing to overlook—*we* are willing to overlook—your transgressions.

'But even though your actions were calculated not to risk life, your plan was ill conceived and reckless. I can understand, Mr Sunderland, your need to defend your honour, but I hope the scar you bear will serve as a reminder of your folly. And Mr Jenkins, I hope you will understand that being a gentleman is what you are, not what others perceive you to be.

'You should also know that I have revealed your deception to Miss Bassett and Miss Chivington—please remain silent!—with the admonition that they not reveal their knowledge to you. I do not know whether their love can overcome their outrage at being deceived. If their love is the stronger and you do wed, then I trust you will honour them as they deserve. And know further that if you misbehave and they do not chuse to wield their knowledge of your duplicity, then *I* can certainly do so.'

After this address, Mr Jenkins and Mr Sunderland were completely chastened and understandably confused. They offered little further objections and in a few minutes were gone. Shortly afterward, Mr Wallace left as well. I think he left still upset at the behaviour of the two men and still upset at Charlotte's request of him. I too was upset.

'You are troubled, Jane,' Charlotte said to me after we were again alone.

'I still cannot understand why you felt it was necessary to threaten those men and further to reveal to them that their future wives will know their secret.'

'I must have my little fun. Oh, do not look so disapproving. Marriage is a delicate balance; neither side can have the advantage. I certainly take no side in these matches and I cannot say these will be happy marriages. There may be genuine love here, but there is certainly a surfeit of selfishness, vanity and self-serving.'

'But the women …'

'The women have almost as much guilt as the men. They have coyly played with the affections of Mr Jenkins and Mr Sunderland because they think that is the only power they have and that it disappears once they are married. I give them a sense of power that survives the wedding night and I give the men fair warning of that power. If the marriages proceed despite my machinations, then they may deserve one another.'

Her words—'deserve one another'—hung in the air. The winter light that had earlier illumined Charlotte's face was now gone and the room was sunk in darkness. In all my time with my friend, I had always thought her motivation for what she did was the joining of like minds and like hearts, but now I realised that her equations of love still worked even when used with lesser values.

'It is all so calculating,' I said.

She did not dispute this and merely nodded and for a space we sat quietly. Then Charlotte said, 'Are you not late for Mrs La Fontaine?'

'Oh my, yes I am. She will be horribly displeased,' I said.

'I should hate to face her ire,' Charlotte said, 'and therefore I shall go with you to blunt her anger and we shall take Mrs Fitzhugh. I am very eager to see her efforts, as I do wish you to look presentable in London. I still can't believe that you have never been.'

You can imagine my feelings as I heard this first confirmation of my accompanying Charlotte. 'I am to go to London?'

'Of course, Jane. And as your plans to have your sister visit us here have never been realised, I have taken the liberty of asking your sister to join us in London. Now let me inform Margaret of our visit to Mrs La Fontaine.'

Charlotte sprang up and left the room and I could hear her bellowing our friend's name up the stairs while I remained alone in the drawing-room. The sudden release of my worries left me quite exhausted and the news that I was to go to London and see my darling sister had me overjoyed. The crash of these two emotions could only lead to one outcome and so for the next few minutes, I happily wept in the silence of the now dark room.

The End of the Affair

A se'ennight later saw us ready to leave for London. The preparations for our leave taking had left me eager for our remove, but now that the day was approaching I realized with what sadness I would be leaving No. 1 Royal Crescent. I had come to Bath under a heavy cloud, feeling friendless and unworthy of friendship. Now I was leaving here for my first ever visit to London with two fast friends. Even all the servants save for Alice would eventually join us, for Charlotte would not lightly give up servants she could trust. #

Our leave taking also included visits to Miss Bassett and Miss Chivington after word of their engagements became public, although neither woman received us warmly. Perhaps they resented Charlotte for placing on them the burden of their knowledge of the duel. But for me, this last business helped me to break my last ties to Bath until our return next season.

And how I warmed to the reassurance of predicting my return. My only sadness was my taking leave of Mr Wallace, but even that was alleviated by his reassurance that he would visit me in London shortly.

The day before we were to leave I was finishing my journals before placing them in the strongbox, where they would remain until our arrival in London. I had just concluded the details of our visits to the two ladies and my last meeting with Mr Wallace. I was about to put my journal away when I returned to those notes I'd written describing the sadness I observed in Charlotte. I also thought of Mrs Fitzhugh's advice to apply Charlotte's methods.

I recalled the number of times when Charlotte had seemed struck by sadness. It was difficult to recall precisely, especially from the time before I had begun my journal, because Charlotte's manner often could turn grave and then happy in the wink of an eye. But without a doubt there were several occasions when she would allow sadness to overtake her and then almost forcibly throw it off. And I reflected of her disinterest in any man.

I was also taken by her look of horror when she thought the duel not a sham and unconsciously I said to myself, 'She has lost someone she loved to a duel.'

But my words were overheard.

'You are correct, Jane. I lost my heart to the man I loved and then I lost him in a duel.'

I turned to see Charlotte standing in the doorway of the drawing-room, having not noticed her arrival while perusing my journal.

'I did not hear you,' I said.

'I knew the servants would be engaged in packing and I let myself in,' she said, removing the gloves from her hand. 'A shocking lapse on Robert's part to leave the door unattended.'

She dropped her gloves on a table, shed her Spencer on the back of a chair and then took a seat opposite me.

'When did this happen?' I asked.

'Oh, many years ago now.'

'You are older than you look,' I said inelegantly.

'I have that good luck, but I will soon see nine and twenty and my luck will soon turn. Ah, that shocks you. I should have told you earlier but I am as vain as any woman. Still, my age is an open secret, just one you did not care to investigate fully.'

'The midshipman, from the sketch? He was your love?' I asked. I looked to the mantel for the sketch in its frame, but it had already been packed.

She nodded. 'Finally a lieutenant ... on the day he died, actually.'

'Was it ... like the matter between Mr Jenkins and Mr Sunderland?'

'Oh no, this was in deadly earnest. Although it was alike in that he was defending my honour, or what he thought to be my honour. And it was aided and abetted by one senior in rank, age and experience to him.'

'I am very sorry. Were you to … was there an understanding?'

'Between us there was, but my father and mother forbade our union because they would not call Edward a gentleman. And then he died before I could defy my parents and marry him regardless.'

As she said this, the sadness that I had registered before took over her whole being and I felt drawn in to her misery and regret.

'How very sad,' I said, 'and you are unable to love again because you lost your heart to him and only him.'

And then she surprised me by a little laugh. 'Such a romantic, Jane. Yes, I could contemplate no other because I lost my heart to him. And because of his child that I bore.'

Colophon

The printed book is set in Adobe Garamond Pro at 11.5/13.8. Linotype Zapfino is used for some of the ornamentation. Edwardian Script ITC is used for the title on the book cover, and the title and drop capitals that start each affair. Zapfino and Goudy Old Style are used in the Mallard Press logotype.

The cover was created in Adobe Illustrator and PhotoShop and the book was created in Adobe InDesign after first being written in Microsoft Word, all proudly created on an Apple Mac Pro.

The EPUB and Kindle versions of the book were created by exporting the InDesign document as an EPUB, adding a table of contents in Sigil (http://code.google.com/p/sigil/) and a cover page in calibre (http://calibre-ebook.com/). calibre was further used to convert to the Kindle MOBI format.

The book was printed on demand through CreateSpace (an Amazon company). For more information about Mallard Press and self-publishing, visit mallardpress.blogspot.com

For more information about Jane Austen and Sir Arthur Conan Doyle, visit www.myparticularfriend.com

NEW

AUG 3 0 2012

CPSIA information can be obtained at www.ICGtesting.com
Printed in the USA
LVOW130900190812

294966LV00001B/19/P

9 780615 597461